GRIPPED WITH FEAR,
TOLLIVER CHARGED AHEAD!

He found the bodies lying near a wagon. They had been shot several times. Barnaby had a gaping hole in the side of his left temple. In a daze, Tolliver stumbled toward the smoldering tepee. In a small clearing he saw the sprawled body of Black Bow. Agonized, Tolliver bent over the boy. Young Black Bow had been shot in the back.

This had been retribution at its worst. Never in his life had he felt more miserable and lonely. As he buried the bodies, he buried his heart with them.

His mind flamed with fury. Retribution? One day soon the perpetrators of this foul deed would die screaming, the skin stripped from their bodies in shreds.

They had destroyed Eden. They would discover Hell. . . .

TOLLIVER

"Fans of historical westerns will appreciate the author's mastery of settings and events and his avoidance of the clichés that plague this genre."
—*Publishers Weekly*

TOLLIVER

by

Paul A. Hawkins

A SIGNET BOOK

SIGNET
Published by the Penguin Group
Penguin Books USA Inc., 375 Hudson Street,
New York, New York 10014, U.S.A.
Penguin Books Ltd, 27 Wrights Lane,
London W8 5TZ, England
Penguin Books Australia Ltd, Ringwood,
Victoria, Australia
Penguin Books Canada Ltd, 10 Alcorn Avenue,
Toronto, Ontario, Canada M4V 3B2
Penguin Books (N.Z.) Ltd, 182–190 Wairau Road,
Auckland 10, New Zealand

Penguin Books Ltd, Registered Offices:
Harmondsworth, Middlesex, England

First published by Signet,
an imprint of Dutton Signet,
a division of Penguin Books USA Inc.

First Printing, October, 1994
10 9 8 7 6 5 4 3 2 1

 REGISTERED TRADEMARK—MARCA REGISTRADA

Printed in the United States of America

last

Book One

Sanctuary

Chapter 1

Fort Connor, Dakota Territory, September 1865

Where in the hell did this buck come from?" asked Sergeant Burns. Sergeant Edward Burns, a medical aide, glared at a dazed, young Oglala brave who was sitting near the door. The Indian was bleeding profusely from a bullet wound above his right knee.

"Two of the boys dumped him there," replied Delbert Carnes. Carnes was a corporal; he was also an aide assisting the two surgeons in the rough-hewn log infirmary at Fort Connor. Corporal Carnes said, "He got shot the other side of camp . . . stealing horses, I reckon. Some of his buddies got away."

After another contemptuous stare, Sergeant Burns said, "Well, drag his ass outta here. We haven't got time to go fooling around with Injuns. It's against regulations. Why in the hell didn't they finish him off in the first place? Damn this place! We got a bunch of idiots 'round here."

With a hapless shrug, Corporal Carnes said, "All right, whatever you say. He'll be bleeding to death, anyway." Carnes moved toward the door.

One of the army doctors at a nearby table turned. As Corporal Carnes lifted under the young Sioux's shoulders, the officer spoke. "Let's take a look at his leg." Then to Sergeant Burns, the doctor said with a nod, "Sergeant, give Carnes a hand. Get the chap on the table."

From a second table, Major Calvin Mudd looked up. Wiping his bloodstained hands on a towel, he said, "Good Lord, Tolliver, whatever are you doing? The sergeant's right. That scoundrel shouldn't be in here, and he's no concern of ours." Major Mudd motioned to Sergeant Burns, then to a heavily bandaged soldier on the table in front of him. "Get this soldier to a bunk, first."

Captain James Tobias Tolliver moved from his table over beside the stricken Sioux brave, knelt, and briefly examined the leg wound. To Carnes he said, "Here, help me get him up." Together, they lifted the young man to his feet and laid him on Dr. Tolliver's table.

"You've gone daft, Tolliver," Major Mudd said, shaking his head. Mudd leaned over and also inspected the wound. "Bone may be shattered. No exit. The lead is still in there. Waste of your time, James . . . against regulations, too."

Sergeant Burns, moving away with Major Mudd's patient, muttered, "Fellows back there ain't gonna be liking a hostile bedding down beside them, Captain. Likely the buck might be responsible for some of 'em being here in the first place." Burns, with the wounded trooper in tow, disappeared to the back where the long room was lined with plank bunks and hay-covered stretchers. A dozen men were there, suffering from an assortment of ailments, ranging from arrow and gunshot wounds to

Tolliver sighed with resignation. So what? The campaign was over. Everyone but two companies of galvanized Yankees was leaving for Fort Laramie. So was he. He was tired. Until the next campaign, he had seen enough young lives wasted.

That night Tolliver was particularly tired and weary. Though only twenty-eight, he had served two years in the War Between the States; he had reason to be weary. With only two years of his commission remaining, assignment to the Army of the West had not been his choice. He had hoped for a post at one of the medical facilities closer to his home in Philadelphia. He went reluctantly to Fort Atkinson, then to Fort Laramie, eventually into the command of Patrick Connor, an ambitious general seeking to enhance his reputation as an Indian fighter.

Tolliver reclined on his cot and listened to his companion, Major Thomas Stubbs. A good cavalryman, Stubbs was one of several aides to General Connor. Stubbs admitted that the Powder River campaign had done little to enhance the reputation of the general. His thrusts against the hostiles had been badly blunted by the cunning of the Hunkpapa chief, Sitting Bull, and Red Cloud, the leader of the Oglala. Not only had the chiefs outwitted him, in most cases they had outfought him. Discouraged and suffering unexpected hardships, some of General Connor's troops had deserted. Others were in such poor physical shape they were unable to fight effectively.

Major Stubbs, puffing a corncob pipe, told Tolliver that undoubtedly General Connor was in for a severe reprimand from headquarters in Omaha. Certainly he wasn't going to get a second star for his effort in the Powder River country.

"That's bad enough," Stubbs said. "Now you go putting salt in the wound by taking one of the enemy under your wing. You've turned out to be a bleeding heart, and the old man doesn't like bleeding hearts. Oh, it's most admirable of you, sure, James, saving the youngster's leg, but it's entirely unorthodox."

"I've always been unorthodox," returned Tolliver.

"You're also one of the best surgeons out here."

"What's the army to do? Boot me out?" For a moment James Tolliver's dark eyes twinkled. "Say, Thomas, I wouldn't mind that."

"Demotion. Ridicule for insubordination. The old man taking out some of his outrage on you. That sort of thing. Unpleasant business, I'd say."

"A pity. Blame the poor doctor for misdirected deeds."

Major Stubbs purred. A blue stream of smoke floated across the dimness of the small room. He looked over at Tolliver. "By the way, how is your young patient? Does he know what's going on?"

Tolliver snorted. "He's on the mend, if that's what you mean. I told some of the boys to take him a meal this afternoon. They didn't. I did. He muttered something entirely unintelligible. Perhaps a thank you, I don't know. Some fool had bound his wrists with rope. I took the ropes off so he could eat. I left them off. I helped him outside to take a leak. I took him a blanket for the night."

"He's a prisoner of war," Stubbs reminded.

"He's not going anywhere on that leg."

"The old man doesn't take prisoners."

"If the boy's my obligation, then that's the way it will be, Thomas. He's not out of the woods yet."

"Yes, and he may not get out of the woods," Major Stubbs replied. "The general wants him off the post. He has no room for prisoners of war. He doesn't want to feed the boy, either. We're short on rations." Major Stubbs took another puff on his pipe. "Rather an either-or, I'd say."

"Either or what?"

"Get him out of here or watch him shot for stealing horses."

"Nonsense!"

"Not my words, James."

"By gadfrey, we'll be leaving here in another two or three days!" said Tolliver. "What difference does it make?"

"Do you want to talk to the old man about it?"

James Tolliver gave Stubbs an incredulous stare. "An Englishman talking to a hotheaded Irishman? Not on your life, not when he has the upper hand, I don't." Tolliver groaned. "Why in the hell does everyone make so much of this? One damn Indian with a bum leg! Good grief, the old man must have more important things to think about the way the hostiles have been kicking his butt."

"That's just it," mused Major Stubbs. "His ass is sore enough already. The fact that he's harboring one of those redskins responsible for his condition just rubs him the wrong way." Stubbs pointed his pipe at the door. "We've got to get that Indian out of here, James."

* * *

Major Stubbs went to eat supper. Captain Tolliver didn't. Instead, he rested back in his bunk and dwelled on what Stubbs had told him. "We've got to get that Indian out of here." Obviously, there was some credence in this, but Stubbs hadn't contributed any ideas of how to get the Indian out. The "we" was only a matter of expression, and Tolliver was resigned to the fact that it was solely up to him to get the deed done. Under normal circumstances the young Oglala probably could escape on his own. Surveillance around the fort was shoddy; with six cannons and two hundred men positioned inside, there was no fear of the hostiles attacking. They only picked on the troopers when they ventured away from the fort, or attacked the supply trains and escorts. This had been their usual game, and they were very good at it. The problem was that Tolliver's Sioux patient couldn't walk. Even riding a horse would be excruciating. And Tolliver had some fear that any extended riding might bring about more bleeding from the young man's wound.

After a few more minutes of deliberation, Tolliver got up from his bunk. He stretched and yawned. He searched around in his duffel and found an extra shirt and pants. He had no spare boots, but he pulled out a pair from under Major Stubbs's bunk. He bundled all of this into a ball and tucked it under his arm. At Major Calvin Mudd's quarters, he spied a cavalry hat; he took this, too. Someone had left a gunbelt with holster and revolver suspended on a wall peg by the door. He quickly fastened this around his waist. Once outside, he cached the clothing at the rear of the cook's quarters. He strode boldly over to the hitching pole next to the teamsters' barn. There was no use in trying subterfuge; this had to appear very deliberate and official. He did have time on his side—it was near dusk and most of the officers and men were at mess.

At the barn, he was greeted with a casual salute from a young man in boots, baggy trousers, and a badly soiled undershirt. "Riding the perimeter for the Officer of the Day," Tolliver said. "I need two mounts . . . taking a scout with me."

"Yes, sir," the man answered. He pointed down the line. "Take any of them, but begging your pardon, don't those Pawnee have their own horses?"

"Chap says his pony is lame," lied Tolliver. Without looking back, Tolliver led the two horses away. He threaded their reins through the wooden handle of the shed, picked up the bundle of clothing, and quickly ducked inside. One small window illuminated the interior. Directly under the window sat the Sioux brave, an empty plate to the side of him. Tolliver smiled. Obviously someone had fed the young man again.

Squatting in front of him, Tolliver placed the bundle of clothing on the floor, then examined his bandage. There wasn't a stain on it, and Tolliver smiled again and said, "Good."

"Good," the youngster repeated. "*Waśte.*"

"Friend," Tolliver said. "I am your friend."

"Friend. *Kola.*"

Tolliver nodded. "Yes, friend. You catch on fast. If you could stay around here a few weeks, you'd probably speak better English than most of the soldiers." Placing the clothes in the brave's lap, he added, "Here, get dressed. Ready or not, we're taking a little ride."

Tolliver made a few motions—riding, going away. He positioned his hands in the shape of a tipi. Home, going home. He touched the brave on the chest. "You go home."

However awkward the sign, the brave understood. He nodded once and momentarily stared at the clothes. He gave the hat a flip with a finger and frowned.

"I know, my friend," Tolliver said. "I know just how you feel. It's a disgrace, but dammit, it's the only way." After a few more gestures, he helped the brave to his feet. He had to help dress him, too.

The brave's mouth drooped and he shook his head. "Good, *Waste*. No good."

Once outside, James Tolliver gave the Sioux a boost into the saddle. In return, he received his first grin. Yes, it felt good to sit in the saddle, but smiles were deceiving. Tolliver knew it hurt like hell. He also knew this young Indian would never admit to pain.

Tolliver said, "*Waste*, eh?"

With a motion, he reined away, and the brave followed. In the evening dusk they rode out from behind the building toward the gate. Here, a salute, the gate wedged open, and Dr. James Tolliver and his scout moved briskly toward the river bottom.

The next morning Captain Tolliver had breakfast with several of his fellow officers. It was to be his last. By nine o'clock he was escorted to General

Connor's office where Major Thomas Stubbs, standing next to the general's small field desk, read off the charges—one, insubordination; two, theft of U.S. Government property, one horse and accoutrements; three, aiding and abetting a prisoner of war.

General Patrick Connor's face was florid. He was a master at brevity. "How does the captain answer the charges?" he asked.

"I helped the young man," admitted Tolliver. "I didn't think he deserved to be shot a second time for trying to steal a skinny horse."

"So you took it upon yourself to steal one for him?"

"Borrowed. I'm not a horse thief, General."

General Connor exploded. "It was an act of treason, goddammit! You're a traitor. That horse you stole was mine!" He slapped his hand on the desk. "Confined to quarters. Court-martial proceedings to be held at Fort Laramie upon return of this command. Dismissed."

Major Stubbs had some sympathy for James Tolliver. They had been friends for more than a year, so he made a brief visit to the captain's quarters that evening. A guard was in front of the door. Despite the gravity of the situation, Tolliver saw some humor in this.

"They think I'm going to borrow another horse and make a run for it," he told Stubbs.

Stubbs sat on the lone chair and lit his pipe. After a moment he said, "The charges aren't all that frivolous, James. The old man can make every one of them stick. They can demote you, sack you, or give you up to five years at hard labor. I suggest when we get to Laramie, we get you the best solicitor in the ranks. We can plead you were irrational . . . duty fatigue."

"We?" snorted Tolliver. "That's what you suggested about the Indian chap. 'We' should get him out of here. Now it's *we* again."

"Figuratively speaking."

"Damn figuratively. *I* got him out."

"I didn't tell you to steal the general's favorite mount."

"Borrow."

"You should have been a bit more discreet about it. Likely he would have given you nothing more than a reprimand for treating the lad. But escape . . . horse theft . . ."

"It was you who suggested 'we' get him out, dammit!"

Major Stubbs casually waved his pipe. "Now look here, James, I entertained no grand scheme of escape like you pulled off. I had a notion we could spirit him out in the dead of night, at least get him out the gate."

"Good grief, Tom, the fellow couldn't walk!"

"A cane . . . only to the river bottom. His friends are always sneaking about down there."

"Hindsight," muttered Tolliver. "You're mad because I stole your boots, aren't you?"

"Not at all. They didn't fit well, anyhow, and no one in quarters wanted to report any thefts. Who wants to compound this by accusing you of being a common criminal?"

"I'd rather not discuss it. I don't like the thought

of facing a court-martial . . . or five years hard labor, either."

Thomas Stubbs smiled. "They used to hang men for treason, you know." In afterthought, he added, "They still hang them for stealing horses."

"You're not much help, Tom."

"Oh, you know I'll do what I can when we get back to Laramie." Stubbs shrugged. "Who knows, maybe this will all blow over by then. If the old man can kill a few hostiles along the way, he might get to feeling better."

"Balls!" scoffed Tolliver. "His game is up. Where in the hell can he find a village to surround south of here? They're on to him, Tom. He'll never get close to another village. When this debacle is aired, he'll be lucky to get another command the rest of his life. The red-nosed bastard is finished. You know it, I know it, and he knows it."

Major Stubbs was pensive. He sighed. "You may be right. I just hope you aren't finished, too. You're a fine doctor, James. What a waste it would be."

"No waste. I'm fed up with this fieldwork. I'll never saw off another limb again, I'll tell you this. Never."

Chapter 2

Fort Laramie, October 1865

During his first two weeks of confinement at Fort Laramie, Captain James Tobias Tolliver received good news and bad news. The good of it was that General Patrick Connor would not be present for Tolliver's court-martial—he had been ordered back to Fort Atkinson to face a board of inquiry. The bad—Tolliver's best friend, Major Thomas Stubbs, received orders to report to a new fort under construction a hundred miles up the North Platte trail—Fort Casper. Major Stubbs's departure was imminent.

Thanks to Stubbs's intervention, Tolliver's detention had been tolerable, if one could consider house arrest tolerable. The captain was confined in a room adjacent to Bachelor Officers' Quarters. There was a sentry on duty at the door, usually a private, occasionally a corporal. All of the amenities were furnished—bunk, washstand, a small table, and two chairs. A window sans curtains faced south, affording Tolliver a view of the stables and the back gate.

Captain Tolliver took exercise twice a day, an escorted walk around the compound each morning and after supper. Meals were delivered regularly to his quarters, and except for his limited freedom, he found little of which to complain. Compared to his recent tour of duty with General Connor, and his short tenure in the ill-equipped infirmary at Fort Connor, his present detention bordered on luxury.

In his daily walks, Tolliver had the opportunity to witness all of the renewed activity at Fort Laramie. He had never seen it so busy. In some of his brief conversations with Major Stubbs, he learned the reasons behind this frenzy of work—construction of another new fort was planned somewhere in the vicinity of the Big Horn Mountains. Major Stubbs explained wryly, the fort was one of several proposed to protect the military road and prevent illegal entry of white civilians into the unceded lands to the north. Another treaty with the Sioux, Cheyenne, and Arapaho was in the making. One way or another, by guise or force, the government was determined to make the Bozeman Trail a less hazardous passage to the territorial mining camps.

Sitting at Tolliver's small table, Major Stubbs confessed that striking a new treaty with the Indians was going to be an onerous undertaking, particularly after General Connor's invasion. The new commandant of Fort Laramie, Colonel Henry Maynadier, had been given the task of calling in the chiefs for a council. His first attempt to recruit emissaries had been a failure. Two of the most trustworthy scouts, Jim Bridger and James Medicine Calf Beckwourth, had come from Colonel Maynadier's office on this very morning. Neither man thought it wise to serve as an intermediary so soon after General Connor's abortive campaign. They would be thrown out of any village, or worse.

Major Stubbs said with a faint smile, "Bridger told him the Indians are as mad as hornets, and the fact that Connor is on his way out wouldn't make a damn bit of difference. Besides, Bridger says it will take a month or two to spread the word about a council. By then, winter sets in, eh? Indians don't like to move in cold weather. So that's the size of it. Maybe next spring they'll sit down and attempt to reconcile this mess. I understand Maynadier is going to see if he can get some of the fort Indians to go north, make some enticements to the chiefs, some ruse to bring them down."

James Tolliver knew who the "fort" Indians were. Most of them were Sioux—Big Mouth, Big Ribs, Eagle Foot, and Whirlwind. They were contemptuously called the "Laramie Loafers," trader Indians who were shrewd entrepreneurs. They made their living arranging trades between the whites and Indians, trades that most often were illicit but very profitable.

Tolliver nodded knowingly and smiled back at Stubbs. "And in the meantime, the supplies for the new fort construction keep rolling in. I doubt Colonel Maynadier will get a new treaty of any kind when the Sioux and Cheyenne get wind of this." In afterthought, he said, "And they will . . . they always seem to know what the hell is going on."

"Yes and no," Stubbs replied. "Most everyone thinks the freight is destined for up the river, Casper, and another proposed fort location somewhere in between the La Bonte stage station and here."

"Interesting," mused Tolliver. "Very interesting. A clever game."

"Yes," agreed Stubbs. "Do you know, after our recent sortie up north, I discovered those chaps Red Cloud and Dull Knife to be quite clever, too. They adapted readily to any game we chose to play." Stubbs placed his hand on the paper and envelopes he had brought. "Well, I must be going, James. I trust this will take care of your immediate needs."

Dr. Tolliver nodded. It would. He had only one letter to write and post—to his parents in Philadelphia. He had no intention of revealing his present poor predicament though. His father, Tobias Tolliver, a prominent doctor, a pillar in the Methodist Church, might not only be grieved; he would be appalled. The captain's letter would only tell them that all was well, that he was on another extended tour of duty on the great American frontier.

Tolliver stopped Major Stubbs at the door. "Keep me advised, Tom."

"Rest assured, I will," Stubbs replied. "I daresay, this affair will drag on another month." He grinned. "At least, the old man won't be able to testify."

"What could he say, anyway? That I borrowed his horse?"

"That's hearsay evidence, James."

"That private told me to take any two down the line."

"The private won't be here, either," Major Stubbs said. "He's still up at Fort Connor with the galvanized troops. Likely, he won't be out of there until next spring." Stubbs stopped and chuckled. "Maynadier's adjutant told me the army's already decided to rename the fort. It's already penned in on the map. Fort Reno." He chuckled again and pulled out his corncob pipe. "A man's career out here can be awfully short, sometimes. Either hero or fool. There isn't much in between."

Tolliver said, "Connor called me a traitor. That's in between."

"It's nonsense, too," replied Stubbs. "What does your attorney say?"

"Lieutenant O'Leary?"

"He said you called him a 'potato eater.' "

Tolliver's dark eyes danced. "I was generous. Of all the officers around this post, you had to get me an Irishman, a counterpart of Patrick Connor. You did it out of spite. You're still sore because I stole your cavalry boots."

"Not true. O'Leary was in army intelligence at Omaha. He's a smart young man."

"He's researching," Tolliver said. "He says to his knowledge General Connor's orders are arbitrary. He hasn't been able to find anything in the books regarding the illegality of treating a prisoner of war humanely. Theft of government property and abetting the escape are different matters."

"A matter of proof on those counts."

With a devious look Tolliver said, "I thought I was rather crafty, you know. That soldier at the gate didn't know I was a doctor. He couldn't identify me, and no identifiable Sioux warrior went out with me, either. It was a man in full uniform wearing a major's hat. It was dark as hell when I returned, too."

"Yes, only the private at the livery . . ."

"If they bring that chap down here, I'm as good as dead."

Major Stubbs grinned. "I thought you wanted out of the army? You said you were tired of dismembering men ... something along that line."

"Oh, I don't mind the sacking, Tom, no, not at all," answered Tolliver. "That hard labor bit you mentioned ... that doesn't appeal to me. That damned O'Leary says it's possible, too."

"Trust him," advised Stubbs. He gave Tolliver a pat on the shoulder and left.

The following morning when Dr. Tolliver was out for his morning exercise, his usual stroll around the perimeter, an older man with a mustache and a scraggly beard approached him near the main gate. He was dressed in a flannel shirt and wore a beaded leather vest. His faded army pants were tucked into cavalry boots. He also wore a black army holster with a Navy Colt tucked in it. Behind him was another man dressed in faded denim pants held up by suspenders. He had on an abbreviated shirt, the sleeves cut off at the elbows. The two men had drifter written all over them.

The man with the beaded vest approached. "Are you Doc Tolliver?" he asked.

James Tolliver's young private escort stepped briskly to the front and said, "This man is a prisoner. He's not allowed to talk with anyone in the compound."

The bearded man took one step back, then placed his hands on his hips and replied, "Is that so?

'Feared I'm gonna fetch him away, are you? 'Feared we'll make a run for the gate yonder?"

"No, sir."

"Well, then stand back."

"Regulations, mister."

The man defiantly stuck out his whiskered chin. "I don't give a shit about regulations, sonny. My name is Bridger . . . James. Most people call me Jim. A few call me Major. I'm chief of scouts for Colonel Maynadier. I was on this post when your momma was wiping your fat little butt. Now, you get on over there to the side a piece so I can talk to this man or I'll tell the colonel you're messing up my work. I guarantee you won't be on guard duty tomorrow. You'll be shoveling horse shit down at the barn."

The private was astounded. He momentarily stared at Bridger and his bedraggled friend, then finally looked over helplessly at James Tolliver. Tolliver shrugged and said, "Perhaps just for a moment, Private. Major Bridger can walk along with us."

"That's right," Bridger said. He nodded at the man with him and said to the private, "That's Luther . . . Luther Willet, eh. You parley with him so you won't feel all lonely-like."

The soldier hiked his brow, hunched his shoulders once, and stepped to the rear with Luther Willet. They all slowly walked past the gate and back toward the parade grounds.

Jim Bridger told Tolliver that a trader by the name of Barnaby Cobb had come to the fort the past evening. They were old friends. Barnaby Cobb, Bridger said, was into some new trading, dealing through two of the fort Indians, the "loafers." He was running rifles to the Indians in the northern valleys. He had just returned from the Powder River country with four mules loaded with furs and hides and an assortment of beaded buckskin shirts and fur-lined jackets.

Well, this was all very interesting, Tolliver said, but what did Barnaby Cobb's trading with the hostiles have to do with him?

Then Jim Bridger enlightened James Tolliver with an amazing story. Barnaby Cobb had stopped overnight in an Oglala hunting village somewhere along the Little Powder. He talked with a brave there called Little Dog, a young man who was still recovering from a bullet wound in his leg. The Oglala told Barnaby that a doctor at the new fort on the Powder had removed the lead last month and had given him a pony so he could return to his people.

"Good grief!" Tolliver exclaimed. "The lad made it! No infection. Why, that's good news, Mr. Bridger! Excellent!"

James Bridger had a clay pipe tucked into one side of his mouth. It wasn't lit; it jumped when he talked. "Well, you made yourself some friends up there, and that's something few whites do, y'know. Those people don't fiddle much with the *wasichu*. That boy's ol' man is Two Coups, a subchief right close to Red Cloud, the head man, himself."

Tolliver was mystified. He said, "How did that youngster know who I was? He didn't know my name. Why, as I recall, not more than ten words passed between us."

"Knew you were one of those medicine men, he

did," chuckled Bridger. "And when ol' Barnaby tells me the story, I knew right off who the boy's talking about. So I tells Barnaby you're in the stockade for that little escapade with the buck up on the Powder . . . had yourself a regular how-de-do with Red Nose Connor, stealing the ol' man's horse."

"I borrowed it," Tolliver said.

"Fixing to return it then, I reckon."

"Borrowed for an extended period."

Jim Bridger cackled. "Best damn story I heard in a long time. Every Injun 'round the fort's been laughing about it. Some crazy doctor patching up an Injun, then stealing the general's pony and giving it to the Injun. By crackee, that's a hot one, Mr. Tolliver, damned if it ain't."

"I didn't realize it was a topic of conversation, especially among the Indians."

"Oh, hell, when they get hold of one like this, it's like wildfire," Bridger said. "Probably already up in the valleys by now. Injuns like a good joke, 'specially when it makes a white man look stupid, which by my reckoning, most are."

"I'd like to talk to this Barnaby . . . Barnaby . . ."

"Cobb. Cobb like corn on the cob."

"Yes, Barnaby Cobb."

"Have to go through the gate back there," Bridger said. "Have to go down the river about twenty miles."

"Then he's already gone."

"Yassir." Jim Bridger winked. "Has what he calls some freight to pick up at a cache. Left nigh dawn, and I 'spect he's already packed and moving north again, back to the villages."

"Freight, is it?"

"Freight. Boom, boom!"

Tolliver gave him a hard stare. "You don't begrudge these people getting illegal firearms?"

"I lived off an' on with 'em nigh on thirty-five years. I begrudge no man what he needs to defend himself."

"Good grief, whose side are you on, Mr. Bridger?"

Bridger scratched up behind an ear and cocked his head. "Well, damned if I know. A chore it is, walking both sides of the trail at once. For a fact, I try not to take sides, Doc. Most times I've always been peaceful-like. Had some good times, mostly bad of late. The omens ain't good, y'know. Bad times a'brewing." His pipe jumped to the other side. "You was in the big war?"

"Yes, two years of it."

"War's ugly business. You don't strike me as one of those glory boys."

"I'm not."

"Why in tarnation are you out here then?"

"It wasn't my choice of duty."

"Reckon they'll bust you to flinderjibs?"

"It's likely."

"Good. I hope they do, pilgrim. You won't be 'round to see the worst of it." The little clay pipe moved again. Bridger asked, "Ever see a prairie fire?"

"No."

"You stick 'round here 'nother five or ten years and you will."

"I won't be around that long, Mr. Bridger, I assure you."

"Good. This whole country's gonna go up in flames. War is gonna kill it and all the goodness the Almighty put in it. She's a dead duck, Doctor, a dead duck. Yassir, lucky you ain't gonna be 'round, 'cause you sure as hell could get your tail feathers scorched."

They were approaching B.O.Q. "Good-bye, Mr. Bridger," Tolliver said. "Perhaps we'll meet again down the line somewhere."

"I hope not. But good luck."

Another two days passed routinely. Then Major Thomas Stubbs stopped by to say good-bye. He was leaving the next morning with a small detachment of troopers for Fort Casper, among them Dr. Calvin Mudd. This news stirred Tolliver's blood. Mudd leaving? At least this was heartening—one less witness to shoot arrows at him. Of course, as Timothy O'Leary had said, Mudd's testimony was irrelevant—the young attorney had been unable to find any rule prohibiting medical treatment of a prisoner of war. Undoubtedly, the prosecution officers were aware of this, too, or Dr. Mudd wouldn't be on his way to a new assignment.

So, Major Stubbs said good-bye. Tolliver gripped the hand of his best friend. "I'll write," Tolliver said. "Maybe when this is all over we can meet again somewhere . . . have a drink and a good laugh. You've been a valued friend, Tom."

"Likewise. We'll be entitled to a laugh. There's been damn few around here . . . among whites, anyhow."

Tolliver managed a smile.

His smile was short-lived. Not more than ten minutes after Major Stubbs left the room, Lieutenant Timothy O'Leary arrived. He came in with a deep frown on his ruddy face. "The hearing has been postponed again ... at least two weeks, maybe three," he said.

"Good grief, what now?"

Lieutenant O'Leary sat down at the table and put a hand to his forehead. He finally said, "They're sending for Private Claypool."

"Claypool? Who in the hell is Claypool?"

"Ulis Claypool. The private at the post stables up at Fort Connor ... Fort Reno. The man who let you ride away with the general's horse."

"Oh, shit!"

Chapter 3

After several days of blustery weather, including a storm of bone-chilling sleet, Indian summer settled in—warm sunny days and brisk nights. Despondency became the companion of Dr. James Tolliver. Major Stubbs was gone and Private Claypool was on his way. Additionally, Lieutenant Timothy O'Leary, the pride of the Irish at Fort Laramie, went on patrol for three days. The army continually searched the North Platte area for signs of hostiles, the unfriendlies who regularly harassed incoming freight wagons.

Tolliver took receipt of two sets of woolen underwear and socks. He shook out his winter coat. He had no idea when his court-marital would begin, but he knew winter was around the corner. He used the coat on his early morning escorted walk. This was a time for conversation, but news was scant. Tolliver's guards passed a few rumors but nothing with any validity, so most often he listened without comment. He had learned that barracks and barn talk was the least dependable of all news.

However, activity at the fort continued. Several loads of military freight arrived, accompanied by two platoons of new cavalrymen. And with winter creeping down from the high country, a few wood trains and hay wagons began to trundle back and forth. Either on his daily walks or from his back window, Dr. Tolliver, beset by anxiety and visions of hard labor, observed this activity. What else could he do? He was a valued doctor; he was a good cavalryman. Confined, his healing hands were useless, and he no longer had a horse to ride. Oh, his plight wasn't all that miserable, and he had never been one to feel sorry for himself. Throughout his recent turbulent life in the tents of the maimed, the wounded, and the dying, he had become well acquainted with misery and sorrow. For others, not himself. His present feelings ranged from apprehension and fear to discontent and loneliness. Most of these aches were his own damn fault, too. He was tired of army life.

Though Tolliver's healing hands were idle, his eyes were not. He watched the wood haulers move into the fort with their mule-drawn wagons. Civilians and troopers stacked the logs in a big pile adjacent to the stable area. Sawyers were there with cross-cut saws. They sliced through the logs and threw the blocks into another pile. It was laborious, shirtsleeve work. The men were rugged and rawboned.

To the other side of the stables, the men with the hay wagons came. They tossed huge forkfuls into the barn loft; other men packed it to the rafters. Dr. Tolliver, a chair pulled up, observed from his window, and in his observation on this brisk afternoon, he saw an unbelievable sight. It was so startling and unnerving, it made his stomach roll. He strained his eyes for another hard look. There was no doubt about it—one of the men tossing hay was the same young brave he had treated more than a month past at Fort Reno! Jim Bridger said the man's name was Little Dog.

Dr. Tolliver leaned forward. Gadfrey, how could this be? There were four or five Indians working the hay. Some were dressed in baggy army pants, black boots, and faded blue shirts. Some wore black hats with broad brims; several had tattered cavalry hats. Little Dog wore a hat, too. And from what Tolliver could see, the hat looked exactly like the one he had stolen from Dr. Mudd's room. Good grief!

Tolliver finally wheezed, rested back, and pondered. There was only one explanation—the young Oglala must have joined ranks with some of the hang-around-the-fort Indians who occasionally worked at menial, back-breaking jobs for paltry wages. But to Tolliver's knowledge, Little Dog wasn't any fort Indian. He was the proud son of an Oglala chief who fought soldiers. Certainly, the young man wouldn't be working for them. It was all too bizarre, too confusing. When Tolliver eased up to the window for a better look, the man called Little Dog was nowhere in sight.

Lieutenant O'Leary, armed with writing materials, arrived at Tolliver's quarters about an hour after evening mess. He was tired from patrol duty; his troop hadn't encountered any hostiles, only signs of where they had been. On the first day out, his Pawnee scouts discovered unshod pony tracks not more than ten miles from the fort, but the sign later became muddled in the heavily used main trail. The Pawnee hadn't been able to determine which way the small party of hostiles had ridden.

However, the lieutenant did return with two prisoners—deserters from Fort Reno. The two soldiers, happy to be alive, had been on the prairie for ten days, most of that time wandering about on foot at night. They had gone without food for the last three days, and only the fact that they had been without horses saved their lives. Three other deserters with mounts were killed and scalped by Indians. O'Leary's men found their bodies on the north side of the river.

Lieutenant O'Leary gave Tolliver a forlorn look. This was something he absolutely couldn't comprehend. He said, "I can understand desertion, Doctor, but under these circumstances, the prairie, the unpredictable weather, and all of the hostiles about, it's sheer stupidity. It's absolutely senseless."

Tolliver shrugged. If young O'Leary had spent some time at Fort Reno he certainly would understand. "Men get desperate," he said. "When they're hungry and cold, they get desperate. Before winter you'll see more desertion out of that fort, if one can call it a fort. It's nothing more than a way station. It's a good six-day ride. In some places one can see five miles in any direction. Getting supplies up there with the Sioux and Cheyenne riding about is not a pleasant chore. It takes brave men to cut wood in the river bottom. In the winter it's going to be worse. I guarantee you, if those men aren't evacuated by December they'll either starve to death or freeze."

"I don't think the commandant will forsake them," sighed O'Leary. "I can understand your bitterness about the place."

"The stupidity was building that stockade in the first place," Tolliver went on. "Second, Connor should have known better than to leave two companies of ex-Confederates to man it. They have no desire to kill Indians. That's one helluva punishment for losing the war."

"You realize," O'Leary said, "Colonel Maynadier is soliciting civilian sawyers and builders for more forts up the Bozeman. The Big Horn Mountains. Spectacular, I hear, very isolated, primitive country. Orders from the commandant in Omaha."

Tolliver grunted skeptically. "So, I hear. It's no secret, Lieutenant. Time will tell how much building the army will get done. Bridger says the Indians will have something to say about it, too."

O'Leary placed his papers on the little table, the pen and bottle of ink beside them. "Yes, I suppose they will since they have first claim on the land, the forefathers' thing and all of that drivel. But if the forts are built, they'll need very large garrisons, won't they? Probably hundreds of men."

Tolliver gave him a curious look. "Well, of course. Good grief, I think even those officers with the thickest skulls may have learned something from General Connor's misadventure. What's on your mind?"

Carefully examining the tip of his pen, O'Leary said, "You realize this Private Claypool has put us in a pickle. His testimony is going to damage us . . . those horses he gave you."

James Tolliver groaned. "Old Red Nose's mount."

"We can't deny you took the horse."

"No, but Claypool didn't see me ride out of the fort with it," countered Tolliver. "And no one saw me leave the fort with an Indian, either."

"Circumstantial evidence? Is that what you're suggesting?"

"Why not?"

"All right, Doctor, but you didn't return the horse, and the Indian escaped."

"He stole it from me when my back was turned."

"Two uniformed officers rode out the gate."

"That they did." Tolliver smiled. "At least, I heard that."

"The duty log shows no record of two officers being authorized to leave the fort," O'Leary said. "I saw the damn log. There is a notation in the log that Private Claypool reported to the officer on duty that one horse was not returned by the captain who requisitioned it."

"Hmmm."

"The prosecution will eat you alive, Doctor."

"Maybe the hostiles will get to Claypool before he gets here."

"He's no deserter, dammit. He's regular army."

"You have a point there, Lieutenant."

"I think we should plead guilty by reason of temporary derangement, your mind was troubled . . ."

"Wait a minute!" Tolliver said. "You're claiming I was crazy?"

O'Leary held up the pen defensively. "Temporarily only, Doctor. Under severe stress . . . General Connor's threat to shoot the young man unless evacuated by the next day. You were impelled, nay, driven, to take action."

"Good grief!"

O'Leary shrugged. "Under the circumstances, it's the best I can come up with, but I talked with your good friend Major Stubbs before he left. He suggested an alternative, something that could have a bearing on the severity of the penalty. A great retreat, as he put it."

"Tom? Tom suggested I plead guilty?"

"No, this is my idea," answered O'Leary. "His idea is sound, a move for leniency. My idea and his go hand in hand, and it just may please the court."

"All right, please me," Tolliver said. "What's Tom's great retreat?"

Timothy O'Leary momentarily hesitated. He took one deep breath and said, "I have statements from both Dr. Mudd and Major Stubbs vouching for your integrity and ability as a surgeon. In fact, Dr. Mudd states you're one of the best he's ever had the privilege of working with . . ."

"We go back to the war . . ."

"Well, Major Stubbs said in his statement that the Army of the West is in short supply of good doctors, men with proven experience, and that a man of your caliber would prove invaluable at one of the new forts up north . . ."

"Oh, Lord!"

". . . That if the court so deemed, Captain Tolliver would volunteer . . ."

"Probably Lieutenant Tolliver . . ."

"Well, a demotion, for God's sake, is a damn sight better than two to five years at hard labor, isn't it?"

"I can't deny that," replied Tolliver. "Tom didn't say anything about the fact that I'm tired of removing lead from young men and amputating their arms and legs, did he? Or that the army foolishly puts these men at risk in these frontier forts and expects us to repair them under the worst conditions possible with inadequate medical supplies and equipment?"

Lieutenant O'Leary sighed. "No, he didn't, Doctor. Look, I was assigned to defend you. I shall do this. I'm in sympathy with you in this ridiculous case. But I'm an attorney, not a supply officer."

"I know, I know," replied Tolliver. He forced a grin. "I'm sorry. I suppose it's because I'm a bit disgruntled . . . deranged, I think was the term you used."

"Shall we try to strike a compromise then?"

Dr. Tolliver shrugged. "What the hell, Lieutenant, why not? Right now I'm so tired of this charade I really don't give a hang what happens. Two years more at some godforsaken post doesn't make that much difference."

O'Leary stifled a small cough. He hesitated, then said, "I've sounded them out on this. They respect the word of Major Stubbs and Dr. Mudd. They wondered about your sincerity in the matter . . ."

"They think I'm crazy, too?"

"No, but they said since your tour is up in less than two years, to show your mettle, you should agree to extend your commission to four years . . ."

Tolliver gave the lieutenant an incredulous stare.

"Four more years! Ridiculous! Those fellows are in a turkey dream. And you were wondering about why men desert this confounded army!"

In the predawn hours, Dr. Tolliver heard a faint scratching at his window. He stirred and turned a bleary eye. There, bathed in the light of a lowering moon, was a face. As Tolliver eased out of his bed another face materialized. For a moment he thought he had been confronted with carousing troopers engaged in some kind of nighttime revelry, but once at the window, he realized this was no prank. Lord, Lord, one of the faces was that of the young man called Little Dog! Little Dog's grinning companion had his nose flattened against the pane. This, along with his wild eyes, gave him the look of some hideous, misshapen ogre of the night. What's more, the man was mouthing words and poking a finger up and down.

Tolliver quietly raised the window. He was greeted by a whispered "*Hau*" from Little Dog.

Astounded and puzzled, Tolliver nevertheless managed to whisper, "*Hau*."

Then Tolliver was further flabbergasted when the other young Indian said brokenly, "You come. We go. Ponies there. Soldiers no kill you. We come take you home. Go free. *Hiya, ku wanna, ku wanna*. No more talk." The man pressed a finger to his lips. Little Dog smiled broadly and nodded approvingly.

Dr. Tolliver recoiled in shock. Suddenly everything came together—the men in the hay wagons, the Indians working with them, Little Dog up in the hayloft. Why, these damn fools had come to free him from captivity! Little Dog and his people were returning the favor. Go free? Go free, indeed! But where? Home. What home? This ruse was so outlandishly foolhardy it bordered on insanity. Hah, that insinuation again, insanity!

"You are crazy dogs!" whispered Tolliver. "We'll all end up in the stockade . . . jail, big bars. You go. Go home. Do you understand?"

The one brave understood but he didn't leave. He said, "Blanket Chief say you no come you go far down big river to soldiers' lodge. Plenty bars, big jail. Maybe they kill you. You come, *Ku wanna, mistaput neotukit.*"

Blanket Chief? Jim Bridger? Bridger was in on this? Absurd, but undoubtedly he had talked with the men. There was only one place down the big river with plenty of bars—Fort Leavenworth! Gadfrey, two to five years there! Or four years in the Big Horns! No, by God! He was going to give the Indians something to cackle about around their night fires. He sure as hell was! And let the damn army brass ponder on his sanity.

Tolliver gave the two men a crafty smile. Likewise, he pressed a finger to his lips, then turned away to fetch his clothing.

Tolliver discovered the two men he now followed through the shadows knew the direction of freedom. It was as though they had been quartered at the fort all their lives. Tolliver had no time to question the plan of escape; his mind was still fractured from his impulsive decision to flee. That his career in the army was coming to a disastrous end, there was no doubt. The two braves creeping ahead of him were still attired in discarded (stolen?) army clothing. Tolliver fearfully followed. In a short time, they were at the west wall. Brief hesitation here—two soldiers were beside the heavy plank rear door. Moments later, Tolliver, his heart pounding, found himself in the blockhouse staring out the aperture of a cannon placement; the sentry was gone; a rope was fastened to the stanchion of the cannon.

In silent awe, Tolliver watched the English-speaking Sioux skinny his way through the opening and disappear. Then Little Dog pointed to Tolliver. The doctor took a quick look, tossed out his small bundle of belongings, and grasped the rope. Moments later he dropped to the frosty ground. Little Dog was right behind. Sprawled in the shadow of the wall was the missing tower guard. Tolliver shuddered. The Indians must have killed the man and thrown him from the tower!

A half-dozen Sioux lodges loomed up in the shadowy perimeter, lodges belonging to the hang-around-the-fort Indians. The three men skirted these, and in a small depression leading down to the Laramie River, three Indians were waiting. They had six ponies. Not a word had been exchanged since the men had slid down the rope at the blockhouse. Now the brave who spoke English addressed Tolliver.

Handing the doctor the reins of a horse, he said, "We honor you Toll-e-veer. Now we ride. *Heya, hechetu welo!*"

Tolliver took the reins. He momentarily stared at the horse. There was no doubt about it. Even in the faint moonlight he recognized it—it was General Connor's piebald mare.

Shortly after daybreak, the Indians stopped at a small creek to water the horses; they broke out a supply of tinned goods from the bundles lashed on behind their saddles. Tinned goods, U.S. Army issue, pears and peaches. They also had several boxes of hardtack. And it was at this point that Tolliver learned the identity of the other four men in the party. The English-speaking brave was Crazy Coyote. Tolliver was surprised to learn that Crazy Coyote was the breed son of the trader, Barnaby Cobb. Crazy Coyote introduced the remaining three, all Oglala, too—Hawk Leg, Eagle Wing, and Fast Runner. A council called by Little Dog's father, Two Coups, had sent the men to try to free Tolliver. They were all members of the Dog Soldier Society. To them, pain was as nothing, death was as nothing, and cowardice was a crime.

With exaggerated gestures, Crazy Coyote spoke and simultaneously translated for his brothers. He told Tolliver that the small party had left Little Powder River country more than ten days ago, shortly after passing trail runners told a story of a *wasichu* medicine man who had been imprisoned for treating a badly wounded Lakota brave. They knew it could only be the medicine man from the new fort on the Powder River. They didn't know Tolliver's name until Crazy Coyote talked with Jim Bridger outside the fort.

After the council, they rode swiftly. They stopped to rest on three nights. They lost some time tracking three bluecoats from Red Nose's soldiers' lodge, but they caught them and counted coup. Tolliver winced at this disclosure. Undoubtedly, these were the three deserters Lieutenant O'Leary had told him about. Crazy Coyote, grandly making sign, said he and Little Dog, after joining the hay crew, hid two nights in the barn loft. They watched the guards; they sneaked around the barracks at dark until Little Dog finally saw Tolliver sitting by his lamp making talk with another man. Tolliver nodded. This had to be Lieutenant O'Leary.

After listening to the story, Tolliver shook his head and said, "You're very brave to do such a dangerous thing. Any one of you could have been shot or captured. They could have hanged you for such a stunt. I'm grateful."

Once again, Crazy Coyote translated for the others. They all mumbled and waved their hands as if to say it was nothing. Little Dog spoke and made sign. The men laughed. Crazy Coyote said to Tolliver, "My brother says this better than stealing long-knife ponies and getting shot in leg."

"You killed a soldier," Tolliver reminded them.

Crazy Coyote said to Tolliver, "Hawk Leg says this plenty good joke. Bluecoats blame you. You counted coup on one of your people to escape."

James Tolliver winced again. The vision of that brief encounter with General Connor flashed through his mind. Connor had called him a traitor. Damn true. Here he was riding with the enemy off to God only knew where, and to do what, he didn't have the faintest notion. Not only was he a traitor, it now appeared that he was a killer to boot.

Tolliver said forlornly, "You didn't have to kill the man."

Crazy Coyote returned, "You want out of soldiers' jail, no other way. We kill him. He gonna yell plenty and bring other bluecoats. You want out. We get you out best way, Toll-e-veer."

Tolliver was exasperated. "Yes, I understand. But I didn't even know if I wanted out. You didn't even give me any time to consider it, dammit."

Crazy Coyote shrugged. "You want take Red Nose's pony back? You no pony thief, eh? Make good. *Waśte wakage*. No more jail."

Tolliver gave him a grim look. "Do you know what a gallows is, my friend?"

Crazy Coyote did. He quickly made the sign of a crossbar, a dangling rope, and put his hands to his throat. Everyone laughed. Tolliver groaned. He didn't see any humor in this at all. He said so.

Crazy Coyote calmly slit the lid of a can of peaches. He peeled back the tin and took a hefty gulp. In between several swallows, he said this was a very good joke on the bluecoats. He was young, but he had heard many good stories. He could not remember one story about a general's horse taken away from a soldiers' lodge two times by the same man. All of his brothers laughed and slapped their thighs in glee.

Dr. Tolliver put on a fake smile. He had no idea where he was going or what he was going to do. One thing he did know—he had a lot to learn about Indian humor.

Chapter 4

Dr. Tolliver's journey north with his five Oglala companions was exhilarating. This was riding free as the wind. By day, Tolliver exulted in the golden landscape of the prairie, the sight of thousands of buffalo and antelope; by night, he enjoyed the camaraderie of the Sioux around the campfire. But the journey was also depressing when Tolliver dwelt on the reality of his situation. He had almost a hundred dollars in his money belt; he had warm clothing; he was strong and robust, but he was entering another world of uncertainty. It looked grim, almost foreboding, and he wasn't prepared for it. Regardless of the trailside friendship with these men, he wasn't one of them. He was a white man out of his element. He was also a traitor, and this put an ache in his mind as well as his stomach.

As they neared their destination, his anxiety mushroomed. It was the fourth day since they had fled Fort Laramie. Crazy Coyote said there was a Lakota winter village ahead in the shadows of the Black Hills, the Paha Sapa. Until Tolliver decided where and when he would return to the white man's civilization, he would be welcome to live with the

Lakota. With apprehension, Tolliver said, *"Waśte."* This was good. It was also a horrendous challenge. He was about to join an alien society and partake in a primitive culture of which he had scant knowledge.

Suddenly, the village was within sight. Comprised of fifty or so brightly painted lodges, it sat on a timbered flat next to a shimmering river. It was beautiful and big, at least Tolliver thought so. Crazy Coyote told him it wasn't big at all. It was a small Lakota winter village. Because of the need for forage for the pony herds, the tribes always split up into smaller groups during the winter moons. In the summer when there was plenty of grass, some villages had over two hundred lodges. Crazy Coyote smiled. The camps during spring festivals *were* big— sometimes five hundred to a thousand tipis. This was a sight Toll-e-veer should see. Tolliver said by spring he planned to be lost in civilization, not on the prairie.

The reception was small but very enthusiastic. Thirty or so men, women, and children, and a multitude of mongrels gathered at the big soldiers' lodge. There were a few high-pitched tremolos from the women who were happy to see their men come home. Tolliver had never heard this unusual scream. It sent a shiver up his backbone. Introductions were made. Tolliver was warmly welcomed, for everyone knew this was the man who had saved the life of Little Dog and helped him escape from the soldiers' village on the Powder River.

Robes were soon spread. A half-dozen chiefs joined the circle, a long, decorated pipe was passed, and another small chill hit Tolliver's spine. The clothing some of these men wore was frightfully startling. All were clad in buckskin, some draped with blankets, but a few wore items of blue tunic— army jackets, a cavalry hat, and one solemn brave sported a necklace of beads, finger bones, and shiny brass buttons. There wasn't any doubt in Tolliver's mind where they had obtained this bizarre assortment of apparel and decoration. Many troopers had paid the ultimate price for General Connor's mad summer escapades in the valleys to the west.

Little Dog spoke eloquently of the journey to the big soldiers' lodge on the Geese Going River. Crazy Coyote whispered a translation to Tolliver. After Little Dog finished there were nods, smiles, several "*hau-haus*," and a few grunts. Everyone was pleased how effectively the five Oglala braves had carried out their mission.

A medicine chief called Red Bone briefly talked. His words were ones of welcome to the man called Toll-e-veer. He also said those people in the village who didn't wish to call this great healer Toll-e-veer could call him Big Black Bear. Red Bone explained this is how Toll-e-veer first appeared in the village wearing his great dark coat and hat and black boots. He was as big as his pony. He was Big Black Bear. When Crazy Coyote translated this, Tolliver was amused. He smiled and nodded, but no one else in the circle smiled. Honoring him with a new name wasn't frivolous; it was a solemn, meaningful occasion. Crazy Coyote told him this, too.

Chief Two Coups spoke next. He was the father of Little Dog. He honored Big Black Bear for saving his son's life. He said it would be wise for everyone in the tribe and all of the neighboring tribes to be vigilant, to seek the far-seeing medicine of Spotted Hawk. He prophesied that many longknives would come seeking to capture or destroy Big Black Bear because he had made fools of them. Watch for these people, he warned. If they come into the land of the Lakota, kill them and leave their bones for the wolves.

Crazy Coyote translated. The man called Big Black Bear shuddered inside.

Some of Tolliver's apprehension dissipated when he learned his new home was in the lodge of Little Weasel, the wife of Barnaby Cobb and mother of Crazy Coyote. It narrowed the language barrier considerably, for Little Weasel had some knowledge of English. It was poorly phrased English and she used it sparingly, but it was adequate. Tolliver guessed Little Weasel was in her late thirties. (Crazy Coyote had told Tolliver that he was twenty years old. He had a younger brother, Black Bow, who was twelve.) When she first welcomed him into her tipi, she wore a long buckskin skirt and a bright red blouse. Her black hair was partially hidden by a red and blue blanket. An attractive woman, she wore many colorful strands of beads. Tolliver had seen Sioux women around Fort Laramie, but he had never seen a woman wearing such an assortment of necklaces as Little Weasel. He commented how beautiful they were. Some were beads of gold and silver. Capa Tanaka, she explained, Big Beaver, was the name the Lakota had given Barnaby Cobb. In his early days on the frontier Cobb had traded in beaver pelts. Big Beaver always brought her gifts when he returned from one of his trading trips.

Tolliver was also fortunate in that Little Weasel kept a tidy lodge. Except for the fire pit in the center of the spacious dwelling, the floor was covered with robes. A variety of clothing was suspended from crossbars lashed to the lodge poles. In one area, several boxes and an assortment of parfleches were neatly stored. (Tolliver discovered later that Little Weasel always had a good supply of dried and tinned foods stashed away in these containers. Much of it was government issue, undoubtedly procured at army posts, either traded or stolen. Tolliver, grateful for the hospitality extended to him, never inquired about such things.)

Little Weasel had a steaming black pot on the fire outside her lodge. On the rocks next to it was a large covered skillet. She said in fractured English she wasn't expecting her son home so soon. It was an honor to have Big Black Bear sharing her lodge. Now it was time for him to share her meal; she had plenty.

The flat cakes in her pan were thick and doughy; the stew (Crazy Coyote said it was antelope) was laced with small pieces of prairie turnip and mushrooms. It was spiced with sage and pepper; her coffee was very strong and bitter with chicory. Tolliver ate heartily and drank sparingly. Physically and mentally exhausted, he went to the pile of robes she had prepared for him; he slept until dawn.

The morning was chilly so Tolliver bundled up in his big dark coat. Crazy Coyote and little brother Black Bow joined him for a walk around the perimeter of the village. Soon following were a few curious children and their dogs. The smaller boys had only seen one *wasichu* in their lives—Barnaby Cobb, the man called Big Beaver, but except for his coat and hat and big black boots, Big Black Bear didn't look much different from any other man in the village. True, his face wasn't too dark but his eyes and hair were. They thought he could look like a Lakota if his hair were longer and he wore buckskins and moccasins. His feet were very big. Big Black Bear would need big moccasins.

The doctor told Crazy Coyote that his dark brown eyes and hair came from his mother's side of the family. They had been colonists. However, his grandfather, George Tobias Tolliver, had been a redcoat, an officer in the regiments of King George. Perhaps his grandfather had big feet. He didn't know because he had never met the gentleman. Crazy Coyote said he knew nothing about redcoats, but he hoped they were better than bluecoats. The bluecoats had been plenty big trouble.

Tolliver didn't elaborate. He didn't tell Crazy Coyote another revolution was about to take place on the prairie. But then, perhaps Crazy Coyote already knew this.

Tolliver made observations. He saw young boys and women bringing in wood from the nearby timbered slopes. He saw older men, too, but there were only a few young braves about. His young Oglala friend explained this. Several days ago, more than twenty warriors went back to the Powder River country. Along with men from other nearby villages, they were planning to attack the supply wagons trying to reach Fort Reno. When Cold Maker came, there would be no food in the fort. The bluecoats didn't know how to hunt, how to take care of themselves on the cold winter prairie. Either they would have to go home or starve to death.

Tolliver reflected. Hadn't this been one of his assumptions? But what difference did it make? If desertions continued to deplete the garrison, the army wouldn't have to worry about feeding anyone. And, after the Fort Reno debacle, it was beyond his comprehension that the army was planning on building additional forts along the foothills of the Big Horn Mountains. But he was a doctor. He was trained to treat ailments of the body, not to comprehend the malfunctions of the army mind.

Dr. Tolliver had two visits this day, the first from Chief Two Coups and his son, Little Dog. Tolliver was seated on a robe enjoying the warmth of the afternoon sun. He politely stood and greeted the chief with a customary "*hau*." Two Coups acknowledged this with a nod. He sat on the robe and beckoned Tolliver to join him. Crazy Coyote explained that Two Coups wanted to talk and smoke; he had come to express his thanks for the attention Big Black Bear had given his son at the big soldiers' lodge during the Moon of the Drying Grass.

Little Dog produced a small pipe. He went to Little Weasel's cooking fire and lit it with an ember. Tolliver and Two Coups alternately took puffs. The sweet aroma of tobacco, red willow, and kinnikinnick permeated the air around them.

After a moment of meditation, Two Coups spoke.

"The breath of this pipe is symbolic of renewed life. This is a stick and a stone but together it is the pipe of friendship. I am honored to share it with you. That you forsook your people to save the life of my son is the greatest honor of all. You have a pure heart, my brother. You travel the Red Road and I will speak of this in the council."

Crazy Coyote had been translating as Two Coups spoke, and when the chief finished, Crazy Coyote looked at Tolliver and smiled. "You make a good friend, Toll-e-veer. This is good. Some chiefs no trust bluecoats, say no damn good. Two Coups make good talk for you."

Tolliver understood. He was a foreigner in the village. Until he somehow proved himself, he would be looked upon with suspicion. Two Coups was a strong ally. This was the underlying message—mistrust. Well, these people had every reason to mistrust him. The very clothes he was wearing were reason enough. He was a bluecoat—or had been. Yet on the other hand, a few of the chiefs must have thought he was trustworthy—they sent five Dog Soldiers out to free him. Tolliver had pondered on this more than once. Had Little Dog died from complications of his wound it would have been an honorable death. Had he been shot or, worse yet, hanged, it would have been a disgrace. Honorable death, dishonorable death, what difference did it make? Dead was dead. And his freedom seemed something more than poetic justice. He was confused. He had to get into the minds of these people, learn to understand them.

Tolliver said to Crazy Coyote. "Tell the chief I'm

not a soldier. I'm a doctor, a healer. I don't shoot people. I try to save them. I thought it was my duty to help his son. And I didn't want him shot a second time for stealing a damn horse. I value any man's life."

Crazy Coyote gave Tolliver a crooked grin. "They gonna shoot Toll-e-veer for stealing the general's pony, eh?"

"Good heavens, no! They put me in confinement—jail. You know that."

Crazy Coyote shrugged. "A joke, Toll-e-veer, a joke." He turned and began translating. Moments later Two Coups spoke again. Tolliver attentively waited. Finally Crazy Coyote said, "Chief Two Coups says he understands. He wants make you welcome with our people. Big friends. He hopes you stay long time, be plenty happy. Bluecoats no want you, Lakota do. You no go away, stay here. Bluecoats coming make more forts. He says we go on warpath. You be big help to Lakota saving lives."

"Good grief!" exclaimed Tolliver. "He already knows about those plans for the forts?"

"It's big secret?"

"Well, I surely thought so."

Crazy Coyote shook his head. "No secret, Toll-e-veer. If hang-around-fort Injuns know, we all know, eh?" He grinned. "How you think Little Dog and Crazy Coyote get on hay wagons work?"

Flabbergasted, Tolliver emitted a great sigh. "One way or another, you people seem to stick together, don't you?"

"Pipe of friendship."

"Is that so," Tolliver said. "Well, I like friendship

a damn sight better than war. You tell the chief I'm happy to be here, but I don't want to join his army. I plan on being out of this crazy country before the shooting starts."

"He has gift for you."

"Oh, Lord."

Crazy Coyote translated again. He smiled and turned back to Tolliver. "Chief Two Coups says maybe you change mind."

Two women approached, one young, the other older. The older woman was Teal Eye, the wife of Two Coups. Beside her, holding a bundle, was her daughter, Red Moccasin. Under their blankets, they both wore long buckskin dresses but their moccasins weren't hidden. They were fringed and beautifully decorated with intricate beadwork.

"Sister . . . mother," Little Dog said from the side.

Tolliver glanced over at Little Dog. Someone had taught him the words "sister" and "mother." Perhaps those sneaky dogs at the fort. Or Crazy Coyote.

Tolliver nodded and said, *"Waśte."* To the two women, he said, *"Hau kola,"* the only expressions he knew.

Red Moccasin shyly stepped forward and placed the bundle in front of her father. Stepping back, she looked at Tolliver and smiled, a very small smile. She was a slender, pretty, young woman, no more than sixteen or seventeen, Tolliver thought, slightly taller than her mother, and small beads and breath feathers adorned the sides of her black hair.

With a twinkle in his black eyes, Two Coups

spoke to Tolliver, then leaned over and placed the bundle in his hands. Crazy Coyote grinned at the doctor. "Chief Two Coups says people call you Big Black Bear. Not so good you go 'round looking like bear. He says this big chief's shirt. You wear. You no chief but you look like one."

Tolliver unrolled the bundle. Indeed, it was a shirt, a long pullover buckskin fringed down the sleeves and across the bottom. It was heavily beaded; it was bleached almost pure white. Under his mustache, Tolliver's smile was broad. Everyone could see he was delighted. They smiled, too.

"Why, this is beautiful!" he exclaimed. He leaned toward Two Coups and bowed several times. He stared helplessly at Crazy Coyote. "How can I thank him for such a fine gift? Why, something like this would bring a fancy price down at the fort. What can I say?"

"*Eya he, pila miyah,*" Crazy Coyote said. "You say, *kola, pila miyah.* Teal Eye and Red Moccasin make this shirt. They make plenty. You go see, maybe make you leggings and moccasins, eh?"

Then Little Dog spoke. Crazy Coyote said to Tolliver, "Little Dog says you welcome in mother's lodge. You big brother now. He has pretty sister. Come eat and smoke anytime. You understand?"

Tolliver nodded and smiled. Yes, he thought he understood. His smile was a weak one.

Not long after Two Coups and his family left, a woman arrived at Little Weasel's lodge. Tolliver could only see her face. Her body was covered by a red and blue blanket. She was short and middle-aged and she scurried about like an impatient squirrel, first to one side of Crazy Coyote, then the other. After a brief conversation, she tossed a look at Tolliver, then hurried away.

Crazy Coyote told Tolliver he was an honored man—one of the *wisca-wakan*, a chief called White Wolf, wanted to talk with him. White Wolf, explained Crazy Coyote, had powerful medicine; like Tolliver, he was a healer, a doctor; he also was a holy man and visionary. Crazy Coyote said he didn't know whether this was good news or bad news. Sometimes White Wolf was a very contrary man.

This piqued Tolliver's curiosity. He had heard stories from several army doctors about the unusual healing practices among these people, some practical, some mysterious. Tolliver gave Crazy Coyote a questioning look. "Do you have any notion why this fellow wants to see me? One night in the village, and I'm summoned to the lodge of a holy man, a seer so to speak. To read my fortune? Nonsense. It's bad, I know that. To cure me of something I don't know I have? To assist him in practice? Why, my friend?"

"We go find out," Crazy Coyote said. "He no want help, I tell you that. He has two women, that old one . . . another fat one. They help. They keep watch. White Wolf's lodge *wakan*. You understand?"

"He doesn't like visitors?"

"He no like *wasichu*."

"Well, who in the hell around here does?"

"I like *wasichu* sometimes."

"I should hope so. Your mother married one."

"Big Beaver?" Crazy Coyote laughed. "My father more Injun than White Wolf. My father lived here before White Wolf. Two Coups likes Toll-e-veer, eh? You *wasichu*. You have friends." He motioned. "Come, go now. You no worry. No sick, White Wolf no make medicine, no hit belly, no make drink plenty-bad-smell potion."

Tolliver folded his new buckskin shirt and set it aside. Getting to his feet, he said, "He does those things?"

"Plenty more," Crazy Coyote replied. They walked. Immediately, a few children gathered. They followed. Crazy Coyote continued, "You fix leg of Little Dog, eh? That before we move village. He come good all right. Plenty sore. Plenty blood from riding pony. White Wolf stop bleeding."

"The lad must have hemorrhaged," Tolliver opined. "I thought I did a good job on that leg."

"You do good job," Crazy Coyote said. "White Wolf tell Little Dog *waśte*. Sew 'em plenty good. White Wolf put on chipmunk tail potion, eh? Wrap on rawhide plenty tight. No more blood."

Tolliver's brow arched. Gadfrey, a potion from the tail of a chipmunk! What kind of a hemostatic alkaloid could White Wolf get from an animal's hind end? Tolliver gave Crazy Coyote a curious stare. "A chipmunk's tail? Did you see White Wolf do this?"

"No see. Little Dog tells me."

"I never heard of such a thing."

Sensing some misinterpretation, Crazy Coyote laughed. He said, "*Mi-ya*, no tail from chipmunk!"

He moved his fingers around in a mad scrambling motion. "No, no, my friend. This plant, eh? You see. In meadows. Many white flowers. Leaves like tail of chipmunk. You understand?"

Tolliver sighed in exasperation. Always, "Do you understand?" Most often he understood. Frequently, he had to digest a subtlety, sometimes solve a riddle, but ultimately, understanding surfaced. He looked at Crazy Coyote. "In English, we call that plant yarrow. It's ancient . . . very old. It reduces the clotting time. It's a mild disinfectant, too. *Herba militaris.*" Crazy Coyote pointed. A large lodge was directly ahead of them, standing in front of it, the same woman who had recently come to Little Weasel's tipi. When she saw Tolliver and Crazy Coyote approaching, she put her head to the lodge flap, apparently to alert White Wolf. The medicine chief didn't appear; it was a rotund woman, instead, and from what Tolliver could make of it, she had a bundle of switches in her hand. Yes, the lodge entrance was fully protected.

She was a large woman, all right, the heftiest that Tolliver had seen in the village, and she immediately went to work with the switches. They weren't switches, Crazy Coyote whispered. They were branches of sage. Tolliver knew sage had medicinal properties, but he didn't know it was used in ceremony. (He later learned it was a very significant plant used in all Lakota rituals.) From head to toe, she whisked the sage around Tolliver and Crazy Coyote.

Finally, Tolliver asked Crazy Coyote, "Do you

know what this is all about? If she keeps this up, we're going to sprout flowers."

"Bad spirits," Crazy Coyote said. "She do this keep away bad spirits. Plenty bad medicine in lodge, eh?"

"Bad spirits, is it?" Tolliver grinned. "I think this has been my problem ever since I arrived in this land. God bless her, but it's a little too late to cure me now."

"I no tell her that."

"No, please don't, my friend."

Once satisfied, the large woman disappeared inside. The little woman motioned to Tolliver and Crazy Coyote to follow. Inside, Tolliver saw White Wolf sitting on the far side of a fire pit. The rocks were arranged in a perfect circle, and a tiny fire burned directly in the middle. Light illuminated the lodge; the vent at the top was open, and the skirts were raised. Tolliver sniffed. The air was delightfully fragrant. Juniper, pine. There were a few small bundles of braided grass suspended from the lodge poles. At one side, Tolliver saw an array of pots, large and small, and many small parfleches all tightly bound with rawhide. Undoubtedly, these were the herbs and ingredients from which White Wolf concocted his potions.

Tolliver and Crazy Coyote sat opposite White Wolf. The two women returned to guard the entry. For a while, there was silence. Outside, Tolliver heard the distant shouts of children, the bark of a dog, and an old woman scolding someone. He had no idea why he had been summoned to White Wolf's lodge until the chief finally spoke.

Crazy Coyote whispered, "He says you are here not by fate or accident. He says a spirit has directed you to the Lakota. He says because of this, you are welcome. He wants to tell you the purpose of his dwelling."

And then as Crazy Coyote continued to quietly translate, White Wolf spoke instructively. "Wakan Tanka, the Great Spirit, made all things. All men are his children. The Great Spirit is our father, but the earth is our mother. She nourishes us. What we put into the ground, she returns to us. Likewise, Mother Earth gives us healing plants and the Great Spirit gives us the wisdom to use them. When we are sick, when we are wounded, we go to Mother Earth and lay the wounded part against her to be healed. Man knows that all healing plants are given to us by Wakan Tanka, and to man he gave the knowledge of how to use them."

White Wolf gestured to the surroundings. "Everything you see here is *wakan*, for everything comes from Wakan Tanka. The wisdom and power to heal comes from Wakan Tanka, and through his spirit is given by the holy man to the people. The holy man counsels, he heals, and he makes charms to protect his people from evil. His power is great. He is honored by his people." White Wolf paused and looked across the ring of rocks. "Red Bone tells me you are a healer. He tells me what I already know. I have seen your healing power on the young man called Little Dog. His wound was deep. Your cut was small, your skill great." Once again, the maker of medicines directed Tolliver to the assortment of pots and parfleches. He said, "If a spirit has brought you here, it must be for the purpose of healing. How great is this spirit? Go forth and tell me about the gifts Mother Earth has given us."

After Crazy Coyote translated this, Tolliver was shocked, not visibly, but a slight chill coursed his body. My God, could this be? White Wolf wanted him to inspect his medicines and explain their curative values! Tolliver whispered to Crazy Coyote, "This has nothing to do with a spirit bringing me here, my friend. I'm a surgeon. This man wants to know if I understand anything about medicine. It's a test. He wants to know how much I know . . . or don't know."

Crazy Coyote gave him a blank look. "Why? Why he do this?"

"How in the hell do I know?"

"Make you horse's ass?"

Tolliver grimaced.

"My father says that."

"Shall I play like I'm a horse's ass?"

"No." Crazy Coyote smiled. "You go look in bags. Tell him plenty good."

Tolliver pulled himself up. He stared up at the open tipi vent. Divine guidance? His days of medical school were far behind. How much did he remember? Tolliver looked down at Crazy Coyote. "You make sure you repeat everything I say loud and clear. He won't understand the English terms. You have to be clever. Chipmunk tail, egads!"

Dr. Tolliver stopped in front of the store of plants and herbs. He knew as well as White Wolf he wasn't going to identify them all, so he chose a few at random. He could ease the unfamiliar ones to the side. Tolliver looked over at White Wolf. The old man was staring into his tiny fire of twigs.

Tolliver removed a leather covering from a pot. He sniffed. Mint. Well, this already was a good one. Mint tea? No, the old man wouldn't be making mint tea. Horsemint? Likely. Tolliver spoke up loudly, "Horsemint, brewed. Believed good for regulating menstrual flow or related female problems."

Crazy Coyote whispered a protest. "I no translate that . . ."

Tolliver went on. "Balsam fir. Balsam trumatick. A wound dressing. Grind needles to powder and mix with grease derivative. Good for infections, a poultice. Sometimes used in tea form for coughs or colds." Ah, here was one! "Yarrow." He stopped and stared at Crazy Coyote. "Yarrow. Disinfects and believed to promote rapid healing. Tea has sudorofic properties, used to break fevers . . ."

"I don't know what you're saying," implored Crazy Coyote.

"That's all right," replied Tolliver. "Neither does he."

And Tolliver continued. He discovered Oregon grape, lovage, alumroot, gumweed, chokecherry, and box elder. He shoved aside a half-dozen other containers. He had no idea what was in them. Ground toenails or some glutinous potion from a buffalo hoof. What did it matter? He had proved himself knowledgeable. Tolliver swung around and faced White Wolf. The old man still had his eyes fixed on the fire.

Tolliver said, "Tell him Mother Earth is great. Many people across the big rivers and the oceans have been blessed by her benevolence . . . and the Great Spirit, Wakan Tanka. Tell him he is wise and powerful. And let's get the hell out of here."

Chapter 5

Indian summer was over. The trees along the river were barren, scrawny skeletons against the first skiff of snow, and geese were on the high wing in the cold buttermilk sky. By James Tolliver's calculation, it was early November. He felt secure in his primitive surroundings; he also felt trapped. He had a few good friends, but as yet none had offered to guide him east toward civilization.

Tolliver realized there were reasons for this—the Sioux were occupied with more urgent matters. Winter was near. Hunters arrived with meat and left for more; braves joined war parties from other neighboring villages to harass the army along the Powder River.

On this brisk morning, six Indians rode into the village from the east. They caused a frenzy of activity in the lodge of Little Weasel. She told Big Black Bear these were Hunkpapa braves en route to join Sitting Bull's winter village on the west side of the Paha Sapa. They had encountered her husband, Big Beaver—he was on the Cheyenne River trail with a wagon and eight mules. The trader, Barnaby Cobb, was coming home.

A joyful Little Weasel began making preparations. She hung fresh boughs of juniper to scent the lodge; she sorted through her food cache for delicacies; a homecoming feast was in the making.

Tolliver's interpreter, Crazy Coyote, who the Oglala occasionally now called Plenty Talk, had left the village at dawn with several others to hunt deer in the nearby hills. Little Weasel told Tolliver that Crazy Coyote was a great hunter; there would be fresh liver for her pot this night. In a way, it was too bad he had gone—if he weren't hunting, he would be on the river trail to meet his father. Black Bow, her twelve-year-old, was listening to this conversation. Though he knew only a smattering of English, he understood some of what they were saying. Tolliver smiled. He pointed a thumb at Black Bow, directed it to himself, and then made a motion of going away. Tolliver told Little Weasel he would be happy to ride out and meet Barnaby Cobb. He was restless; he needed some activity; a good ride would suit him fine. This pleased her. Then he suggested to Little Weasel that Black Bow saddle two horses and accompany him. She spoke to her young son. With a gleeful shout, he bounded away to fetch the ponies.

Shortly, the *wasichu* called Big Black Bear and his young friend, Black Bow, were on the trail heading east. Tolliver had on his great coat and dark cavalry hat. Little Weasel had given him a bright red wool scarf. He wore this around his head to protect his ears. He was on the piebald mare sitting a McClellan saddle. He looked exactly like what he no longer was—a U.S. cavalryman.

They rode until shortly after the sun had reached its highest point. At a distant bend near the river, they finally saw a mule-drawn wagon and a small wisp of bluish smoke. It appeared that Barnaby Cobb had stopped to rest his stock and brew a cup of coffee.

Black Bow reined up, pointed, and smiled proudly. "*Ateyapi, Capa Tanka.*" He looked across at Tolliver. "He Papa, eh?" Then with a shrill scream, he kicked away hell-bent for the distant bend. Pulling his hat low, Tolliver charged after him.

Barnaby Cobb was a stalwart frontiersman dressed in boots and buckskins and a wolverine-trimmed coat. He wore a furry hat banded by bead-work. He had a rifle resting against a rock near his smoke-blackened pot. His bronzed cheekbones flared out from a dark brown beard. He had been living with the people of the plains for thirty years, but there wasn't a speck of gray in his hair. He was out of the mold of Jim Bridger and Tom Fitzpatrick. That he still had his hair was amazing in itself.

Barnaby wasn't surprised to see his younger son ride up. He lifted him off the ground in a mighty hug. But he was both astounded and puzzled when he saw James Tolliver dismounting. Black Bow partially explained. This *wasichu* was a friend, a guest in their lodge.

This was the extent of the introduction, for in a deep, rumbling voice, Barnaby asked, "How in tarnation did you get way up here, soldier? There ain't been a white man on this trail 'cept me in years! For God's sake, what you doing here?"

Tolliver extended his hand in friendship. Barnaby Cobb gave it a hardy shake. Tolliver replied, "Some of the men in the village brought me ... I'd say close to two weeks ago. My name is James Tolliver, and I'm not a soldier, at least not anymore."

"Tolliver!" exclaimed Barnaby. His whiskers jumped. "Tolliver, the doctor fellow ... Fort Laramie? ... that Tolliver?"

"Yes, sir, the one and the same."

"Good God, man, the whole damn country is looking for you!" Barnaby Cobb leaned over and rummaged around in a cloth sack. He handed a tin cup to Tolliver. He gave his own cup to his son. Barnaby went on. "Why, I hear tell there's patrols running the North Platte all the way to Atkinson looking to arrest you. Reward on your head."

Tolliver gingerly tipped the coffeepot and poured. The tin cup was stinging hot against his cold lips. "I didn't think they would miss me that much," Tolliver said. "You've heard all about it, then?"

"Who in hell hasn't! You're the crazy bastard that stole General Connor's horse, ain't you?" He stared over at the piebald mare. "By God, you're still riding the critter, too. Why, that's pure gall if I ever saw it! Lookee there, you ain't even smudged the brand. U.S.!"

Tolliver grinned. "There's quite a few with this mark on them back at the village."

"No general's horse, I'll bet."

"That's some kind of an honor?"

"A real coup, by God! You made a laughingstock out of the army, son. Every Injun 'round knows the story. Hell, they oughtta give you a feather for that stunt." Black Bow returned the cup to Barnaby. He took a long draught and said, "You made a fool out of 'em getting outta the fort, too. Some shavetail down on the Platte trail told me they ain't figured yet how you got over the wall . . . even how you got away. Never found sign of your horse. Only what you left behind, that dead fellow, his throat cut ear to ear. That lieutenant says he never figured you for something like that."

"I didn't kill that soldier," protested Tolliver. "One of your brothers from the village killed him . . . maybe your son Crazy Coyote or Little Dog . . . maybe both of them for all I know. I never asked."

Barnaby Cobb's eyes exploded white. "Great balls of fire! My boy was in on it! Little Dog, too? How in the hell did they get tangled up in this mess?"

Tolliver said, "Look here, Mr. Cobb, I sure didn't get out of there by myself. Five of those men came down and got me out . . . thought the army was going to hang me, or send me down the river to break rocks for five years. I understand the council gave them the approval."

"Damn fools!"

"They seemed to take great enjoyment in it."

"Crazy dogs!"

"Yes, so I found out." Tolliver gave Barnaby a curious look. "I thought you might have had a hand in it. Just a thought."

"No, by God, not me."

"You saw Little Dog after he was shot. That's what Bridger said."

"Well, yes, I did," admitted Barnaby.

"You told those people I was in the stockade."

"I did that," Barnaby replied. "I said it was a dirty shame, but I sure didn't go saying nothing about going down and jerking you outta the goddamned place." His face was all innocence. "Y'see, Mr. Tolliver, I have to work in and out of that fort, trading and such. Now I wouldn't be able to trade a bean down here if someone got the idea I had something to do with this. Y'see my point, boy?"

"Yes, I surely do, Mr. Cobb." Tolliver took a sip of coffee, then said, "By the way, that lieutenant you talked with on the trail . . . did you get his name?"

"Looked in my wagon, he did." Barnaby grinned. "Thought maybe I had you stashed away under the canvas."

"His name?"

"Larry . . . Leary . . ."

"O'Leary?"

"I reckon that's right. O'Leary. Said he knew you right well."

"Army intelligence."

"Yassir, he seemed right intelligent."

Tolliver and Black Bow tied their mounts behind and joined Barnaby on the seat of the wagon. It was a leisurely ride back up the river trail, the trader in no particular hurry. The sky had cleared; it was sunny, and he knew he would reach camp before dusk.

Though Tolliver was disturbed by the news that the army now considered him a killer, he wasn't too surprised. Crazy Coyote had already warned him of this possibility. And since he had taken up residency with the Sioux, albeit temporarily, he was a traitor, too. This was a chilling thought—out here there was no distinction between killers, traitors, and horse thieves. Their ultimate reward was a rope, and in the short span of two and a half months, he had become all three, an outcast, a man without a country.

Barnaby Cobb talked. Black Bow handled the reins, and Tolliver listened. Barnaby said he didn't see much promise in the peace talks proposed by Colonel Maynadier. Rumors of more forts along the Bozeman Trail were already circulating among the tribes. He thought it unlikely that any of the big chiefs, namely Red Cloud, Sitting Bull, or the Cheyenne leader the Lakota called Dull Knife, would agree to any concessions about forts in the buffalo grounds. Barnaby saw nothing ahead but trouble— a major conflict between Indians and the army.

Tolliver had heard rumors, too, probably more than rumors. What chance did the Indians have if the government decided to put more troops in the field, accelerate its campaign? Barnaby had given considerable thought to this possibility. He opined the Sioux and Cheyenne were too elusive for the bluecoats. The Indians were better fighters. They were dedicated to protecting their land. As had been the case with General Connor, they would make the army's presence in the valleys a miserable one. But Barnaby also had reservations. The defense of the buffalo grounds would come at a terrible price for his red brothers.

Though Barnaby supported his people's cause, he said he was reluctant to participate in it. The thought of his brothers, particularly his family, suffering grieved him. But these were his people; he had lived with them all of his adult life; he had smoked, eaten, and lodged with them; he had counted coup with them. He couldn't forsake them, nor could he take his family from the tribe and move north out of harm's way.

Oh, he had thought about this more than once. He could exist anywhere. He had white blood. But his wife and children? Why, they might wither on the vine like frostbitten leaves if they left the village.

Barnaby Cobb's flinty green eyes narrowed, eyes deeply lined at the corners from years of fighting the wilderness sun. He said to Tolliver, "I had me a notion of giving up the trading . . . moving up to the gold country and going into the freighting business. She's booming, y'know. Good trail down from Fort Benton to the mining camps. Right peaceful-like, too." He put an arm around Black Bow. "I reckon notions don't mean a bean when it comes to family, though." He stared at the white landscape. "Take one of those bushes, Mr. Tolliver. Pull that sucker up and try and plant those roots somewhere else. By damn, she don't grow worth a hang." Back to Tolliver. "Y'see what I mean?"

James Tolliver nodded. He had some sense of the meaning, himself. He had foolishly torn out his own roots, and consequently had half of the Army of the West on his tail. "Yes, I do, Mr. Cobb. We all have to deal with fate, I suppose."

The silence of the afternoon was broken only by the clop-clop of hooves against the frozen, winding trail. After a moment Barnaby said, "Now take you, son. 'Less you find something to do with these Oglala, it's gonna be a damn long winter." His laugh was husky and deep. "Sure as hell, you don't look like no mountain man."

"I don't plan on staying the winter," Tolliver said.

"Well, now, just where in the hell do you plan on spending it? In Mexico?" He laughed again.

"I want to go down the river," answered Tolliver. "All the way . . . maybe New Orleans for a start."

Barnaby scoffed. "New Orleans, is it? Son, you set foot on that river and likely you'll end up wintering in Fort Leavenworth. 'Sides, 'nother two weeks, ain't no boats coming up the Mizzou. Water's down and she'll be icing up." He thumbed to the back. "I got this load outta Pierre. Might well be the last 'til spring."

Tolliver sagged in the fur-covered seat. Lord, Lord, six months with these people? This was preposterous. "How about overland?" he asked hopefully. "How about a stage or a freighter . . . Saint Joseph?"

"Freeze your ass off if you don't get caught first," Barnaby returned sourly. "Course you could do what I was thinking . . . maybe make it to the gold camps. Those bluecoats ain't likely to be looking for you to go the other way, the Montana Territory. You might be touched but not that touched."

"I'm not touched," sighed Tolliver. "Irrational at times, certainly not touched."

"Those boys at Laramie think you're crazy."

"I'll freeze my butt trying to get north, won't I? How do I get up there? Have one of your spirits guide me?" His lips dragged. He gave Barnaby a disgusted look. "That's how I got here, you know.

Dammit all, old White Wolf says a spirit led me here. All of this was meant to be."

Barnaby Cobb grinned. "Ah, you met the head shaman already, eh?"

"I surely did. The old bugger tested me on my medical knowledge."

"Worried about his own medicine, he is," explained Barnaby.

"Worried?"

"Ehyup. Guards his power right close. Most of these holy men do that, y'know."

"Zealous?"

"Don't know that word, son, but if it's meaning jealous-like, that's right. Someone goes knowing more'n he does; he's likely to lose some of his medicine. That means he loses face ... business, too. White Wolf don't cotton to that."

Exasperated, Tolliver said, "Good grief, man, I don't intend to usurp his authority or business. How can I? I don't have a single drug or instrument with me. All I have are the clothes on my back ... and that dratted mare that everyone seems to gloat about. I don't even own her. She's stolen." With a touch of irritation, Tolliver asked, "How can I reach the mining camps?"

"Ride like hell," chuckled Barnaby. "Carry fire in your saddle and watch your backside. Pray to God you don't run into Blackfeet ... or some of Ben Tree's Mountain Crow. Three to four weeks up that way."

"Who is this Ben Tree?"

"A contrary breed chief who hates whites."

"You know him?"

"Sorta know him."

"Then you take me. I'll pay you."

"Next spring," replied Barnaby. "Next spring I'll think about it. I ain't going nowhere but home for now. I'm tired of trailing and trading."

"I'm doomed," moaned Tolliver.

"Now don't go getting all sorrowful on me. You ain't doomed. Alive, ain't you? Eating my woman's food right regular, ain't you? Not all skinny like a beggarman's bitch, are you?"

"No," sighed Tolliver. "No, but I'm worthless as a beggarman's bitch. I'm nothing but a charity case."

With a little snort, Barnaby said, "Reckon that woman of mine ain't made you all that welcome, mebee thinks you don't take to Lakota women."

"On the contrary," Tolliver said, "she's treated me like one of the family."

"Ain't bedded you, has she?"

Tolliver was mortified. "Heavens, no! What kind of man do you take me to be! I'm no cad, Mr. Cobb."

Barnaby simply shrugged and grinned. "She likes white men. Always has my permission to bed who she chooses. Keeps her happy this way when I'm gone so confounded much."

Tolliver blinked in disbelief. This was incredible! His black eyes widened. "White men? For God's sake, I've been the only white man in the country until now. And besides, isn't that adultery? I can't believe this."

Barnaby nodded. "Consorting? Sorta, I reckon, I don't mind. Nothing to go 'round preaching 'bout, but it happens among these Injuns now and then.

Some like a bit of sharing. Oh, I recall ol' Fred Jennings staying on with us one fall. Snow chased him out, say 'bout seven years ago. I went out for a couple weeks fetching bear hides. Came back and he has a big grin on his face. That's all, just a grin. I didn't ask, neither, and my woman, well, that's her business."

Tolliver shuddered.

Barnaby Cobb chuckled. "Well," he concluded, "if you're no account in the robes, I'll make a hunter outta you. We'll go out with some of the boys and fetch meat, get some elk . . . makes for good eating in the cold months, better'n dried buffalo and that goddamned *wasna*. Valuable hides, too. Earn your keep this way and you won't go 'round all mealy-mouthed."

"I don't even own a rifle, dammit."

Barnaby Cobb thumbed to the back again. "Got me some fancy ones hidden in the packs of those long-eared mules. Latest things from the U.S. arsenal, they are. Carbines, by God! Rim-fire percussion. I can loan you one . . . sell it to you, if you want."

"Good grief! You *are* running guns then!"

Barnaby Cobb stiffened as though shot by an arrow. He gave Tolliver an innocent look. "It's just on the side, boy. Most of this freight is flour'n beans'n coffee, some dry goods, and a little raw whiskey for my personal use when I get the ague. That's all. Oh, I get a few rifles now and then when I can make a deal, y'know, but it's chancy business. Get myself caught and I'd likely end up down the river where they want to put you."

My God, thought Tolliver, this man was impossible! Very clever, too. Muzzle loaders, old Hawkens, a Sharps or two, but repeaters? Tolliver said, "May I ask, Mr. Cobb, how you traded for those weapons? Or did you procure them some other way?"

"Y'mean thieving?"

Tolliver shrugged. "Whatever."

"I'm a trader, not a thief . . . discounting ponies. Course, my people don't consider fetching up a few ponies as thieving. More of a coup. That's the way they look at you taking that mare, y'know. 'Cept taking the horse of a big chief is a powerful coup."

"The army doesn't look at it that way."

"Oh, I know that."

"How did you get the rifles?"

Barnaby Cobb thoughtfully rubbed his beard. He cocked his head and said, "Now, you wouldn't go spillin' the beans, would you? Spoil my game?"

"How in the hell can I spoil anyone's game in this godforsaken country?"

"You don't see the land like we do, son."

"Mother Earth. I know. White Wolf told me all about Mother Earth."

Barnaby grinned. "'Cept for stealing the general's horse, you look like an honest man, Mr. Tolliver."

"I consider myself so. I have scruples."

"Some of your army boys don't," replied Barnaby. "Trick is to find one who's looking for a little cash on the side, say like a sergeant or a sergeant major in ordnance supply. Smart fellows, they are . . . know how to rig a bill of lading right well, they do."

"That's terribly dishonest!" exclaimed Tolliver.

"It's stockade time or dismissal from the ranks. It's worse than stealing a damn horse."

"Hardware or horseflesh, don't make much difference, does it? They just lose track of a few rifles is all. I pay 'em half price for finding 'em, and I move on out."

"Gadfrey!"

"Course," Barnaby said, smiling, "a fellow can get himself a good supply of guns when a string of supply wagons is on the trail. Takes a helluva lot of my brothers to do it that way, though. Bigger risk. Likely someone's gonna get shot . . . like Little Dog when they caught him in the pony herd at Fort Connor."

"Fort Reno," Tolliver corrected.

Barnaby was surprised. "Fort Reno? Changed the name, did they?"

"They did. The army didn't think it was an appropriate name."

This didn't surprise Barnaby Cobb.

Trader Cobb had many friends, and with the exception of a few old men everyone seemed to have turned out to greet him. His arrival was heralded by tremolos and lusty shouts. Tolliver wondered what a furor and tumult this rascal would cause in a large village.

Little Weasel climbed on the wagon. She had tears in her eyes. Crazy Coyote, one arm raised high, led the mules around in a big circle. To Tolliver, it was heartwarming to be a small part of the homecoming. Big Beaver could well have been a gladiator making a triumphant appearance in front

78

of the Forum. He was an honored man. Tolliver soon learned that some of the celebration had materialistic connotations.

It took almost half an hour to unload the wagon and pack train. Half of the supplies, including Barnaby's blanket-wrapped weapons (twelve Spencer and Henry rifles), went into Little Weasel's big lodge. An orderly line of men and women formed, and Barnaby and Crazy Coyote passed out an assortment of items previously ordered, everything from food staples to beads, trinkets, cotton and flannel cloth, and woolen blankets. Tolliver, quietly observing by the lodge entrance, marveled at this. No one grumbled or complained; everyone was happy, and most left with smiles on their faces. He suddenly realized that either by chance or divine purpose, he was among beautiful and caring people.

Later, James Tolliver, the unemployed doctor, joined Barnaby's small family circle around the fire inside the lodge. The excitement of the trader's return had passed; it was warm and peaceful. Little Weasel scurried back and forth bringing in her meal from the outside cooking fire. There were strips of liver basted in cornmeal; a large bowl of steaming, stewed fruits from her larder of tinned goods, these mixed with dried wild berries she had preserved in tallow. She also had a pan of flat cakes.

Shadows danced on the golden walls of the lodge. Tolliver relaxed and took comfort. Then to his astonishment, Crazy Coyote began singing. It was a happy sounding little chant, and when he had finished, everyone clapped, including Crazy Coyote.

He explained to Tolliver his song was customary. It was a song of thanksgiving he always sang when his honored father returned home.

The meal was delicious. Tolliver, in English and a few words of Siouan, complimented Little Weasel. She was pleased. He explained that in his land it was always customary to compliment the cook.

Another compliment followed, this one directed to Tolliver by Barnaby Cobb. Tolliver's elk skin shirt was very handsome. However, he thought it would be more appropriate if worn with leather pants and leggings. Tolliver said he wasn't certain but he thought such apparel might be forthcoming from the lodge of Chief Two Coups. Two Coups seemed to have taken a fancy to him.

Little Weasel and Black Bow had brought several pots of water from the river. She caught part of Tolliver's comment near the entryway. She spoke a few words in Siouan, and Barnaby smiled. "She says if you shaved off your mustache and combed your hair back you'd look like a Lakota." He pointed to Tolliver's boots. "I'm afraid those would have to go. You need winter moccasins."

"I need a haircut, that's what I need," said Tolliver. "I need a good shave, too, but my razor is as dull as an ax. I surely don't need to look like an Indian, which I'm not."

Barnaby tossed his shoulders nonchalantly. "Oh, I don't know. It might be a good idea, son. One of these days some bluecoat or bounty hunter may catch up to you. If they saw you this way, they might take you down the river to hang, eh? Who knows?"

James Tolliver grimaced. "You have a helluva way

of making a man feel comfortable, don't you? Your people brought me here to escape such incivilities. I'm supposed to be safe here."

Barnaby wagged a warning finger at Tolliver. "My friend," he said, "don't ever be fooled by this land. You have much to learn this winter if you hope to go north next spring. What looks good can turn very ugly in a matter of moments. There's a lot of men out there looking for you. Before you leave this village you're gonna have to look like an Injun and think like an Injun. You ain't gonna make it 'less you do."

James Tolliver thought about this for a while. However, by the time he climbed into his robes, he had forgotten it. He was warmly content and safe. He had one of his best sleeps in months.

When he awoke to the crackle of burning branches and twigs, he was still comfortable and warm. Stretched out beside his pallet were heavy winter moccasins, buckskin pants, a fringed, fur-lined leather jacket, and a gleaming pearl-handled razor. He stared around. Only Little Weasel was in the lodge. Tolliver gave her a sheepish grin. He said slowly, "All . . . Big Black Bear . . . needs . . . now . . . is . . . a . . . feather. *Hi ho,* feather."

Little Weasel nodded approvingly. "Maybe Toll-e-veer get."

Book Two

The Black Hills

Chapter 6

His brothers called it the Moon of the Strong Cold. The month was aptly named. A two-day blizzard swept through the valley, behind it came bone-chilling cold. Within three days the cold front passed to the east; the weather moderated, and the small Lakota camp returned to normal. Hunters and wood gatherers went out to prepare for the next frigid breath of Winter Man.

James Tolliver, weather permitting, hunted by day. Along with his reputation, his contributions to the village grew. Tolliver was an excellent marksman, Barnaby Cobb a good teacher. Barnaby gave the doctor a Henry rifle, and with this far-shooting thunder iron Tolliver killed elk, deer, and antelope. He also gained fame by shooting an enraged grizzly bear mistakenly stirred from its den by Little Dog and Crazy Coyote. They had believed it to be the den of a black bear.

Tolliver also learned to pack mules. He had a new purpose in being; his life had been enriched, and he felt some worth in himself. There were always a few scouts out searching for migrating buffalo. Tolliver now entertained thoughts of hunting the big blackhorns. He wanted to assert himself; he wanted to prove to his red brothers that he was as good as any of them.

By night, Tolliver sat by the fire and talked with the family of Big Beaver, Barnaby Cobb. Visitors came, too. Tolliver listened to many legends, and through the interchange of conversation, he began to learn Siouan. Young Black Bow admired the man called Big Black Bear, and he often sat near him. It was a trade—Black Bow and Tolliver, making sign, sometimes laughing, began to teach each other their respective tongues.

One evening toward the end of the Hungry Moon, a woman appeared at Little Weasel's lodge. Her blanket was drawn tightly around her body. She bowed in the presence of Tolliver and Barnaby. Tolliver saw she was gripped by anxiety; her eyes were wide, and she talked so rapidly he barely understood a word. After this excited exchange, the woman cried out once, parted the heavy hide flap, and disappeared.

Little Weasel spoke hurriedly to her husband, and once again Tolliver only understood a fragment or two, but Barnaby enlightened him. A young woman named Slow Runner was in the throes of labor but was unable to deliver her baby. The healer, White Wolf, had sent for Big Black Bear to see if he could help.

Tolliver immediately slipped into his moccasins. Certainly, he would see the woman. Little Weasel already had pulled her big coat around her. Tolliver, preparing to follow, turned and told Barnaby to come with them. If anxious old women were about, he needed someone who could keep them quiet. He had witnessed several heated exchanges between village women before. He wasn't about to be a party to such harangues while treating a patient.

Within moments they were in the lodge of Slow Runner. Her husband, Black Wing, and several older women were crouched over the moaning woman. White Wolf was not present. Black Wing said he had just left; he didn't want to see the medicine of Big Black Bear.

Bending over Slow Runner, Tolliver moved his hands slowly back and forth across her abdomen, then down to her pelvis. The attending women were whispering and moaning, and Tolliver told Barnaby to tell them to stand aside and keep quiet. If he needed them, he would call.

After a moment Tolliver looked up at Barnaby Cobb. "Ask them how long this woman has been in this condition."

Barnaby did. He said to Tolliver, "Two suns . . ."

"Good grief!" moaned Tolliver.

Black Wing spoke. He told Barnaby that White Wolf had made medicine for one sleep and one sun. He had been unable to bring forth the child.

Tolliver understood enough of this. He didn't wait for a translation. Instead, pointing at the fire, he shouted, "Get that fire up so I can see! Build another one by the flap. I need all the light I can get. Barnaby, tell Little Weasel to bring me that new razor . . . her needles . . . gut . . . yes, and a bottle of your damn raw whiskey."

Barnaby's jaw went slack. "What the hell . . ."

Little Weasel understood every word. She left immediately. One of the women began stirring the fire.

Tolliver, running the palm of his hand over Slow Runner's damp forehead, said, "Dammit, Barnaby, if I don't open her up, she's going to die before this night's over, probably the child, too." He carefully rested his fingers against Slow Runner's neck, then came away with another groan. "She's exhausted. Good grief, two days of this! She barely has a pulse. God, I'd give my leg for a vial of morphine . . . anything."

"Whiskey?"

"Disinfectant, the best we can do. She can't drink it now."

"She can stand the pain," Barnaby said. "These people never complain, eh? Never."

Tolliver gestured to a gawking woman. "Go make hot water, plenty of hot water. Make firebrands for more light."

Barnaby Cobb repeated what he had signed, and the woman scurried away. He stared down at Slow Runner. Her jaw was rigid, but the muscles were jumping. She heaved up once, and Tolliver took hold of one of her hands.

Barnaby asked hesitantly, "Have you . . . have you done this, Doctor . . . cut a woman before?"

"No. I've seen it done . . . twice." Tolliver said nothing more. Slow Runner's eyes were open. She was blankly staring at him. Tolliver smiled at her and nodded reassuringly. He wasn't reassured himself. He had watched cesarean operations twice, one successful and one pathetically terminal—both the infant and mother had died. And this was under the best of circumstances. Only God could help now, God and Barnaby Cobb.

Tolliver said, "I'm going to need some help, Barnaby. When that hot water gets here, wash your hands . . . thread some of the needles with the gut. Saturate them with the whiskey. And get one of the women to bring some cloth . . . clean or new, but plenty of it. If this doesn't go well, we're going to have a bloody mess on our hands."

The husband, Black Wing, spoke. What could he do?

Tolliver looked up. He said brokenly, "Go outside and make a prayer to Wakan Tanka."

Barnaby Cobb heaved a sigh. He gave Tolliver a helpless look. "I don't feel so good."

"Neither do I," confessed Tolliver.

Dr. Tolliver told Little Weasel to lie over Slow Runner's chest to keep her from moving, to talk to her, to tell her it was going to be over very soon. After this, Tolliver swabbed Slow Runner's abdomen with Barnaby's alcohol. He saturated the razor, too, then with careful precision made a horizontal cut several inches above Slow Runner's pelvis. Blood trickled down the woman's belly.

Tolliver said, "Get your cloth moving, Barnaby."

From Little Weasel there was a gasp. Slow Runner had gone limp.

Tolliver also sensed it from below. "She fainted," he said. "Slow Runner is all right." And for the moment, it *was* all right. The woman's unconsciousness was a blessing. Tolliver swiftly cut through to the uterus. He tossed the razor aside and probed back and forth. Another rush of blood bubbled up, and Barnaby quickly put cloths to each side of the long incision.

Moments later Tolliver shouted, "By gadfrey!" He pulled gently and slowly—out came a little silvery, slippery bloodstained sack. Little Weasel spun 'round and came to her knees. Tolliver plucked and pulled tissue. He dumped a tiny little girl into her outstretched hands.

Tolliver said, "*Wachin ksapa yo! Mistaput!* Clean . . . nose . . . make air . . . mouth. Make breath! Hurry now!"

A great sigh escaped Barnaby Cobb. "Oh, Lord," he gasped. "I'm shaking all over. I can't do this. I . . ."

"Stop it!" demanded Tolliver. "Stop it, dammit. I need you now more than ever. Needles . . . hurry, get down here. Put your thumbs up here . . . one there. Pry, man, pry. I've got to get in there in a hurry. She's hemorrhaging! Get a firebrand down here. I need more light."

Tolliver bent low. From the other side of the fire, a joyous shriek came from Little Weasel. A tiny jerky cry split the tenseness of the lodge. The baby was alive! Dr. Tolliver didn't smile or draw a breath of relief. His delicate fingers flew. He finally sutured the uterine wall; he swabbed with alcohol; he cleaned, a clot here, another there. He did all he could, and then he closed. He bathed the incision once again with Barnaby's raw whiskey.

Tolliver tightly bandaged Slow Runner, four wraps around her hips and across the swath at the incision. He checked her pulse. Slow but steady. He bathed her forehead and put a cold rag in back of her neck, and he patted her cheeks. Her jaw began to tremble; her eyes opened. For a moment she greedily gulped air as though her lungs had never tasted it.

Tolliver finally looked across at Barnaby Cobb. The trader's shoulders sagged; his bloodstained hands were palm up in his lap; his eyes were filled with tears. Tolliver said, "Tell these women to give her broth, hot tea, nothing else. Tell them not to let her move from the robes all night, not so much as a muscle." He turned to Little Weasel and smiled. "Put the baby on her breasts. Let this mother feel her baby. This is where the Red Road begins, eh? The source of life."

Outside the entry, James Tolliver drew a big breath of the cold night air. He was going to ask the Lord to take care of Slow Runner, to let her live so she could play with her daughter during the Summer Moon. He didn't. Standing next to him was Black Wing. He said to the young man, "*Hau kola. Wagnikte. Hechuta welo.*" Yes, for now it was finished. He would return. It was good.

Black Wing smiled and nodded. "*Pila miyah, Toll-e-veer.*"

Tolliver walked away into the night.

He heard Barnaby calling. "Hey, pilgrim, where in the hell you going? We gotta have a drink on this."

"Over to White Wolf's lodge," replied Tolliver. He thought he would ask the medicine chief if he could borrow some chipmunk tail for Slow Runner's dressing in the morning. He thought the old chief might like this.

*   *   *

At dawn, Tolliver was awakened by several twicks on his ear, this followed by a whisper. "Toll-e-veer. *Ku wanna, ku wanna.*" It was Little Weasel. He heard the fire crackling; he smelled coffee. It was time for him to make the first house call of his career. As he dressed, he said a silent prayer of thanks for the miracle of life. Slow Runner had survived the night. No one had come to roust him as he had ordered in case she showed signs of distress.

After several sips of Little Weasel's coffee, he pushed out into the chill and went to the bushes near the river. He then washed his hands in the frigid water and dried them on his face. This was primitive, but he had to make do. The only hot water he ever received was from Little Weasel's kettles on the night fire.

Black Wing and an older woman were waiting for him. They nodded and stood aside. Tolliver knelt to examine Slow Runner. She was in a deep sleep. She had a wool blanket over her shoulder, and under it was her newly born baby. Wrapped in a tiny blanket and nuzzled up against a breast, the infant was also asleep. Tolliver put his hand to Slow Runner's forehead. Normal. He detected only the warmth of the lodge. Her breathing was regular, too.

Tolliver made sign to the attending woman. Had Slow Runner eaten anything? The woman pointed to the fire. Soup. One bowl, she signed. "*Waśte,*" Tolliver whispered.

The lodge fire was too low for adequate light, so Tolliver slipped his hand under the robes and gently felt the abdominal bandage. He traced his fingers across the area around it. With a smile, he looked up and nodded. "*Waśte,*" he whispered again. Black Wing came forward and placed both hands on Tolliver's broad shoulders. "*Cilagon, misunkala. Pila miyah,*" he said.

Yes, Tolliver was his honored brother. This was good. With a broad smile, Tolliver left. "*Watinkte,*" he said to himself. "I will eat now." He felt wonderful. God was great. How miraculous this was, this blessed birth. And he wondered. This was late in the Moon of Sweat in the Tipi—December. He had no way of knowing the date. He had lost all track of time. Christmas, perhaps?

For one week, Tolliver closely monitored his patient. Slow Runner told him she had no pains, or if she did, she declined to admit it. Her big, dark eyes were filled with adoration for the man called Big Black Bear. He had saved her life; he had saved her baby's life; Big Black Bear had powerful medicine, *wochangi otapi.* Slow Runner honored him—she named her daughter White Medicine Woman.

Others honored James Tolliver, too. The men in the village already recognized him as a powerful hunter. In the eyes of the women, his medicine was *wakan,* the birth of White Medicine Woman spiritually invoked. When Tolliver walked the perimeters of the camp, the admiring eyes of the women followed him. They whispered behind their blankets. Toll-e-veer was indeed *wichaska wakan.* With his hands he had brought forth a child from a woman's belly. The child was alive and the woman walked. This was remarkable; this was *wakan.*

But when Barnaby Cobb and Little Weasel told

Tolliver how the women now regarded him, he was distressed. He implored both of them to tell the people his medicine had been learned from years of practice; it was a special kind of medicine, but it was not spiritual, nor was it infallible. Sometimes it failed. Through many prayers, Wakan Tanka had blessed Slow Runner, not James Tolliver. There was much talk about this. Not everyone was convinced. After all, hadn't the two village healers agreed? Red Bone and White Wolf both said that Big Black Bear had come to the village by a purposeful and divine design, not by accident. To them, this meant Toll-e-veer had been spiritually guided. Though the *wasichu* was ignorant of tribal customs, the sacredness of rituals, and the power of Wakan Tanka, they respected his knowledge of surgical medicine. Red Bone and White Wolf also honored Toll-e-veer. In time, they would teach him to become Lakota. Once Lakota, the man called Big Black Bear would never leave his new people.

On the heels of a late winter blizzard, four scouts rode into the village. They had news. During the past moon, the hang-around-the-fort Indians had made contact with some of the belligerents. Red Cloud, Spotted Tail, and Standing Elk had met with Colonel Maynadier to arrange a great peace council during the Moon of the Green Up Grass. Representatives of the Great White Father in Washington were going to be present. But nothing had been said by Colonel Maynadier about opening the Bozeman Trail; nothing had been said by Red Cloud about Fort Reno.

Both James Tolliver and Barnaby Cobb received this news about the peace council with skepticism. What they (and a few chiefs as well) knew was that the army already had plans under way to build more forts along the North Platte and Bozeman Trail. Under this threatening cloud, no peace treaty would be concluded. Instead, both men predicted a bloody war was in the offing, one that would make General Connor's invasion look minuscule.

One of the four returning scouts was Hawk Leg who had helped Tolliver escape from Fort Laramie the preceding fall. Hawk Leg told Barnaby Cobb that information about the proposed treaty had come from two Hunkpapa runners who were relaying the news to Sitting Bull up near the headwaters of the Belle Fourche River. Then, making sign and speaking slowly, Hawk Leg said to Tolliver the bluecoats had information that the doctor was living in one of the Lakota winter villages. The bluecoats wanted him returned to Fort Laramie; they were offering many wagons of supplies to any tribe that disclosed his location. The fort people also made threats—if they discovered Tolliver's whereabouts, they would send out soldiers to destroy the village harboring him.

This alarming news caused Tolliver's brow to furrow. Good grief, this was preposterous! But Barnaby Cobb scoffed and dismissed the Hunkpapa report as nothing more than typical army coercion, an idle threat. He was no military man. He was a man of common sense. If the army had been unable to sustain Fort Reno properly, how could it possibly spare a company or two to chase down the doctor in some remote winter village? And why jeopardize the new peace opportunity by undertaking such a hazardous military adventure? No, Barnaby Cobb allowed that Colonel Maynadier probably was attempting to ascertain Tolliver's location for other reasons—the doctor could be used as a pawn in later negotiations, or could be captured in spring or early summer when troop reinforcements always came west from Fort Atkinson.

Barnaby puffed on his pipe several times, then said, "Ain't no doubt about those boys wanting to get their hands on you, James, but after the mess Connor left behind, they're gonna be damn careful just how they go about it. Searching up here now with a couple of columns, most likely would get 'em nothing but their bones picked apart like crow bait. Every village within a hundred miles of here would know about it. Catch those bluebellies out in the flats and they'd be dropping like flies in the frost." He chuckled. "Time the grass is green, you can be on the trail north to the diggings. Hell, they'll never know where you went. And time next summer comes, they'll be in such a goddamned war, they won't have the time of day for the likes of you. When Red Cloud tells 'em there'll be no more forts, all hell is gonna break loose. Mark my word, pilgrim, mark my word."

James Tolliver said, "I don't doubt your word, Barnaby, not in the least. What I now wonder is how they found out I'm living with Indians. Egads, I thought this place was the end of the world! Now those Hunkpapa bucks say I'm on the trading block for a few lousy loads of staples, for God's sake."

Barnaby grinned. "My friend, you're too famous to hide forever. Hell, these people like to tell good stories. First, how you saved one of their brothers, the coup of stealing One Star's horse, eh? How Little Dog saved your life . . ."

Tolliver cut Barnaby Cobb short. "Hold it, hold it," he sighed wearily. "They absconded with me. I told you this. It certainly wasn't a case of saving my life. The fact is, those crazy dogs put my life in jeopardy. You talk about crow bait. Well, that's what I am now, dammit!"

"I know," agreed Barnaby. "But everyone thinks the Oglala saved your life. Besides, these people like heroes."

"And I'm no hero. I'm a damned outcast."

"And the woman and child you saved," Barnaby continued. "So you see, sometimes these stories get back to the *wasichu,* and they say, aha, that missing sawbones is up there turning Injun. Aha, so he is, but finding you is one thing, catching you another. I'll tell you this, son, ain't no Lakota gonna turn you over to a bunch of bluecoats."

"I'm not turning Indian, either."

Barnaby Cobb chuckled. "I've been living with 'em all my life, boy, for a fact. Now I don't look Injun, but you sure as hell do. Got your hair all combed back. Got yourself some beads, even. Heh, heh, heh. All you need is some feathers."

Tolliver fondled the beads, several multicolored strands interspaced with ivory elk teeth. "You know these are a gift from old Chief Two Coups. It's proper to wear them. It would be dishonorable not to. You should know this!"

"Thinking like an Injun, too, ain't you?"

It was at this moment of consternation when another revelation by Hawk Leg sent Tolliver's whirling mind spinning off in another direction. The Hunkpapa, the scout said, had reported finding six supply wagons abandoned in four-foot snowdrifts along the Powder River trail. From old pony tracks, it appeared the troopers had packed their mules with all the food and valuable hardware and had forged on to Fort Reno. Other unshod tracks indicated that Indians had plundered what the bluecoats had left behind—but not all of it.

The Hunkpapa told the Oglala scouts there were also crates of bottles, tins, and small boxes. Some of these smelled rotten like the hot-mud-stinking-waters. The Hunkpapa didn't touch these things. It was bad medicine. Hawk Leg signed that since Big Black Bear made powerful medicine, he might be interested in what the two Hunkpapa runners had told the Oglala scouts.

Tolliver and Barnaby exchanged surprised looks. Tolliver, his dark eyes wide, said, "Good grief, sulfur! Medicine, all right, but not necessarily bad. It sounds like they were resupplying the infirmary . . . pharmaceuticals. My God, they must plan on keeping that hellhole operational!"

Barnaby Cobb scoffed. "No, my friend, I don't think they'll do that. The Injuns don't think so, either."

After a moment, James Tolliver said, "Then it could be only one thing, Barnaby. It has to be the shipment Dr. Mudd and I ordered last July . . . August. Hell, I can't even remember now, but that's the only answer. And if the army plans on abandoning the fort, why are they still trying to move supplies?"

"Because it's a good jump-off for the valleys next spring," replied Barnaby. "My friend, a new fort or two north, and who needs Reno? So our bluecoat friends keep a toehold on the Powder, eh . . . for the time being?"

Dr. Tolliver signed to Hawk Leg. "Did the Hunkpapa say how many suns from the big soldiers' lodge to the wagons?"

Hawk Leg thought for a moment. He finally held up two fingers.

Barnaby gave Tolliver a dark look. "Wait a minute, pilgrim. Now you just wait a minute. You ain't getting a notion about picking up that stuff, are you? Why, that's a two-day ride from here, a cold ride. And what would you do with it in this place?"

"You have a short memory," countered Tolliver. "We sure as hell could have used some of it two months ago."

"Ah, little Slow Runner?"

Tolliver sighed. "Yes, Slow Runner. We were lucky, Barnaby. Lucky and by the grace of God."

"No, my friend, by your grace, your medicine."

"What's dangerous about riding over there?" asked Tolliver.

Barnaby pointed his nose out the lodge. "The weather. It's damn contrary. It ain't tolerable at times. Winter's still hanging on."

Tolliver nodded at Hawk Leg. "He and his boys tolerate it, don't they? They hole up somewhere when it gets nasty . . . ride it out, don't they?"

"Injuns," commented Barnaby dryly. "You ain't no Injun." He grinned through his whiskers. "Like I said, you might be looking like one, but you ain't Injun, pilgrim, and don't go getting the notion you are. There's bones of the *wasichu* all over the prairie because of fool notions."

"It's not a fool notion. If those are the supplies Cal and I ordered, there's enough to take care of a battalion for six months . . . everything from pneumonia to gunshot wounds, new surgical supplies, anesthetics, too. They shouldn't be wasting out on the prairie, I can tell you that. It's a travesty."

Barnaby grinned. "Planning on setting up a practice, are you? Thought you was getting out of here come spring."

"I haven't changed my mind about that," answered Tolliver. "You and White Wolf and Red Bone could put some of those medicines to good use."

"Me!" exclaimed Barnaby. "Balls of fire, man, I ain't no healer, and the ol' chiefs, why, they wouldn't touch the stuff."

"Dammit, I can show you . . . show all of you. You people aren't that hardheaded and foolish."

"Some notion that is," Barnaby sniffed. "'Sides, can't get a wagon across that stretch with all the snow. Even in the best of weather, she's a poor trail. Likely break an axle."

"I wasn't thinking about a wagon. Mules. Those mules you have. We could pack the entire load with six or seven mules."

"That's stealing U.S. property, you know. It's thieving."

Tolliver snickered. "Against your scruples, I suppose."

"Against my better judgment, it is."

"When can we leave?"

Barnaby Cobb thoughtfully rubbed his whiskers. His green eyes narrowed. "Most likely in the morning." He looked at Hawk Leg standing impassively to the side. The young brave hadn't understood one word of this brief conversation. Barnaby said, "His boys just got back, y'know. Have to rustle up a few of the others to protect our backsides case some of those bluecoats get the same crazy notion you have."

"Nonsense!" huffed Tolliver. "If it's not something edible they won't be back until spring. When it's safe, they'll retrieve their wagons and make a bee-line for Laramie. It surprises me Maynadier even tried to get freight up that trail this time of the year. Perhaps your friend, Red Cloud, struck a deal with the colonel, got something in return while he was visiting down there."

"Ehyup, likely," nodded Barnaby. "He ain't never been one for giving the bluecoats much for nothing. Maynadier'll get no bargains next spring, though."

Chapter 7

Against the shadowy backdrop of the Black Hills, the small file of Oglala rode out. This was early in the Moon of Ice Going Away. It was midmorning, brisk but not cold. Captain James Tolliver marveled. If this were his end of the world, God had made it the most beautiful. How magnificent! The touch of *anpetu wi* painted a glossy patina of gold along the tops of corn snowdrifts rimming the coulees. These were big drifts undercut by shades of blue and purple shadows. Juniper, clumps of sage, frosty buffalo grass, and dun-colored rock vied for attention in the winnowed snow patterns of the prairie. Yes, what Tolliver once saw as foreboding was now paradoxically magnificent. Little wonder these people were so protective, so covetous of their Mother Earth. Tolliver thought they had much to love and appreciate here. One didn't have to be Lakota to appreciate it, either.

The trail east had been clear-cut the previous day by the ponies of Hawk Leg's returning scouts. Barnaby Cobb, collar up, wolverine hat pulled low, had his horse moving in a brisk walk. Tolliver was directly behind him, and bringing up the rear with the six mules were Black Wing, Fast Runner, and a brave called Crazy Horse, by Barnaby's word, a young warrior inappropriately named. Crazy Horse was intelligent, fearless, and cunning, and he mistrusted bluecoats. Tolliver himself knew something of this mistrust. During his first two months in the small village, he had become acquainted with most of the men. Not Crazy Horse. Crazy Horse had avoided him like the pox. Ultimately, two of Tolliver's exploits had changed this—the slaying of the big grizzly and saving the lives of Slow Runner and her baby. Killing the silvertip bear was bravery; saving the lives had to do with blood of the clan. Also Black Wing, Slow Runner's husband, was the first cousin of Crazy Horse. Blood was very thick among the Lakota.

Except for the late winter beauty of the landscape, the first day's ride was uneventful. Several small bands of antelope were sighted but the men had no need for fresh meat. They were traveling with a man called Big Beaver, and Big Beaver never ventured too far from camp without adequate supplies. He was a very knowledgeable plainsman. Tolliver had observed that Barnaby was as much Lakota as any man in the village. Barnaby always reminded him that despite the beauty of the prairie, it could be as contrary as the weather.

On this little journey, the man called Big Beaver had one of his mules packed with a quarter of smoked elk and an assortment of tinned goods. Another mule was packed with tarpaulins and blankets. The other four carried bundles of wood. Tolliver thought this was prudent; the three Oglala chided

Big Beaver for making wood like a woman. But this first night when Barnaby struck his fire under the protection of a great sandstone ledge, Tolliver observed that his chiding companions were the first to warm their hands and behinds.

Big Beaver poured water from one of his big canteens. He made coffee in his black pot, and everyone shared. Then Big Beaver reminded them that without wood there would be no fire; without fire there would be no hot water; without hot water, no coffee. It was good to drink fresh coffee with his brothers, Barnaby told them. Who among them now thought making wood was the work of a woman? The three Oglala grinned at Big Beaver. Tolliver thought their grins were rather sheepish.

Near noon the next day, Barnaby came to a halt on a small windswept rise. He pointed ahead. Far below at the neck of a coulee were the snowbound wagons. Immediately there was a swift exchange of talk and sign between the men. Tolliver caught some of the sign. His friends weren't excited; they were confused. Tolliver surveyed the scene—beyond the wagons in the haze of the river bottom barren cottonwood and elm trees poked eerily through the mists like black skeletons. The trail along the bottom was no more than a thread, but it was visible. Crazy Horse gestured emptily with his hands. Why, he asked, had the longknives driven their wagons so far from the usual trail? He thought this was strange. Barnaby Cobb reasoned that the troopers probably had chosen the foothill route because they feared an ambush from the deep cover of the trees.

Crazy Horse wasn't convinced, but in another several minutes the five men closed in on the wagons. With exception of the two sets of Hunkpapa tracks heading northeast, most of the sign had been obscured by blowing snow. On Hawk Leg's trip he had crossed trails with the Hunkpapa near the sandstone bluffs. Barnaby rode around the wagons. It was obvious that the two Hunkpapa had been the last to visit the site.

Tolliver had already dismounted and was busy probing the boxes and crates. All had been opened and inspected, but surprisingly nothing appeared to be damaged. Reasonable, Tolliver thought, for there was nothing edible here for Indians or soldiers. But it was a rich treasure of medicinal supplies, everything from disinfectants and balm to rolls of gauze and surgical instruments. Enough to supply a fighting battalion.

It took the men no more than a half hour to pack the mules. Barnaby was turning the pack string into a file when Crazy Horse suddenly wheeled about on his pony. Pointing to a faraway knoll, he exclaimed, "*Ma-ya, wachin ksapa yo!*"

The distant hill was splotched with juniper and buckbrush. Tolliver caught nothing more than several small but brilliant flashes.

"*Wikmunke?*" Crazy Horse asked. A trap?

Barnaby Cobb squinted. He turned and stared toward the river bottom. "I doubt it," he replied. "But someone's keeping an eye on this cache, and I reckon we've done and gone and picked up the bait." Barnaby's next move was calculated and deliberate. He said casually, "Let us pretend we have seen nothing, my brothers. Make no fuss about this. We shall see what these men are doing here, what they have on their minds." To Tolliver, he added, "Appears to me, pilgrim, this was a ruse to draw you out, get a fix on you. We've done gone and obliged these buggers."

"Preposterous!" Tolliver said.

Barnaby clucked his horse ahead. "Not so," he replied. "You're the only one out here who knows how to use this stuff, ain't you? Sorta explains why the wagons were left here 'stedda down on the trail. They were planted, goddammit. Crazy Horse had it figured, too. See everything from those little ridges yonder. Can't see a lick along that river-bottom road." He turned and grinned. "Oh, they're watching us, all right. No troopers, I reckon, or they'd be charging out here on the double."

To Tolliver, all of this was beyond belief. "Who then?" he asked.

"Can't say for certain." Barnaby tucked his pipe back into his pocket and began slipping on his mittens. "Spies, I reckon. That's what all that signaling was about. Probably a small camp tucked away in the bottom someplace."

"Indians? Good heavens, man, this is Lakota and Cheyenne country, isn't it? What the hell are they doing spying on their own people?"

"Hired fort Injuns, maybe. Trackers. Can't say yet."

James Tolliver stared back at the river bottom. "Well, what do you plan to do about it?"

"Just mosey on out, that's all," answered Barnaby. "Watch our backside for a spell, see what they're up to. Hell, we took the bait. Rest is up to them. Not much of a trick following our trail in this snow."

"This is ridiculous, a fool's game, Barnaby."

"No, son, sooner or later they aim to tack the hide of Big Black Bear on the post wall. Heh, heh, heh."

Tolliver grimaced. This was not funny. It was absurd, yet he was beginning to get the feeling it was also a tad dangerous.

Barnaby Cobb continued, "Oh, our boys here, they ain't gonna let us be the fools in this game, as you call it. No siree bob. No, y'see, they already know what they're gonna do. If we're followed, they're planning on counting coup on those buzzards back there. Yep, down the trail aways, they'll spill some blood. Y'see, James, if we was outnumbered, we'd be fighting our fool heads off behind those wagons right now, and that's a fact. I figure this is one of them intelligence things you was telling me about, just getting you all located, that's all."

Tolliver's eyes widened. "Then you believe they'll send out a company to raid the village? You think they actually want me that badly? Why, I can't believe it, not a smidgen of such a conjecture. The army has too many irons in the fire to be preoccupied with the likes of me, too many other things to worry about. Good grief, man!"

Barnaby Cobb just grinned. He said, "It only takes one thorn to make a jackass wild, one porky-pine quill to rile a griz. Take it from me, James, you're one big pain in the ass to the bluecoats."

Several hours passed. Uneasy ones for James Tolliver. Barnaby Cobb was headed for the sandstone ledge where he had cached some of his wood. Once again this was to be camp for the night. There had been no sight of anyone following, but Barnaby told Tolliver he saw nothing unusual about this. Unless there was a heavy snow to backfill tracks, these men were likely to hang behind anywhere from several hours to a half day. Or they could come in at night and mount a surprise attack.

Tolliver abhorred this possibility. He hadn't come on this trip to fight. He was a doctor, or had been. He had been trained to save lives, not destroy them. Now he was wondering if he shouldn't have let well enough alone. This damned medicine! The possibility of bringing grief to his new brothers over a load of medicine, medicine about which they knew absolutely nothing, had now become a thorn in his own butt.

At this juncture of Tolliver's fret Crazy Horse abruptly left the pack string. Urging his pony into a brisk trot, he rode off to the south. Barnaby explained that Crazy Horse was going to circle back to see if there were any sign of the enemy. He was to catch up with the train before sundown at the sandstone ledge. But long before the party reached the campsite, the young Oglala came galloping back. Indeed, they were being followed—about six miles back he had circled behind five riders. From what he could determine, four of them were Indians, the fifth man, wearing a heavy dark cloak and a buffalo hat, was on a big brown horse.

Barnaby, with an apprehensive glance at Tolliver, said, "Just like I figured, James. U.S. Army spies . . ."

"Intelligence."

"Not so intelligent," countered Barnaby. "Damn fools. 'Less we get a chinook, this time tomorrow they'll be all stretched out in the sage stiff as lodge poles."

"Oh, no!"

Elevating his hand, Barnaby said, "The gospel." He then pointed to the east. The sandstone camp was another five miles away. He briefly spoke in Siouan to his brothers, then translated for Tolliver who had only partially understood. A trap for the interlopers would be set at the bluffs. Barnaby and the three Oglala were to dismount at the edge of the rocks. They would leave no tracks. Tolliver was to continue on with the pack string and ponies. It was a perfect setting for ambush, Barnaby explained. If the trackers hesitated they would be shot from their mounts at long range; if they passed, the attack would come from behind.

"Good as dead, they are," Barnaby finished. "After you hear the shots, you just mosey on back." He grinned. "Allow you'd rather be the decoy than shooter, eh?"

Tolliver shuddered.

James Tolliver, full-time fugitive, part-time healer, lost all track of time. The vastness of the prairie was as timeless as it was endless. The lowering sun, however, told him it was getting late in the afternoon. It was cold, too. He thought he had been riding alone for hours; it was less than a half hour. A series of muffled shots brought him around, shots that sounded like tiny pop-pops from a sputtering fire. He listened for several moments. Nothing, not a sound in the prairie stillness except the creak of cold leather, the shuffling of hooves in the skiff of snow and frozen ground. He slowly made a half circle with the string of horses and mules; he doubled back on his trail.

Half an hour later Tolliver saw blue smoke rising above the reddish-brown outcropping of rock. He soon saw several figures moving about. He also saw five horses with empty saddles.

When Tolliver approached the camp, he never would have known the area around it had been a killing field. The men were busy at the fire preparing the evening meal. Nothing seemed amiss. After casually greeting him, Black Wing and Fast Runner hurried out to secure the ponies and pack string. Crazy Horse was hunkered beside the fire. A big kettle and a coffeepot were steaming.

Haltingly, Tolliver asked, "Where is Big Beaver?"

Crazy Horse motioned to the darkness of the ledge undercut.

Indeed, Barnaby Cobb was there, crouched next to another man, the man who wore the buffalo hat and dark coat. But the man was stretched out; he wasn't wearing the big wool coat; his coat covered him like a blanket.

Barnaby waved. "Crazy Horse saved this one for you, pilgrim. Pawnee scouts other side of the rocks, they're dead as doornails. Bluecoat here. Shot up a bit in the shoulder. Says he knows you."

James Tolliver hurried up to the shelter. True, the man was a soldier, but before Tolliver could pull away the great coat and inspect the wound, the man spoke. "Good afternoon, Captain. It's been a long time. Sorry it's come down to this. A lousy detail."

"By gadfrey!" Tolliver exclaimed. "Sergeant Abbott! Here, let me take a look at that." Tolliver knew Frederick Abbott from his days in confinement at Fort Laramie. Abbott was a sergeant major, the top man in Lieutenant Timothy O'Leary's platoon. He was a veteran trooper; he also was very knowledgeable about intelligence operations. Frederick Abbott had a wad of bloody cloth pressed against his right shoulder. Tolliver pulled the sergeant's clinched hand away to examine the wound.

Barnaby Cobb said, "There's a hole out the back, too."

Tolliver's hand went behind the shoulder. It came back bloody and gritty with bone splinters. "Damn!" cursed Tolliver. He quickly pulled off his woolen scarf and balled it. Thrusting it against the exit hole, he rested Abbott against the wall. "I'll see what I can do. At least, there's no lead in there, but it bloody well nicked your scapula."

"Is it . . . is it bad? You know, that bad?"

"Bad enough," Tolliver replied. "Bad enough if we don't get this bleeding under control." He shook his head. "Was this O'Leary's brilliant idea?"

Abbott nodded. "They've been on his ass, Captain. He had to make a move of some kind. Rumor's you been hanging tough in some village. Thought something like this might draw you out."

Barnaby Cobb said, "Just like we figured, eh?"

Abbott grinned weakly at Tolliver. "Well, bleeding to death is better than what those ornery bastards did to my scouts. A couple of 'em had repeaters, goddammit."

Tolliver said, "Yes, a few of them have repeaters, Mr. Abbott." He pushed away from the overhang. "And you're not going to bleed to death." Tolliver left. He hurriedly searched through several of the bundles that Black Wing and Fast Runner had unloaded. He couldn't remember where anything had been packed, and many of the small boxes and bottles were without labels or markings. He rummaged for almost five minutes before he found what he needed—disinfectant, a few rolls of gauze, salves, and several suture packets. Somewhere in the cache were vials of morphine and syringes, but time was precious. Pain wasn't. Tolliver told Barnaby to give Abbott a cup of coffee. A good slug of his private brandy would help, too.

With assistance from Barnaby, Dr. Tolliver had Abbott's wound cleaned and patched in short order. There was minimal bleeding. Tolliver told the sergeant that after a good night's rest he could ride out the next morning for Fort Reno, his best bet for further assistance.

Abbott was surprised at this. Setting his coffee mug to the side, he said, "I'm not a captive? You're letting me ride out?"

Barnaby laughed outright. "Captive! What the hell for? You ain't no use to the Lakota, man. Just one more mouth to feed. Why, you won't be worth a lick for more'n a month, maybe worth nothing if you get all infected." Barnaby pointed his pipe at Dr. Tolliver. "You take James, here. The Lakota call him Big Black Bear. He ain't much for fighting but he's a meat-getter now. Cures ailments, too, like the collywobbles and ague. Earns his keep and the Injuns tolerate him. No, you're going back to the forts, and this ain't me'n James's decision, soldier. It's the boys over there, those ornery bastards as you call 'em. They want to make an example out of you . . . tell the brass a thing or two when you get back." He stuck his hairy face close to Sergeant Abbott. "You hungry? Feel like eating a little elk stew? Be needing all the strength you can get to make it outta here, y'know."

"Yes, sir, I know, and I'd appreciate some of your stew."

Barnaby called out to the braves below. Crazy Horse shortly returned with a heaping tin plate of stew. He handed it to Big Beaver, not Abbott. It was beyond his dignity to serve a bluecoat. Crazy Horse stood back and watched Abbott as he awkwardly maneuvered the wooden spoon with his left hand. Tolliver had tightly bound the sergeant's right arm up against his chest so he couldn't flex his shoulder muscles.

Crazy Horse had removed his fur hat. He wore a beautiful Hudson Bay coat decorated across the breast with a dozen ermine tails. His hands were on his hips and his head almost scraped the underhang of the ledge.

In between mouthfuls, Abbott asked Barnaby, "Is this buck the leader, Mr. Cobb? Is he a chief?"

"He's a leader, Mr. Abbott. That he is. He's not a chief. His name is Crazy Horse. Best you remember his name 'cause he'll be a chief one of these days. Yassir, you ever meet up with him again, your stew-eating days will be over. Fact is, you wouldn't be eating now if it wasn't for me'n James here."

"I understand, Mr. Cobb. I owe my life to you."

Tolliver said, "And one shot askew of your heart."

Barnaby went on. "Crazy Horse don't cotton to bluecoats, Mr. Abbott. Don't cotton to Pawnee, Comanche, Shoshoni, or Crow, either. Can't say rightly in what order, but that's the nut of it. He's polite, though, just waiting for you to finish eating before he dresses you down."

"A reprimand, eh?"

"Heh, heh, heh. Ass-chewing's more like it."

"I'm a soldier, Mr. Cobb, just like he is," said Abbott. "I follow orders."

"Oh, I reckon he respects that much of it," acknowledged Barnaby. "Hell's bells, ain't no dishonor in that. He's the highest rank here in feathers, y'know, and he has to speak his piece. Wants you to take a message back to the brass, that's all."

Sergeant Abbott swallowed. He scraped the tin plate with his spoon. He looked up at Crazy Horse and said, "Well, soldier, start chewing ass. If I make it back, I sure as hell can tell 'em what you say. Likely they won't give a shit. They never do, but I'll tell 'em."

Barnaby translated what Abbott had just said. It brought a wry smile to the usually somber face of Crazy Horse. He replied that this was the problem with the bluecoats—too many chiefs talking and not enough listening. He pointed to Tolliver and made sign. To the side, Barnaby began translating.

"This man Toll-e-veer is our friend. Our people honor him. I honor him. I am called Tashunka

Witco. One day I will be chief. Go back and tell your leader at the soldiers' lodge we do not want any more pony soldiers on our land. If you bring pony soldiers to our village we will destroy them. There will be no peace in the council of the Green Up Grass. There can be no peace when all your people know is war. We hear you want to build more soldier lodges on our land. The land is sacred. It is the land of the buffalo. The buffalo is sacred. Who gives you the right to destroy what is sacred? We do not sell this land for the rights of a few greedy white men. They have no rights. One does not sell the earth upon which people walk. We have a good life here. Who gives you the right to come here and make our life miserable. We are not savages as many of your star chiefs claim. We are free. We will not make peace with you at the price of our freedom. We will fight. This man is called Big Black Bear. He is free, too. He is one of us. This is the way it will be. You go back and tell your chief at the soldiers' lodge this. Tell him he will come to know Tashunka Witco with each passing moon if he does not listen better."

Crazy Horse bent down and picked up Abbott's tin plate. He held it with both hands and bent it double.

Quote this pg.

Chapter 8

By the Moon of When the Ponies Shed, James Tolliver had his own lodge, a gift from the clans of Two Coups and Black Wing, benefactors of his good medicine. It was a sturdy tipi built of fourteen lodge poles and thatched with the thickest of buffalo hides. The figure of a big standing bear had been painted over the entry; the tipi faced east toward the rising sun.

Inside, the great furry hide of the grizzly he had killed served as a carpet where he made his bed of robes. All of the army medicines and surgical supplies were neatly stacked to each side of the entry. The villagers called Tolliver's dwelling Lodge of the Bear. Some considered it *wakan*. There were many mysterious potions with great healing power here. They were of great interest to everyone. The two village healers, Red Bone and White Wolf, were especially intrigued, more so when Tolliver revealed the ingredients in his wares. Many were nothing more than derivatives from the herbs and plants that Indians had been using for ages. This pleased Red Bone and White Wolf. While they learned from the man called Big Black Bear, they also taught, and

Tolliver began to understand some of the spirituality and psychology in their methods of healing.

All of this was good. In seven months James Tolliver had acquired knowledge and understanding, new friends, and moderate wealth. He owned five horses, the four Pawnee ponies that Crazy Horse had given him after the ambush at the sandstone bluffs and General Connor's piebald mare. He was soon to have seven—the piebald and one of the Pawnee mares were about to foal. The faithful attendant to his stock was Black Bow, his language teacher.

On this warm day in early May, Chief Two Coups and his son, Little Dog, sat with Tolliver in front of his new lodge. At first, they smoked, talked, and made sign about several impending events, the proposed peace council at Fort Laramie, and preparations for the winter village moving to the Powder River valley for the spring ceremonies and buffalo hunts. Ultimately, Chief Two Coups pointed out that Big Black Bear had everything he needed now—everything except a woman. Toll-e-veer needed a woman to take care of his lodge and other necessities of village life—the making of wood, the gathering of food, the cooking, sewing, and washing, yes, and companionship in his robes at night.

Tolliver shifted uneasily on his robe. True, a woman was something he didn't have, and under the circumstances was something he didn't want, either. In fact, he had purposefully avoided and stifled romantic inclinations. Oh, he knew what Two Coups had on his mind—Red Moccasin, his winsome, doe-eyed daughter. Even Little Dog had tossed out a suggestive morsel—his pretty sister had just turned seventeen winters. She was ready for marriage, and his father had been casting about for someone suitable and worthy. But James Tobias Tolliver? No, this was outlandish, absurd, and impractical.

But Tolliver didn't say this. He wasn't about to offend the chief and his son. He had to be diplomatic. Making sign and laboring in Siouan, he said, "My days with your people are growing short. When the grass is high again, I will return to my village. My home is far across the Mother River. It is where I belong. It would be unwise to take a woman. She would not be happy away from her people. It would not be good medicine to take a woman and then leave her so soon."

Two Coups was silent for a moment. He puffed several times on the pipe and passed it to Tolliver. "What you say is true," he finally said. "I find it strange you want to go back to your people. They want to punish you. The bluecoats want to kill your medicine. They want to put a rope around your neck. This is dishonorable, Toll-e-veer. Is this not so?"

Tolliver took a long drag on the pipe, blew smoke, and said, "I do not plan to go where the bluecoats live. Until the bluecoats forget me, I will journey north to one of the villages where men dig for gold. Big Beaver says there is a need for doctors at these places."

Little Dog's face brightened. "Those places," he signed, "are beyond the Yellowstone, less than a moon away. You could do as Big Beaver does. He goes away to make trade. He always comes back. This would not be so bad, my brother."

Barnaby Cobb? Little Dog was comparing him to Barnaby? Good grief, Tolliver thought, he couldn't tell them that Barnaby was facing a dilemma of his own, how to extricate his family from the village before hostilities erupted again. And Barnaby was certain a war was to come. Tolliver attempted to explain. "It is not the same. This is Big Beaver's home. His business is trading with the white man. He makes trades and returns to his home. I am a doctor. This is my business. I have to live where the people need me."

Two Coups said with a smile, "A good woman makes a man happy. You have plenty work here, Toll-e-veer. If you had a good woman maybe you would not want to leave, eh? My people honor you. I honor you. We need you. It would be wise to think about this."

Chief Two Coups received the pipe again and took one final puff. He carefully doffed the ashes to the side, then stood and pulled his red blanket around his shoulders. He motioned once with his hand, palm outward, and left.

Little Dog smiled at Tolliver. "*Hechetu welo.* My father has spoken."

"Yes," Tolliver said with a nod. "Yes, he has spoken. But has Red Moccasin spoken? Does she know about this?"

Little Dog feigned surprise. "My sister? Who said anything about my sister?"

"Come, come, my brother, I am not the ass of a

pony! When your father speaks about a maiden, he has only one in mind, Red Moccasin."

Little Dog shrugged. "What does it matter? It is the decision of my father and his eldest son. I am that son. I have kept away my sister's suitors for six months because of you."

"Gadfrey!"

Little Dog grinned like fox eating crayfish. "You always say that word, gad-free. I am curious, my brother. What does it mean?"

"It means . . . it means something like . . . by the power! Or smoke that is holy . . . or by the Great Spirit!"

"Ah, you are surprised."

"I am struck by lightning," Tolliver signed. "That you would do such a thing to Red Moccasin, to give the maiden no say in such affairs is not honorable. She should have the choice of a husband."

"Hmmm," mused Little Dog. "Yes, I sometimes forget you are not Lakota. Our ways seem strange to you. But you see, my brother, in this case there is a difference. Since the very day she and my mother brought you the shirt of lights, Red Moccasin has had her eyes on you. She says she wants a husband who is a man of peace, a great peace chief. She does not want a warrior like myself or some crazy dog who risks his life all the time. She is a smart woman. She does not want to be a widow too soon, eh? She wants a man like Big Beaver. He has been with the Lakota thirty winters. Red Moccasin admires you. She would be happy to be your woman."

"Good grief!"

*   *   *

At least in one respect, Tolliver considered himself fortunate. Except for his usual breakfast of meal and berry mush and black coffee, (which he prepared in his own lodge) Little Weasel insisted he be present at her lodge for supper. He didn't object to this, for he had no foodstuffs of his own. Occasionally some of the people who felt indebted to him (or sorry?) gave him a choice portion of meat or a stack of flat cakes made from meal and *wasna*. But it was Little Weasel's cooking that sustained him.

Tolliver, Barnaby, Crazy Coyote, and Black Bow sat in a small circle outside the entry on this evening. They served themselves from a huge pot of prairie chicken stew Little Weasel had prepared. Tolliver listened intently when Barnaby began discussing plans for a trek across the eastern prairie to the trading post at Fort Pierre, a round-trip journey that was to take the better part of a month. Cobb had enough hides, furs, and Oglala-made garments to make the trip a profitable venture. By the time he returned, the village would be camped at the confluence of Crazy Woman Creek with the Powder River, a good place to guide Tolliver north to the mining settlements.

Tolliver, pricked by the thorny suggestions made by Two Coups and Little Dog earlier in the day, was struck with a sudden notion, one he thought might get the burr out of his seat. This was his first good chance to bolt and it couldn't have come at a better time. He would volunteer to accompany Barnaby; he needed to get away, forever if possible. Risky business showing his face along the big river, but time was running a short wick. His exit would be honorable, offensive to no one. There would be no dishonor to Two Coups's clan, no shame to Red Moccasin, and much relief to himself. Social customs be damned, he had to nip this marriage business in the bud before it had time to bear fruit in the summer.

Yes, this was his chance to clean country in honorable fashion. Civilization! Tolliver soared like an eagle. Then pow! He was stricken in midair. Before he could offer his services to Barnaby Cobb, the trader said he was taking Crazy Coyote with him to Fort Pierre. It would be Tolliver's responsibility to help Little Weasel and young Black Bow in the journey across the Thunder Basin to the summer camp. Black Bow beamed at this; Big Black Bear was his idol.

Tolliver, however, cringed inside. "But . . . but," he sputtered, "I have no experience in such affairs, this moving, trailing the prairie."

Barnaby replied, "You're gonna have to learn then, boy. 'Sides, that's your direction, anyways, ain't it? Like I said, when me'n the lad get back, we can head out for the Bighorn. Just a whoop and a holler from there to the Yellowstone. Hell's bells, two or three weeks and you're in the settlements. No more bluecoats, eh? Get rich in the diggings, y'can."

Tolliver grunted. "I'm no miner."

"Learn that, too," returned Barnaby with a grin. "Nothing to it. Just scratch 'round in the cricks a tad, flip a few rocks, and look for color."

"I don't even have a grubstake."

"Hell you don't! Got yourself a string of ponies, don't you? Five hundred dollars' worth, I reckon. And you still got your money, 'nuff to get you started right proper. Take all those doctor tools, too. Why, in no time you're in business."

"Very simple," Tolliver sighed wearily. "It's always cut and dried with you, nothing to it."

Barnaby Cobb smacked his lips. He dabbed at the sides of his mustache. He got up and disappeared inside the lodge. When he returned, he tossed a leather pouch to Tolliver. It fell in the doctor's lap. "Getting a little gold is simple, boy. Ain't so simple keeping it secret, though. Have to be sneaky as a jaybird when you're looking for yellow iron."

James Tolliver peeked in the pouch. Good grief, it *was* gold! A bag full of shiny nuggets, some quite large. Aghast, he stared up at Barnaby. "Where did you get this? Why, there's a small fortune here!"

Barnaby Cobb grinned. With a wink he said, "Like I said, have to keep things secret-like, James. Go showing up at a trading post with too much of that and people start getting right suspicious. Someone's likely to start sniffing your trail like a dog." He winked again. "I always tell 'em I met up with a miner or two and did some fancy trading."

Tolliver carefully knotted the rawhide strip around the pouch. Giving it a toss back, he said, "I've known you for seven months. You've never said a thing about digging gold, not a word. Gold, Barnaby, gold. That's what drives men mad. They kill for it, and you don't seem to attach any importance to it whatsoever. You're a very unusual man, Mr. Cobb, very strange."

Barnaby said, "Stuff is bad luck 'round here. Never talk about it, pilgrim, never."

Crazy Coyote added, "Bad medicine, Toll-e-veer."

Tolliver looked puzzled. "Bad medicine? I don't understand."

Barnaby tucked the pouch up under his buckskin shirt. He quietly explained. The year he arrived on the land, Fort Laramie was called Fort William. It was nothing more than a trading post established by the Sublette brothers, and named after one of them—William. He recollected it was about 1837 when a trapper named Maselino came with his pelts. Maselino also had a few pokes of gold. Soon afterward, Maselino mysteriously disappeared.

Stirred by Maselino's discovery, other trappers ventured into the mountains seeking to locate the Spaniard's strike. A Lakota legend was that five men did find the lode. However, none lived to tell about it—they were all killed not far from the discovery site.

Barnaby went on to say that as late as one year past, seven Swedish miners struck a vein of gold in one of the small valleys near the Big Horns. The Lakota caught them, too. Five were killed; two escaped. They lived to tell about it. But to Barnaby's knowledge, the miners never returned. With a raised brow, the trader looked at Tolliver. "Nope, never came back."

Tolliver said, "With good reason."

"*Heya,* bad medicine," Crazy Coyote repeated.

Nodding at the bulge under Barnaby's shirt, Tolliver asked, "If they don't like miners poking around, how did you come by that?"

"Hell's bells, James, I ain't a miner, either," protested Barnaby Cobb. "Look here, sometimes when I'm coming through the hills back there, I wash up in one of the cricks, rinse out my pots, that sorta thing. Sometimes I run my spoon under a gravel ledge just t'get it all shiny-like." He grinned. "Damndest thing when one of these little yellow chunks rolls over. I save 'em. They buy rifles, y'know. Now to my notion, this ain't mining and riling up the crick. It's more like keeping things tidy."

Tolliver grinned back. "You said 'hills.' What hills?"

Barnaby pointed his nose toward the dark mountains in back of them. "Those hills . . . where I reckon Maselino used t'do his washing up. Sierra Negra. That's what the ol' Spaniards called them. Our brothers call 'em the Sacred Hills. Spirits back in there all over the place. Buggermen, too. No fit place for a white man. I reckon a dozen or so found that out. Ain't like that up in the diggins, though. Least, that's what I hear. No spirits or buggermen to worry about."

"Or Indians."

"Ehyup," replied Barnaby. "Like I said, it's simple up there. Just get yourself a sluice box and a shovel. Hell, you're in business. No time at all y'got yourself a stake and you're a doctor again. Y'know, in Alder Gulch or Virginia City, those places."

Exasperated, James Tolliver said, "Good grief, Barnaby, I can't even get out of this place. Worse yet, I have new problems. Now, Two Coups wants to give me his daughter . . . wants me to take care of her. Damn, I can't even take care of myself! He thinks I'm going to live here the rest of my days, come and go as I please, like you. Or some damned crazy dog Indian."

"*Mi-ya!*" exclaimed Crazy Coyote. "Toll-e-veer takes a woman! Red Moccasin!"

"Not on your life! It's preposterous!"

Barnaby Cobb guffawed.

Tolliver glared at him. "What the hell's funny about this?"

"Another squaw man in the tribe."

"By gadfrey, are you in on this, too?"

"No," Barnaby replied. "No, but you shoulda known, pilgrim. Soon as you start turning Injun, they get notions, and Two Coups owes you a debt of gratitude, don't he? Saved his boy's life. Makes you a tall stalk in the bean field, it does. He's paying you the highest honor, that's what."

With a deep groan, Tolliver said, "I don't want the honor. And I keep telling you, I'm not turning into a Lakota."

Barnaby sniffed. "Humph! Well, let me tell you, James. If one of those bluecoats came in here looking for you, he'd have a helluva time finding you. And like *I* keep telling you, you look Injun and you damn well talk like an Injun, now."

"Nonsense!"

Barnaby Cobb grinned. "Tell you another thing. You start bedding down with that little Red Moccasin and you're gonna be all Injun. Likely you'll be striking gold all right, but it ain't gonna be in the settlements. Gonna be in your lodge, that's what. Might change your mind about being all so antsy 'bout getting outta here, too. That's a notion to think about, ain't it?"

"Damn your hide, it's a horrible notion!"

Tolliver wasn't an unhappy man. How could he be unhappy among people who treated him so kindly, so humanely? He was a tad disappointed that Barnaby Cobb was leaving him behind, though. He forced a smile and gave the trader and Crazy Coyote a cheerful good-bye at their departure. Barnaby had his long pack string loaded with hides and furs; he had four ponies behind; Crazy Coyote, a rifle across the front of his saddle, rode at the point. They were off for the spring trading at Fort Pierre.

Tolliver's face was long. Within another few days, he would be off, too, but in the opposite direction, headed for the great valleys to the west. By army standards he was a fugitive. That foolish escapade at Fort Laramie had put a price on his head. *Fate* hadn't placed him in the middle of the Lakota nation; it had been his own impetuous frivolity in following Crazy Coyote and Little Dog over the fort wall. But even more crazy was that he had changed sides. Barnaby was right. Tolliver had converted, had turned Lakota. He threw back his head and laughed bitterly, then self-consciously looked around to see if anyone had noticed his peculiar behavior. With a little kick at a sniffing dog, Tolliver skulked away to the edge of the village. He sat on a boulder and watched two black eagles soaring the pale blue sky high above. Oh, that he had such powerful wings!

Deep in his thoughts, he hadn't paid much attention to the two riders who just returned from a scouting venture to the south. Someone was always coming and going, bringing in scraps of information gleaned from trailside encounters. He was constantly amazed at how news moved from village to village across the broad expanse of prairie and, yes, even over the mountains. Barnaby Cobb called it the Indian telegraph. Tolliver recalled that in his own case, it was only a matter of several weeks before everyone knew he had stolen One Star Connor's horse and spirited a Lakota brave away upon it.

Behind him, he heard a few excited voices. When he turned and squinted across the *hocoka*, he saw a small group of men gathered in front of Two Coups's lodge. Several subchiefs had arrived. They were impassively listening to one of the scouts who occasionally gestured toward the south. Curious, Tolliver got up from his big rock and walked over to investigate. He just managed to get in on the last of the talk, a few words from Two Coups. The chief wanted some men to leave immediately and find out what so many bluecoats were doing on the Platte River trail.

And this was a case of fate. Young Crazy Horse tapped Tolliver on the shoulder. He smiled. He spoke and made sign. "Chief Two Coups wants you to go with us to see some pony soldiers. He says you know about these things. He says it may be plenty important. Chief Red Cloud and Man Afraid of His Horses are in a village one moon west of here. Two Coups says if what we discover is bad medicine, we must ride over there and tell them before the big peace council."

Tolliver went limp. Bluecoats! Soldiers on the move! Gadfrey, whatever value could he be on such a scouting adventure? What kind of a clever game was the chief playing here? How ironic! Frightful, too. Two Coups wanted him to spy on bluecoats, the very same bluecoats who wanted to nail his hide to one of the walls down at Fort Laramie. Good Lord! Tolliver winced. He managed a weak grin. He said to Crazy Horse, "I am honored." He wasn't honored at all; he was weak in the knees. Gesturing to the nearby lodges, he asked, "Such a journey will take four or five sleeps. What will I do about Little Weasel and her son? The lodges will soon be struck for the move to the summer village?"

"Nyah," replied Crazy Horse. "We move six suns from this one. We will have plenty time to go see these pony soldiers and return."

Tolliver tried again. "What did the scouts say? These pony soldiers may be taking the star chiefs to the great council meeting. It may be nothing more, my brother."

"Our men saw nothing," replied Crazy Horse. "Some people of the Brule told them about the bluecoats. They said there were plenty soldiers, plenty wagons and *wasichu* with them. The Brule say these people may be coming this way."

Mystified, Tolliver frowned. "How do they know this? Maybe these people are immigrants. During the summer moons, they always go across the mountains to the Idaho and Oregon country."

Crazy Horse said, "The Brule told our men they saw many big thunder irons."

"Gadfrey! Cannons?"

"I ask you, my brother, do the *wasichu* movers take these big guns with them to the Land of the Winding Waters? Do they take these big guns with them to the Land of the Shining Mountains?"

James Tolliver swallowed once. "*Nyah*," he replied. "*Nyah*, they do not do this. The bluecoats do this when they plan to make war."

Crazy Horse smiled. "You are wise, Toll-e-veer."

"Not so wise," Tolliver replied. "What if the bluecoats see me? What if they discover who I am?" He sliced the edge of his hand across his throat.

Crazy Horse spat to the side in contempt. "Hah, they will not see any of us. We will watch them. We will listen to the voices at the night fires. You will understand, eh?" Then, with a quick motion of his hand, Crazy Horse's contempt was displaced by grim humor. "You are no longer the foolish doctor who came to us during the Moon of the Falling Leaves. Your big feet no longer make noise. Your pony no longer looks cross-eyed when you ride it. Your eyes see farther than your nose. You are Big Black Bear. You have become Oglala, my brother, and no bluecoat will know otherwise. This is what I say." Crazy Horse proudly folded his arms across his expanded chest. His black eyes were ablaze. "It is good to be Oglala, Toll-e-veer. What do you say?"

The afternoon had become warm, but James Tolliver felt a cold chill run up his spine. He nodded. He cleared is throat. He placed a hand on Crazy Horse's blanketed shoulder. "You say it well, brother," he said gamely.

Little Weasel prepared a parfleche of food for Tolliver; Black Bow brought in one of the Pawnee ponies; Tolliver packed a few belongings and shouldered his Henry rifle. Within an hour, Crazy Horse, Little Dog, and the doctor were riding south. Ultimately, they crossed the Niobrara and made camp. The next day they headed for Loup Creek, and riding at a steady pace were in sight of the main valley by late afternoon. Crazy Horse decided to ride toward the north fork of the Geese Going River. He reasoned that the pony soldiers sighted by the Brule had been below the forks at least four or five days past. By now, the men and wagons probably were headed up the Big Medicine Trail to the soldiers' lodge at Laramie Creek.

Toward dusk, just about the time the three scouts were ready to make camp, Little Dog, who had been searching the east perimeter, returned. He reported the bluecoats had stopped for the night on a big bluff overlooking the river. He had seen the smoke from their fires. He thought it might be a good idea to circle back and camp in the river bottom below them. From experience he had learned the soldiers never paid much attention to where they had been, only to where they were going.

That night, much to Tolliver's chagrin, Crazy Horse elected to investigate the camp; he was anxious to get a closer look at the troop train. Though Tolliver believed it more prudent to observe from a considerable distance in daylight, he didn't share his opinion with Crazy Horse. He wanted no doubts about his loyalty. So shortly after dark, Tolliver and his Oglala brother walked about a half mile following the same trail made by the wagon train. Little Dog stayed behind with the ponies. If there were any shots or shouts, he was to bring up the mounts in a hurry.

There were a dozen small fires along the line of tents and wagons. These weren't fires for warmth or cooking—they were smudge fires. Tolliver allowed this was for a good reason. The spring hatch of Platte Valley mosquitoes was out in force. The humid night air hummed with them. Night hawks and tiny bats were everywhere in the air gorging themselves on the singing hordes.

Tolliver and Crazy Horse crept behind big shadowy clumps of blossoming sage and observed two of the nearest sentries. They were leaning on their rifles, smoking pipes, and chatting. Beyond the sentries, Tolliver saw a few men wearing large floppy hats; from the rest of their dress, he ascertained they were mule skinners. There were many other civilians present, too, and in one group he saw a half-dozen women. This momentarily puzzled him until he concluded they must be the wives of some of the officers. No immigrants here, he whispered to Crazy Horse. Except for a few heavy-duty flat-beds, these were army wagons. The cannon the Brule had reported were lashed inside a few of the large freighters; most of these guns were eight-pound howitzers, excellent armament to place atop a log stockade. Tolliver groaned. No doubt about it, this was a fort-building expedition. His Lakota brothers were going to be angry as hell about it, too.

On the lower side of the camp toward the river, several hundred horses and mules were pastured, most of them hobbled or picketed. The tinkling of a few bell mares mingled with croaks of the river-bottom frogs and the cries of feeding bullbats over-head. Tolliver and Crazy Horse carefully skirted the big remuda, for there were six sentries posted along the perimeter. Crazy Horse smiled and tapped a finger to his temple—these teamsters were smart; they knew the consequences of leaving stock unguarded.

It was an hour before the two men returned to where Little Dog waited with the ponies. The men mounted and rode a mile north to a grassy coulee. While they ate a cold meal of elk jerky, flat cakes, and a can of pears, Tolliver explained the meaning of what he had observed. Both Crazy Horse and Little Dog were expressionless, but Tolliver knew they were burning inside.

The three scouts were up and away before dawn, riding northwest. Shortly after sunup, Little Dog, who unlike the bluecoats always watched his back-side, reined up and pointed. Silhouetted on the horizon were two riders, small vertical shapes on an otherwise horizontal plain. Crazy Horse dismounted and pulled out a small cylindrical-shaped bag. It was what he called his "Long Eye." Emblazoned on the leather was "U.S. Army." It was the small telescope he had confiscated from Sergeant Major Abbott after the sandstone ambush, and he was now using it on the enemy.

After a moment, he grunted and passed it up to James Tolliver. "Blanket Chief," he said.

Tolliver focused in on one of the figures, a buck-skin-clad man who rode his pony as though he had been melted into it. With the scope still to his eye,

Tolliver grinned and said, "Mr. Bridger! Why, the old fellow must be scouting for that contingent." He handed the telescope back to Crazy Horse and made sign. "Chief of scouts. I know that man you call Blanket Chief. The wagons are far behind. You want to know about those bluecoats, eh? Now we will ride over there and make talk."

Oblivious to any thought of danger, Tolliver kicked away. Mr. Bridger was a man of his word, one man whom he could trust.

Within a minute, Tolliver and the two Oglala had closed the gap to within yards, and directly Bridger crooked his arm and elevated a hand, palm outward. He moved ahead ten yards or so, and his companion, a man clad in blue tunic, held fast.

Tolliver called, "Mr. Bridger, we want a few words with you." Tolliver moved his pony at a walk until he was almost abreast of Bridger. "The best of the morning to you, sir," he said with a smile. Tolliver then tipped his fingers to his beaded headband.

Bridger's jaw jumped. He pushed back his faded gray hat and squinted. "By crackee, is that you, Mr. Sawbones! Tolliver, I recall, Dr. Tolliver?"

"Flesh and blood."

Jim Bridger threw back his head and guffawed. "Well, if this don't beat all! Why, I heard stories 'bout you holin' up with the Sioux. Never figgered you'd last it, boy. Figgered you'd be 'cross the big Mizzou by now. Dadgum, you ain't lookin' poorly for it either. You look lean and fit for a long'un, y'do."

"I feel fit," Tolliver replied. "If I had known you were heading up this outfit, I think I could have built a fire this morning and had a cup of coffee without worrying about someone jailing me again." He motioned to the east. "With all of that coming up behind, I can't tarry." Tolliver then quickly introduced Crazy Horse and Little Dog. Little Dog immediately spoke and made sign to Bridger.

Bridger nodded and smiled at Little Dog. He then said to Tolliver, "The buck says you saved his life last fall. Says he got you outta the fort. This is the one, eh?"

Tolliver smiled. "I know everything he signs, Mr. Bridger, and most of what he says. Yes, he and several other young men decided the army was mistreating me. Not exactly true, of course, but after all they had gone through getting into the place, I didn't want to disappoint them."

"Damndest story I ever heard," Bridger said with a wrinkled grin. His keen eyes, not quite as sharp as they once had been, were narrowed into two dark slits.

"Everyone down there still looking for me?" asked Tolliver.

"Under rocks," Bridger replied. "Know you're up here. Likely ain't gonna send the soldier boys out now with birds on the wing again. My notion, they're bidin' their time. Got the trails closed off. That Abbott feller came back all shot up." Bridger chuckled. "Said wasn't for you, varmints'd be pickin' his bones. Much ado 'bout nothin'."

"I wish you would convince them of that."

"Mos' times, they pay no mind to what ol' Gabe has to say."

Tolliver said, "You realize news of this army is all the way up the valleys to the north?"

"Figgered it would be," said Bridger, nodding. "Saw a few feathers half a dozen times along the trail. Always rattled the greenhorns."

"This doesn't bode well for the peace council. Your spokesmen understand this, don't they?"

"They's figgerin' on bargainin' for passage rights up the Bozeman," Bridger said. "No settlin', just passin'-through-rights to the diggings. Boss man of this outfit is Colonel Carrington. Follows orders just like I do."

"Obviously, this is before the fact, Mr. Bridger, the cart before the horse, as it were. Henry is an engineer, a builder, not a cavalryman or peace-maker."

"You know him?"

"I do," replied Tolliver. "We met twice, once during the war and once in Omaha."

"Army wants those forts along the trail."

"The Lakota and Cheyenne don't. I have no idea what the army's inducement will be, but from what my friends tell me, Red Cloud and Dull Knife won't abide any forts along the trail north. Reno is going down before the summer is over, I can tell you that."

Jim Bridger grinned. "No matter. They're plannin' on 'vacuatin' it, anyhow. Miserable place." He chucked at his chin whiskers and winked. "Reckon you should know 'bout that, eh?"

"Amen."

"Well, I told 'em that last year," Bridger continued. "Told 'em forts ain't needed. What's needed is some parley, somethin' to keep the Injuns off the mover's backs. Y'know, keep the pilgrims movin' and not tarryin' 'long the way. But you damn well know the army ain't much for listenin'. Bluebellies don't put much stock in what anyone out here says. Never have 'til they gets their asses whipped. Reckon General Connor gave 'em a cock and bull story, for certain. Back again, they are." He scrutinized Crazy Horse for a moment. "Mean-looking buck," he said to Tolliver. "His brothers say anything 'bout sittin' down to parley next month?"

"Intentions, that's all," answered Tolliver. Nodding toward the distant wagons, he added, "I doubt they'll even sit down for a smoke when they see that mess coming into Laramie. Pure and simple, Mr. Bridger, that's a fort-building unit. Many of those rigs are lumber wagons, wood trains, and there's a big contingent of mule skinners and sawyers. Officers' wives along to accompany their men to their new headquarters. Good grief, man, my friends here aren't stupid!"

With the mockery of a man unheeded, Bridger sighed wearily. "I know it, Mr. Tolliver. I know it and you know it, but the bluebellies, they don't know it. They just keep gettin' their learnin' the hard way. Half blind and rocks in their ears."

Tolliver politely tried to translate this for Crazy Horse and Little Dog. Little Dog said nothing. Crazy Horse spat once to the side and cursed. "*Shunka witko!*"

Jim Bridger raised his hand. "Kee-rect. *Heya, waon welo.*"

James Tolliver elevated his hand and said, "Goodbye, Mr. Bridger. We must move along."

"Keep your powder dry, Mr. Sawbones."

"No longer necessary, Mr. Bridger." Hoisting his Henry repeater high, Tolliver wheeled about and kicked his pony into a trot. Crazy Horse and Little Dog, emitting high-pitched screams, followed.

Bridger turned and walked his horse back to the young officer. The man asked, "Anything important, Major Bridger? Who were they?"

"Sioux scouts just pokin' 'round, that's all."

"But that big fellow, he called you out in English. You addressed him as 'Sawbones.' "

"A breed. Hills are full of 'em these days."

"But did you see his rifle? A new Henry carbine! My God, Major Bridger, most of our troops out here don't even possess that weapon yet!"

Jim Bridger grinned. "Smart breed, I reckon."

"They looked like troublemakers."

"Not to my notion."

James Tolliver breathed easier. What a wonderful day, cloudless, the endless tumble of greening prairie sprawled out before him, two sturdy companions at his side. Mr. Bridger was right—he was lean and fit for a long race. He was relieved, too, damn relieved to be riding home. Home! Judas priest, what was happening here? He had completed a spy mission against the army. Now he was calling some remote Indian village "home."

The morning sun caressed his bronzed face; his lungs filled with the fresh, clean air. Tolliver mumbled to himself, "What the hell, I'm my own man now. I'm Big Black Bear! Big Black Bear of the Lakota! Home! I can spread my blanket anywhere in these great valleys. Home is where I choose to make it!" Tolliver let out a tremendous scream. His horse jumped, and Crazy Horse and Little Dog gave the doctor curious stares. With several thumps against his chest, Tolliver grunted, *"Wagh!"* His two friends broke out in smiles. They nodded in approval. Big Black Bear felt plenty good about himself.

Chapter 9

Bordeaux, a boisterous post north of the Niobrara River, at one time had vied with Fort Laramie for trade with the Indians, trappers, and a few hardy mule skinners. However, by the mid-fifties, less hazardous routes to the south bore the brunt of the westward traffic, and Bordeaux withered on the vine. Only a few Indians and an occasional drifter now visited the old post. Crazy Horse told Tolliver it was a place of bad bargains and rotten whiskey.

Tolliver, who had tired of Barnaby Cobb's charity, wanted smoking tobacco. He had a few coins in a small pouch fastened to his black army belt. After a short discussion, his two Oglala brothers agreed to make a brief stop. It was near sundown. They wanted to ride another ten miles to a place they had made camp on the trip down.

The main building at Bordeaux, built of hewn cottonwood and chinked with gray prairie mud, faced east. A small barn and adjacent pole corral were on the south side near the slough of a creek. This was the direction of approach by Tolliver and his two brothers. It was a lucky approach. The men made a half circle, then, whoa! Crazy Horse abruptly reined up and pointed. Tolliver saw nothing irregular; two mules were grazing at the edge of the corral; three picketed ponies were standing at the edge of the small slough.

After Crazy Horse grunted disdainfully, Tolliver saw the reason—two of the horses were big bays, undoubtedly army stock. The third was considerably smaller, big head, lean body, and spindle-legged, an Indian pony. Curious, Tolliver moved closer. There on the flank of one of the bays he saw the simple brand "U.S."

Alert, Little Dog nodded toward the trading post. Making a few quick signs, he indicated he would dismount and take a look in front to see if it was safe. He knew this man who owned the post, a Cheyenne breed called Iron Head, Iron Head Comstock. Little Dog handed the reins of his pony to Tolliver, who with Crazy Horse went around to the north side of the building. They were out of sight, only awaiting a signal from Little Dog.

The signal wasn't what they expected. It came within moments, a high-pitched scream, followed by several shrieking "yi yis.' Crazy Horse kicked away around the corner, closely followed by Tolliver. A fight was under way. On the ground not far from the small porch was Little Dog, thrashing about in the dust trying to avoid the slashing knife of a Pawnee. A white man clad in an undershirt and wearing red suspenders was kicking at Little Dog's head.

Aghast, Tolliver dropped the reins of Little Dog's pony. He pulled his Henry rifle clear. Before he could swing into shooting position, Crazy Horse, wielding his hatchet, charged into the melee. In one swift blow he split the skull of the white man.

To a horrified James Tolliver, everything seemed like a nightmare in slow motion. Temporarily paralyzed, he suddenly found his voice.

"Get away! Move out!"

In a mad scramble, and clutching at a bleeding arm, Little Dog rolled to the side. The hooves of Crazy Horse's rearing pony came down on the Pawnee. The man came to his knees once but fell on his back. The pony's hooves came down again, once, twice, again and again until the Pawnee moved no more.

Then a lazy blur from the front porch caught Tolliver's wide eyes. Another white man, this one shouldering a rifle! Tolliver reacted instantly; he leveled down and triggered his Henry. He heard the sickening thud. Simultaneously his pony reared, almost throwing him. When the doctor wheeled about, the man he shot had disappeared; the impact of the slug had knocked him from the porch.

A whiskered face appeared in the doorway, then ducked back. A shout came. "What the hell's going on? We under attack?"

Tolliver quickly dismounted and hugged the side of the building. Crazy Horse was off of his pony, trying to shelter his wounded brother. Tolliver called back, "You better come out of there, mister . . . hands high. You have some explaining to do, I'll tell you that."

"I'm Iron Head," the muffled reply came. "Damnation, I don't want my place all shot up. Don't you shoot, you hear? Goddammit, my wife is in here having a conniption. She ain't coming out, mister, no way!"

Tolliver alerted Crazy Horse with a wave. Rifle at the ready, the doctor stepped around to the stoop. Arms outthrust, Iron Head appeared in the doorway. His eyes bulged at the sight of James Tolliver.

"You . . . you the one making all the talk? Why, you're a white man!"

"Yes, and a damned scared one," Tolliver said.

"Good gawd, you must be the one these ol' boys been asking everybody about. You're sure as hell are the one, ain't you? . . . the one who escaped."

Tolliver eased to the side and peered down at the man he had shot. He was dead. The bullet had penetrated the right side of the rib cage. Looking back at Iron Head Comstock, Tolliver asked, "Anyone else about?"

"Crazy wife, that's all."

Tolliver emitted a mighty sigh. He was trembling like a wind-whipped aspen. He was also horrified. Crazy Horse and Little Dog were scalping the dead white man and the Pawnee! That the Pawnee was dead, there was no doubt—the side of his dangling head was shattered. Gasping for air, Tolliver slumped on the steps and started at the lowering sun. My God, what had happened to his beautiful new world? Within moments, it had collapsed like a puffball, his brain and stomach with it. His head throbbed; he felt like vomiting.

"Lord, Lord," he moaned. "All we wanted was some tobacco."

Mystified, Iron Head threw out his hands. "A fight like this! Tobacco? All this for a lousy chaw?"

"Smoking tobacco. We came to buy some." Tolliver looked up. "They jumped my friend, tried to kill him. Why? Why don't you tell me why? For God's sake, they didn't even know I was here!"

Iron Head shrugged innocently. "Probably thought that Sioux was fixing to steal something. Hell, who knows what these scamps think? Course the Pawnee don't hanker much for Sioux being 'round, either. Coup maybe. Wanted to count coup. They fight all the time."

"Those other men? Soldiers? Bluecoats?"

"I don't rightly know," replied Iron Head. "One called himself Tracker. Other one was John. They come every two or three days. They ride back and forth, always looking, asking questions. Never do I see army clothes. Who knows?"

Tolliver sighed again. Intelligence, he thought. Some of O'Leary's men. Tracker? Probably a nickname. Or maybe they were bounty hunters; as Bridger had said, watching the trails. Well, in due time he would identify them. To Little Dog, he called out in Siouan, "Ho, get over here. I want to see your wound."

"By gawd!" exclaimed Iron Head. "You speak their lingo!"

"One learns, my friend. One learns."

And for the second time, Dr. James Tolliver went to work on Little Dog. He had help. The Cheyenne wife of Iron Head was named Minnie. Ridiculous! Minnie! What her tribal name was Tolliver had no time to ask. But she did regain her composure. She quickly brought a needle and some black thread and

144

a few strips of white cloth. Good enough. It took eleven stitches to close the gash in Little Dog's upper arm. As had been the case at Fort Reno, the young brave never complained. However, he made one observation that disturbed Tolliver's already muddled mind. He saw some spiritual significance in this. Twice he had been near death; twice Tolliver had saved him. And by killing the *wasichu* with the rifle, Tolliver had also saved the life of Crazy Horse. Big Black Bear had counted coup. He was big medicine. There was no doubt about it now—Little Dog's sister, Red Moccasin, belonged to Big Black Bear.

Directly, Crazy Horse came with papers from the pockets of the two dead white men. True to what Iron Head had said, one was John—John Mendoza. He had clearance papers for Fort Laramie, signed by the commandant's office. He was not a soldier. The other man was army, or had been. His name was Jacob Morgan. One of the papers in his pocket was a memo from Lieutenant O'Leary, requesting his service at surveillance duty for a period of ninety days at sergeant's pay. It began: "Tracker, my good friend . . ." Obviously, "Tracker" had been discharged sometime earlier in the year. Ironic. His discharge was now permanent.

It was almost dark by the time Tolliver and his companions rode off. Tolliver had his smoking tobacco, a big pouchful, a gift from Iron Head Comstock. He bought a sack of coffee beans. He also had another horse to add to his string—one of the army bays. Little Dog claimed the other, and Crazy Horse took the Pawnee pony. They confiscated two breech-loading Spencer rifles and a Navy Colt revolver. And Tolliver had a token hanging from his bridle, Tracker Morgan's scalp, courtesy of Crazy Horse. The good doctor's look of abhorrence was obvious to the proud warrior.

Crazy Horse slapped his chest several times. "*Wagh!*" he mimicked.

Tolliver's grin was a weak one.

There was a flurry of activity at Red Cloud's winter camp near the headwaters of the White River. Preparations to move to the buffalo grounds were under way; some of the tribe had already left for the western valleys. Tolliver listened quietly as Crazy Horse told him that by the beginning of the summer moons some of the Lakota villages along the Powder and Tongue rivers would contain as many as five hundred lodges. This was the time of the food gathering, making meat, and the great renewal rituals. This was the time everyone came together to share in common causes. Crazy Horse predicted a common cause this season would be the war on the longknives if they dared invade the buffalo country. Tolliver saw no qualifying "if" about it. The presence of Colonel Henry Carrington's huge contingent and Jim Bridger's disclosure of its purpose made it a deplorable fact.

Tolliver and his two companions led their string of horses through the usual village traffic, busy women, yelling children, lean dogs, and a few dozing old men who seemed oblivious to the confusion. Except for a few youngsters who ran alongside asking about the two big army bays, the trio attracted very little attention. During this short walk, Tolliver realized he had crossed the line of demarcation. These Oglala were strangers; if they had heard about him, at least they hadn't seen him; he walked along as one of them without drawing a single curious stare; he looked like one of The People; he felt like one of The People.

Near a large, impressive lodge, two men came up and greeted them. Introduced to Tolliver as Yellow Eagle and High Back Bone, they were good friends of Crazy Horse and Little Dog. Tolliver learned they all had shared time harassing General Connor's soldiers the previous year. Yellow Eagle was especially happy to meet the man called Big Black Bear, for he had heard the stories about the doctor's good medicine. He, like Crazy Horse, was a member of the same clan as Black Wing. Tolliver wasn't surprised at this—everyone he met seemed to be related in some way.

As in the army, Tolliver had learned there was protocol among the Lakota. Chief Red Cloud had a lieutenant, a tall, handsome fellow named Man Afraid of His Horses, and it was he who sat with the men in a small circle and listened to their report. Tolliver pulled out his pouch of tobacco, a very polite move that pleased Man Afraid of His Horses. As Crazy Horse related the story of their trip, they passed the pipe. Several men and women and a few children stood silently to the side and listened. Occasionally, Man Afraid of His Horses looked over at Tolliver and smiled. Tolliver thought Crazy Horse was gilding the lily a tad; the young brave went into every minute detail, even to the scalps decorating the bridles of their ponies.

When he had finished, Little Dog said approvingly, "*Hau, hau!*"

Everyone solemnly nodded and emitted a few more "*hau haus.*"

Moments later, Man Afraid of His Horses stood, pulled his blanket close, and entered the lodge. He then reappeared, followed by the big chief himself, Mahpiua Luta, Red Cloud. Now Tolliver saw the man he had heard so much about during the past two years. The chief nodded as Man Afraid of His Horses introduced each man in the circle, and if Red Cloud was surprised to meet the former blue-coat healer, Big Black Bear, he did not show it. His eyes were coal-black. They penetrated each man and passed on. Red Cloud was dressed simply, a light robe, one strand of red, blue, and yellow beads, buckskin pants, and moccasins decorated at the tops with multicolored beadwork. His hair was as long as any Tolliver had seen among the Oglala, well down below his shoulders. It was parted in the middle. Red Cloud wasn't an old man. Tolliver guessed that the chief was in his early forties. He was impressive, no doubt about that. His eyelids were heavy, his lips broad and unsmiling, and his nose was somewhat like Tolliver's, hawk-like and long. Man Afraid of His Horses immediately handed Red Cloud the pipe and began relating what Crazy Horse had reported.

This discourse, however, was much shorter and directly to the point. Red Cloud received the news about General Carrington's big wagon train impassively. He interrupted Man Afraid of His Horses once—when were the bluecoats arriving at the big soldiers' house on Laramie Creek? He wanted to be there to confront them, to make a show of force, to convince the white chiefs it would be bad medicine to pursue any plans to travel up the Powder River trail. But as he promised, he would attend the peace council. He wanted to hear with his own ears what lies the white chiefs would tell.

Then Red Cloud said calmly, "We will listen, that is all. We will go to war if the bluecoats go to the buffalo grounds to build their big lodges. I see now what they are doing. They want to pretend to talk about negotiating for rights to our land while they prepare to take it by conquest. I will listen. I will leave. I will fight. I have spoken." He stood, acknowledged each man, and disappeared inside his lodge.

The men in the circle exchanged a few grim smiles. Tolliver rubbed his chin thoughtfully. What the Oglala leader had just said was no more than he and Barnaby Cobb had expected—the peace council was doomed even before it was to begin.

Man Afraid of His Horses spoke again, this time directly to Tolliver. Making sign, he asked, "Do you know where these pony soldiers will ride to make their big lodges?"

Speaking slowly, choosing his words, Tolliver answered, "I only know it will be on the trail to the gold country somewhere near the mountains we call Big Horns."

Man Afraid of His Horses looked surprised. "You said it well for a white man," he said with a small smile. He nodded at Crazy Horse. "This one speaks well of you. He says you are more Lakota than white. You are a good pony thief, a healer, and a man who already has gained honors three times. Is this true?"

Honors? Good grief, three times! Tolliver hesitated. What could he say? Whatever had he done three times that was honorable?

Crazy Horse intervened. "Big Black Bear is too modest, my brother. He stole One Star's pony, eh? Everyone knows this story. He saved the lives of his brothers. He counted coup on a bluecoat spy. Big Black Bear has proven himself to be a warrior. Let him be judged. I say no more."

Little Dog agreed. *"Hau, hau!"*

A little tick of nervousness touched Tolliver's jaw. Judged for what? He caught Little Dog's smile from the side. Oh, he already knew what was on Little Dog's mind—that sister of his!

Man Afraid of His Horses finally said, "How say you to this, Big Black Bear? Are you a warrior?"

Tolliver's mouth was dry. He swallowed once. Making sign and once again speaking slowly, he replied, "I was trained to be a doctor. I am a doctor first. I want to save lives. I am only a warrior when I have to be."

"You must be a brave and honorable man."

Tolliver nodded. "When one lives with the Lakota, it cannot be otherwise. *Heya,* I honor The People."

Man Afraid of His Horses said something aside to Yellow Eagle. Yellow Eagle nodded and smiled. Then Red Cloud's chief lieutenant stood, and with a flourish of his hand dismissed the small gathering.

Yellow Eagle approached Tolliver and placed a hand on his shoulder. "We will have a small ceremony in the Dog Soldiers' Lodge before you leave for your village," he said. "Some of the chiefs will be there. All of us will be there. Our people honor brave men. You are entitled to wear three eagle feathers, my brother. Man Afraid of His Horses has decided. This is good."

Little Dog was elated. "*Hau, hau!*" he cried.

This was good? Tolliver was stunned. An *ozuye*? A Lakota warrior! Judas priest, this wasn't good. It was ridiculous!

By afternoon, what had been an otherwise pleasant but surprising day began to turn muggy. A gray blanket of clouds from the west settled over Red Cloud's village. It soon began to drizzle. Crazy Horse said the feather ceremony would delay their departure for home. Home. That word again. Tolliver sighed. It was the only home he had. Whatever, the delay was opportune. Tolliver disliked riding in the rain. It was chilling, and afterward his wet leathers always reeked; he smelled like the very beast he was riding.

And there was the matter of Little Dog's wound. The young brave was feeling pain. He said nothing but it was obvious to Tolliver. So with Little Dog in tow, he went to the lodge of Sun Runner, one of the village healers. Sun Runner was another man who had heard about Big Black Bear's medicine. He welcomed him. Near the light of the lodge entry, the two men of medicine chatted as they inspected Little Dog's slashed arm. Sun Runner was impressed with Tolliver's suturing. He grunted in approval, but he was unhappy about a small area of festering yellow at the lower end of the cut. Poison here, he told Tolliver. Tolliver wasn't happy either, but down at Bordeaux the only disinfectant available had been Comstock's rotgut whiskey. Though it had the burn of hell, it hadn't quite done the job.

Sun Runner shouted, and a woman appeared out of nowhere. She stirred up the coals on the little fire, brought some dead boughs, and placed a small pot of water on the rocks. Sun Runner busied himself with a few pouches. He continued to talk with Tolliver and Little Dog as he worked. Shortly, the pot began to bubble. He came to where Tolliver and Little Dog were sitting and waved his ingredients under the doctor's nose. Ah yes, Tolliver nodded. He smelled the fragrance of balsam, then detected the aroma of Oregon grape, probably a compound from the roots. And there in the palm of Sun Runner's hand was the old favorite, the hemostatic disinfectant, "soldier's woundwort."

"*Waśte,*" Tolliver said.

Sun Runner doffed all of his ingredients in the hot water; he covered the pot and let the concoction steep for five minutes. And after he bathed Little Dog's wound, he hunched back on his heels and predicted, "In two sleeps this poison will be gone." He added, "I shall make prayers to Wakan Tanka."

In one sleep, Tolliver knew he would be back in Two Coups's village where he could administer some of his own drugs. Not that Sun Runner's medicine was faulty, not in the least. He just wanted to take precautions. In his time he had seen lesser wounds turn gangrenous. The prayer? Nothing new in this. His medicine friends in Two Coups's camp did a lot of chanting and praying to invoke the blessings of the spirits. "I understand," Tolliver said, making a final knot in the rawhide-strip binding.

Sun Runner closely eyed Tolliver. He finally said, "I hear you took a child from a woman's belly. What possessed you to do such a thing?"

Tolliver got up. He could see it was still raining, but he instinctively put the palm of his hand out the entry to check. Then back to Sun Runner, he replied, "The woman would have died, the child, too. What else could I do?"

"Hmmm," observed Sun Runner with pursed lips. "To do such a thing, one must possess great faith, faith in himself and the Great Spirit."

"I never thought about it," Tolliver said. "I never thought about my faith."

Sun Runner politely advised him. "You should dwell upon this, Big Black Bear. Meditate. You should be in communion with the Great Spirit and learn the true meaning of faith."

"Faith. A powerful potion."

"Yes, my brother," Sun Runner said. "If you listen to the songs, if you listen to the whispers of the wind, one day you will learn that without faith all the clay of the prairie is worthless to heal anything, even the bite of one little yellow fly."

"*Hau, hau,*" muttered Little Dog. "Everything has a song to sing."

Tolliver gave Little Dog a sidelong glance. He said, "I would like to hear one of these songs instead of your *hau haus.*"

* * *

To Tolliver's relief, the ceremony awarding him three eagle feathers was brief and without too much pomp. He thought there were at least fifty men packed in the lodge; a few women and children were at the entry where the hides had been raised for better viewing. He was pleased to see Chief Red Cloud among those seated at the back. After a holy man had blessed the lodge and presented the sacred pipe to the Four Great Directions, Man Afraid of His Horses summarized the deeds of Big Black Bear. Tolliver understood most of the incantation, which was delivered in a solemn monotone. Finally, Yellow Eagle came from the side with a red cloth. On it were the three feathers. The base of each one was bound with rawhide strips. Tolliver stepped forward, and with a few more words of praise, Man Afraid of His Horses tied them to the locks of Tolliver's long hair. He could wear them this way anytime he chose. If he went to battle, they were to be worn crossed on the top of his head.

"*Wochangi otapi!*" someone shouted.

"*Hau, hau!*"

"*Hechetu welo, hechetu welo, Mato Wichaska!*"

Tolliver turned and opened his arms to The People. Those closest warmly embraced him. Tolliver felt good. He was no warrior, but he felt good, damn good.

Book Three

The Bozeman Trail

Chapter 10

How exciting! James Tolliver thought. Such a sight! Two Coups's village forged ahead. Like a moving picture, it stretched out almost a quarter of a mile across the undulating prairie—mounted men and women, small children riding atop travois, dogs racing ahead, the great herd of ponies trailing behind. Anticipation was high. The animals anticipated, too. They heard the calls of the youngsters, "Grass aplenty ahead, meat aplenty ahead!"

Tolliver rode proudly. He was part of this magnificent mass of beautiful people in their annual exodus to the buffalo grounds. To the side was his good sister, Little Weasel, and his little brother, Black Bow. They were driving Barnaby's wagon. They had reason to be proud, too—Toll-e-veer, the Bear Man, as Little Weasel had predicted, now wore feathers; he was an adopted member of their family. This was good.

Though Tolliver enjoyed this warm feeling of family unity and the friendly companionship of his red brothers, there was a chilling aspect to it. Since Tolliver's triumphant return from the Platte River Valley three days past, he had been honored and feted by Chief Two Coups. The chief's wife, Teal Eye, and his pretty daughter, Red Moccasin, hovered around him like honeybees seeking nectar. And to Tolliver's dismay, the chief was now convinced Big Black Bear's medicine was *wakan*. Could it be otherwise? Hadn't his son, Little Dog, benefited from this powerful medicine on two different occasions? Wasn't there something beyond the realm of Mother Earth in this?

James Tolliver winced when Little Dog had related his father's latest spiritual beliefs. Two Coups believed (Tolliver scoffed) that the man known as Big Black Bear was destined to be a wisdom-seeker, that Toll-e-veer already had begun a journey around the Great Hoop. As sure as *Anpetuwi* ruled the heavens, Big Black Bear was moving to each of the Four Great Directions. Spirits had directed him to a remote Lakota village in the East. (Tolliver recalled that it had been Oglala scouts, including Little Dog.) To the West, Toll-e-veer had gone and brought back powerful medicine to The People. And to the South, he encountered the bluecoats; he fought white men; he defeated them; he returned with great honors. Now Big Black Bear was headed in the Great Direction of the North. Two Coups reasoned that none of this was accidental.

Tolliver thought it nonsense. Pure coincidence. Furthermore, had he gone with Barnaby Cobb to the Great Direction of the East, he would be on a steamboat headed the Great Direction of the South—to St. Louis or even New Orleans. Of course, this hadn't been his reply to Little Dog. God forbid, he wasn't about to dispute the spiritual connotations of these good people. Nor did he care to offend Two Coups. Tolliver was already treading slippery moss. This Red Moccasin business had him in a quandary. And these three feathers he wore certainly hadn't helped matters, either. The damn feathers had enhanced his eligibility. He was no warrior. Red Moccasin knew this, but with a shy smile and fluttering eyelids, she had called him "*ozuye.*"

Oh, he was happy riding along in the Great Direction of the North. Why not? This was the direction of liberation, his escape route to some boisterous mining town where he could begin practice again, a new man, a new identity. He was a tad apprehensive, though. His present situation was tenuous, really quite impossible. Everything that had happened to him this past year was impossible. And now Chief Two Coups had set an enticing trap for him. Sweet bait, indeed. Like forbidden fruit—one bite and he was doomed.

In five days Two Coups's village reached the confluence of Crazy Woman Creek with the Powder River. It was a rigorous but pleasant journey but not without minor incidents. Tolliver, Little Weasel, and Black Bow stalled for more than an hour on the second day repairing an axle. The third day, they fell behind again while Tolliver set and put a plaster cast on the broken ulna of a young boy named Crow Foot. Crow Foot, helping with the pony herd, had taken a bad spill. When he reappeared at the camp that night, his brothers promptly gave him a new name—Big White Arm.

On the fourth day, the villagers passed through a vicious swarm of buffalo gnats. Tolliver thought several minutes in burning hell could have been no worse. Women hastily covered the smaller children with blankets; ponies bucked and snorted; at least a hundred in the herd fled across the grassland. It took nearly an hour to retrieve them.

Circumstances took a turn for the better on the last day. Several bands of Miniconjou and Hunkpapa joined the Oglala. They were packing a heavy load of fresh buffalo meat from several random kills they had made along the trail earlier in that morning. This wasn't meat for drying and smoking. Meat making would come later. This was camp meat for immediate consumption. So this first night in the new village the Hunkpapa and Miniconjou prepared to share their bounty with the Oglala in a feast celebrating the return of the Lakota to the buffalo grounds.

Most of the lodges went up in a great semicircle. They were staggered in two rows. Other lodges were set by the river, a few along the creek. The ponies were pastured in the blue stem and grama grasses a half mile below the camp. Little Weasel wisely selected the site for her lodge and Tolliver's. It was about fifty yards up Crazy Woman Creek in the shade of a few bull pines and a grove of alder. She explained to Tolliver that within another two moons, *anpetu wi*'s golden touch would scorch the land. Though Toll-e-veer might be in the Land of the Shining Mountains by then, her man, Big Beaver, wouldn't. Her man would enjoy his afternoon naps in comfort. Indeed, this was a shady glen, and less than a stone's throw from the cool water of the brook. Tolliver tapped his temple. Little Weasel was a smart woman. She smiled at him and nodded. Of course she was.

Tolliver thought the site was splendid. Aside from the comfort, it afforded more privacy than the lodges located within the perimeter. And with respect to enjoying an occasional afternoon nap (free from the shouts of the youngsters and their yapping mongrels) he considered himself no different from Barnaby Cobb. Indeed, there was a moderate touch of isolation here. So he thought.

Tolliver and his family were adjusting the two vent poles of his lodge when his constant shadow, Little Dog, appeared. Directly behind him with a fat grin on her face was Chief Two Coups's wife, Teal Eye. Peeking around her shoulder was Red Moccasin, the sweet morsel of temptation. Her smile was not fat; it was thin, mischievous. Her hungry eyes looked like two big ebony bonbons. Red Moccasin had become another one of his shadows. By gadfrey, five days on the winding trail, and at almost every bend, she and a few of her smiling friends always popped up like prairie posies. Worse yet, Little Weasel had noticed. One night when the little parade had passed by, she slyly winked.

"Before the Moon of the Red Cherries," she said with a smile, "one of those maidens intends to be keeper of your lodge."

"Not so," Tolliver reminded his sister. "By the Moon of the Red Cherries I plan to be far away."

Tolliver, Little Weasel, and Black Bow politely greeted the visitors. Pleasantries were exchanged.

Little Dog's appearance wasn't unexpected, for Tolliver had examined the young brave's knife wound daily. It was time to remove the stitches.

Tolliver planted the second vent pole firmly. A while later, he went to work with tiny scissors and tweezers. He plucked the last shreds of Minnie Comstock's black sewing thread. The ugly red scar stretched midway from Little Dog's biceps down to his elbow. It was a mark of bravery. To Tolliver's dismay, Little Dog admired it.

Flexing his arm, Little Dog said proudly, "*Wagh!*"

Tolliver held up a finger of warning. "Two times I have repaired you, my brother. I want no more of this. Stay out of trouble, eh? The next time you may not be so lucky."

"What!" exclaimed Little Dog mockingly. "Stay out of trouble? You expect me to die like an old man? . . . An old man with a toothache and sore feet? *Nyah*, this is not my way."

"To live a long life is not dishonorable," Tolliver retorted. "It takes a clever man to do this, not a foolish throw-away-life crazy dog."

Little Dog smiled. He stared up at the tipi vent, then down to the entry. His keen eyes surveyed the surroundings, the blooming spring foliage, the shadowy boughs of the pines. Two gray jays already had perched above the two lodges. They had their heads cocked as though listening to the conversation.

Little Dog said, "I think *you* are a clever man, Toll-e-veer. You have chosen a good place for your lodge. The old women cannot watch you, eh? They cannot pretend they are just passing by. Ei, one who comes here comes for one purpose only . . . to seek your medicine." He grinned. "Plenty smart, Toll-e-veer. No gossip."

Gesturing toward Little Weasel, who was talking with Teal Eye and Red Moccasin, Tolliver replied, "She chose this place, my friend, not I. It will be peaceful, she says. No bad-luck dogs to piss on our tipis."

Little Dog puckered thoughtfully. "Yes, she is a very clever one."

After a few more words, Teal Eye and her pretty daughter prepared to leave. Red Moccasin glanced back over her shoulder at Tolliver and faintly smiled. "Toll-e-veer," she said huskily. That was all. With the grace of a swan, she glided away behind her mother.

Little Weasel began arranging a few big rocks for her fire pit. She looked over at Tolliver and Little Dog. "Chief Two Coups has honored us. We will sit with him at the feast tonight. *Mi-ya,* a good place to hear the songs, to watch the dance."

Tolliver stared daggers at Little Dog. The brave merely shrugged. He said, "My father is very clever, too."

Once again, James Tolliver observed. He did share in the feast, but other than that, he was an interested spectator seated with an admiring host and a doting family. Yes, Tolliver observed. So did Red Moccasin. Most of the evening, her dark eyes were flashing signals; he was the recipient.

During the galloping buffalo dance when several of the dancers (one decorated with a set of horns) pretended to copulate, the crowd laughed hilariously. Red Moccasin smiled; she smiled at Tolliver. Though he thought this particular sequence of the dance to be a bizarre display of crudity, Little Dog explained otherwise. No, this was very symbolic; it had great significance. The Lakota's very existence depended upon propagation of the buffalo, Wakan Tanka's greatest gift to The People.

Tolliver nodded. Yes, he understood. From those eyes of Red Moccasin came suggestive significance.

Little Weasel observed, too. Tolliver realized this. Nothing escaped her sharp eyes. Though she was likewise sympathetic to Tolliver's plight, (even protective, he thought) his fate was out of her hands. He was aware of this.

After the celebration, Tolliver and Little Weasel walked back to their lodges up Crazy Woman Creek. Black Bow and a few of his companions were doing their versions of the dance back at one of the ceremonial fires. Little Weasel asked in English, "What will Toll-e-veer do? . . . this maiden?"

He shrugged. He certainly had given this question some heavy thought. Somewhere in the tremendous void of his mind there was a solution. Tolliver finally said, "Stay out of sight. Go with Crazy Horse and some of his brothers. Scout for the best herd of buffalo. Wait until Barnaby returns. Another week."

"Week?"

"Seven sleeps, eh?"

"Twelve . . . fourteen sleeps. Maybe . . . late for you." Then in Siouan, "Chief Two Coups has made up his mind. Soon he will give Red Moccasin to you. What he does now is present her, to show you her worth. Next, he will make a gift, a very honorable gesture, the daughter of a chief."

Tolliver shook his head. "No, I do not think he will do such a thing. I have explained. He knows I will soon leave, find the trail to the white man's place in the north. I told him this."

"He will say Red Moccasin can go with you."

"She would be unhappy."

Moonbeams played across Little Weasel's pretty face. Her strands of beads sparkled. Likewise, the dark glade around the lodges sparkled with rays of silver. Tolliver looked at her and asked, "Would Little Weasel be happy in the white man's village? Away from her people, would she be happy?"

"I am thirty-seven winters, Toll-e-veer," she replied. "I am too old to leave my people. My man comes and goes. It has always been this way. Red Moccasin is a maiden. She can learn the ways of the white man."

Tolliver smiled. "Thirty-seven winters is not old, my sister."

Little Weasel laughed. "Not too old to take pleasure in the robes, no, but too old to learn the ways of the white eyes. Big Beaver has told me stories about these villages where they live. It would be good to see these places. Maybe it would not be good to live there."

"If war comes to this land, Big Beaver may want to find somewhere safe for you and your sons. You should think about this."

"I have thought about it," she replied. "If Big Beaver wants us to go, we must go. Then I would have to pretend I am a maiden and learn. This is a land of plenty. Big Beaver once said it would not be so bad to make a trading place on the River of Yellow Stones. The fire boats now go to such a place below the Powder River. The Hunkpapa and Miniconjou have seen this."

James Tolliver made no reply. Barnaby Cobb probably hadn't told her the days of the trading posts were getting shorter each year, reason enough for his entertaining thoughts of entering the freight-hauling business up north. Obviously, he hadn't said anything to her about this.

They were in the shadows of the two lodges. Little Weasel plucked a handful of twigs from her pile of dead limbs. She was going to make a little fire, she said. Did Tolliver want to make some coffee and smoke his pipe?

Tolliver smiled. He had plenty of coffee; she knew it, for she had pounded the coffee beans he had brought at Bordeaux, ground them with her pistil. "Make fire," he said. He strode away. By the time he returned from the creek with water and had doffed out a portion of the coffee, Little Weasel had fire. She was piling on a few of the larger limbs.

Soon there was leaping light around the lodges; the coffee was boiling. Tolliver set it aside and poured a touch of cold water in the pot to settle the grounds. Black Bow came and joined them, and for the better part of an hour, they sipped black coffee and talked as a family. After stifling a few yawns, Black Bow finally went to his robes. And as though this were a cue, Little Weasel gathered the cups and the pot. She, too, went to the creek, but when she came back she was draped in a damp robe; her hair was in long wrinkles streaming down both sides of her cheeks. She bowed politely and disappeared inside her lodge.

Since his arrival in the village, James Tolliver had lost track of time, the days, the months. This was a timeless place. Time was irrelevant, only the seasons mattered. However, he was aware that he hadn't been resting on his robes more than ten or fifteen minutes when he heard a rustling at his entry. And then he heard a tiny whisper. "Toll-e-veer." Good grief! Red Moccasin! He almost swallowed his tongue.

"Go home!" he whispered harshly.

Nothing, nary a sound.

Tolliver came up on his knees. He tried again. "Look here, this is no time to be playing such a game. I cannot believe either your honorable father or your mother sent you. Your brother, yes. He is a crazy dog and knows no better. And if you have done this on your own you have no more sense than he does."

A throaty laugh, then the sound of someone crawling toward him. Gadfrey, that laugh! Little Weasel! She came close, touched his shoulder, and whispered, "Were you asleep, my brother?"

"No I was not asleep," he sighed.

"I did not think so."

"And you should not be here either!" Tolliver said. "What is happening in this place? I think everyone has gone mad. Now you!"

"Shh! You will awaken the Owl Maker."

"*Mi-ya,* who is the Owl Maker?"

"A witch who throws ghosts of the unworthy back

to Mother Earth when she is displeased with them. She may be displeased with me someday. I do not know."

"She would have reason to be," retorted Tolliver.

Little Weasel only laughed. It was that low, throaty laugh again.

"Are you crazy?" whispered Tolliver.

"No, my man. Why do you think I chose this place for our lodges? Because of the Owl Maker? Because of the old women who gossip? For many reasons. Because of you."

Tolliver suddenly felt a band of heat across his forehead. His mind ricocheted with a barrage of thoughts. One jumped out like a big black toad, a black thought—"She likes white men." Right out of Barnaby Cobb's mouth, the conniving lout! "Big Beaver!" he croaked. "What about Big Beaver?"

Little Weasel sighed. "Big Beaver says it is not good medicine to be jealous about the happiness of another."

"He's a contrary fool."

"Big Beaver says you know nothing about Lakota women. Red Moccasin is a maiden. She knows nothing about men. If she becomes your wife, you will have to be patient with her."

Tolliver groaned again. "If Red Moccasin finds out you came to my lodge in the middle of the night, she will not be patient, woman. She will take a big stick to me . . . maybe you, too."

Undaunted, Little Weasel said, "She knows nothing. I know plenty, Toll-e-veer. I will teach you about Lakota women. *Eeeyah*, you do not have to be patient with me, I tell you this."

"Gadfrey! You . . . you intend to go through with this? What if Big Beaver protests? How can you tell what he will do?"

She replied softly, "If he knows, he will not care. As a man is pleased, so must a woman be. If I say nothing, you say nothing. If Red Moccasin throws a stick, this will be good. You will be rid of her. You will not have to take a wife, eh?"

"You are a fox. You think of everything and everyone. You even think of the consequences."

Little Weasel whispered, "The consequences will be plenty good for you, plenty good for me. No more talk. Now we please each other."

Tolliver felt her palm caress his damp forehead. He reached up and pulled her into his arms. In the sweet smell of fresh pine boughs, the delicate aroma of her minty body scent, in the darkness of his lodge, he envisioned a mighty herd of galloping buffalo. They were moving swiftly across a golden plain. *Ozuye!* Warrior!

Tolliver eyed the open vent. He squinted against the shafts of sun rays illuminating the peak of his wonderful home, then stretched once. Crawling to the entry, he poked his head out. No one in sight. Somewhere beyond the creek a dog barked and Tolliver heard the gleeful shouts of the small fry. A glance at the sun told him it was nearly ten o'clock. He allowed that the women and older children had gone to the fields to forage. Edging back, he slipped into his pants and moccasins, and finally entered the new day. The gray jays swooped by to greet him. They emitted several whistles—"wheee, wheee."

169

In front of Little Weasel's lodge a fire smoldered. Tolliver saw a covered bowl and the blackened coffeepot. Ah, the good woman had left him breakfast. Gadfrey, he had earned it!

After a quick bath in Crazy Woman Creek, he ate—several small cakes, a mush laced with dried plums, plums that had swollen to the size of big marbles. In between spoonfuls, he spat the tiny pits into the ashes of the dying fire and contemplated his dilemma.

What was to become of him now? Good grief, he was a philanderer! Little Weasel *had* come willingly. Forbidden fruit? Nonsense! Barnaby Cobb, the absentee landlord, had stifled such notions long ago. "What she does is her own business." If this were Barnaby's idea of happiness in his absence, Tolliver believed he would have to oblige his trader friend— at least for another two weeks. Red Moccasin? Definitely not. Avoid her like the plague.

Though Tolliver knew most of the women were at work, he had no desire to stroll the new village. Despite some new assurances from Little Weasel (betrothals took several weeks to be arranged and fulfilled), he was still wary about another encounter with Chief Two Coups. He decided to keep to his quarters until his little family returned. He had a few chores, one of them rearranging his medicines. He did this. He also diluted a big jug of overpotent iodine with alcohol to attain a more suitable bacterial disinfectant. The new solution still had a sting but it was better than frontier red-eye or some tipi concoction.

His final chore was washing a few pieces of clothing. He did this some distance up the creek, and in fear of embarrassment hung the wash on bushes far from the trail. Washing wasn't the work of a warrior. Tolliver retreated to the shady glen where he rested under one of the big evergreens. He dozed.

Near midafternoon, Little Weasel finally returned. She was alone. She carried a large bundle filled with turnips, mushrooms, and several types of greens. A happy James Tolliver greeted her.

Setting her bundle and dibble to the side, she bowed politely. "Toll-e-veer," she said. "What have you done this day?"

He gestured toward his lodge. "I made medicine." He whispered, "I thought about last night."

Little Weasel frowned and passed her hand back and forth several times. "It is good to make medicine, my brother, but what happens by night should not be a part of the day. It should be forgotten. As each day is different, so is each night. Night cannot dwell with day."

Tolliver's mouth drooped. "Forgotten?"

Little Weasel pressed a finger to her lips. "Shhh. I have work to do." She disappeared into her lodge and directly returned carrying two parfleches.

"But ... but I would like to help," a perplexed Tolliver sputtered. "To show my appreciation, I would like to help you."

Her smile was thin. "That is not necessary, my brother. And it would be improper." Little Weasel gathered her bundle of food and swayed down the trail leading to the creek.

Improper? After last night? James Tolliver scratched his head. Damn, this wasn't the kind of greeting he expected. Ah, discretion! Yes, this was it. The Owl Maker was about, and always the eyes and ears of the villagers, too. Yes indeed, what seemed highly improbable by day was most probable by night. Patience, a lonely rider until the cry of the nighthawk. Until further orders, carry on as usual, soldier. Dismissed.

Chapter 11

To many Lakota, the *wasichu* called Toll-e-veer was an honored brother who had proved himself. He wore three feathers. To others, he was a healer, a man of powerful medicine. A few even believed him to be *wakan*, destined to become a man of wisdom and great knowledge, perhaps even a chief. One woman considered him (secretly, fortunately) *wachangi wicasa otapi*, a man with plenty good medicine in the robes. Admittedly, James Tolliver's heady adventures lent credence to all of this acclaim. He had fared well.

A knowledgeable scout, he was not. Yet on this day in early June, here he was stretched out alongside Crazy Horse and Little Dog observing three mounted figures in the valley below. By dark, it would be three nights since his amorous adventure with Little Weasel. If she had "forgotten," he certainly hadn't. He now discovered he would rather be with Little Weasel than on the trail with his brothers.

Crazy Horse passed the spyglass. He said, "That is Whirlwind, one of the hangs-around-the-fort Lakota. His brother, I do not know, and I have seen

173

that white man only once. He was with the Blanket Chief two summers ago."

Tolliver put the little telescope up to his eye. After a moment he handed it back. "We should go down and have a smoke with them. We have seen no sign of pony soldiers up here."

Little Dog spoke. "Maybe those men carry a message from the soldiers' village."

Skeptical, Crazy Horse grunted. "Who would they talk to around this place? The chiefs have gone south to the fort to hear the bad-medicine talk of the white man's government. Hah, if these men do any talking it will be among themselves or to the birds in the trees."

"They search about like they are looking for birds," Little Dog said. He grinned. "Maybe they seek a good campsite, eh?"

Tolliver observed. The three men had separated, two riding along a meandering creek. The other disappeared in a forest of pine. Tolliver finally asked, "How far are we from the trail north to the mining camps?"

Crazy Horse laughed. "Big Black Bear, what you see below *is* that trail. You follow it north and in less than one moon you will be at the place where the white men dig their gold. *Hi ho*, the very village where you wish to go, eh?"

Tolliver nodded. He replied wistfully, "Yes, friend, by the Moon of the Red Cherries I will be at that place, the Great Spirit willing." He stared through the sage and splinters of cheat grass. "What is that creek down there?" he asked.

"We call it Water of the Big Pine," Crazy Horse

said. "Our people sometimes camp there. Big Piney, eh. The water comes from the Big Horn Mountains."

Tolliver studied the broad expanse of land, the lush foothills, the grassy meadows and creeks and nearby timbered ridges. He finally said, "I think it is important, my brothers. It is time we ride down and have a talk with those men."

In a cordial exchange of "*haus*" they met near a stand of greening aspen. The white man introduced himself as John Phillips, known to everyone as Portugee Phil. As Crazy Horse said, Phillips was frequently hired as a scout out of Fort Laramie and was a friend of Jim Bridger. The two Lakota were Chief Whirlwind and Crow Wing, traders, often used as intermediaries by the army. None recognized James Tolliver. Tolliver had been introduced by Crazy Horse as Big Black Bear of the Oglala.

The men sat on their blankets and smoked. But Crazy Horse, suspicious of any *wasichu*, got straight to the point. With a flurry of sign, he asked the men the purpose of their visit, why they were so far north of Fort Laramie, a ride of ten sleeps. What Tolliver had assumed, Portugee Phil confirmed. The white man's government had sent him and the two Lakota to search for suitable sites for one or two forts along the Bozeman Trail. This place was a good one.

Crazy Horse, reading sign closely, reacted violently after Phillips's last flourish. "*Wagh!*" he cried. Leaping to his feet, he shook his rifle and glowered at Chief Whirlwind and Crow Wing. "You traitors!" he shouted. "The peace talks have not begun and you seek a place for a soldiers' village! I tell you there will be no fort built here! We will fight any bluecoats who come this way. You hear my words, brothers. We have seen the wagons of the bluecoat builders. We will not be fooled by crooked words."

Chief Whirlwind said calmly, "There have been no crooked words."

"The star chiefs always make talk from both sides of their mouths!" yelled Crazy Horse. "And you . . . you hear with only one ear!"

Whirlwind countered, "Young man, you do not speak for the council."

"I speak the mind of The People!" Crazy Horse stomped his moccasin. "You go back and tell the star chiefs this is the land of The People. It will be bad medicine to come here." For further emphasis, he jacked a cartridge into the chamber of his carbine.

Aghast, Tolliver leaped from his blanket and held up a hand in peace. "Wait, my brother," he said to Crazy Horse. "These men are not our enemies. They did not come to make bad medicine. They are not bluecoats or builders. We must talk, eh?"

Surprised, Chief Whirlwind stared up at Tolliver. This man was Lakota, true, but he had a strange way of making talk; his tongue was stiff. Whirlwind asked, "Who are you, brother? From what village do you come?"

Portugee Phil had been scrutinizing Tolliver, too. "Why, by damn, he's some kind of breed!" He made a few signs to Whirlwind and Crow Wing.

"I'm not a breed," Tolliver said. "They call me Big

176

Black Bear. I live with the Oglala. Down below the Platte they call me Dr. James Tolliver."

"Doc Tolliver!" exclaimed Phillips. "By gawd, they thought you'd cleaned country!"

"I plan to," Tolliver said. "Very soon."

"They said you were looking to cross the big river . . . you killed some men down at Bordeaux, one at the fort . . ."

Portugee Phil paused and signed to Whirlwind and Crow Wing. Within moments, the two Lakota had smiles on their faces. This stranger was the bluecoat who had stolen Star Chief Connor's pony. Many men were now searching for him. He was a clever fox. He had eluded them all.

Tolliver said to Portugee Phil, "Look here, dammit, what you've heard is a pack of lies. In all the time I've been gone I have shot one man . . . one! Had I not, he would have killed my brother, here." He nodded at Little Dog. Little Dog seemed to understand. He put a thumb on his breast and grinned. "*Hau, hau.*"

"Damnation, you're a big bone to pick on now, Doctor. You're Injun for sure."

"Bone or not," retorted Tolliver, "what my brother says is true. It would be a waste of time to build a fort here. The soldiers would be beleaguered from the day they set foot in it. It will take freighters the better part of two weeks to get up here, and these people own the trails. Your superiors better consider this because when winter comes there'll be a lot of empty bellies and cold feet."

For the benefit of the Lakota, Tolliver flashed a

few signs. Little Dog smiled. "*Hau, hau,*" he said again.

Portugee Phil said to the doctor, "Now look here, Doc. That's what this big parley is all about. Army boys figure they'll talk some sense into the Sioux and Cheyenne, make a deal." He grinned. "Hell, if I was to go back and tell 'em you're doing some big talking, they might just laugh in my face. Crazy damn doctor."

Making sign, Tolliver reverted to Siouan again. "These words are not those of Crazy Horse and Big Black Bear. These are the words of Red Cloud. He already knows about the wagon train of the bluecoats. He has said if the bluecoats come there will be war. There will be no peace until the bluecoats are defeated and return below the Geese Going River."

Whirlwind was not swayed. He replied impassively, "Red Cloud is on the trail to the peace council. We saw him on our way. You look Lakota, Big Black Bear, but you are a white man. You have been honored but your words have no meaning. Red Cloud has not spoken."

Crazy Horse jumped in front of Whirlwind and leveled his rifle at the chief's head. "Do you have stones in your ears?" he hissed angrily. "Red Cloud *has* spoken! One moon ago he said these words. I was there. Big Black Bear was there. Little Dog was there. We were the ones who took the message to him about the soldier-builders! You are a fool Whirlwind! The next time I see your yellow eyes I will shut them forever. I talk no more." He strode away and leaped on his pony.

Crazy Horse rode in stony silence. It took an hour before his anger subsided. Little Dog alternatively chomped on elk jerky and cursed the longknives, ready for battle, eager to get revenge for the hole in his leg.

Tolliver listened half heartedly. Lately he always sought a rationale for his adventures. (Misadventures?) Was it impudence or foolishness to disclose his identity to Portugee Phil? Did it matter? If and when the army arrived in the Powder country, he certainly didn't plan on being around for a confrontation. He had some sense of direction now; he had seen a portion of the Bozeman Trail. Within another ten days or so, he planned to be on it, long before troopers were about. Of course, there was the other side of the coin—army intelligence would know he was still on the prairie. Chief Whirlwind and Crow Wing would boast about this. For the army, more salt in the wound. Also, more rationale here, the Indian kind. Tolliver mumbled to himself, if the bluecoats lack the medicine to catch one horse thief, how can they find the medicine to control six hundred miles of lonesome trail? He grunted. Worry about me?—with a thousand Indians on their tails! Gadfrey, it will take sheer luck, a catastrophe on my part, a bungle of the worst kind. Improbable. But wait! Not impossible. Luck, always the unknown ingredient. Take care, Dr. Tolliver, take care, don't become too damn self-assured.

Young Crazy Horse kept to the front; he was the leader; he carried the pipe. He finally broke his silence when Little Dog pointed out they were riding the wrong direction. Not so, Crazy Horse told him.

The day was growing short. Crazy Horse had heard of a Cheyenne village camped on Goose Creek, only several hours' ride, a good place to take food and shelter for the night. Tolliver readily approved. With an early start the next day, they could be back in Two Coups's village the following night.

A small celebration was under way when they reached the Cheyenne camp. Tolliver learned it was twofold—a successful buffalo hunt had been conducted that day, and new arrivals from the Southern Cheyenne south of the Platte River were being honored. (Tolliver later discovered some of these people were survivors of the Sand Creek Massacre led by Colonel John Chivington.)

The overnight stay proved eventful for the three visitors. They were guests of Two Moons, one of Dull Knife's young subchiefs. Dull Knife himself had gone south to join Red Cloud, Spotted Tail, and Red Leaf of the Lakota tribes in the Laramie peace council. Two Moons was outraged by the news that the longknives were planning to build forts along the valley trail. This was contrary to messages delivered during the Moon of the Ice Going Away. Two Moons declared there had been no mention of forts by the hang-around-the-fort Lakota who delivered the peace council invitation. Chief Dull Knife had gone to the meeting only to approve a new treaty regarding unhampered use of the trail to the mining camps of the *veho*. He would be furious when he learned of this treachery. As others did, Two Moons predicted war.

Several of the Southern Cheyenne who watched

this exchange of sign between the Oglala visitors and Two Moons angrily made sign themselves. They shouted and shook their fists. They welcomed war. They had good reason. One hundred five women and children and twenty-eight men in Black Kettle's peaceful village had been killed by Chivington's soldiers.

Shortly after dawn, Tolliver and his two brothers left the Cheyenne village and rode into the rising sun. By midday they had crossed Clear Creek, and without incident arrived in camp near midnight. The moon was high, and except for one barking dog and two young boys watching the distant pony herd, the camp was quiet.

Tolliver, spirits rekindled, saddle across his shoulder, and carbine in hand, trudged across the moon-lit paths to his lodge up Crazy Woman Creek. Home, he was happy to be home. The four-day scouting trip had been successful, noteworthy in several ways—the parley at Big Piney Creek, the sighting of many buffalo, the meeting with Two Moons at Dull Knife's village, and most important, he had seen the Bozeman Trail.

After stowing his gear, Tolliver went to the creek and washed. He had a four-day bristle; he needed a shave, but this would have to wait until morning. His big pallet of robes welcomed him, and he stretched out and found comfort, restless comfort. Sleep was as elusive as the glittering stars framed in the vent above him. Very quiet. He heard the tiny song of a lone mosquito as it did a ballet across his forehead. Whap! Quiet again, only the voice of his fertile mind. Little Weasel. The lovely woman's ears were as good as her eyes. She missed nothing. Tolliver coughed several times. *Hau,* good sister, I'm home! Somewhere in the dark piney woods an owl answered him, nothing more. Tolliver waited expectantly, for naught.

Finally, he silently crept from his lodge and with the tread of a cat's paw approached the shuttered entry of Little Weasel's tipi. "Night cannot dwell with day," and this was night, the very dead of it. Good woman, he had to alert her of his return to the fold.

Tolliver cautiously parted the flap, immediately detected a heavy, blubbery snore. Black Bow? The lad was a heavy sleeper. Like the fox he was, Tolliver moved softly ahead on his hands and knees. His shoulder brushed against something, a box, a parfleche, and it fell with a sickening thud.

A voice from the darkness: "Ho! Who comes?"

Paralyzed, Tolliver came to point like a bird dog. Crazy Coyote! Barnaby Cobb and Crazy Coyote had returned!

"Who is it?" Crazy Coyote demanded.

James Tolliver retreated, from fox to a stiff crawdad. "Tolliver," he whispered.

"Ah, Toll-e-veer, you come back? What is it?"

Tolliver vainly reached for words. Nothing. He gulped once. "Has . . . has anyone seen my razor?" Razor! Good grief! He heard the deep, resonant snore, also a low, throaty laugh. Backing outside, the cool night air filtered up his blanket; it played against his hot ears. He gave the entry flap a gentle pat and fled.

*   *   *

Dawn. Another beautiful spring day on the Powder. After several sidelong glances at his neighbor's lodge, James Tolliver bounded away to the creek to attend his personal chores, a hasty dip, a lather, a shave, and a brushing of his long hair. A half hour later he returned with an air of bravado. Gadfrey, how else! He was heartily greeted by Barnaby Cobb, embraced by Crazy Coyote, who casually observed that Toll-e-veer had found his razor.

Little Weasel, as usual, politely bowed. She poured him a cup of coffee. He thought he detected a small smile. Smirk? Tolliver, his mind askew, heard Barnaby. "Came back earlier than we figured, James . . ."

"Yes, so I see," Tolliver replied.

Barnaby continued, "Trading went fast, it did, no waiting or chasing 'bout for my special people and supplies. 'Cept for rifles, we did right good, plenty of staples anyhow. Got a few Springfield breechloaders and some ol' muzzle irons, two Sharps, some shells and powder and shot, 'nuff to keep a few of the boys happy."

Tolliver immediately stiffened when Barnaby added that he had encountered a column of soldiers and two Pawnee scouts on the lower Cheyenne River, "a far piece from home."

"Routine patrol?" asked Tolliver. "Or . . .? No, not me?"

Barnaby Cobb chuckled. "I'd say a bit of both. Seems like there was some ruckus down at Bordeaux, some fellers getting their hair trimmed by some Injuns and a white man . . ."

"Oh, Lord."

Crazy Coyote laughed and put a thumb to his chest. "What you think, Toll-e-veer? They come, aim guns at me. They think me Toll-e-veer, eh. Come give plenty good look. Nyah, no whiskers, no big feet, no Toll-e-veer."

Barnaby nodded. "Said they had a report you was running with me somewhere on the prairie. Figger that's from the feller Abbott, the one you patched outta Reno that day."

"Well, what the hell did you tell them?"

Barnaby grinned between his bushy beard. "Said I dropped you off at Pierre two days past. You was waiting for a steamer." He slapped his hands together and cackled. "Assholes rode off hell-bent for leather to the east. Didn't even check my packs."

"A piece of luck there," Tolliver commented dryly. "I appreciate the subterfuge but I doubt that it holds up that long."

"Subterfuge?"

"Your outlandish lie. You see, two days ago I was on the Bozeman Trail talking to two Indians from the fort and a fellow named Phillips."

Barnaby cackled again. "So much the better, I'd say. They'll think you're a goddamned ghost." He stroked his beard thoughtfully. "Phillips? Wouldn't be ol' Portugee, would it?"

"The same." And Tolliver went on to explain the purpose of Phillips's mission and the slight altercation between Crazy Horse and Chief Whirlwind. He also told Barnaby about the scouting trip along the Platte River and details of the unexpected fight at Bordeaux.

Barnaby smiled. "Been earning your keep, haven't you? Staying outta mischief, eh? Ain't got that Red Moccasin in your wigwam yet?"

"Certainly not!" Tolliver replied indignantly.

With a little chuckle, Barnaby Cobb said, "Well, I reckon that's a piece of luck for you. When I left I figgered time I got back you'd be a part of Two Coups's clan and you'd be packing that little woman off to the gold diggings."

"Humph."

Barnaby sat cross-legged on his robe and eyed the bowl of mush Little Weasel had placed in front of him. He spooned in and took a bite, smacked his lips once and looked up at Tolliver. "Just like we figgered, James, the roof is 'bout to cave in. Reckon we better get our tails outta here in a couple of days, move north a piece. That's what I figger."

Surprised, Tolliver said, "Move? You mean your lodge? . . . the family?"

"Yassir, pack the whole shebang, that's what," Barnaby replied.

He looked over at Crazy Coyote. "Oh, he'll probably want to stay 'round a piece, count some coup with his brothers. Stay with one of the wife's clan if he wants so he won't go starving to death."

Crazy Coyote suddenly came to a crouch, a fighting stance, and carved the air once with the flat of his hand. "*Hi ya!*"

"He's ready," Barnaby said.

"But . . . but what the hell are you planning to do?" asked Tolliver. "Are you going all the way? . . . up to that landing?"

"Fort Benton? Not likely, least ways not yet. Have

185

to do these things easy-like, sort like breaking in new mocs, eh, so as no one gets sore and out of sorts." Barnaby stirred his mush and gulped several spoonfuls. He flicked a dribble off his beard and said, "No, I figger I can keep in touch. I don't hanker this fighting, y'know. Did my share of it. Just keeping the Bloods and Big Bellies off my back was enough. Oh, I reckon I'll move up one of the canyons, the big mountains over there." His thumb flashed to the west. "That upper Tongue country. See how she goes down below. Man can make do up there, y'know. Hole up for the winter even. I did it a couple of times in the old days, me'n the woman. The boy, here, he was a taddy-pole. He don't remember, and Black Bow was a piece of dust."

"Good grief, that's isolation! The end of the world!"

Barnaby's face wrinkled in amusement. He said, "Damn sight better'n hanging 'round a war village, maybe getting rubbed out by a soldier's boot. Right peaceful in the mountains."

"No," Crazy Coyote said. Moving his foot back and forth across the dirt several times, he glowered. "No, Papa, we rub out bluecoats first. *Heya!*"

"Cocky bastard, ain't he?" Barnaby said with a grin. "A crazy dog."

Tolliver sadly shook his head. "No, he's not crazy. The crazy ones are down below the Platte. They just don't understand what they're getting into up here. Good grief, that Two Moons said if his people join with the Lakota and the Arapaho, they can mount a cavalry of three thousand warriors?"

Barnaby Cobb gave Tolliver a skeptical stare. "You doubt it?"

"No, I don't doubt it," replied the trader. "Trouble is, always takes Injuns a couple of months to get their asses moving. Too much smoking and talking, not enough listening and doing. Fact is, if they'd joined up last year, ol' Red Nose woulda been wiped out in two weeks." He grinned. "And I wouldn't have to be dragging you up the trail a piece. You'd likely be fertilizer for wild mustard."

James Tolliver shuddered. "That's not a pleasant thought, Barnaby."

"Ain't nothing pleasant about war, pilgrim. Damn poor excuse for settling arguments, but when you keep getting pushed, I reckon there just ain't no other way."

Chapter 12

Four young women carrying bundles of green willow limbs came down the creek. One tarried, the others laughed and chided her and disappeared toward the village. James Tolliver gave Red Moccasin a courteous welcome. She nodded politely and sat in the shade of his lodge. Perspiration pebbled her brow; her bundle was heavy, the day warm. It was hard work cutting willows and fighting mosquitoes at the same time. She hoped the hunters would bring back plenty of meat to smoke on the lattices to make all of her work worthwhile. Tolliver assured her they would; he had seen many buffalo west of the village.

Red Moccasin was seated in a half-reclining position, her long legs bent and hidden under her skirt, this the polite, subservient pose of a maiden. After a while, she spoke again. "My father says you travel two roads, Toll-e-veer. He says you are confused."

Confused? Tolliver went about sorting his medicines, those he planned to take north, others he promised to his friends, Red Bone and White Wolf. Identifying the medicines in Siouan for the two healers had been a painstaking ordeal. With a quick glance at Red Moccasin, Tolliver said, "I honor Two Coups. He is a wise man. I travel the road north. I am not confused about this. I know my direction."

Red Moccasin hid behind a small smile. Lowering her eyes, she said, "I do not believe my father meant confused in direction."

Tolliver stared blankly at a brown bottle labeled "salicylate." "Ah, my mind! Is that it? Confused in my mind. Now, my sister, can you explain this? Do I look confused?"

"You will miss our people?" she asked.

"Yes," he confessed. "I am known as a brother. How can I not miss these people?"

"You are leaving tomorrow?"

"Yes."

"You have been plenty happy, eh, content?"

"Happy? Yes, I have been content." Tolliver's eyes lit up. "Ah, you probe me by deduction." He could think of no Siouan word for "analysis."

"I seek the truth," she replied. "Is it not strange one can be happy and sad at the same time?"

Tolliver moved to the side and hunkered down across from her. For a moment he eyed her critically, her shy demeanor, wondered if a tawny catamount lurked behind it. Such a pretty doe-like creature. He said, "For one so young you are very perceptive. You think I am sad, eh?"

"I see sadness in your face. And I am not so young. I am seventeen winters."

Tolliver asked, "Confused, eh? sad? Are these your words or those of your father?"

"What my father says is what I already perceive," she replied softly. "You are happy to leave but you have a heavy heart. What you have here is good. What you may find at the end of the North Road you do not know. You are a seeker, Toll-e-veer."

"You only repeat what your father told me. He said I was a seeker. He also said I was *wakan*. I do not think I am either."

"It is good to be modest," Red Moccasin said. "A man who goes about with a high nose cannot see the ground upon which he treads."

Tolliver laughed. "What I seek is freedom," he said. "I seek to be free of men who hunt me, to be at peace, to be with my people again. War displeases me, my good little sister."

Red Moccasin gracefully rose. She swept a few pine needles from her skirt. Her broad lips parted, exposing her upper teeth, a touch of a small overbite but charming to Tolliver. She picked up her bundle and bowed. "I must go," Red Moccasin said.

"So soon?" Tolliver asked. "You speak so well."

Her usually evasive eyes came to a direct stare. "Had you talked with me in the many moons you have been in this village you would already know this." Hoisting the willows to her shoulder, she added, "One day, Toll-e-veer, you may discover the Oglala *are* your people. You may discover everything you seek is within reach of your arm. Do not hold your nose too high." Red Moccasin bowed her head again and left.

A perplexed James Tolliver returned to his work. A touch of melancholy swept over him. Good grief, warrior, healer, seeker, *wakan*. What more could these people expect of him! He was a white man. "*Wagh!*"

A small, throaty laugh! Tolliver turned. He saw Little Weasel shaking out a robe in front of her lodge. His smile was weak. Ah, good neighbor, once his woman of the night, soon to be his trail-riding companion of the day. He picked up another brown bottle. It glistened. It had no label. Holding it to the light, he saw his distorted image gleaming on the shiny surface. Warrior, healer, seeker, was he a pharmacist, too? Within minutes he had concocted a bittersweet potion of nostalgia and melancholia. Or had he? Tolliver's eyes probed the shadows of the big pines. "Owl Maker?"

Early the next day, Little Weasel struck her tipi; Tolliver, Barnaby, and his sons helped. Since the doctor had no use for his lodge, he gave it to Crazy Coyote who, as Barnaby predicted, had elected to remain with his brothers. By midmorning, the wagon and mules were backed out. A large crowd gathered at the village perimeter. Amid many tremolos, shouts, and a few tears, farewells were made. Tolliver saw Chief Two Coups with his hand raised in a salute, next to him Teal Eye and Red Moccasin. Close by stood Slow Runner cradling her daughter; she held her aloft. Tolliver turned away. Misty-eyed, he sighed in relief. The move to Wolf Creek canyon was finally under way. Barnaby handled the wagon; Tolliver and Little Weasel rode to the side, and young Black Bow brought up the rear with the pack string and trailing ponies. Far to the west the Big Horn Mountains loomed high. They were etched in purple against a golden sky.

*   *   *

Because of the cumbersome wagon, Barnaby Cobb had to make several detours, but the delays were minor. In the balmy spring weather the journey was more like a camping trip. Game was plentiful, Barnaby's larder fat, daily progress inconsequential. Slumped, molded into the saddle, Tolliver rode leisurely, often nodding off under the gentle gait of his mare.

On the third afternoon, Barnaby coursed a few brushy foothills, swung to the left alongside a willow-lined creek. Directly ahead was a narrow defile where the rushing creek glistened with white and golden riffles. After several bends, the neck of the canyon widened into broad meadows covered with colorful patterns of flowers—lupine, yarrow, paintbrush, and elk thistle. Birds were everywhere. Groves of fir, pine, and aspen hugged the hillsides. The new grass was already above the hocks of the mules and horses.

Barnaby finally reined up at the edge of a lush meadow flanked by a stand of stately timber. A scent of pine and bear grass was in the air. Little Weasel pointed. "I will put my lodge over there."

James Tolliver sidled his horse next to the wagon and smiled at Barnaby. The trader, one boot propped against the footboard, was biting into a plug of tobacco. Tolliver said, "My friend, this is magnificent!"

Barnaby's chin whiskers jumped once as he shuffled the chaw to the side of his mouth. Squinting at Tolliver, he said, "Isolation, pilgrim. End of the world. Ain't that what you said?"

Tolliver shucked the gentle barb and grinned.

"My apologies. I only imagined, Barnaby. No man believes out here until he sees. This very well could be the beginning of the world, an Eden of sorts."

Barnaby pointed. "Yonder, other side of the trees, is a cold-water spring. Good for drinking, no good for a bath. Freeze your balls off." He spat to the side and hopped down. "Yassir, this'll make do 'til the dust down below settles, 'til the first frosts."

Dismounting, Tolliver asked, "And then . . . ?"

"Snow gets ass-deep up here, James. Go back across the valleys, I reckon, below the Sacred Hills, upper White or Cheyenne. Winter village. Mebee do some robe trading over on the Mother River." Barnaby nodded to the north. "Hell, James, if I take a notion, mebee I'll follow you. Land's changing. Catch on to freighting before it's too late. Just a notion."

Tolliver patted Barnaby on the shoulder. "A good notion, I'd say. Something for the future."

"Yassir, I'm thinking she's a short wick, pilgrim."

Dr. Tolliver stayed at Barnaby Cobb's mountain-meadow retreat for three days. He rode the splendor of the high country with young Black Bow. It was truly spectacular, the breath of life everywhere, birds and animals he had never seen—woodpeckers the size of small crows, grouse that pecked along the paths oblivious to the tread of a moccasin, sheep, tiny rock rabbits, marmots, and dusky squirrels that constantly chattered. Tolliver opined this was a virgin land where no man had set foot. Not so. Black Bow reminded him that The People had been here forever. But when The People passed through, they never left sign.

Yet another farewell. They accompanied Tolliver several miles up the North Trail. The doctor was grateful. Barnaby had prepared him the best he could, rations, a trade of two mules for one of the mares and a colt, a rough map of the country, and one precious, little pouch of gold, his grubstake. Blessed friends. Tolliver felt blessed.

Though Barnaby hadn't been beyond the Yellowstone in ten years, he knew the land and its dangers. On the map he marked suitable river crossings. The streams would be running high from the spring snowmelt in the high country. With the exception of getting lost, Barnaby saw little else to cause Tolliver any worry. Indians? A few, but most of them would be busy hunting buffalo, making meat. Tolliver was already acquainted with the Lakota and Cheyenne. The Blackfeet, once a threat, seldom ventured below the Yellowstone River anymore, and the Crow were friendly toward the whites. However, Barnaby did think it might be prudent if Tolliver removed his Lakota trimmings when he crossed the Little Bighorn. His last gift to the doctor—a floppy, old white man's summer hat. With a smile, Tolliver stuffed it into one of his bundles.

James Tolliver was ready to move. He had two mules, an extra horse, the piebald mare that he was riding, and her spindle-legged colt. After a few final reminders from Barnaby, a shake of hands, and an unexpected embrace from Little Weasel, he rode off to freedom. He had a lump in his throat, a rather large one, for fear had crept into his heart to join sorrow.

James Tolliver seldom indulged in song. Because he couldn't carry a tune, he relegated himself to listening. Exception. Alone on the trail, encompassed by a vast, lonely land, he *tried* to sing. It provided him with self-assurance, at least a small measure of bravado.

Toward evening on the first day north, Tolliver suddenly discovered the land was not as lonely as it seemed—his fractured song attracted visitors. As he wound his way down a creek-side trail, there they were directly in front of him: three mounted braves, two bare-chested, another wearing a beaded vest. Ye gods, what a bumbling idiot he was, stumbling into a confrontation like this! A blind man could have done better.

Tolliver's alarm was short-lived. The vested brave moved his pony broadside blocking the trail, but simultaneously crooked his arm in a friendly salute. He smiled. As Tolliver's song trailed off into a sick hum, the other two riders also smiled.

Elevating his arm, Tolliver returned the greeting. He grinned sheepishly and said, *"Hau. Hi ho, kolapila."* He waited. They only nodded. They didn't understand Siouan. Ah, they must be Cheyenne. Then to his astonishment, one of the bare-chested fellows said, "Toll-e-veer."

"Eyah," the doctor returned, touching a thumb to his chest. "Tolliver."

A brief exchange of sign revealed the young men were from Dull Knife's village on Goose Creek, one a brother-in-law to Chief Two Moons. His name was Tall Elk, and he remembered Tolliver as the white Lakota who had visited Two Moons earlier in the spring. Tolliver learned the three Cheyenne were trail runners, headed for a village of buffalo hunters on the Rosebud. The news they carried, though disheartening, did not surprise him. The peace council had ended in failure. Red Cloud, after delivering a stinging accusation of army underhandedness, stalked from the meeting. The rest of the chiefs followed. The tribes were moving back to the valleys to hunt and conduct their annual Sun Dances and Rites of the Arrow Renewal. By late summer, they planned to congregate in the Powder River valley and make war on the fort builders.

That Tolliver was unaware of the aborted talks surprised the men. They knew the bluecoats wanted to capture him. Since the fort builders were coming up the North Trail, the three scouts presumed he was now fleeing to avoid capture.

With an indignant look, Tolliver expanded his chest. *Nyah,* this was untrue, he signed. In ten moons the soldiers had been unable to capture him. He had made fools of them, but he was tired of playing the fox. It was time for him to go north and seek a new place free of soldiers.

Tall Elk smiled grimly. He signed, "By the end of the Hungry Moons there will be no bluecoats in this land, only their bones." His two companions nodded.

They made more sign. They advised Tolliver to follow the creek trail. It would lead him to the

Tongue River. He gave them tobacco. As they prepared to leave, Tall Elk's hands flashed. "Tread
softly, my brother. You may be the fox but your song
is that of a crow."

Tolliver quickly discovered there was no such
thing as a Bozeman Trail, at least not a marked one.
It was a mishmash of paths, an occasional rut, and
it wandered from wash to coulee as though first trod
by a drunk. This first night he rode into a hollow
and spread his blanket in a grove of cottonwood
within sight of the Tongue River. This was his first
mistake. Shortly, his bedroll swarmed with big red
ants. He had chosen a pathway to the sticky excre-
tions of the budding cottonwoods.

Tolliver moved to the edge of the glade. Mistake
two. By nightfall, hordes of no-see-ums and mosquitoes struck up a humming symphony over the grassy
meadow. Many were hungry. Many attacked Tolliver. He fled this site to a bench-land knoll where
he curled up in the rocks.

Dawn came without the sun but with rain, the
first in more than two weeks. Tolliver crawled from
under his tarp and retreated to the cottonwood
grove. The ant migration had come to a standstill,
but he had a terrible time striking a fire. Barnaby
Cobb would have laughed. It was times like this
when a man needed a good woman. Little Weasel
never would have chosen such a miserable
campsite.

After coffee, tinned beef, and hard biscuits, Tolliver packed and headed up the river trail to find a
suitable ford. As Barnaby predicted, the stream was

turbulent and over its banks. Luckily, it took only ten minutes of riding before he made a belly-deep crossing in slack water at the end of a long, murky pool.

By late afternoon, the drizzle moved east leaving behind isolated shrouds of mist. Not good. Tolliver could no longer see his two most important reference points—the sun and the Big Horn Mountains. He let his piebald mare follow another small stream. It gradually widened as several creeks emptied into it. Was he lost? He finally paused to check Barnaby's map. It appeared this stream was a fork of the Little Bighorn. Relieved, Tolliver breathed deeply. Oh, happy day, he wasn't lost; he was right on course.

Tolliver breathed deeply again. *Wagh!* He smelled like wet dog. He hadn't sung a song all day, either. Enough was enough. Wielding his hatchet, he hacked dead limbs from a few bull pines and built a big fire. He rigged a willow rack and dried his buckskins. Blanket-wrapped, he drank coffee and ate a can of Barnaby's U.S. Government peaches. He also swatted a few foraging mosquitoes. This was the extent of his evening.

After banking his fire with green willow, Tolliver rolled up in his robe and slept. Not too soundly. He knew the difference between the mournful howl of a wolf and the yip-yip of a coyote. Wolves were about. Once during the night he thought he detected the soft tread of their big paws circling the camp.

*   *   *

James Tolliver awoke to the warmth of the sun and the calls of the birds, whistling jays, a guttural cluck from a raven, and a few raucous squawks from crows. He shoved aside the canvas. He saw a tiny wisp of smoke curling above his nighttime smudge. In the nearby meadow his two hobbled mules flicked their ears and stared at him. Tolliver suddenly bolted from the bedroll. The horses! His piebald, her colt, and the Pawnee paint were gone!

Barefoot, Tolliver bounded away, his neck craned like a gander. He scanned the countryside, the willows, the distant rolling landscape, and the banks to either side of the creek. Nothing. He hopped through the damp grama over to the mules. He addressed them. "You bray all day, you beasts, why not at night?"

Bent low, he probed the grass, soon discovered what he had feared—a single file of pony tracks heading out to the north, and among them the faint imprints of a moccasin. Some bastard had counted coup, had stolen his horses, someone who had little use for mules—an Indian. Gone, gone, gone.

James Tolliver eyed the two mules apprehensively. It wasn't a matter of indignity, that of riding a flopeared beast; it was dire necessity. Despite the nighttime thievery, Tolliver wasn't destitute. He had his tack, his rifle, pistol, and packs. With some shifting about he still could ride to freedom on his mules. Misfortune spawned determination. He could do it.

However, he forgot one critical matter—cooperation from his two packers.

Tolliver shortly discovered why his Lakota brothers disdained mules. Obviously, one of his critters had never tasted a bit. It put on a display of head tossing, baring of teeth, and ugly lip curling. Tolliver finally bridled it and mounted. A long bray and several stiff-legged leaps quickly followed. Tolliver landed on his back. His success with the other mule wasn't much better. He settled comfortably into the saddle. Despite gentle nudges, then several hefty kicks in the flanks, the animal refused to budge. Determination gave way to frustration. Tolliver grudgingly repacked the mules, tied on lead ropes, and headed back up the Bozeman Trail the way he had come. The alternative was worse—walking five hundred miles to Virginia City was entirely beyond his endurance. He was a fox, not a beast of burden.

Five miles up the trail, he discovered moccasins were inadequate footwear for hiking. It was impossible to keep a lookout for trouble and guard his footing against rocks, downfall, and prickly pear. He shucked his moccasins and put on his old military boots. Boggy areas he once had plodded through with the piebald he now had to avoid. His route was circuitous, worse than the trail itself. Time chewed at him. By the end of the first day, he had only covered half the distance of the previous day. At this rate, Wolf Creek canyon was three more sleeps away. He was lonely. He had forgotten all about the comfort of song. How he wished his Cheyenne friends would reappear.

But Tolliver doggedly trudged ahead, covering more ground than he had anticipated. On the third morning, he reached the Tongue River. His spirits soared again. To shorten the last miles he trailed close to the foothills, away from the meandering ruts in the bottom. He threaded his way through small forests of alder, aspen, and cottonwood, into green coulees and across sagebrush flats. The Cheyenne scouts never reappeared. A galloping column of cavalry did, fortunately a good distance below him. Tolliver heard the pounding of hooves and cracking brush. He quickly led the mules behind a juniper and sage-covered knoll. Moments later he peered over the rim. Several hundred yards below, the troop came into view, bluecoats riding two by two, led by an officer with a rakish hat and mounted on a big gray.

Two men dressed in leathers were beside him. Heading north, the column suddenly swung to the right toward the bottomland and slowed. One of the men dressed in buckskin dismounted and slowly led his horse down the trail, Tolliver squinted. At this distance, he couldn't be sure, but it appeared the soldiers were searching for tracks or following them. Puzzled, he ducked and flopped on his back. Strange they were so far north, so far from Fort Laramie. Fort Reno? Had the army reactivated that sorrowful bastion? Another thought struck him and he took a second hard look. The troopers appeared to carry nothing more than their usual accoutrements, no extra supplies, and there wasn't a pack animal in the line. Deduction here. Somewhere within a day's ride the bluecoats had established a supply base, and that "somewhere" was probably where Colonel Carrington had decided to build his fort. The army had arrived in the Powder River basin.

As Tolliver stared at the cloudless sky he heard a distant shout, then the faint clatter of hooves. When he peeked from his cover he saw the soldiers riding away to the southeast. Leading his mules out of the coulee, he grinned. It would take two days of hard riding to find anything in that direction. Unlikely. Only a fool would put his hand in a hornets' nest. Two Coups's Oglala, some of Sitting Bull's Hunkpapa, and a hundred Miniconjou were camped over there, soon to be joined by a thousand of Chief Red Cloud's people. Poor place for a bluecoat picnic, Tolliver surmised.

James Tolliver felt a joyous surge. In the distance to the left, he saw a silver ribbon winding down from the mountain meadows. Wolf Creek! He topped a rolling hill, stood on a grassy ride, and stared down. Far below were the faint imprints of Barnaby's wagon wheels, more than a week old, but there they were, etched in the moist earth pointing the way to Eden.

Tolliver descended, scalloping the long hill with his huge, leaping footprints. His chest heaved, his legs wobbled at the knees when he bottomed out. Homecoming, it was glorious! Sensing familiar haunts and old pasture mates, the two mules trotted ahead. Tolliver, however, stalled and stared at the ground in silent shock. The grassy bottom was heavily pocked with fresh horse tracks, shod stock, going both directions. Good grief, this was no mystery! Cavalry! The bluecoats had ridden up the canyon, undoubtedly the same column he had observed not more than two or three hours past. Gripped with fearful anxiety, Tolliver charged ahead.

When he saw the distant camp smoke and a few horses and mules grazing in the meadows he sighed in relief. This was short-lived. Suddenly he was overcome by dread—Little Weasel's lodge was gone! No, not gone. In shambles! As he jogged closer, he saw the lodge poles poked out like jackstraws, loose hides hanging from them like shrouds. A thin film of smoke covered the campsite, and no one was in sight. Tolliver's heart turned to molten lead.

He found the bodies of Barnaby Cobb and Little Weasel lying near the wagon. They had been shot several times. Barnaby had a gaping hole in the side of his left temple. In a daze, Tolliver stumbled toward the smoldering tipi. In a small clearing ten yards from it, he saw the sprawled body of Black Bow. Agonized, Tolliver bent over the boy. Black Bow had been shot in the back.

Tolliver cradled his little friend and wept.

High above, shards of gold knifed through the towering pines. Heartbroken, gnawed by guilt, Tolliver sat down below in the purple shadows of twilight. He observed the three mounds in the darkening meadow, this the horrible, sickening reward for sanctuary, friendship, and love. This had been retribution at its worst. Never in his life had he felt more miserable and lonely. Tolliver had buried his loving family. He buried his heart with them. As devastated as he was, his mind flamed with fury. Retribution? One day soon, the perpetrators of this foul deed would die screaming, the skin stripped from their bodies in shreds. They had destroyed Eden. They would discover hell.

Chapter 13

James Tolliver left Wolf Creek at dawn. He rode one of Barnaby Cobb's fast ponies and trailed his own two mules. He needed no more. Herding the rest of the trader's stock was out of the question. Rations were enough. He had done all he could in the shattered camp, sorting through the debris, salvaging tins of food, flour, sugar, beans, and a tin of coffee. He hid most of this in the crevice above the cold-water spring where Barnaby had fashioned a rock-covered cooler for fresh meat and bacon. The soldiers had looted all the clothing and hardware in the lodge. Tolliver found no sign of Barnaby's little pouches of gold; his revolver and Henry rifle were missing; the bluecoats had even stolen Little Weasel's necklaces. Somehow they had missed a strand of red and white beads, and these Tolliver reverently draped around his neck. He thought Crazy Coyote might want something that had belonged to his mother. Without looking back, Tolliver trotted across the meadow of flowers. One last tear rolled down his tanned cheek.

He crossed the main trail in a hurry. Obviously, the bluecoats had given up on his tracks to the north. They were too old; he had been too far ahead of the soldiers and they hadn't been equipped for a ride of any great distance. Well and good if they believed he had eluded them, but he knew they were in the vicinity. He had to be cautious. In a steady trot, he rode due east, the direction he believed safest. Somewhere across the prairie he would strike the lower Powder River and ride up the trail to the village of his Oglala brothers.

Tolliver no longer desired to seek freedom in the north, once a bright illuminating thought. He now entertained black thoughts of death and destruction, thoughts as black as a moonless night. Flee now, yes, but by the Great Power, he planned to return to this sorrowful site—riding beside a thousand Lakota warriors. *Ozuye, ozuye, ozuye!*

Whenever possible, Tolliver kept to the highest, most tortuous route. Young Crazy Horse, a superb scout, had counseled him about this—"A bad trail is the safest. Never relinquish the high ground to the enemy." The cavalry was the enemy. Troopers loved to ride the flats; they detested the rocks, sage, and buckbrush.

Late afternoon he came down from a series of rocky knolls to a small stream. (He later learned it was called Buffalo Creek.) It coursed east so he followed it and by evening was on the banks of the Powder. In thirty or so miles of riding he had crossed only three sets of pony tracks; they were made by Indian stock.

The creekside camp was free of mosquitoes, wolves, and pony thieves, but Tolliver, haunted by the violence in Wolf Creek canyon, slept restlessly.

The thought of riding into Two Coups's village bearing such sorrowful news pained him body and soul. Crazy Coyote, my God, his family wiped out in one fell swoop! In his own miserable state, how could he comfort anyone? He wasn't *wakan*. He was a Judas bull. Good medicine had turned sour. This had to be rectified, put right again. His indebtedness to The People for their aid and comfort had increased twofold. But in his white mind he knew salvation for such a tragedy was impossible. In the red man's mind, retaliation, yes. Vengeance, yes, and he was obligated to follow. In their culture, the Lord had no claim on vengeance.

Tolliver's morning was as bitter as his thoughts. He saw a black eagle soaring the high currents, winging away to the south. Black. Well, the color was right.

Since this section of the river was new to him, Tolliver had no idea of the distance to the village. After several hours of riding, he was surprised to see mounted figures on the horizon. He quickly moved into the shadows of the trees. Ah, no troopers, these! Hunters, meat-makers, men and women, and they were moving south. He could see the travois, the huge mounds atop them, hides, meat. Heartened, he rode out from his cover sorely aware this sudden euphoria soon would be smothered by lament and fiery anger.

Moments later one of the hunters spotted Tolliver and began to close in on him. Tolliver waved. It was Hawk Leg, one of the men who had participated in his escape from Fort Laramie. The appearance of the Medicine Maker, Big Black Bear, surprised Hawk Leg, but he was stunned when Tolliver related the reason for his unexpected return. Hawk Leg said the village was less than a half sun away. He held his bow high, screamed, and galloped away.

Shortly after the sun was at its highest, a group of braves pounded down the trail. Led by Hawk Leg, they made a big sweep around Tolliver and flanked him, five riders to each side. Their faces were painted and streaked in yellow, crimson, and black. Black Wing was among them. He carried a small pouch. Hawk Leg screamed again and shook his scalp stick. Everyone moved ahead in a brisk trot.

On the flat ahead, Tolliver saw the pony herd, behind it the faint outlines of the Lakota lodges, the cottonwoods, and the spires of the evergreens. Closer now, many people moved toward them, from the meat racks women brandishing their knives, from the ripe hides women with fleshing tools, children, barking dogs. Tolliver sucked wind. Where were the wails of lament? The shrieks and tremolos were deafening.

A wide path opened at the *hocoka*. At the end of it stood a group of men, in front, Chief Two Coups holding a decorated crooked lance, a symbol of authority. He held the staff high. The villagers screamed. He presented it to the Four Great Directions as he would a ceremonial pipe, and at each point the crescendo grew in intensity. Tolliver's spine tingled. This was no lament; it was a savage outcry for revenge.

Chief Two Coups lowered the feathered stave. Silence. Tolliver dismounted and the chief beckoned him forward. Placing a hand on the doctor's shoulder, Two Coups said, "You have come home, Toll-e-veer. It was foretold. You have returned from the North in the fourth sun of the Black Eagle." The people shrieked. After another wave of the staff, Two Coups continued, "Your medicine is from the North. Chief Red Cloud has already spoken. He said if the bluecoats come, war will come with them. The bluecoats have come. They struck the first blow against our people in the Canyon of the Wolf. The Canyon of the Wolf is a holy place. Toll-e-veer has brought the message of the Black Eagle. War!" The ground suddenly shook with the stomping of moccasins, and the air reverberated with renewed screaming. "Now, my brothers," cried Two Coups, "make your moccasins ready. War, war, war!"

Defiant shouts echoed across the rolling prairie. Tolliver cringed. The Black Eagle? My God, war was a forgone conclusion! It always had been. He had fled to escape it! Certainly, war was foretold, but he and this mysterious, high-flying bird had nothing to do with it. Just a moment here. Clarification, a few words of explanation? People closed in, touching, slapping his back. Young boys darted to and fro, fingers poking, stealing his medicine.

That night, a disconsolate James Tolliver sat with Crazy Coyote in front of the lodge on Crazy Woman Creek. How painfully sad not to see the splendid lodge of Little Weasel, but they were brothers; they watched the carmine sky; they shared food, and they shared misery. Tolliver was guilt-stricken. He must bear the blame for the tragedy on Wolf Creek. Not so. Crazy Coyote gave him solace. It had been sheer fate, an outright accident. The bluecoats had stumbled on his father's wagon tracks. And who knew what prompted the disaster that followed? Complicity in hiding Tolliver? The killings at the sandstone buttes? Barnaby Cobb's gun-running? Any one of these, the young brave said.

Crazy Coyote sighed. He placed a twig on the little fire. "He trades for plenty long time. They know this. Guns, maybe. They see repeater. How he get repeaters, eh? Injuns get Springfields. How get Springfields, eh?"

Tolliver nodded. To a point, this was believable. Though most Lakota used bows, rifles of various makes and calibers were commonplace now. The army knew what the white traders were peddling, but few had been caught. This didn't explain the wanton killing of Little Weasel and Black Bow. Tolliver said, "They could have arrested him. Good grief, it was murder, your mother, Black Bow."

Crazy Coyote leaned close to Tolliver and stared. "What difference?" he asked. "They do this before. Papa tells us one time if bluecoats come, run, go hide. We called lice. Kill 'em all, no more come. Papa says this what star chiefs tell bluecoats."

Tolliver shuddered but made no reply. Barnaby Cobb had spoken the truth. Such stories always got back to the Indians. General Connor had ordered his men to kill all male Indians over twelve years of age. Worse, Colonel Chivington's words: "Kill every Indian, infants included. Nits make lice."

Tolliver felt sick. His stomach rolled. At length he said, "I'm no Black Eagle. Everyone knew this mess was coming when that train of builders came up the Platte River trail. Red Cloud said there would be war. Your father predicted it. So did I. It was none of my doing, this eagle business. Your father and I were trying to get away from war."

"You come back to make it your doing, eh?"

"Yes," confessed Tolliver. Then: "What else could I do? Damnation, if I hadn't come back no one would ever have known what happened up there in that canyon."

Crazy Coyote said in Siouan, "Our people believe in the signs, my brother, the omens, the visions. It was not the vision of Chief Two Coups today. It was the medicine of your doctor friend White Wolf. It was he who said you would return from a storm. *Eyah*, he saw the Black Eagle fly three times north to south. Little Dog heard him speak with his father, Two Coups. White Wolf said on the fourth day, a sign would come. The Black Eagle came again. So did you."

"Coincidence," scoffed Tolliver. "Eagles fly around here very day. I see them all the time."

"Tomorrow you will not see one. You will see Red Cloud. Red Cloud and the rest of his people come. We will go to war."

Tolliver stared into the embers of the dying fire. He removed the red and white beads from around his neck and placed them over Crazy Coyote's head. "These belonged to your mother," he said. "She was a good woman. You should be proud to wear them."

Chief Red Cloud and his followers did arrive. They pitched their lodges swelling the village to over two thousand. A war council was held that night. A number of chiefs spoke, including Man Afraid of His Horses, Two Coups, and Swift Bear. Tolliver sat by Yellow Eagle, Crazy Horse, and Hawk Leg. He listened to the oratory condemning the crooked talkers at Fort Laramie, and heard several suggestions how Little White Eagle (the name they had given Colonel Henry Carrington) and his fort builders should be fought.

Finally Red Cloud spoke. A prudent but ferocious warrior, he predicted a prolonged war with the bluecoats but saw no necessity to rush into battle. Before war, the Lakota must prepare for it. Let the men and women continue with their food gathering. When the annual ceremonies and meat making concluded, let the warriors come together fully ready for war.

Red Cloud was aware that Little White Eagle had already begun his fort building on Big Piney Creek, that he had many cannons positioned around the construction. He had no inclination to assault the site and get his warriors mangled by shrapnel.

Red Cloud pointed to the south, the direction of Fort Reno. He asked scornfully, "What use is a big soldiers' lodge when men do nothing but live in it? Those men do not fight. The village has no importance when the bluecoats cannot leave it to ride the trails and protect the wagons." His broad mouth tightened in contempt. "The star chiefs have learned nothing but deceit and deception." He held up his palm and dramatically squeezed it into a fist. "A snake cannot eat when it is choked.

212

We will not waste lives attacking these soldiers' lodges. By the Moon of the Falling Leaves, we will have three thousand warriors on the trails. We will isolate the bluecoat lodges. When wagons are on the trail, we will attack them. When the bluecoats come out from their hiding, we will attack them. The star chiefs will not make war. We will. We will make war on our terms, not the terms of the star chiefs."

Red Cloud drew his blanket close. He had spoken. A few rumbles came from the gathering, some *"hau, haus"* but no dissents. Red Cloud's heavily lidded eyes met with those of James Tolliver. Tolliver nodded. This was going to be a war of attrition, one the army would be hard-pressed to win.

Several of Crazy Coyote's Dog Soldier brothers declined to wait until the Moon of Falling Leaves to initiate punitive action against the soldiers. They had a grievance, a petition for a small war party to avenge the deaths of Crazy Coyote's family. The council approved it. Hawk Leg promptly recruited six warriors. James Tolliver was shaken out of his robes at dawn. Would he join a war party? Without protest, he was the eighth volunteer.

After packing enough rations for a four-day journey, they headed up Crazy Woman Creek, making directly for the Bozeman Trail, a ride of one sun. Eight men! This wasn't what Tolliver had envisioned when he had vowed to return to Wolf Creek. Gadfrey, he had dreamed of riding beside one thousand angry braves! Though somewhat dismayed, he also knew eight clever Lakota braves were capable of creating a lot of havoc and panic.

Hawk Leg, organizer of the party, had been elected leader, the pipe carrier. Among them, only Tolliver, Crazy Coyote, and Crazy Horse had rifles. The rest were armed with bows. All carried knives, war clubs, or hatchets.

Since the departure had been hasty, Tolliver learned nothing definitive about Hawk Leg's plans. The young warrior had only told the group he wanted to circle the construction area around Big Piney Creek, then scout the main trail. As they rode along, an apprehensive James Tolliver sought more information. Hawk Leg obliged him. Hawk Leg wasn't foolish. He realized they were too few to mount an attack on a wagon train or troop column. He thought an ambush or a swift hit-and-run tactic might prove successful if the right opportunity presented itself.

Reassured, Tolliver said nothing more. With the exception of Crazy Coyote, he wanted retribution probably more than anyone, yet he abhorred the thought of these crazy dogs risking their lives needlessly in some foolish skirmish. As Red Cloud said—this was going to be a long campaign.

An hour before dusk, the eight warriors came to the main trail between Crazy Woman and Dry Creeks. Sign was everywhere, tracks of wagons, mules, and horses, even oxen. Most were old, but they were all headed in one direction—northwest. All of the grass in the area had been cropped short; the water down at Dry Creek, what little of it there was, had been fouled with excrement. A short conference occurred. The decision: make camp on Crazy Woman Creek; in the morning, make a circle to the left and come back on the trail below Big Piney; see if there are any bluecoat patrols in the vicinity.

They camped, shared a meager meal of jerky, dried cakes, and coffee. They sat in a circle around their tiny fire and told stories, ones heard, ones created. They spread their blankets for sleep.

Crazy Coyote, settling in next to Tolliver, stared up at the star-studded sky. He asked in English, "You see Black Eagle fly up there since you come back?"

"No."

With a little chuckle, Crazy Coyote said, "Sleep good, eh?"

The next day the Oglala bore slightly to the left, often within sight of the main trail, and finally crossed it late in the afternoon. The rolling hills and timbered ridges sheltering the Big Piney Creek bottom were only three miles away, close enough for precaution. The men rode into a coulee, dismounted, and climbed to the crest. Crazy Horse focused his small spyglass on a ripple of ridges to the north and west. He mumbled several times, then handed the telescope to Tolliver who likewise made a slow sweep of the area. At one point, he paused.

Surprised, he said in Siouan, "A wolf lookout!" A small platform had been erected on a knoll overlooking the bottom from the south and east, precisely on the spot he, Crazy Horse, and Little Dog had once observed Portugee Phil and the two hangs-around-the-fort Lakota. The lookout appeared to be more than a half mile away, and Tolliver barely made out a small, black splinter atop it. A horse alongside was clearly visible. From this vantage point (later named Pilot Hill) the lookout had a sweeping view of the Virginia City road to the right and the southern approaches along Big Piney. The top of the hill had to be within view of the fort site, but from the Oglala's position, they saw no sign of any building.

After several other men had taken a look, Hawk Leg said, "It would be good to see what that blue-coat does when the enemy comes into sight. *Eyah,* see what happens on the trail below." He pointed to another knoll. "You see, if the bluecoats came, men could hide over there. Someone could ride across the trail the other way, eh?"

"A trap," said Crazy Horse with a faint smile. "A decoy."

Tolliver said, "A trap only good with rifles, my brother. That is too far to shoot a bow. If a column of bluecoats came down the road we could do nothing but watch them ride by. We are too few to take up a chase and make a fight."

Hawk Leg agreed. "What you say is true, Toll-e-veer. What I say is also true. Maybe not for this day, but it will be something to remember when we are many." He smiled. "Come. A few of us will play a little game with that wolf on the hill. We shall see what he does."

"He will call others," Tolliver said. "That's what he will do."

"*Wagh!*" grunted Crazy Horse. "Who will see us? By the time the others come, we will be in the mountains over there." He handed his spyglass to Tolliver. "You watch, Toll-e-veer. We will ride to the side of the hill where no one can see us, eh? If the bluecoats come, you make a signal. We will ride back the way we came plenty fast."

Crazy Coyote asked, "If no one comes, then what?"

Hawk Leg replied, "We will cross over there and hide in the mountains. I want to see this place from the back."

He ran down the side of the coulee, leaped on his pony, and screamed. Crazy Horse, Hides Alone, and Turkey Leg were right behind. With several more whoops, they swung away directly for the lookout.

Tolliver positioned himself and squinted through the aperture. When the four warriors were within two hundred yards, the dark splinter materialized into a leaping little man frantically waving a flag. Moments later he jumped from the platform and bounded away on his horse. "Gadfrey!" exclaimed Tolliver.

"What that man do?" Crazy Coyote asked.

"He ran like hell, that's what he do," replied Tolliver.

Hawk Leg's braves made a half circle and came to a halt in a gully on the south side of the hill. The empty platform was above them out of sight. All they could see were the dark outlines of their comrades watching them from the distant coulee. They waited.

Somewhere in the timbered bottom a bugle finally sounded, this followed by an eerie silence. Tolliver trained the little telescope on the north trail where it disappeared in the trees. Nothing.

After a short while Tolliver motioned to his brothers. It was time to go. He signaled to Hawk Leg's men. They came riding down the hill to the saddle where everyone met. Within five minutes they picked their way through the shadowy pines west of Big Piney Creek, ultimately crossed over a small hill to Little Piney where they made a cold camp. By this time it was dark. After a meager meal without the benefit of hot coffee, the men made their beds in cushions of pine needles at the base of the big trees. That no soldiers had come rushing out from the fort didn't surprise them. Crazy Coyote said this was because of a disease called "yellow streak." The bluecoats at Fort Reno had it, too.

At daybreak Hawk Leg and his warriors moved across Little Piney to the northwest following an old game trail, one as ancient as the great mountains behind it. Hawk Leg told Tolliver that one of these paths led to a mysterious place used by the old ones. A great medicine wheel built of huge stones was up there somewhere. His grandfather had told him about it. No one went there anymore. No one knew the rituals, only that it was sacred and represented the Circle of Life.

Walking their horses down through the cover of trees, Hawk Leg finally came to a stop and held up his hand. He cocked his head. Everyone turned an

ear to the strange sound "zeez-zuah, zeez-zuah."
Hawk Leg stared curiously at Tolliver.

Tolliver whispered, "The white man's saw to make
wood. A very big saw. They call it a crosscut. It
takes two men to use it, eh."

Nods all around. Directly, a huge, splintering
crash echoed across the bottom. Several more saws
set up the chant "zeez-zuah, zeez-zuah." Hawk Leg
motioned to Hides Alone and Turkey Leg to sneak
down and take a look. Moments later the two braves
were nothing more than shadows. They fused with
the brushy foliage and disappeared. The rest of the
party dismounted, listened to the rhythmic saws,
and waited.

Within five minutes the two men returned. Turkey Leg reported there were ten *wasichu* below making wood. They had wagons and mules. Eight pony
soldiers were there, too, only they were not making
wood. They were guarding a big black kettle on a
fire, making big talk and laughing.

For a moment Hawk Leg stared thoughtfully toward
the bottom. He finally went to his pony, got his
bow, strung it, then carefully adjusted his bundle of
arrows. Passing a hand for silence, he beckoned the
others. In whispers, he quickly explained his plan—
bowmen to the front, Tolliver, Crazy Horse, and
Crazy Coyote directly behind. A barrage of rifle fire
would alert the soldiers too soon. The silence of the
arrow was its greatest power. The ponies were then
tethered, and the eight men moved toward their
positions.

James Tolliver heard the thump of his heart. He

took a deep breath to steady himself. Once again those thoughts of riding proudly beside one thousand warriors. *Wagh,* here he was sneaking through the brush like a dog. He paused to check his Henry one last time. The bite of the crosscuts picked up, became louder, now intermingled with voices. A few leafy boughs made whispers against his leggings.

Tolliver picked up the hand signals from Hawk Leg—spread out, the enemy was now in sight. Moments later the doctor peeked from behind a big pine. Twenty yards away two men were pulling the sharp teeth of a crosscut through a fallen tree. Other sawyers worked closer to the small road, and one man was behind a team of mules skidding three logs to the bottom. Tolliver crouched, tiptoed to his right another ten yards. He saw Turkey Leg and Hides Alone notching arrows. The bluecoats, rifles propped together nearby, circled the small fire. Several held cups. Another was bent over the black pot. Good grief, one was an officer wearing a rakish, dun-colored hat! Tolliver's eyes widened. He knew this man! The killer of his family! He leaned forward and squinted. About twenty yards down the narrow logging road were the wagons and ponies, and there was the big gray!

At this crucial moment a long neigh from one of the tethered Lakota ponies cut the early-morning air. Tolliver winced. The officer whirled about and stared. Several of the men grabbed rifles. Simultaneously a bush parted and Hawk Leg materialized like a ghost. *Swish!* From down the line another *swish.* Tolliver heard two solid thuds.

"Indians!" someone yelled.

Panic. The bottom erupted; confusion reined. The sawyers made a mad dash through the timber, hell-bent for their wagons. The soldiers shouldered rifles but they didn't shoot. They saw no targets so they ran for their horses. Several hid behind one of the wagons. Another flight of arrows zipped from the brush. Tolliver heard two return shots and the whine of a bullet. Two palls of smoke drifted from behind a wagon. Two answering blasts sounded to his left. Crazy Coyote and Crazy Horse were into the fight. Yet another boom next to him. Several of the mules reared throwing their harnesses askew, but two wagons jolted forward, men trying to clamber aboard at a dead run.

The officer had mounted his gray. Brandishing a revolver, he whirled about and got off two rounds, but most of his troopers, two with shafts stuck in their sides, were slapping leather alongside the trundling wagons. One of the mules had an arrow flagging from its butt.

The rakish-hatted bluecoat took another shot at the hillside, spun around, and kicked off. Tolliver stepped from behind his tree, aimed between the man's shoulder blades, and fired once, twice. The officer jolted violently. His hat flew to one side, his pistol to the other. Slumped limply over his saddle, he disappeared around a small bend in the trail.

"Die, you sonofabitch!" Tolliver shouted. "Die!"

Nearby, Hawk Leg screamed at the brilliant sky and shook his bow. He made the sweeping gesture for retreat, but Tolliver took one last look. He saw two soldiers and a woodcutter on the ground. Some of the escapees had been painfully hit. He reasoned the officer on the galloping gray was dead, or would be by the time he reached the fort. Good enough. This was the beginning of the wood train skirmishes in Red Cloud's war.

Chapter 14

The ambush behind the fort altered plans to retrieve Barnaby Cobb's hidden provisions and stock in Wolf Creek canyon. Hawk Leg reasoned that the little war party had stirred up a hornets' nest in the fort; a few patrols might be riding the trails. Herding Barnaby's mules and ponies could put his warriors in jeopardy. Instead, Hawk Leg took to the game trails southwest of the fort and led his men to safety through a wilderness of timbered draws and verdant meadows.

James Tolliver marveled. None of his brothers had ever ridden in this region of the mountains, yet there was a keen sense of presence among them. They knew where they were and where they were going. He was lost. Only the sun scorching the high peaks indicated direction. On one grassy ridge, Crazy Horse killed a young sheep, a remarkable shot at almost a hundred paces. Within minutes, Crazy Horse and Hides Alone dressed out and quartered the animal.

As the sun died behind Cloud Peak, the eight men wound down a trail into Rock Creek canyon. In a flowering meadow beside the creek, they made camp. Tolliver thought it was a splendid location, somewhat reminiscent of Wolf Creek.

In due time, the men had a big fire; rocks piled high, a lattice of sturdy willow boughs arranged across the top. Meat aplenty, here. A few "ahs" and nods of approval came from the men when Tolliver withdrew a small tin of mixed salt and pepper from his bundle. This had belonged to Barnaby Cobb who had never been able to tolerate unseasoned meat.

It was a simple but hardy feast, the men consuming two quarters of the young ram and a few meal cakes. The remainder of the meat was cut in strips and smoked over a night fire of slow-burning green willow. Hawk Leg and Crazy Horse built a larger fire in a stand of pine and stacked a few big chunks of downfall beside it. This was the "talk-around-the-fire." The morning attack on the bluecoats was the talk, each man relating his version of the fight. Tolliver's brothers were surprised when he ended his story with a short prayer to Wakan Tanka. He gave thanks that no one had been wounded or killed. The men smiled at Big Black Bear. They thought this was good.

Toward midnight Tolliver discovered this was also the "keep warm fire." The mountain air turned frigid. He spent most of the night curled up like a wooly worm, his back to the hot rocks and smoldering logs. Tolliver learned later the altitude at this camp was seven thousand feet.

The next morning near Clear Creek Hawk Leg held up his hand. Approaching from the south were two riders. Appropriate moves and gestures were made, the sidled ponies, crooked arms, and shouts of tribal affiliation. The two parties closed. James Tolliver blinked in surprise. The braves were Cheyenne, one of them Tall Elk, the scout who had ridiculed his singing up on the fork of the Little Bighorn.

And that subject was the first sign passed. Tall Elk in a grand flourish signed to Hawk Leg: "My brothers, what happened? The Song Maker of the North rides with you. Now he flies south. It is good you clipped his beak. Your approach would have been a poor one."

Hawk Leg had no idea what this sign meant. He simply shrugged. Crazy Coyote shot Tolliver a questioning look.

Tolliver said, "Sometimes I sing. When I ride alone, I sing."

"I did not know this."

"That fellow does." Tolliver moved to the front and made a few flourishes. He had encountered trouble up the North Trail. Bad medicine. He decided to return to the Oglala. That was the extent of his explanation.

Everyone dismounted. They sat in a circle in the shade of a cottonwood and Hawk Leg distributed the strips of smoked meat. He related the story of the fight with the bluecoats. The Cheyenne were surprised war had begun. Hawk Leg said the war hadn't begun—the tribes weren't organized yet. He went on to explain that Crazy Coyote had a grievance against the bluecoats; the fight had been necessary, a matter of family honor.

Tall Elk then told the Oglala more longknives

were on the trail, that he and his companion, Gray Bull, had seen fifteen of them escorting several wagons. They were unfriendly. When he and Gray Bull approached to make talk and ask for some food, one of the longknives had fired his thunder iron. There were a few laughs.

Tall Elk signed to Tolliver, "You once lived with these people. You were a bluecoat. Why do they act this way?"

Tolliver was pensive for a moment. He couldn't think of a word for "ignorant." He finally gestured, "They are afraid of The People. They believe The People are savages without learning."

Tall Elk signed, "What is there to learn but to survive, to live honorably and die honorably?"

Tolliver signed back, "They do not perceive. They do not understand that on this land they are the ones without learning. There is fear in their hearts. Many lose faith in themselves and what they have been taught. When this happens they become what they call us . . . savages."

Crazy Horse signed, "This man Toll-e-veer speaks well, my brothers. He is a warrior. The bluecoats are not warriors. It is true. They fear death. They run from us like frightened rabbits. They shame themselves. Death is as nothing, pain is as nothing, but cowardice is a crime. Disgrace is a worse punishment than death. This is what we perceive. This is what the bluecoats do not perceive."

Tolliver smiled at Crazy Horse. "You say it well, too, my friend."

Hawk Leg signed to Tall Elk, "Where on the trail did you meet these unfriendly bluecoats?"

"Far beyond the place where many of the white people make their camps. One half sun from Dry Creek."

"They will not camp at Dry Creek this night," signed Hawk Leg. "What little water there is lies in a dirty hole. It is filthy from too many big wagon cows, too many mules and ponies. *Wagh!*"

Crazy Coyote gestured. "They will stop at the Creek of the Crazy Woman. This is the place they will camp tonight." He looked around the circle.

Tolliver said in English, "What the hell are you suggesting? We made our fight. I thought we were heading home . . . good food, comfort. I need a bath with soap, a good shave."

Hawk Leg stared at them. "What does Toll-e-veer say?"

Crazy Coyote quickly answered. "He asks me if I want to go greet these bluecoats, give them an unfriendly welcome."

Tolliver nodded. In Siouan he said, "I thought my little brother might have sore backsides from too much riding, eh? He says he has plenty hard backsides."

Everyone laughed. Tolliver tried to smile.

Later this day Hawk Leg's warriors filed down the brushy bottom of Crazy Woman Creek. When they reached the main trail leading to the fort on Big Piney (it had been named Phil Kearny), they discovered fresh wagon tracks but no sign of any camp. This led them to believe the bluecoats seen by the Cheyenne had decided to push on down the Bozeman Trail. After a discussion, Hawk Leg moved ahead to a grove of cottonwoods below the Middle and South Forks to camp. It was agreed that if no bluecoats appeared by dark, they would return the next morning to their village.

The next morning a bizarre set of events unfolded, so startling that James Tolliver could hardly believe he was both a participant and witness. Crazy Coyote and Hides Alone returned from scouting the South Fork, Hides Alone with a fresh scalp suspended on the end of a new Springfield rifle. The men had encountered a lone soldier walking the prairie. Hidden in the sage, they watched to see if other bluecoats were with him. They finally decided he was hunting for game. From where he had come they didn't know. They killed him with their hatchets and dragged his body behind their horses to one of the rutted trails.

While the warriors discussed this strange happening and daubed their faces with victory paint, down through the willows came another lone bluecoat. He was atop a big black horse and by appearance was an officer. Turkey Leg spotted him first. In a hurried whisper, he alerted the rest of the men. Tolliver groaned. Good grief, by the minute, his return home was crumbling like stale cornbread!

Oblivious to any threat, for there had been no sign of Indians, the bluecoat came closer. He seemed to be inspecting the creek bottom, sizing up the terrain. Tolliver finally whispered to Hawk Leg, "Either this man is lost or he searches for a campsite. I believe there must be other bluecoats somewhere between here and the forks . . . the man hunting, now this one . . ."

Hawk Leg only nodded. He turned and motioned to Turkey Leg, Long Mane, and Hides Alone. In sign, he told them to move out and position themselves to each side of the trial. Stringing their bows, they disappeared. Moments later Hawk Leg stepped out. Legs spread wide, hands on his hips, his face grotesquely aflame in streaks of red and yellow, he startled both the soldier and horse.

The big black reared. The officer shouted, "God Almighty!" Hawk Leg raised an arm, brought it down in a swift chop. Zip, zip, zip! Clutching frantically at his side, the stricken man emitted a tremendous wheeze. Three more arrows swished from the brush. One went awry and hit the horse in the rump. It bolted. The officer flew to the side and landed in a clump of gooseberry bushes and the big black thundered away. The soldier desperately clutched at the thorny shrubs. More arrows. When his body went limp, Turkey Leg dashed out and seized the man's hair. In several quick cuts and a little tug, he held out the bloody scalp for everyone to see. *"Wagh!"*

Tolliver grimaced. If this weren't enough, a shout from above brought the warriors whirling about.

"Lieutenant?"

Across the path, Long Mane hurtled from his hiding. Notching his bow, he leaped away through the willows.

Tolliver saw a flash of blue tunic moving ahead of Long Mane, nothing more. Gadfrey, another soldier! Why hunt the bastards? They were homing in on the willows like nesting magpies!

Moments later came a whoop and the sound of

galloping hooves. Moments later Long Mane trotted back down the path. One of his arrows had caught the bluecoat in the back but the man had escaped.

Tolliver was breathless. The speed and deadly precision of his brothers had been awesome, yet not at an end. Hawk Leg immediately ordered Crazy Horse and Hides Alone to ride above and investigate. Where were these crazy bluecoats coming from?

Motioning to the rest of his braves, Hawk Leg pointed to the right. Mount up. They were going to cut through, bisect the main trail, and ride up to meet Crazy Horse and Hides Alone. They never made it. Halfway across the grassy flat, they heard rifle fire. Reining back to the left, they topped a small knoll and looked down. On the other side of the creek, a half-dozen wagons were being moved into a tight circle. Men dressed in denim and homespun brown tried to slip the harnesses from mule teams. Bluecoats were behind a few wagons, their rifles popping away at two fleeting figures. Crazy Horse and Hides Alone had their ponies in full gallop heading for cover in the big cottonwoods.

Tolliver swung his pony around and yelled at Crazy Coyote. "Draw their fire, man!" He shouldered his Henry and fired three quick rounds at the distant compound. Crazy Coyote managed to get off two shots. He saw a man fall. Immediately a few bullets came whining through the sage.

"Get the hell out!" Tolliver shouted. He kicked away and everyone followed. Tolliver led them out of range and made a big circle for the distant cottonwoods. He saw two dark figures leading their ponies into the thick foliage. Crazy Horse and Hides Alone were safe.

The rest of the day was a standoff. Hawk Leg couldn't mount an attack without coming under fire from the beleaguered soldiers. And at a distance of eighty yards, the bluecoats had very poor shooting, even when one of Hawk Leg's shadowy warriors did move. The rifle fire was sporadic. Tolliver, Crazy Horse, and Crazy Coyote occasionally changed positions and set off a round or two to keep the enemy guessing. Seldom did they receive return fire. Hides Alone's Springfield was of little use. The soldier he had taken it from only had five shells in his cartridge case.

Using Crazy Horse's small telescope, Tolliver counted eleven soldiers. He allowed the one shot in the back by Long Mane was out of commission. He knew three others were dead. One was still lying outside the compound. He also counted six civilians, probably mule skinners or fort carpenters. And he was surprised when he saw several women and children occasionally peek from an ambulance wagon in the center of the enclosure. One woman was black, a Negro. He assumed these were dependents of officers at the Big Piney fort.

Hawk Leg was patient. Though outnumbered two to one, he had much the superior position. His warriors were in the shade and could get water in either of the two forks of Crazy Woman Creek. The bluecoat party was exposed to the sun. It was a hot day, and the creek was forty yards from the wagons. Fetching water was a deadly game.

Hawk Leg reasoned a barrage of shots at night might give a few of his men a chance to sneak around the backside and do damage, perhaps fire some of the wagons. Tolliver didn't think much of the ruse. The sight of any flame around the perimeter would draw an immediate response, one that might prove fatal. What Hawk Leg really needed was twenty-five more men equipped with rifles and plenty of ammunition. One charge from four sides and the wagon complex would collapse.

The night was long and sleepless. Tolliver, Crazy Horse, and Crazy Coyote crawled through the bunch grass and sage within forty yards of the wagons. Several times bluecoats attempted to reach the creek only to be chased back by a shot after which the shooter rolled away to a new piece of cover.

But any thoughts of further strategy wilted in the prairie heat the next morning. A small cloud of dust appeared far up the trail, and one look through Crazy Horse's spyglass convinced Hawk Leg it was time to move out. A long column of cavalry was approaching. The Oglala melted away through the trees, crossed Crazy Woman Creek far below, and headed home. Hawk Leg showed no shame in withdrawing. The first day had been victorious; the entire journey had been victorious.

Withdrawal was prudent, in this instance good strategy.* Hawk Leg smiled at Tolliver. "Each pass-

---

*In later years, the U.S. Army referred to this skirmish as the "Battle" of Crazy Woman Creek. Killed in action were Lieutenant N. H. Daniels, Sergeant T. Ferrell, Private Terrence Calley. Three people in the party were wounded, including Lieutenant J. M. Templeton who was shot in the back with an arrow.

ing sun is different," he said. "It is one thing to be brave. It is another to be foolish. No battle can be won by foolish men. Today we are not foolish. Tomorrow is another sun, and plenty more will follow. In our time, we shall see plenty suns. The bluecoats will only see darkness. This is what I believe. One must be a true believer."

Tolliver nodded. Eight men. Only eight men. If such a small war party could create such havoc in four days, good grief, what was an army of three thousand likely to do?

Crazy Coyote shouted. He pointed to the sky. The Black Eagle! It was moving north again! *"Hi-yah, yi, yi, yi, yi!"* he screamed.

Chapter 15

James Tolliver handed the small bundle of cut red willow to White Wolf. The healer-visionary tucked the boughs into his leather pouch. It was late morning, very warm and humid, and the two doctors had spent the better part of it gathering raw material for the pharmacy. White Wolf called this wood red willow, but Tolliver knew it as red-osier dogwood, *"bois rouge."* It had no medicinal qualities. White Wolf used it as a smoking mixture in his ceremonial pipes.

White Wolf enjoyed this river-bottom foraging. He enjoyed the companionship of the man called Big Black Bear. His early suspicions of the *wasichu* healer had long since vanished, and though Toll-e-veer did not listen to the songs, he was an honored colleague, a man of good medicine. White Wolf made good medicine, too, both practical and spiritual. When he had doubts about the practical side of his profession, he always could turn to Big Black Bear. White Wolf was at peace with himself. Though war had come, his life was pleasantly in order.

James Tolliver's life was in disarray, the complexi-

234

ties of it troubling, frazzled like the brittle ends of an old rope. War, always war, and this war had barely begun. What a muddle of confusion, such a paradox, how he abhorred it, yet how he had fed on it like a voracious wolf. Good grief, he wasn't a crazy dog. Violence wasn't his game. He had only participated when the lives of his brothers were at stake or justice demanded it. For his most recent contribution, he had been awarded another eagle feather.

Tolliver still planned escape to the north, freedom, peace. If he possessed the medicine of the Black Eagle, why hadn't some of this majestic bird's magic of flight rubbed off on him? Had temporary sanctuary become permanent commitment? Had his soul been invaded by the red man? Certainly, his renewed presence was a matter of concern to others as well as himself. Both White Wolf and Chief Two Coups now contested over his proper place in the village social structure. They had completely forgotten he had been trained to be a doctor in the white man's world. Or chose to ignore it.

Tolliver and White Wolf talked as they led their ponies along the brushy river bottom. They stopped to harvest a few licorice plants, stripped leaves, and dug some roots, good medicine for earaches and infections of the mucus membranes, good tea for children's fevers. Tolliver sniffed a stem. "*Glycyrrhiza lepidota*, Purch," he said, surprised at his Latin recall. "Good smell, my brother."

White Wolf smiled and shook his head. "Too many names for such a simple plant." He rolled several of the greening burrs around in the palm of his hand, seeds of propagation when ripe. They adhered to the fur of passing animals and were carried for miles. White Wolf said, "I will tell you a legend about these," he said. "It will relieve your mind of your troubles, if only for a while. Good medicine."

"I told you," Tolliver said, "my biggest trouble is getting out of here, not whether I am a doctor or a warrior."

"You cannot be both," said White Wolf. "Soon we will have too many warriors, eh, but not enough doctors." White Wolf grinned. "Two Coups is a selfish man. He wants a warrior for his son-in-law, one who has big medicine, someone worthy of Red Moccasin. *Eyah*, plenty of warriors in this village, only three doctors."

"What am I to do?" asked Tolliver. "Until I can arrange to ride north again, this is my home. When my brothers ask me to go on a ride, I go. They believe it is a matter of honor. So do I. This is my contribution for the friendship everyone has shown me."

"Yes, this is good," agreed White Wolf, "but in time, your contribution could be more important in the village than on the warpath. As Two Coups is selfish, so am I. I want you to stay awhile. You have become one of us. There is more danger on the trail than here, this I tell you. And you speak of honor. I ask you, my brother, what good is honor to a dead man? Honor only sustains one in life. Yes, the crazy dogs say death is as nothing. What use to our people are dead men?"

Tolliver shrugged. "The People honor the dead."

"Better to honor a man while he lives. Honor

makes no difference to him when he is dead, eh?"

"They say the spirits of the dead sometimes talk," Tolliver replied. "At night, high on the mountain."

White Wolf scoffed. "*Eyah*, those are legends! I have been in the mountains many times. I have heard songs from the living around me but I have not heard one song from a spirit of the dead. Spirits do not speak. Sometimes they listen."

Tolliver pointed at the cockleburs. "What songs do those burrs sing?"

White Wolf held his hand close to Tolliver's ear. "Listen," he said. "Do you hear? Do you hear what they sing? 'Take us away, good friend. Take us away to another place where we can find new life again.' This is the song! This is the song of the universe, my brother."

Tolliver said, "I think that is my song. Take me away." He smiled, reflecting on his trailside singing, the chiding of Tall Elk. "A Cheyenne brave told me my song was that of a crow. I cannot sing the song. I cannot carry a tune."

"Everyone has a song. It comes from within."

"For me, that is most fortunate," Tolliver said with a smile. "I do not claim to be a singer any more than I claim to be a warrior. A humble doctor, yes."

"It is good to be humble," said White Wolf. "Sometimes a warrior can think too highly of himself. Sometimes a vain man may become too proud. He thinks himself pleasing to everyone, yet in truth he may be nuisance to everyone." White Wolf took one of the burrs between a finger and a thumb. "In the old days, there was a handsome warrior, eh, who believed his hair was the most beautiful of all. It was longer than Chief Red Cloud's. This brave boasted his hair was the best, and each passing sun he combed and fixed it in different ways. One day some maidens discovered this brave asleep under a great tree. They must have been touched by Old Man Coyote. While the handsome brave slept, they fixed his hair yet another way. They tangled his hair with licorice burrs. The man could do nothing. The burrs were embedded from the roots to the end of his great locks. He cut his hair. He scalped himself."

James Tolliver smiled. "This is the legend of the cockleburs?"

White Wolf nodded. Placing his palm to his mouth, he blew the fuzzy pods away. "Yes," he replied. "I suppose there are other legends. I find this one amusing. What do you perceive?"

"Vanity is a false virtue."

"What more?"

Tolliver looked at White Wolf thoughtfully. He finally broke out in a grin. "Yes, I think I see what you mean. Perhaps it is better to be a humble doctor than a warrior with no hair."

"You perceive."

Later in the day, a guarded grievance cropped up. Though everyone considered the recent ambush behind the fort a coup, Crazy Coyote was disappointed. Hawk Leg's tactical change, that of making his exit to the southwest instead of the north, had spoiled Crazy Coyote's plan to retrieve his late father's stock in Wolf Creek canyon, stock that represented considerable worth—nineteen head of ponies and mules. With the welfare of the war party paramount, it would have been dishonorable to grouse about Hawk Leg's decision. Crazy Coyote kept his mouth shut. Until now.

Sitting in front of their lodge, Crazy Coyote told Tolliver he was determined to recover the stock. All he needed was some help, two men to help him, that is all it would take. And the recovery had to be soon. Though the upper canyon was isolated, there was always a chance some wandering Shoshoni or Crow might accidentally stumble upon the four-leggeds. And by early winter when they moved to the valley floor, the bluecoats could even claim them, that was the worst of probabilities.

Tolliver listened to his brother's lament. He finally said, "Two men, you say. And since you tell me this, I assume you wish me to be one of them. Is this so?"

"You have been there," Crazy Coyote said. "It would be wise to have a good guide. You have the medicine of the eagle. This is good. Besides, you are my brother, a warrior."

"Hmmph! Is there anything I am not?"

Crazy Coyote grinned. "The Cheyenne say you are not a very good singer. I cannot say. I have never heard your song."

"I doubt if you ever will, either."

"We can make the trip in three sleeps," Crazy Coyote said. "Do some riding by the moon, and have those fresh ponies to ride home."

"I need three more sleeps to recover from the last ride I took with you and your brothers."

"The bluecoats sleep at night," Crazy Coyote went

on. "We can cross the North Trail by dark. It will not be dangerous."

Tolliver scoffed. "Any ride up that way is dangerous."

"I long to see the graves of my family. I wish to make my prayers, to honor my loved ones."

Tolliver turned. It was as though he saw Crazy Coyote for the first time, not as a warrior, a daring young man who climbed fort walls and laughed about it, or one who unswervingly followed the pipe carrier and risked his life for others. Tolliver now saw him as a little brother whose jaws were locked on the bitter blade of grief.

Tolliver said, "Honoring your family should have been your first wish, my brother."

The young warrior's dark eyes suddenly flooded. "It was," he said softly. "My song is a silent one."

And there was silence. After a while Tolliver said, "I am with you. When do we leave? Who will join us?"

Crazy Coyote collected himself. He said he wished to leave the following morning. Who better than Little Dog to accompany them, cunning, courageous, dependable, one of the best riders in the village. The hunting was at an end. Little Dog would be happy to go. *Hau, hau, hechetu welo!* They would make a good threesome.

Then after another thoughtful pause, Crazy Coyote completely stunned James Tolliver. "You also have a wish. We could put you on the trail to the white men's settlement again. Go seek your place. You have the medicine of the Black Eagle. Perhaps this time you will find that for which you are searching, Toll-e-veer."

For a moment Tolliver was at a loss for words. What a splendid idea! Yet he suddenly felt the gentle brush stroke of misgiving. These good people. And Crazy Coyote, his lodge companion, his little brother. Oh, how death had strengthened this bond. Tolliver hated the thought of another sorrowful departure. Yet sooner or later the cord had to be severed. The *iktomi*, the tiny spider men, began spinning their little webs of deception.

Tolliver finally said, "Yes, it is my wish to leave, to find my own place. It always has been my wish, but I cannot abide saying good-bye to my friends again. I find it a painful ordeal. You, I will miss most of all. So I say, let this be a journey to make prayers and fetch ponies. Let nothing be said about my intentions to ride north. No one should know."

Crazy Coyote nodded. He understood. "Yes, sometimes it is better to just go and say nothing. My mother never liked to say good-bye to Papa when he went trading. She was sad. He always came back. Then she was plenty happy."

"*Wagh*, happiness," Tolliver said with a sigh. "What is one day is gone the next. I worry about you, what is to become of you."

"Do not worry, Toll-e-veer," Crazy Coyote replied. "I have many brothers in the Soldiers' Lodge. When winter comes I will keep a fire in this lodge. If you do not like your place in the north, there is warmth here. There is always warmth in my heart for you. I will think about this."

Tolliver said, "You cannot be a warrior eating

241

wasna and roots the rest of your life. You should bring back that wagon, do some trading like your father did. You speak enough of the white man's tongue to get by."

"My father said the trading will soon be over."

"The white men pay good money to haul freight to the mining camps," suggested Tolliver. "Your father had that in mind. You have his blood."

"Yes, this is true. I also have the blood of my mother. I am Oglala. So I will remain. I do not like what I have seen in the people places of the white men. Some of those white eyes act crazy."

Tolliver smiled. He replied, "So do some of your brothers. That is another reason I have some worry about you. There is bad company throughout the land wherever one goes. There are crazy dogs everywhere."

"Yes," agreed Crazy Coyote. "Yes, I know this. Papa taught me to be brave among my people, brave but not foolish. Among the white men, he taught me to be smart but to play dumb. Do not show too much gold to a white man. Papa says he will follow you to hell to get it."

"They followed me up Wolf Creek canyon," Tolliver said. "They did not want gold. They were bluecoats. They wanted me. But they were thieves and murderers. They got your father's gold, his guns, and they stole your mother's beautiful necklaces. These are the same soldiers who come to make the trails safe. You will serve justice each time you kill one, for most of them serve no one but themselves. Just remember what your father told you . . . be brave but not foolish."

"They did not get Papa's gold," Crazy Coyote answered. He jerked his thumb toward the lodge. "The gold is in there in a bundle. He was a smart man. He only carried one small pouch when he went to trade. He left the rest. He told my mother that one day he might not come back from trading. He did not want to leave her with nothing but a lodge and two children. This is why she never liked to say good-bye to him. She told me she would rather be a poor wife than a rich widow. *Eyah*, a mad dog pissed on my tipi, Toll-e-veer. I stayed behind to fight thieves and my family died by the hands of them."

Little Dog, Tolliver's first Oglala friend and patient, readily agreed to accompany him and Crazy Coyote to Wolf Creek canyon. He was indebted to Big Black Bear; Big Black Bear had saved his life; he was a brother. With the temptation of Red Moccasin, Little Dog had hoped to make Tolliver his brother-in-law. He had given up on that hopeless quest. He understood the doctor's desire to return to a village of his own people; he saw nothing unusual in this, for it was the way of all creatures, the winged and four-legged. All possessed the want of like companionship. All possessed the homing instinct. His brother, Tolliver, had good medicine. It would be valued anywhere he chose to go, and after all that had passed between them, it would be bad medicine not to help him.

Early this morning Little Dog made his moccasins ready. Two Coups had gone to talk with other chiefs in the big medicine lodge, and Teal Eye was already in the fields foraging. Red Moccasin tarried over the small cooking fire. Little Dog packed a parfleche of food, checked his bone-handled knife, and strung his small medicine pouch around his neck. He took bridle and reins and went for his pony. Red Moccasin observed. She finally turned away, pulled her blanket over her hair, and headed for the trail to Crazy Woman Creek.

Red Moccasin was a soft shadow on the trail. The bushes whispered as she passed. Tolliver, busy packing the last of his two mules, heard nothing until he looked up and saw her. He politely nodded and gave her a smile and a cheery "hola." Crazy Coyote also greeted her, then led his horse to the creek to drink.

Red Moccasin said, "I came to tell you to take care of my brother. He has good medicine but sometimes he forgets he is a human being. He carries two scars for being so forgetful."

"I will do my best," Tolliver replied.

Red Moccasin hesitated, then added, "Since you have no woman or family to wish you a safe journey, I come to do this, too."

"You are very thoughtful, very kind."

"I will say one more thing," she went on. "You spend too much time making medicine. When you are not riding with your brothers, you are picking flowers."

James Tolliver grinned. "I am not a lazy dog. I do what I must to please others, make medicine, help my brothers."

In soft admonishment, she said, "You do not

please me, Toll-e-veer. You avoid me like I am a plant of poison."

Tolliver's smile faded and he felt a tinge of warmth at his ears. Good grief, the maiden made him feel guilty! She was a beautiful woman. He adored her—from a safe distance. How could he explain he avoided her out of necessity, that any involvement outside of a few pleasantries would lead to nothing but misery and regret. He already felt miserable. Under the circumstances, he mustered up the best he could. "You are a good medicine plant, young woman," he said. "You are the fairest flower in the field, and if I were able to choose anyone, it would be you."

Deception is the art of men, perception that of a woman. Red Moccasin suddenly took cognizance of the two pack mules. Her big eyes grew wide, went from the mules to Tolliver. She searched his face, then sadly shook her head in realization. Almost in a whisper, she said, "You are leaving, Toll-e-veer. You are not just going to fetch ponies. You are packed for a long journey. Is this not so?"

Guilty again. Tolliver cleared his throat. He didn't want to croak like a sun-spanked frog. "I thought it best this way. Less trouble for everyone . . . to go quietly."

Red Moccasin gave him a deploring look. She moaned and shook her head again. "Without the touch of a hand? Without a small good-bye? Nothing more than to ride up the trail with your back turned?"

Tolliver shrugged haplessly. "I am truly sorry.

What more can I say. I have to leave. Even with a heavy heart, I have to leave."

Her voice trembled. She said, "You have been with The People many moons. What have you learned? What have you seen? In all this time you have been unable to reach out and touch the goodness around you." Tears rolled down her cheeks. She turned away.

"Wait . . ."

Red Moccasin hurried. She called over her shoulder. "How can a blind man be a doctor? Good-bye, Toll-e-veer, good-bye."

Without fanfare, the three men rode up the Crazy Woman Creek trail several hundred yards, then turned northwest, Tolliver paradoxically looking to the future but haunted by the past. Red Moccasin's unexpected visit had spoiled his game. He now felt like the traitor he already was. But she was right—he had been blind, blind on purpose. What he *had* been was prudently virtuous. Luckily, what could have been, was not. Had it, the parting would have been more than painful. It would have been downright cruel. Bittersweet visions drifted through his ragged mind—Red Moccasin, White Wolf, Two Coups, and Crazy Horse, all dear to him in different ways. And most of all, Barnaby, Little Weasel, and his little brother, Black Bow, loved ones etched in his memory forever.

They rode the drying coulees, the barren washes, and through sage and juniper, grama and blue stem. They camped and rode again. Near the Bozeman Trail, caution gave way to quiet alarm. They faded into the cover of the tall sage to observe. A long military train heading north trundled by, freighters and wagons with soldiers perched on top, mules, horses, and cannons. Watching the file disappear around a bend, Little Dog and Crazy Coyote looked at Tolliver for an explanation. Why were these bluecoats leaving the big soldiers' village on Piney Creek? Was this another campaign? Could they be so foolish?

Tolliver had no immediate answer, but remembering what Lieutenant O'Leary had long ago mentioned about the army's plans to build "forts" and the fact that Portugee Phil had been searching for "sites," it didn't take him long to make a conclusion. Now it was obvious. There wasn't more than one troop of cavalry, and there must have been at least two companies of infantrymen in the line, what his brothers called "walk-a-heaps." These men weren't part of the complement at Fort Phil Kearny as it had been named. Not at all. They were fort builders.

Tolliver finally spoke. "Somewhere below they plan to make another fort, probably on the Bighorn. Those are the men who will build and protect it. Only a few pony soldiers, eh? Most of them are walk-a-heaps."

Little Dog exclaimed, "Another soldiers' lodge! *Eyah,* too many. Bad medicine."

Tolliver smiled. "Bad medicine for the soldiers, my brother, not us. They do not know what your chiefs plan to do after the Moon of the Falling Leaves. When Winter Maker comes, most of those soldiers will be sick and hungry. If they come out from behind the walls, their bones will be picked apart by warriors. Inside, they starve. Outside, they die."

"*Mi-ya*, you make it sound too easy," Crazy Coyote said.

"It will not be easy," Tolliver replied. "It will be a long winter, but this is the way it will be. Chief Red Cloud is no prophet but said it well. When one chokes the throat of a long snake, it cannot eat."

The dust began to settle. Tolliver nudged his pony ahead and glanced back to check on the two mules. Little Dog suddenly reined up and whispered harshly, "*Hiya!* More come!"

Once again the men took cover, and once again dust began to rise above the trail. This too was a big train but of a different kind, fifty or more wagons, some of them pulled by oxen. A few lusty shouts floated across the long flat. Bull whackers, mule skinners, wagons with dust-covered canvas flapping against bony ribs, emigrants, sodbusters, miners, grit in their ears, fear in their eyes, hope in their hearts, all looking for the land of milk and honey.

"Good grief!" whispered James Tolliver.

In English, Crazy Coyote said observantly, "They follow bluecoats. Trouble comes, they yell like hell. They go dig gold, eh?"

"Or dirt," commented Tolliver dryly. "Some of them are farmers."

"How you know?"

"Cows," replied Tolliver. "They have milk stock trailing along."

After a moment, Crazy Coyote said, "Plenty peo-

248

ple, no bluecoats." He glanced over at Tolliver. "Maybe good you trail along, too, eh?"

"What!"

Crazy Coyote turned and explained to Little Dog. Little Dog nodded and said, "What he says is good, Toll-e-veer. You will not have to travel alone." He grinned. "No one can sneak up on you in the night and count coup."

"*Wagh!*"

"Those are your people," Little Dog said. "They go where you want to go. It is something to think about. The bluecoats will not go beyond the Bighorn where the Crow are. The Crow are thieves but they do not make war on the bluecoats. With all those people you would be safe. This is what I think. So I have spoken and I will say no more."

Tolliver stared at the wagon train. "Those are not my people," he said. "Just because they are white does not mean they are my people."

Crazy Coyote smiled. "For one moon, maybe less, you could pretend. You cut your hair, eh. You put on my father's big hat and your big boots. *Wagh*, who would know you?"

Tolliver eyed him closely. "You want to get rid of me too soon."

"The Canyon of the Wolf is only a short ride from here anyhow," replied Crazy Coyote. "We can find the tracks of my father's wagon. We do not need a white man to show us the way." He gave Tolliver a crooked smile and said in English, "We Injuns, eh?"

Tolliver chuckled. "Crazy ones to boot."

It was decided. The plan was a good one, so they

dismounted, exchanged embraces, and made a few promises. Somewhere down the trail . . .

Choked up, fearful of spilling a tear, James Tolliver rode out.

Tolliver came up to the rear of the plodding civilian train in midafternoon. As Crazy Coyote had suggested, he had made a few appearance changes. His hair was cropped just below his ears; he wore the old hat Barnaby Cobb had given him; he shed his moccasins for military boots, and stowed his Sioux beads and pony trappings. In his buckskins, he looked like a trail guide. He drew several curious looks and several waves as he passed the first ox-drawn wagons. A man riding a big, skinny black mare directed him to the wagon master, one Hugh Kirkendall. Tolliver soon found Kirkendall riding at the head of the mule train alongside two other whiskered, bedraggled pilgrims.

Tolliver edged up beside the men. "Hugh Kirkendall?" he asked.

"Yes, sir, you're looking at him," was the casual reply. But then after a second look at James Tolliver, a mountain man if there ever was one, Kirkendall said, "Where in the hell did you come from?"

"Up there," Tolliver answered, nodding toward the Big Horn Mountains. "Down the old Bridger route . . . safer, not so many hostiles around. I'm heading west and I wondered if I might ride along with your outfit. I have my own rations."

"All alone!" exclaimed Kirkendall. "You been riding that country all by your lonesome?"

"I surely have. Damn sight safer than the Bozeman."

"Well, you're certainly right about that," agreed Kirkendall. "We've had Indians on our tail most of the way. Fellow heading up those bulls back there got killed two weeks back. We've been under attack two times, and a troop of soldier boys escorting some wagons got jumped back at Crazy Woman crossing. Three of 'em killed." Kirkendall sized up Tolliver again. "You look fit enough, all right. What's your name?"

"James Tobias," Tolliver said readily, using his given name. "I'm a doctor by profession. Seeking my fortune west."

"A doctor you say!"

One of the men riding next to Hugh Kirkendall exclaimed, "By gawd, we could use a doctor, Hugh!"

Kirkendall looked at the two heavily packed mules. "You have potions in those packs? . . . potions for healing?"

Tolliver smiled. "Yes, I have some medicines."

Hugh Kirkendall reached across his horse and extended a hand to Tolliver. "Dr. Tobias, we'd be pleased to have you. Damned if I can figure how you made it this far by yourself, a doctor. Well, you're welcome. Yes, if you want to move along with us, you're welcome."

"I'm much obliged," Tolliver said. His heart skipped a beat, but his handshake was firm and steady.

Book Four

Gallatin Country

Chapter 16

Virginia City, Montana Territory,
September 1866

Barney O'Keefe, a fledgling rancher down on the Stinking Water River, bought three dozen longhorns from Nelson Story. Story and a few brave men had brought fifteen hundred head up from Texas, moving them across the Bozeman Trail in midsummer with only minor interference from the Sioux and Cheyenne. There were a few thefts resulting in a skirmish or two, but Story, a crusty, resolute entrepreneur who packed a brace of pistols, parleyed, cajoled, and fought ahead to the Gallatin Valley. Story was lucky, too. Under such circumstances, it was a monumental cattle drive, one never to be repeated.

Nelson Story was the first of the big-time ranchers in the territory. Barney O'Keefe was a small player but he had a big idea—to sell beef to the miners and settlers between Bannack and Virginia City. There were ten thousand hungry mouths to feed in the gulches of glittering gold—for a while.

Albert Terkle, a rotund, middle-aged widower who came with the gold-seeking deluge, was a doctor. He was also a drunkard and gambler who in his spare time sluiced gravel for scads on two claims between Virginia City and Nevada City, cities only by name, not by appearance.

In the short time since Dr. James Tolliver, alias Tobias, began his new practice in town, he had met all three of these men, Barney O'Keefe, aspiring rancher, Nelson Story, cattleman, and Alfred Terkle, part-time doctor. Only Story favorably impressed him. Story had his head on straight; he knew where the territory was headed, and he was at the front of the pack. He saw a future in the abundant grass and crystal pure water. It was on the surface, not underground.

Toward evening on this warm September day, two men in a buckboard hurtled up the ruts of the narrow street. They halted in front of Con Orem's saloon. Some of the bystanders supposed the two men had a terrible thirst to slake. Not so. The men leaped off and lifted a blanket-wrapped body from the wagon box. Several men rushed to help.

"He been gunshot?" someone asked.

"Hell no, he ain't been gunshot! He's been hooked by a critter, right through his gut."

"By damn!"

"What's his name?"

"Dobie . . . Dobie Bennett, one of Barney's hired help. Goddamned longhorn got him up agin a chute."

They carried the moaning Dobie Bennett into Dr. Albert Terkle's little office next to Con Orem's saloon.

Another man shouted, "Where's Doc Turkey?"

"Out diggin', I reckon."

"No, he ain't digging. He's right next door boozing."

They flopped Dobie on the plank table. He moaned. A big wrap of linen around his middle was soaked with blood.

"Well, get the sonofabitch in here," a man cursed.

Directly, Dr. Terkle, coatless, the sleeves of his white shirt rolled high, came puffing into the room. His florid cheeks poked out above his muttonchops like two bawdy-house lanterns. With a flourish, he yelled, "Stand back, boys, stand back!" After one look at Dobie Bennett's torn belly, he said, "This lad needs a drink. Get a bottle in here. By gawd, I think I need one, too." Dr. Terkle bent over and took a second hard look. He parted the torn skin with a forefinger. With a bubble of blood, an intestine popped out of the hole. Terkle quickly stuffed the wad of cloth back. "He's a goner, boys." The doctor staggered back, belched once, and passed out; the floor came up and smacked him in the face.

Dr. James Tobias was eating supper in Beaudry's boardinghouse when a man stuck his head in the door and called out his name. After a brief explanation, the two men hurried up the boardwalk. Dr. Tobias's temporary office was across the street in the back of Pfout's mercantile. The entrance was from the alley. He had one room. His examining table was by the lone window, and all of his medicines and surgical supplies were neatly stacked on several rows of makeshift shelving. He had a small sheepherder's stove that until cold weather arrived he utilized for one purpose—to boil water. The creek water, though used by a number of people along the gulch, was contaminated. Who in Virginia City drank water? So a few outhouses were perched alongside it. Did it make any difference? What the hell, they used the water for bathing, not drinking!

Four men carried Dobie Bennett back to Dr. Tobias's quarters. He gave the men a few orders while he began examining the wound. A lantern was lit for better light, and the little stove fired. Tobias thought it might be a long night; his patient, if he survived, would have to be kept overnight; warmth was imperative. Dobie was in a state of shock, and not from the whiskey the men had dumped down his throat.

"Is he a goner?" one of the men asked. "He's mumbling. Those ain't his last words, are they?"

"A bit irrational, that's all," Tolliver replied. He placed his instruments to the side. He swabbed the wound area with iodine.

One said, "Ol' Doc Turkey said he's a goner, dead-finished."

Another scoffed, "Turkey's soused. It's only when they put you in that wooden kimono you're dead-finished. Dobie ain't ready for no such thing. He's a good ol' Georgia boy."

"Wash your hands in the basin," Tolliver told the man next to him. "I'll need a little help here directly."

Moments later he went to work. He gave Dobie Bennett a shot of morphine. Later, he probed and found the small intestine ruptured. He did some cutting, patching, and tucking, ultimately sutured the stomach wall, and closed. Another swabbing of disinfectant followed, then a compress and bandage. The operation took forty-five minutes.

"It looks good," Tolliver told the men. "He's asleep, not dead."

They all smiled and started slapping each other on the backs, Tolliver included. They also agreed they needed a drink of rye. They thought Doc Tobias should join them, but he declined. No, he would keep an eye on young Dobie the rest of the night. In the morning, if all was well, they could move him down the street to a room in the Fairweather Hotel for three or four days.

"That'll cost a heap of money, bedding and grubbing him," one commented.

"Yes," Tolliver agreed. "A few dollars, I'd say. It's better than one of those wooden kimonos, isn't it?"

"Have to pay you, too," another said.

The doctor smiled. "You can all pitch in. That's what friendship is all about, taking care of one another. Pass the hat over at Con's place. Let everyone contribute. Spread the wealth, boys."

They nodded. One drawled, "Hell yes, what's money? It's like cow shit, ain't it? Only does a lick of good when you spread it 'round." He slapped Tolliver once more on the back. "Thanks, Doc. We'll be remembering you."

The Georgian, Dobie Bennett, survived the longhorn goring. Except for a diet of liquids, his recovery at the hotel was the best vacation he had ever had. In fact, it was the only vacation he had ever had. Friends came to see him every evening, including several of the lady entertainers who worked the back rooms of the Shades Saloon. Dobie also received gifts, a new pipe, stogies, and a tempered steel skinning knife from his boss, Barney O'Keefe. O'Keefe said Dobie could use it to castrate the bull responsible for his misery.

After four days in the hotel, Dr. Tobias dismissed Dobie Bennett. Dobie hobbled out between two cowhands to an awaiting wagon. One of the men gave Tolliver a soiled sugar sack that the doctor later emptied out on the table in his office. The assortment of coins and greenbacks totaled forty-eight dollars, his collection-plate compensation for the operation. However, the surgery, witnessed by four of the locals, had more than this meager monetary significance. Word of Dr. Tobias's unerring skill quickly spread throughout the community, and by mid-October his practice flourished; his medicines dwindled. It took twenty-six days for his first supplies to arrive from Salt Lake City.

In the meantime, Dr. Tobias made do with what he had on his shelves and what he could manufacture. Crusty miners, a few drovers, businessmen, and women with feverish children appeared at his door. He sometimes rode a circuit to outlying cabins and the few budding ranches in the frosty flats. He treated a variety of illnesses, ranging from mountain fever to bronchial disorders; he amputated one man's infected finger in order to save his hand. He concocted brews for fever out of salicylate compounds from the creek-bottom willows, made teas from thyme, linden, and chamomile. Dr. Tobias often thought of his old friend White Wolf. Ah, the Lakota. He reflected at night when he went to his room at Beaudry's boardinghouse. Bone-tired and lonely, he fondly thought of Red Moccasin, too.

One afternoon in mid-November, Sheriff Neil Howie entered Dr. Tobias's office. Howie was a good friend, one of the small group of men who shared coffee and conversation each morning at Con Orem's place. The sheriff had a sour look on his face. He was accompanied by two whiskered men dressed in fur hats and big hide coats, one an old trail guide and roustabout named Luther Willet, the other a freighter-trader, one Jubal McComber.

Sheriff Howie politely and respectfully explained to Dr. Tobias that the two men had just made their marks on a paper attesting the doctor was a fugitive from justice. He wasn't Dr. James Tobias; he was Captain James Tolliver, an escapee from the stockade at Fort Laramie. Luther Willet and Jubal McComber were claiming the one-thousand-dollar reward for the capture of James Tolliver.

Quietly stunned, Tolliver said nothing.

Sheriff Howie said, "You understand, James, I have to investigate the matter, look into the allegations."

Tolliver only nodded. Willet and McComber were gloating. Tolliver couldn't remember seeing either of the men at Fort Laramie or anywhere on the trail. They were absolute strangers. He was still at a loss for words, but he knew he was in jeopardy. He had to make the best of it.

Sheriff Howie looked at Luther Willet. "Are you sure this is the man?" Willet nodded.

Tolliver finally spoke. "I don't know this fellow. I don't know how he comes to such an accusation."

"Don't remember me, eh?" Willet asked. His little smirk was accentuated at the corners by tobacco stains.

"No, sir, I can't say that I do." Tolliver then stared at McComber, a hoggish fellow with a red nose and beady, green eyes. "I don't know this gentleman, either."

Diplomatically, Sheriff Howie said, "Your word against theirs, James."

Willet stuck out his hairy face. "Know Gabe Bridger, don't you?"

Tolliver's heart jumped. "An acquaintance."

"Well, you ain't forgetting that little parley you and him had one afternoon down at the fort, are ye? I sorta was tagging along with that soldier boy who was guarding you. Now I made no talk, Doc, but I ain't one to forget a face, 'specially one that's worth a thousand bills. Heh, heh, heh."

Sheriff Neil Howie looked at Tolliver questioningly. "Well, like I said, it's your word against his. Do you deny the man's story?"

The sheriff was surprised when Tolliver replied, "I do recall that particular incident. If this is the unkempt fellow who was in the company of Mr. Bridger, he hasn't changed." James Tolliver stuck his long nose close to Willet's hairy face. "You're a vulgar, unprincipled lout! What's more, you have no understanding of the legalities in this matter."

Willet bristled. "I don't cotton to insults from a horse thief."

"I don't cotton to bounty hunters," retorted Tolliver. He reached up for his holstered revolver hanging on a peg by the door. "I should put a hole in your head for this stupidity."

"Hold it, hold it!" shouted Neil Howie.

Luther Willet ducked behind a chair; Jubal McComber backed up against the examining table. He shouted. "By gawd, the man's dangerous! Guilty as sin, he is! Take him in, Sheriff, take him in! I'll see him hang."

"Nonsense!" exclaimed James Tolliver.

Sheriff Howie held up his hands. "Now calm down, everyone. We can go over to my office and get this straightened out. See what the right and wrong of it is . . . what's to be done about it."

"Now you're talking, Sheriff," huffed Luther Willet. "Get his ornery hide behind the bars, that's what. Cool him off."

Tolliver lashed out with his heavy boot and caught Willet a resounding blow in the shin.

"Jesus!" he yowled. He leaped high and danced on one foot.

"Out the door!" shouted Sheriff Howie. "Out, out, out, all of you!"

Cursing, Willet limped out into the cold afternoon air, spewing steam like a puffing locomotive. Jubal McComber followed. He said over his shoulder, "That's bodily assault, y'know."

"Good grief!" Tolliver took a swipe at McComber but missed. As hefty as the big man was, he was nimble.

They walked. More like strode. Willet hippity-hopped. A few passersby observed, one of them Dr. Tobias's attorney friend and coffee-drinking companion, Wilbur Fisk Sanders. More than friend. His wife, Harriet, had been an influenza patient of the doctor.

As they approached the sheriff's office, Neil Howie said aside to Tolliver, "What the hell is this horse thief business about? The old fart called you a horse thief."

"He's right. I am a horse thief."

"Oh, for God's sake, James!"

"I stole a general's mount back at Fort Reno," confessed Tolliver. "No, I borrowed it. I loaned it to an Indian boy."

"That . . . that was you!" exclaimed Neil Howie. "You're the one? . . . General Connor's? . . ."

"You heard the story?"

Sheriff Neil Howie exploded in laughter.

Willet and McComber turned and glared. This was no laughing matter! It was a matter of one thousand dollars.

Wilbur Fisk Sanders had knowledge of both the law and lawlessness in the territory. He had been present during the reign of the vigilantes several years back when they took charge and dispatched two dozen road agents and killers on the hanging tree. To the dismay of Luther Willet and Jubal McComber, Sanders said the case of Dr. Tobias or Tolliver, whatever his name, was a military matter. The territory had no jurisdiction. The men's only recourse for compensation was at the nearest fort, and that unfortunately would be over on the Bozeman Trail.

There were other contingencies and complications. "For instance," Sanders said, "there's the matter of delivering the good doctor to the fort. I daresay, with conditions what they are over that way, this presents a serious problem."

Willet protested. "You keep calling him the 'good' doctor. He ain't good, goddammit. He's a horse thief and a traitor."

Wilbur Sanders patiently held up a hand. "A matter for the court to decide, my friend. Dr. Tobias is a respected citizen of our community." He paused, cleared his throat, and then continued, "As I was saying, once the good doctor is delivered there is no assurance any reward can or will be paid promptly."

McComber said, "They can come here and get him. Who says we have to cart him over there through a passel of screaming redskins?"

Sheriff Howie replied, "It'll be a cold day in hell when the army sends a patrol through three hundred miles of battlefield to pick up anyone, Red Cloud included. And furthermore, I don't intend to leave my office to deliver him. As Mr. Sanders pointed out, this is out of my jurisdiction."

"Well, for chrissakes," Willet cried, "you can keep him in the pokey, can't ye? Ain't no law agin that. Someone'll come along t'fetch him when the news gets out."

"That could be months," sighed Howie. "We'd never be able to collect on his board and room bill from the army, never."

Wilbur Sanders said, "A man is entitled to a fair and speedy trial, even a court-martial."

"He's a wanted man," Jubal McComber put in. "Dangerous as a mountain cat. You just can't let him roam the road."

James Tolliver groaned.

Sheriff Howie said, "As far as I can see, there's only one way you can handle this, and it's still going to take a month of traveling. But for a thousand?"

"How's that?" asked Willet eagerly.

"Yeah, a thousand bucks is a real wad," chimed McComber.

"You boys take the doctor to Fort Laramie," the sheriff said. "Catch the Overland out tomorrow. Rope his hands. Take him yourself."

Luther Willet looked at McComber. "Can we do that?"

"Cost a bundle of swag, it would. I can't get fare for even one, Luther."

Sheriff Howie reminded, "Food and lodging along the way, too."

"We *can't* do that," Luther concluded. "We're busted."

"Sell some of your mules and freighters," Sanders suggested.

"Oh, no," Jubal McComber replied. His jowls jangled. "No, no, no. No, we ain't that dumb. This rascal gets away on us and we ain't got nothing to come back to 'cept our shanty. I ain't one to go without my vittles, y'know."

Tolliver said dryly, "Anyone can see that."

"You're a prisoner, man!" shouted McComber. "You ain't supposed to be talking, jest listening, so shut your clapperclaw."

James Tolliver smiled. "I won't be a prisoner long if I ride back to Laramie with you two idiots, either on a stage or one of your wagons."

Sheriff Howie intervened again. "Quiet, the lot of you. No one is riding anywhere yet."

Tolliver suddenly slapped his hands together and said, "Say, why don't you fellows borrow the money? Get it from a few of your friends and pay them back with interest? Everyone likes the smell of money."

"Money thinks I'm dead," grumbled Luther Willet. "So do my friends."

"Well, this is your big chance," Tolliver countered. "You get enough in your pockets and it's going to be all the better for me. I can eat and sleep well on the trip. And if I decide to cut your throats, well, I'll have a little grubstake to help me along the trail."

"See there!" Jubal McComber exclaimed. "I told you! He's a wild one, a regular wolf hiding in a woolie's clothing. You better cage him, Sheriff, keep him tied good 'til we get our trail money."

Exasperated, Sheriff Neil Howie sighed and looked over at Wilbur Sanders. "How long can I hold him legally?"

Sanders shrugged. "Until the army is notified and has a reasonable amount of time to respond." He pulled out a cigar, bit the tip off, and spat at the spittoon. "With all the patients he has, do you figure the good doctor is going someplace other than to work?"

"I hadn't thought about that."

"Whoa, whoa, whoa!" McComber interrupted. "Me'n Luther here got one thousand invested in him."

Sheriff Howie said, "Mr. Sanders is right. The good doctor isn't going anywhere. Besides, someone will be around to keep an eye on him."

"You bet your ass!" Luther Willet said. "We will."

Chapter 17

James Tolliver treaded mossy rocks. Though the support of Sheriff Neil Howie, Attorney Sanders, and Mayor-landlord Paris Pfouts dispelled some of the fright of his unmasking, he knew he wasn't entirely out of the water. Howie was preparing to notify the army, and Luther Willet and Jubal McComber were still skulking about town trying to arrange transportation. Sheriff Howie refused to deputize either man claiming such a proposition "ludicrous." Howie had done all he was obligated to do—he had placed the doctor under arrest. It was now the responsibility of the U.S. Army or a federal marshal to assume control.

Time was on the side of Tolliver. As Wilbur Sanders pointed out, the army presently was out of reach as well as occupied with more pressing matters, such as an Indian uprising, which according to the Montana *Post* dispatches had become one of major proportions. This news didn't surprise Tolliver, but he never disclosed to anyone that he played a role in the uprising during its conception. Though he was apprehensive and guardedly cautious about his plight, no one regarded him as an outright criminal.

No one seemed concerned about troopers appearing on the scene to spirit him away to a court-martial. In fact, a few wags saw some humor in the doctor's predicament.

The next morning after the altercation, Con Orem shouted out a warning when the doctor appeared for midmorning coffee with his friends in the saloon. "Watch your horses, men, here comes Doc Tobias." Granville Stuart, one of the city stalwarts and another coffee companion, referred to Tolliver as "Rustler Jim." Some citizens thought it was much ado about nothing. In their time the denizens of Alder Gulch had witnessed shootings, robberies, beatings, and dozens of hangings. Who cared about some discredited army doctor who had stolen a general's horse? It was a joke.

To some a joke. To others it was an outrage. The news floated down the valley of the Stinking Water to Barney O'Keefe's spread where the Georgian, Dobie Bennett, now back in the saddle, immediately took umbrage. Who were these foul men who had peached on his savior, Dr. Tobias? Another bunkhouse drover, a Mississippi boy named Brevard Bell, knew Luther Willet. Willet was a no-account. Additionally, Luther was a Yankee. Or had been. Made no difference if the big war was over. Dogs never change spots. In a hotbed of Southern sympathizers and ex-Confederates, Luther Willet's ignoble pursuit of reward money was downright disgusting. It was denigrating to the honorable Dr. Tobias.

"But what about Doc?" asked Dobie. "He's a Federal, ain't he?"

"Was a Federal," corrected Brevard Bell. "It's the

damned Federals making his life so poorly. 'Sides, any man who steals a Yankee general's hoss has grits in his blood."

"You know that McComber fellow?"

"Never met him," replied Bell. "Seen him some. Big lard-ass mule skinner, but if he's thrown in partners with Luther he's a boll for certain, two peas in a pod, I'd say."

"Doc's a good man," opined Dobie Bennett. "He's too good to be bothered by that white trash. Likely I'd be six feet under smelling pine if it wasn't for him."

"Reckon so."

"He's a caution."

"Law, law."

Dobie Bennett stretched and scratched at his belly scar. "We oughtta ride in and have a word with Luther and that fat man."

"We oughtta get loading this hay, that's what," Brevard Bell replied. He leaped from the flatbed wagon and mounted a pole ladder leading to the barn loft. He called down, "What you meaning, having a word with Luther and that fat boy?"

"Tell 'em to crawdad . . . back off."

"Tar and feather 'em?"

Dobie grinned. Tossing up a pitchfork, he said, "Ol' Sheriff Howie wouldn't like that. It's agin the law, boy."

"Don't need to know, does he?"

"You mean do something secret-like?"

"I reckon we could figure out something."

"That's vigilante stuff," replied Dobie Bennett.

"Get ourselves in real gumbo doing something like that."

"Shoot fire, Dobie, Sheriff Howie was a vigilante himself. So was ol' man Pfouts, and Story and Sanders. Hell, half of the goddamned gulch was. So what are we talking about, agin the law? Who cares?"

"This ain't the ol' days, boy," reminded Dobie Bennett. "That's what we're talking about."

Brevard Bell threw down several forks of hay. He stopped. "If we don't put the run on those boys, we're gonna lose Doc. Some damn marshal'll come in here and snatch him up by the tail like a possum. That's not tolerable, Dobie." He pitched another load and stopped again. "I say we go in tonight and talk to Josh, see what he thinks about all this chicken hockey. He always has an idea or two. 'Sides, Luther owes him a feed bill."

"A feed bill!" exclaimed Dobie. "Luther's a Northerner. How in the hell did he get credit from ol' Josh? He never gives credit to Yankees."

"Maybe he was drunk," replied Bell. "Leastways, maybe he can figure out a way to take it out of Luther's hide. That's the idea, ain't it?"

Josh Reynolds was a lanky pole of a man who owned the Virginia Cartage Company. He had wagons, mules, a few big horses, some freighters plus a livery, all of which he had won in a poker game. The previous owner, Cyrus Foggarty, never grieved over the loss. Foggarty had established the business as a cushion against poverty. At the time, his Alder Gulch claim was only turning a modest profit. He finally struck a shelf of white quartz streaked with veins of pure gold. He went on one big toot, lost the livery, but went back to Virginia with a half-million dollars.

Josh Reynolds, hailing from Petersburg, Virginia, took pride in the cartage company, particularly the name. It expressed his sentiments so he didn't change it. Most of this customers liked the name, too; they were true-blue cousins from Dixie. Few had fought in the great war, but they never forgave or forgot. In bellicose resentment they bonded together like sweet summer molasses, and there were plenty of them in the territory. To a man they disliked bluebelly Federals or anyone who associated with them.

Reynolds's left forefinger was missing above the second knuckle, a recent loss. A gregarious sort and imbued with tall tales, he had various stories about the loss of the joint. For the urchins of the neighborhood, and there were about a dozen, either a snake, bear, or a bugger had bitten it off. For the men, he had a bawdy story concerning one of the women of The Shades called Quick Cora. In truth, his finger had been amputated by Dr. Tobias. Most knew this. Threatened by blood poisoning, it was either the finger, arm, or his life. Reynolds quickly opted for the finger.

Josh Reynolds admired the doctor, and after a discussion with Dobie Bennett and Brevard Bell, it was decided that Alder Gulch would be better off without Luther and Jubal around, particularly Luther.

Reynolds rested his long frame against the side of a stall. A sprig of hay stuck out the side of his mouth. "Now we aren't about to lose the best doctor in the territory because some scallawag goes pointing the finger at him," he said. "If Luther is the only man in these parts who for certain can identify Doc Tobias, then it figures we have to get rid of him. In my way of thinking, Fats Jubal don't count much. He's backing Luther's play. Like most 'round here, even those bluebellies, no one could tell Doc Tobias from Adam, and Jubal never saw the man before in his whole crooked life."

"They're both crooked," Dobie Bennett said.

"Well, now, I know it and you know it," replied Josh Reynolds, "but the law doesn't know it. There's still two crooks around here to every honest man. That's the problem trying to get rid of these two Yankee peddlers. They're bad for the gulch but it's not legal getting rid of them. Have to play our cards right, boys, and we need some help."

"Help?" asked Brevard Bell. "What kind of help?"

The little stick of straw in Reynolds's mouth dangled. "Well, it's not gonna do us a lick of good if Howie gets off his dispatch to the army. Sooner or later someone's gonna come poking around, and it might just be someone who knows Doc. Luther or no Luther, we lose him, don't we?"

"You can't bribe Sheriff Howie," Dobie said. "He's as honest as the day is long."

"Naw," drawled Josh, "but we can see to it that message never gets out of the territory."

Dobie said, "That's a right onerous chore, Josh. Why shoot-fire, we'd have to rob the stage, steal the damn mail pouch to do that. And, hell, he'd likely just send another dispatch."

273

"And we might get shot," added Brevard Bell.

It was then concluded that this was indeed an onerous task. Josh Reynolds said this is why the extra help was needed. He told them to go round up two more Confederates, Arthur Caufield and Marva Biggs.

A former Gray soldier, Arthur Caufield was a glazier and part-time miner. He was also a good locksmith. Marva Biggs, a jack-of-all-trades, frequently dealt cards at Con Orem's place, hauled freight, was a carpenter, and helped Edgar Tompkins sort mail at the one-room post office in the Lott Brothers mercantile. Tompkins had poor eyesight.

When Dobie and Brevard returned with Caufield and Biggs, Josh Reynolds pulled the shades in the livery office, turned up the coal-oil lantern, and presided over a meeting that lasted until nine o'clock. Marva Biggs said right off no dispatch from Sheriff Howie had left the post office yet. Reynolds left it up to Arthur Caufield and Biggs to intercept the sheriff's post. The Oliver coach left at eight o'clock each morning for the Idaho and Utah territories. Promptly at five minutes before eight, the mailbags were picked up at Lott's mercantile, which meant that if Biggs couldn't pocket Howie's dispatch during the afternoon sorting, Caufield would have to pick the back door lock of the Lott building before dawn.

"Dangerous business," concluded Arthur Caufield. "Never figured I'd get into robbing a post office."

"We might not have to," Marva Biggs said, "if I

can sneak that post out from under ol' man Tompkins's thick glasses."

Dobie Bennett stared at Josh Reynolds. "What do the rest of us do?"

"Well," said Reynolds, "since you and cousin Brevard are working those critters daytime, that means we do our part at night. We're gonna scare the shit outta Luther and Fats Jubal. Yes suh, and if that doesn't work, we're just gonna have to get Arthur and Marva to help us. We'll hang those two scamps on one of the cottonwoods along the river. Be a good lesson for anyone else who gets the notion of peaching on our doctor."

After deliberation, Luther Willet and Jubal McComber reneged on the idea of delivering the doctor to an army post. It was downright hazardous; the forts were too far; it was too cold, and they couldn't raise a cent of credit. They would have to hold fast for a while. To make a little grub money, they decided to haul a few logs out of the hills down to the sawmill. What the hell, Dr. Tobias wasn't going anywhere. The sheriff had his eye on him. Luther and Jubal figured they could wait a month to get their reward. If all went well, they could have the money by Christmas, a fine yuletide present, five hundred dollars each, almost as much as they made in a year in wages, no work, either.

The men donned their big, shaggy coats, pulled their scarfs high and their hats low, and hitched up two mule teams. It was cold, frost on the cruppers, steam over the river, and a skiff of snow on the river bottom. About two miles from their shanty, they wound up a rutted trail leading to the timber, mostly fir and lodge-pole pine, trees with sturdy, straight trunks suitable for building logs as well as mill material.

They found a healthy stand, and soon were busy with their big crosscut saw, hard work this, good honest labor, but worth about five dollars a load if a man could cope. They barely could. Jubal had the weight but not the stamina. He looked like a bloated stump toad covered with grizzly hair. His jowls flared; he coughed; he wheezed, and he cursed. Luther fared little better. His bones were stiff before he started, his crusty skin as taut as tipi hide. He cracked all over when he moved. The cold air colored his crooked nose yellowish-white. It looked like an eagle's beak.

By midafternoon, the men had dropped six tall trees and cut them into twelve-foot logs. Using one team, they skidded the poles into position on an incline where they could roll them into the wagon beds. The green logs were heavy, the work laborious, the bright afternoon sun a delusory fraud. The men's feet were cold and their fingers numb. Jubal McComber waddled around to the side of the first flatbed and eyed the awaiting logs. He was tuckered but with his ponderous arms he still could lift. Luther Willet couldn't do much of anything. He ached all over and the sweat inside his long johns was turning to ice.

Jubal said, "I'll roll 'em in, Luther. You man the stays and get the chains ready." Jubal McComber heaved and shoved. The wagon shuddered as he rolled in one log at a time. He built a second row, and then a precarious third.

Luther Willet, cringing from the cold, hobbled back and forth across the mounting logs. "I think we got a load here," he shouted.

"Well, throw over the chains and we'll tie 'em down," answered McComber. Moments later two lengths of chain came winging over the logs. Jubal McComber let his ends dangle. He climbed atop the logs and looked down at Luther Willet who was trying to secure one of his chains to an iron bar under the wagon frame. Jubal heard a creak, a splintering creak. Luther Willet heard it, too, and immediately straightened like a war rooster.

Staring at the stay, Luther said, "She's cracking, ain't she?"

Jubal McComber replied, "She sure is." He lashed out with his boot against the pole and leaped clear. It split apart, so did the stay, and twelve big logs exploded from the wagon bed. Luther Willet let out one hoarse screech. When the last log flipped over, only one booted foot stuck out from the tangled mess.

Jubal McComber peeked around from the end of the wagon. "Luther?" he called softly. "Luther?" Jubal shook his head and clucked his tongue. He let out a big sigh and grinned. He started pulling away the logs. Dangerous business, this working in the timber.

The burial service for Luther Willet the next day was small, only eight men in attendance, six of them miners recruited as pallbearers. The Methodist minister said a few kind words, and Jubal McComber, the eighth man, finished with an "Amen." "He was a good ol' boy, best partner I ever had."

This same afternoon, Marva Biggs showed up at Josh Reynolds's livery office. He had a big smile on his face; he also had a brown envelope inside his coat pocket. He placed it on the cluttered little table. "Provost Marshal. U.S. Army. Fort Laramie, Dakota Territory."

Josh Reynolds grinned like a baked possum. He didn't bother to open and read the post. He simply walked over to his potbellied stove, gingerly opened the lid, and let the flames devour Sheriff Neil Howie's letter.

"A good piece of work, cousin," Josh Reynolds said. "Another matter resolved. The South lives again."

"Yes, suh," drawled Marva with a nod. "I hear they just planted Luther Willet on the hill."

"Unfortunate. Unfortunate, but timely."

"Sometimes the Lord acts in mysterious ways."

Josh Reynolds smiled grimly. "The lord saved us some work."

Marva Biggs sat on the wooden bench by the stove. "Praise the Lord in all His goodness."

"Yes, suh, He giveth and He taketh away."

"What about that fat one, the Jubal boy?"

"You mean are we gonna taketh?" Josh asked.

"Some such notion. Yes, suh, and we could all rest in peace."

Josh Reynolds withdrew a plug from the top pocket of his overalls. He offered a chaw to Marva who waved it off. Josh took a bite, moved it to the side of his jaw, and said, "Cousin Brevard and Dobie'll be coming in tonight. If you can rustle up cousin Arthur we'll have a little meeting, see what we can do about ol' lard bucket."

"Don't seem mannerly to bother a fellow when he's in mourning," opined Marva.

Josh Reynolds spat at a nearby can. He said wryly, "I wouldn't bet a huckleberry against a persimmon that ol' boy's mourning. Mos' likely, he's already got his tally stick out toting up the leavings, figuring out how he's gonna spend a thousand dollars."

"What thousand? He won't be getting a thousand dollars."

"No, suh, he won't. Those chicks he's toting up just won't hatch worth a damn."

Jubal McComber had a couple of belts of rye at the Mint Saloon. He paid for one. The barkeep, aware of the trader's grief, poured another one on the house. There were six or seven men in the saloon, most of them standing near the big stove. Except for one fellow at the bar whining for a drink, they were an unsociable lot. Downing the last of his whiskey, Jubal McComber pulled up his coat collar and left. No one even said good-bye.

The one-room shanty that he and the late Luther Willet had appropriated was located beside a creek in the foothills several miles east of town. It didn't amount to much. It had a rock fireplace, a dirt floor, one window covered with a double width of muslin, and a rough-plank roof. Furniture consisted of a table, two chairs, and two hay-filled bunks. To Jubal McComber it was his temporary home. His home eight months of the year was a wagon on the prairie. The outbreak of hostilities on the Powder River and adjacent valleys had cut his trading season short. Fearing a raid on his wagon and pack string, he hightailed it up the Yellowstone Trail in late summer and latched up with Luther along the way. With Indians on the warpath, neither wanted to risk the ride back to the Platte River country.

After putting the wagon and mules in the corral, Jubal struck his lantern and fed his fire. It didn't take long to warm the small cabin. He fried some potatoes and bacon, reheated the breakfast beans, and made a pot of coffee. He ate well. Jubal always ate well. He gave his big belly several pats and pulled a chair over by the fire. He farted loudly and contemplated. He knew what he had to do; he had to hold on for another month or so; get those logs down, maybe haul a few loads of freight, and when his fortune came in, pack up and head for the Lemhi, a good place to winter, not so damn cold. He had a few friends down that way, one or two, anyway, and there were always a few wandering Bannock and Shoshoni around. They usually had an extra woman or two with them. Pleasurable. Too much work wasn't good for his constitution. But one more month? He could do it. His mark was on that paper in Sheriff Howie's office. His mark was worth one thousand dollars. Hell, anyone could wait a month for that.

Jubal McComber thought he hadn't been asleep more than an hour. The big log in the fireplace was still spitting and crackling. He rolled over and pulled his rifle close, then cocked an ear. Sure enough, he heard the sound of hooves moving about, then a shout. Someone yelled, "Dead meat!" A mad clattering followed, horses pounding away, and it was silent again. Horse thieves?

Jubal hastily slipped into his boots and big furry coat. Rifle in hand, he went to the back of the cabin and looked toward the pole corral. A dozen mules and horses stared at him in the frosty moonlight. Someone was pulling a prank on him. Once back inside, he threw another chunk of wood on the fire and went back to his bunk.

Early the next morning, Jubal once more replenished the fire. He dressed and prepared for his usual visit to the privy. Stepping out into the brisk air, he closed the heavy plank door behind him. The door! Good God Almighty! Why, someone had defaced his door! The night riders! The night riders, they were the culprits. He took a hard second look. Scrawled in black across the door were the numbers "3-7-77." Jubal scratched his head. Then it hit him. Vigilantes! That was the sign of the vigilantes, a grave measurement, three feet wide, seven feet long, and seventy-seven inches deep. Jesus! He had until sundown to move out! He started packing.

Chapter 18

Jubal McComber's disappearance from Alder Gulch barely raised a brow. Fact was, hardly anyone missed him. Few knew he had gone and those who did cared less. The freighter, Jim Sheehan, who often passed McComber's place said the cabin was deserted. Some joker had painted a vigilante sign on the door, but this hadn't kept the pack rats from moving in. The sign was a joke, all right, for everyone knew the "Exterminators" hadn't been active in the area for almost three years.

Barely raised a brow? At least two brows hiked at the news, Sheriff Neil Howie's and Dr. James Tobias's. Howie, in fact, went out to McComber's shanty to take a look. Indeed, the place was deserted and the ominous figures "3-7-77" had been painted on the door with black axle grease.

Sheriff Howie had one less problem, actually two. He was rid of both McComber and Luther Willet, and unless someone from the U.S. Army contacted him, the case against Dr. Tobias was a dead duck. Just as well. He liked the doctor. So did everyone else in town. Curious as well as amused, he dropped by to see James Tobias.

"What do you make of it?" Howie asked. "Those boys were so all-fired concerned about putting you away and now they're gone, Luther in the ground and Jubal taking off without a word."

Without hesitation, the doctor replied, "I think it's great, Neil. Those two louts were an embarrassment to me. More to the point, they were a pain in the ass. What do I make of it? I don't know. It's damned ironic, I can tell you that, after all the fuss they made over me to end up with empty pockets. Fate, I suppose. If it's some kind of joke, no one let me in on it."

"Well," concluded Sheriff Howie, "that piece of paper they marked isn't worth a damn now. They're gone, but you're still not all the way out of the woods, you know. Those bastards put me on the spot and you as well. What the hell are we going to do if the army shows up? Someone who can identify you?"

Tolliver grinned. "I don't know. There's one thing that might help matters. Get some of your friends to quit calling me 'Rustler Jim' and the 'General's Groom.'"

"Levity, James, levity," replied Howie. "Those men are your friends, too." Howie warmed his hands over the small stove. "You must admit, you do have friends. I don't believe Jubal's leaving was of his own choice. From the looks of that cabin, he left like a hen in a hailstorm. Someone shagged him."

"Vigilantes?"

"That's jaybird jabber," Howie replied. "We quit that a long time ago."

Tolliver said, "If someone threatened him, he should have come to you or your deputy. That's what he and Luther did in the first place, isn't it? Go to the law to file a complaint or seek protection?"

Sheriff Howie grunted. "Now what the hell could we do about it? Follow the big fart around day and night? We couldn't even do that with you, and there's a thousand bucks on your head."

"I hadn't planned on leaving."

"I know, I know," said Howie. "But, I'll tell you what, James. If some soldier comes up here nosing around, you *better* plan on leaving. I'll turn my head the other way and you skedaddle. Get over to the Orofino country. Or over to Bozeman City or Last Chance Gulch, somewhere the army isn't." Sheriff Neil Howie tucked at his hat and fingered into his gloves. "Balls! All of this over a lousy horse! I can't believe it."

"I stole a pair of boots, too," Tolliver said. "They went with the horse."

"Good God!" Shaking his head, Howie left.

The Christmas season arrived, a lonely time for some of the men who were seeking fortunes far from home and loved ones. The saloons were crowded, the best place to work off loneliness. As a guest of Wilbur and Harriet Sanders, Dr. Tobias attended the Christmas Ball at Leviathan hall, a fashionable event attracting the town's social set. On another evening, he had several hot rums with Sheriff Howie. During their conversation, Howie disclosed that he never received a reply from the army regarding the doctor's status. As far as he was concerned, the case was closed. Merry Christmas, Dr. Tobias!

Dr. Tobias generously gave a few gifts to his closest friends. Sam and Emma Beaudry, owners of the boardinghouse; Con Orem, Granville Stuart, and Wilbur Sanders. He received presents, too, a beautiful knitted woolen scarf from Harriet Sanders, and suspenders from the Beaudrys. One of his presents completely mystified him. After attending Sunday services at the Methodist Church, he stopped by his office to check the fire in his little stove. On his examining table he found a small box, the card attached simply reading "Doc." Inside, wrapped in a piece of white linen, was a silver watch. Such a pleasant surprise! Such a wonderful gift! From whom? He snapped open the cover. Engraved on the inside cover were the words "To Doc. The Confederate Five." Gadfrey! The Confederate Five! Now who were these generous people? Winding the watch, he listened to it tick. He would never know who these people were, but they were friends, clever one, too—they had picked the lock on his door to leave the present.

One cold morning after the new year, Dr. Tobias as usual joined his jovial friends in Con Orem's place for coffee and hot biscuits, only to find them less than jovial. They were at a table near the front window, a copy of the latest Montana *Post* before them. Several of the men were bent over reading the newspaper. A few men sipped their coffee with sour looks on their faces as though the hot brew were all chicory. Dr. Tobias received a few somber greetings before Bill Lambert, a freight-line operator, piped up. "The worst of news this morning, Toby. Some of our boys in blue at one of the forts were massacred by the red devils of Red Cloud."

"Aye, she's a tragedy," Jim Sheehan said.

Dr. Tobias looked over the shoulder of Granville Stuart. The headlines were big, black, and ugly. "MASSACRE! Gallant Troopers Killed. Losses Heavy at Fort Phil Kearny." Dr. Tobias felt a knot in his stomach. It rolled around like a big lump of bread dough. He leaned closer. The dispatch was several weeks old. The action occurred shortly before Christmas, more than eighty soldiers and a few civilians killed in a fight with the Sioux and Cheyenne. Between snatches of conversation and condemnation, he read on. His brain was on fire. From what he could make of the dispatch, cavalry and infantry led by a Captain William Fetterman had been ambushed between some hills a few miles north of the fort. A wood train had been under attack by a party of Indians. Fetterman had chased the hostiles only to be attacked by a thousand warriors. Not one of his men had escaped. Good grief, this was no massacre! A vision swept before Dr. Tobias's eyes. He was Big Black Bear. He was hiding on a ridge with his Oglala brothers. Two braves named Hawk Leg and Crazy Horse pointed to the little valleys to the north. *Wikmunke.* A good place for a trap. Decoy. Never attack the soldiers' lodge. Attack the bluecoats on the trail. How can a snake eat if it is choked?

Dr. Tobias heard Wilbur Sanders speaking. "A

bloody mess. What do you make of it, James? You once had the Sioux around you. It appears they aren't the cowards one has been led to believe."

James Tobias Tolliver poured himself coffee. He felt the men's eyes on him. He said with a faint smile, "I was a doctor at Reno . . . and a horse thief." A few chuckles here. "I didn't meet many of the chaps, but the few I did meet weren't cowards in the least. They were cunning and very clever, damn good thieves. I had one steal a horse right from under me. In a gesture of mercy, not to General Connor's liking, I removed a ball from a young man's leg. He was bleeding to death. He didn't whimper, not once. No, the few I knew weren't cowards. They were as brave as any man at this table." He pointed to the newspaper. "This? This was no more than what Red Cloud promised. Yes, a horrible disaster for our soldiers, no doubt about it, but from what I can make of it, it was a well-executed battle plan. They led our boys right into a trap, and knowing some of the army command over there, it's a mistake that won't be made again. Deplorable. General Connor went down the river for less. Someone's likely to get sacked for this blunder."

Jim Sheehan said, "What they'll do is call out every laddie in Omaha. There won't be a redskin in the country when they get through. Aye, that's my notion on it. They'll kill every last one of those savages."

The other freighter, Bill Lambert, said, "There's nothing coming up the trail from the Platte. Injuns got that whole country sewed up. Why, if you paid me double I wouldn't bring a load up that way, not on your life, I wouldn't. Fat Jubal came outta that place last fall. He said those soldiers didn't give a hang about the movers on the trail. Stayed in their forts outta harm's way. That's what he told me."

Dr. Tobias split a hot biscuit. A little wisp of steam wafted up. He looked over at Bill Lambert. With a smile, he said, "As you know, I never put much stock in what McComber said, but in this case, he spoke the truth. That's Red Cloud's tactical advantage. He told the peace council at Fort Laramie he would fight for that land, attack anything moving on the trails. He doesn't have to attack those forts. All he has to do is isolate them, keep anything from going in or out. He has three thousand warriors to do it."

"Three thousand!" exclaimed Paris Pfouts. "Good heavens, Toby, how do you come by that figure?"

"It's not my figure, Mr. Pfouts. Their numbers were calculated by Gabe Bridger and another scout by the name of Phillips. Bridger knows Red Cloud personally. Bridger isn't on the best of terms with the Cheyenne, but he knows Dull Knife's strength, and there are a few hundred Arapaho in this, too. They have a long-standing quarrel to settle because of General Connor. When he couldn't make a fight of it with the Sioux and Cheyenne, he raided some Arapaho villages. So Bridger adds them all together. Three thousand, at least."

Lambert looked at Jim Sheehan. "You're right, Jimmy boy. They'll need every laddie they can get out of Omaha to put this one down."

The discussion continued for another half hour. The Indians caught hell, and it was the same dialogue Dr. Tolliver had heard many times. The redskins were impeding progress. They had no right to block the trails to the white settlements. And the land didn't belong to them anyhow; it belonged to the United States Government. The doctor kept his mouth shut. Arguing over poorly conceived treaties had always been futile. If the treaty makers themselves couldn't understand them, how could a few barroom coffee drinkers?

Whatever, everyone agreed someone committed a terrible blunder at Fort Phil Kearny. Never underestimate the strength and tenacity of your opponent. This conclusion brought a touch of humor to an otherwise grievous discussion. Everyone looked at Con Orem and smiled. Despite his ownership of the saloon, Con was a teetotaler. He was also feisty, an Irishman who had a penchant for fisticuffs. The previous winter he had fought Hugh O'Neil, a miner from the old sod who loved whiskey, in the territory's first boxing match. After 185 one-minute rounds, the fight was called a draw, the supporters of each participant urging the match to be ended. Hugh O'Neil was five feet nine inches tall and weighed 180 pounds. Con Orem was five feet six. His weight—138 pounds, soaking wet.

Dr. Tolliver went down the street to the Montana *Post* and bought a newspaper. In all the furor and the heat of the conversation at the saloon, he hadn't been able to read the dispatch thoroughly. By the window of his office, he reread it, not once, but several times. The names of a few officers were mentioned, none of whom he knew. Other than sev-

eral references to Chief Red Cloud, there were no
Lakota names in the story, and no mention of Indian casualties. Who but the Indians would know
such a thing? If they had annihilated the bluecoats
as reported, they undoubtedly resorted to their usual
tactics—recover their dead and wounded, strip the
enemy victims, and retreat. He stared vacantly out
the window at the snowy landscape. What a sorrowful state of affairs, soldiers dying needlessly for a
cause they didn't understand, his Lakota brothers
dying to protect their right to exist. Good grief, on
their very own land! He wondered how many friends
were lost, who they were, and if they had left
women and children behind. Where was the great
war village? White Wolf? Was he mending the
wounds properly, using disinfectant, using the new
instruments properly? Did he need help?

A woman knocked on the door. She had a little
girl bundled in her arms. The infant was feverish,
her cough metallic and harsh. "She has the croup,"
Dr. Tobias finally said. "Don't worry, I'll take care
of it. We'll fix up a few things here, a little of this
and a little of that, and when you take her home,
keep her in bed, hot broth, lots to drink. You tell
me where you live and I'll drop around tomorrow
morning to check on her, see how things are
working."

"Bless you, Doctor."

Josh Reynolds, without benefit of a wife or a
woman, always had his supper at the Virginia Hotel
dining room. Arthur Caufield, whose status was similar, often joined him. It had become habit with

Reynolds to take his seat at the front table next to the window so he could observe the boardwalk traffic. On this late afternoon, the two men had just finished supper and were talking over coffee and a dessert of bread pudding. The Oliver stage from the Idaho Territory appeared and stopped at the Lott building station across the street. New arrivals were always a curiosity, whether residents returning from business or shopping in Salt Lake City or strangers making a first-time visit. Not many strangers visited during the winter months. It was a very unpleasant time of the year, frostbite and the chilblains common occurrences.

Without comment, Reynolds and Caufield watched the passengers step down, briefly mill around, several stomping their feet on the frozen ground, others swatting their hands, all blowing little puffs of steam while they awaited their baggage. Directly, two of the men toting canvas duffel bags made for the hotel. The door opened and a cold draft whisked through the hall and into the dining area. The strangers, after making their marks on the register, struck up a brief conversation with Martin Becker, the manager of the Virginia. With tips to their fur hats, they picked up their bags and mounted the stairs to the second floor.

All of this was duly observed by Reynolds and Caufield, observed suspiciously because these strangers were unusually dressed, their demeanor very precise, almost military.

"The boots," said Josh Reynolds.

"Army as the day is long," Arthur Caufield replied.

"A buffalo coat on the big fellow."

"Buffalo soldier?"

Josh Reynolds nodded. "A good notion, cousin."

The two men returned stares, pursed their lips, and edged out from their chairs. Reynolds put two greenbacks on the table by his plate, and with a toss of his head went for the registration counter. Caufield followed. Martin Becker was shoving the coins from his new guests into a metal box.

Josh Reynolds asked politely, "Businessmen, Marty? Investors? Certainly didn't look like muckers."

"Who knows?" Martin Beck said with a shrug. "Gentlemen at best, not rounders. Friends of Dr. Tobias, I think. Asked about his good health . . . if he still had a house in town."

"Is that so?" Reynolds said. "Well, they can't be close friends, can they? The doctor doesn't own a house."

"Hmm," mused Becker. "Never gave much thought to that."

Reynolds turned the registration book around, and both he and Caufield looked at the signatures, broad scrawls, heavy and bold. "T. Callahan. George Finnegan."

"Wearing of the green," Reynolds commented dryly.

"Northerners," muttered Caufield caustically.

Martin Becker raised his brow. "How do you know that, Artie?"

"We didn't have any names like that in my regiment, that's how."

Josh Reynolds plucked his hat from the nearby coat rack. He said to Martin Becker. "Well, I hope they have a pleasant visit in our fair city, whatever their business is. If they need a carriage, send them over to my place, Marty. Always do my best for new-comers, make them welcome."

Josh Reynolds and Arthur Caufield casually left, but once outside on the boardwalk they stared at each other. "Over to my place," Reynolds said. "Soldiers or bounty hunters, one or the other, I'll stake my bottom dollar on it. Wearing revolvers under those coats, I'll bet."

"Gentlemen. That's what Marty said."

"For chrissakes, Arthur, Marty's a blind squirrel. Can't tell the difference between an acorn and a walnut."

"We have to make sure."

"That's exactly what we're gonna do," replied Josh Reynolds.

There was only one lantern hanging in the hall. At the end of the passage where a door led to the back stairway, Josh Reynolds and Arthur Caufield huddled against the wall in the dim light. After a half-hour wait a figure appeared from one of the rooms. It was the shorter of the two strangers. He went to an adjacent room and rapped on the door. The other man appeared, closed and locked his door. They disappeared down the hall. Josh Reynolds followed and watched as the strangers entered the dining room and took seats. Back in the hall, Arthur Caufield was busy with several keys, and in short order had the room of the small man unlocked.

Josh Reynolds turned up the lamp and cast his

eyes about. The man's duffel bag had been opened. A few articles of clothing were on the bed, nothing significant, nothing military. He spotted a belted holster hanging from the bedpost, a black holster with a flap covering the handle of a revolver. Reynolds leaned close. Aha! a "U.S." was emblazoned into the leather. At the small table, Caufield found a small manila packet. He whispered to Reynolds. Reynolds quickly loosened the string wrap and shook out a few papers. A few lines of bold print at the top of one paper leaped out and bit like a rattler. "U.S. Army of the West. Fort Atkinson . . ."

"Land o' living!" he whispered. 'We've hit pay-dirt!" He thumbed through several more papers. Another one caught his eye. "Look here, Arthur. Look at this." Reynolds stuck the stub of his amputated finger under a line. ". . . confirm the location as indicated by Mr. McComber, and will duly proceed and apprehend Captain Tolliver as speedily as possible."

"That fat bastard!" hissed Caufield. "Now didn't I tell you we shoulda mangled him when we had the chance? Look what he's done! He's gone and peached. Oh, Lord, Lord."

"That's spilt milk, Arthur," whispered Josh Reynolds. "We got work to do, a whole goddamned night of it." He shuffled the papers and placed them back in the big envelope. "This ol' boy's a first lieutenant, Arthur. Timothy O'Leary. He's no Callahan or Finnegan. Maybe you can say 'yas suh' and 'no suh' to him. You always liked that kind of military shit, didn't you?"

"Never had the pleasure of talking with a Federal officer, Josh."

"Well, I think we better do some talking with Confederates, then," Josh said with a sly smile.

"Call out the troops?" asked Arthur.

"That's right, cousin. The South rides again."

Dobie Bennett and Brevard Bell curled up in the office of the Virginia Cartage Company. Wrapped in horse blankets, they were asleep. Nearby, dozing in a chair by the stove, was Arthur Caufield. He was still thawing out from the ride down to Barney O'Keefe's spread. It was frigid outside. A skinny moon and a million stars studded the heavens but offered no warmth. Inside the livery by the light of a dim lantern, Josh Reynolds and Marva Biggs harnessed up a team. About a half hour later, Dobie and Brevard shucked their horse blankets, went into the big barn, and mounted up. The little party moved slowly up the alley to within twenty-five yards of the Virginia Hotel. The wagon was turned and Arthur Caufield, a wool scarf covering all but his eyes, a shotgun beside him, was left as lookout. The other four men sneaked up the back stairs.

About five minutes later, three of the men reappeared. A fourth figure dressed somewhat differently was in between them, a man wearing long johns, nothing more. His hands were bound and his face was hidden under a swirl of toweling. The men flopped him into the back of the wagon, covered him with a piece of canvas, and remounted the stairs. Directly, the procedure was repeated. Atop the stairs, Josh Reynolds hissed. Marva Biggs turned and deftly snatched a few pieces of clothing and two duffel bags out of the air. After tossing them in the back of the wagon, he carefully covered the load with the canvas. Dobie and Brevard rode point. Directly behind came the wagon, Josh Reynolds at the reins. The Confederate Five, only the whites of their eyes showing, slowly moved down the frozen road. It was three o'clock, a cold, cold morning.

Toward noon, Sheriff Neil Howie appeared at Dr. Tobias's office. He was bundled in a sheepskin jacket. A scarf was wrapped around his head and tied under his chin.

Tolliver momentarily eyed him. With a smile he said, "Best thing for frostbite is slow warmth. Nothing too harsh, and for heaven's sake, don't rub your nose. Makes it worse. Fractures the cells."

"I'm not frostbitten," Howie said.

"You look it," countered the doctor. "You're bow-legged, too. You look stiff, like you can't bend your knees."

Sheriff Neil Howie said, "I've two fellows across the street that are a helluva lot stiffer, I can tell you that."

"Real stiffs? Inebriated? That kind?"

"Frozen stiff. Dead stiff."

"Good grief!"

"I want you to come over and take a look," Howie said.

"Well, what the hell can I do?" asked Tolliver.

"Dead is dead, Neil. Gadfrey, I'm no resurrectionist! I'm nothing but a country doctor. Who are they? Who were they?"

"Damned if I know for sure," replied Howie. "Two gents who took rooms at the Virginia last night. Callahan and Finnegan. That's what they marked. Don't have a bit of identification. Don't know where they came from or what they were up to, but someone sure as hell done them in, in cold-blooded fashion. They froze to death about six miles west. Tied to a goddamned tree."

Tolliver shuddered. "That's cold-blooded, all right."

"Bound head to toe."

"Gadfrey!"

"Come on," said Sheriff Howie. "I want you to see this."

"Why me, for God's sake?"

"Because all they had on was long underwear, U.S. Army issue, that's why." He jerked on his hat. "Dammit, Toby, I got a notion they were here to get you. Those friends of yours with the grease pot somehow got wise to 'em."

Hands up, Dr. Tolliver backed against the examining table. "Whoa, don't blame me, Neil. You advised the army, I didn't. And you told me the case was closed. I distinctly remember you telling me that over hot rum last Christmas. What's more, you told me you'd turn your head and I could run the other way if someone came. That's exactly what you said."

Exasperated, Sheriff Howie sighed mightily. "I

know what I said. Now will you come along and see if you know these gentlemen?"

"Not if you think I made them stiff."

"I don't."

The doctor donned his coat and hat and pulled on his big mittens. A half-dozen men were standing around a wagon in front of the sheriff's office. When they saw Dr. Tobias coming, one yelled, "Hey Doc, you ain't gonna try rubbin' some life into 'em, are ye?"

Another shouted, "All they need is some of Con's red-eye, that's all, a snort or two and they'll be jiggin' the two-step."

Tolliver stared in the wagon. They were stiff, all right, a deadly bluish-white pall on their skin wherever not covered with mustache or whiskers. He scrutinized their features for a moment. The younger one! Good grief, it was poor Timothy O'Leary! Lieutenant O'Leary, once his appointed legal counsel, then the intelligence officer named to bring him to justice. Never underestimate the strength and tenacity of your opponent. The doctor felt sick. Would these fools never give up?

"Ever see 'em before?" asked Sheriff Howie. "Soldiers or just pretending?"

Dr. Tobias shook his head. "No, I can't recall seeing either one of them." He looked closer, the slight smudges on their foreheads. "What are those marks?" he asked.

"That's what I was telling you, dammit!" Howie replied disgustedly. "Grease marks. Axle grease. Either a five or the letter S marked on 'em. I can't tell which, and I sure as hell don't know what it means." He looked at the doctor. "What do you make of it?"

Tolliver swallowed. "Who knows? Could have a dozen meanings. Saints? Suckers? Five, a full hand?"

Sheriff Howie snorted. "Full hand, all right. Two dead ones."

Chapter 19

Jim Sheehan came over from Virginia City. He disliked moving empty freighters so he had five big wagonloads of good dry lumber, twelve-foot planks, he would sell in Helena before moving on to Fort Benton. The first Missouri River steamers were due in April, and he had contracts to haul merchandise back to Bozeman City.

Dr. James Tobias was happy to see Sheehan, the first of his old friends from Virginia City to pay him a visit in his quarters on the second floor of Nelson Story's mercantile. Though Sheehan was impressed with the doctor's office (two front rooms, one of which was used as a bedroom), he didn't think too highly of the town. It hadn't grown much since he was in the Gallatin a year ago to pick up three loads of potatoes. It was a conglomeration of clapboard and log buildings, not a stone structure in sight, and there were no more than thirty or forty houses in the area. Most of these were homesteads owned by Missouri and Kansas sodbusters, not one of them Irish.

Jim Sheehan had paused to feed his mule skinners and deliver two boxes of medicines to Dr. Tobias, freight that arrived in Virginia City after the doctor's departure in February. After Tolliver took receipt of the medicine, he and Sheehan sat down in the Antler Saloon for stew and cornbread. Sheehan dipped and ate heartily. The doctor drank coffee and heard the latest trail news and Sheehan's usual harangue about the hostiles north of the Platte River. The savages were still raising billy-hell. And apparently winning. Also, Colonel Henry Carrington, the commander at Fort Phil Kearny, had been replaced. Progress of the war, or lack of it, hadn't pleased the generals in Omaha.

Jim Sheehan wasn't surprised when the doctor said business was slow, his patients few. "Aye, the place is lacking people," Sheehan said. "And these sodbusters don't have a dollar to pay for your services, Toby. You'd been the wiser to locate in Helena and take some of the gold dust. Or just as well, you coulda stayed in the gulch and done better, not that anyone's blaming you for up and leaving. A man has t'do what he thinks is right."

"Problems."

"Not one of our lads in blue has shown his face in the town."

Tolliver shrugged. "It was only a matter of time. One of these days you might be leaving. The placers are finished over there. When the mining plays out so will the town. Story left. Granville's going to the Deer Lodge Valley, and Sanders told me he's planning a move, probably to Helena." He pointed his nose to the window. "Not much here yet, Jim, farms, ranches, but there will be. Adam Stuart's building his herd, and the farms are producing good crops. They're putting in more wheat. It's only the beginning." Tolliver pulled out a packet from his coat pocket and placed it front of Sheehan.

"This is part of the beginning," he said. "A favor, Jim. Put it in the post, first boat going back."

Jim Sheehan eyed the envelope. It was addressed to the Gibbons Furniture Co. in St. Louis. "Ah, you're planning a home, eh? Sending for the little woman."

The doctor laughed. "Not a home. Not a wife. I can't afford either. I'm a poor man."

"That's a pity, lad, " said Sheehan. "That's the trouble out here. A man needs a house and a good woman, something to come home to. If I didn't have my Maggie, I'd have nothing but my mules, my little sweethearts." He hummed and broke into song. "Oh, I drive 'em with lines and on the wagon I sit, I chew and I spit, all over my little sweethearts' behinds." He cackled once and said, "Aye, the two-legged ones, y'dare not spit on their behinds." Then, "If you're so damned poor, my lad, how can y'be ordering furniture? And if not for a house, what? That is, if y'don't mind me asking."

"I don't mind in the least," Tolliver answered. "We have a little infirmary planned. Six beds, an office, a room for surgical work . . ."

"A hospital! Here? Oh, m'God, Toby, you're daft!"

"On the contrary, I'm sane and serious."

"And who's the goose laying the golden egg for you?"

"John Bozeman."

"Bozeman?"

"Do you know him?"

302

Mopping up the last of his stew, Jim Sheehan nodded. He swallowed and whacked his hands together. "I know him," he said. "A high-stepping rooster, he is. Has his hand in a bit of everything. Charges six dollars a wagon to use that ferry of his down on the Gallatin."

"Good grief!"

"Oh, I don't pay six dollars," Jim Sheehan said. "Pilgrims following the ruts do." He grinned and picked at his teeth with a fingernail. "I take my rigs up the river a mile. Big gravel bend up there. 'Less the water's running high. I don't wet the hubs of my wheels. Aye, he's a high stepper, he is, but he's off the mark on his trail to the Powder. 'Less she's opened up, I fear he'll be high-stepping in mud. There'll be no pilgrims coming through here, laddie."

The rancher Nelson Story had introduced Dr. Tobias to John Bozeman and they enjoyed each other's company from the start. Bozeman said the community named after him needed a good doctor. Story had already told Bozeman about Dr. Tobias's problem with the U.S. Army, the fact that it had all started over a "borrowed" horse. Bozeman had heard the story. He laughed heartily. Bozeman considered himself an influential man on the frontier, was a personal friend of the former governor, Sidney Edgerton, and he knew General George Crook in Omaha. If Dr. Tobias encountered any problem with the military in Bozeman City, he promised to intervene. He could muster plenty of support; he could bring the whole Montana Territory down on the head of the army.

John Bozeman did have prominence. He was considered a trailblazer, which was a misnomer. What he had done was no different than pioneers before him had done—followed long-established trails used for centuries by animals and Indians. At one time or another, all of the tribes in the northern plains traveled the trails along the Powder, Bighorn, and Yellowstone rivers. These were ancient migratory routes for trading and hunting. Jim Clyman, Joseph Walker, Tom Fitzpatrick, and Gabe Bridger followed the same trails. None claimed to be trailblazers. They were mountain men, long runners, and trappers who took long chances in the wilderness, another misnomer. To those who inhabited the land, there wasn't anything wild about it except the animals.

Though Tolliver admired Bozeman's courage and foresight, he had some reservations about his integrity, his transgressions on land long inhabited by the red man and, indeed, accorded to them by the white man's government. There was no doubt in Tolliver's mind that the warring Sioux and Cheyenne impeded trade and progress in the settlements, particularly the terminus at Bozeman City. His contention with Bozeman was that the army had taken the wrong course by using a show of force in attempting to solve the matter.

John Bozeman wasn't swayed in the least. Somewhat like Nelson Story, he was an enterprising fireeater. Trespassing be damned, his eyes were on the future, Bozeman City's future. The land was bountiful and those who settled would prosper. White men in the Mississippi and Missouri River valleys shot each other over trespassing; he didn't see what difference it made to eradicate redskins. Though the doctor thought this was somewhat of a "might makes right" theory, he had to agree—for centuries some civilization was always stomping another into submission.

Several days later, Dr. Tobias accompanied Bozeman and Tom Cover to Donald Blodgett's blacksmith shop to get some horses shod. Cover, an exminer, was a close friend and sometime business associate of Bozeman. The two men were planning a trip down the Yellowstone to the beleaguered outposts Fort C. F. Smith and Fort Phil Kearny. Military contracts were lucrative. Bozeman saw an opportunity to supply the forts with badly needed beef, flour, and potatoes from the northwest end of the trail—from the rich Gallatin Valley. With exception of the ninety miles in between the two forts, the Yellowstone leg of the route was in traditional Crow country. No trouble here. Bozeman knew the Crow. He envisioned the forts as permanent fixtures on the road, the keys to its future success as a gateway to the Northwest. People always settled around the forts. People and soldiers needed food and other supplies. If the Platte River traders were unable to deliver the goods, he could, much to the benefit of the farmers in the Gallatin. Everyone would profit, particularly the main contractor, John Bozeman.

Just about the time Donald Blodgett was nailing on the last shoe, a rider came galloping in from the southwest. Reining up beside the men, he said, "Indians. A whole herd of 'em coming this way."

The men exchanged a few anxious looks. John Bozeman asked, "Did they chase you?"

"Made no move to do that," the young man replied. "I saw 'em first and I rode."

Donald Blodgett said, "There's been no report of hostiles in this country."

"There's no Indians in *this* country," Tom Cover interjected. "They're probably just passing through, heading for the prairie to hunt."

Bozeman took the reins of his horse. "I know Indians. You boys want to join me, we'll go take a look, see what they're up to. No use getting excited." He looked up at the rider. His name was Clay Moore, one of Adam Stuart's drovers. Bozeman said, "You go on up the street and tell some of the people. Tell them to stand easy. I don't want any ruckus. Like Tom says, this is probably no more than a hunting party." Bozeman glanced at Dr. Tobias. "You want to ride along, Doctor? See what some real Indians look like?"

Yes, he certainly wanted to see what *real* Indians looked like. Donald Blodgett threw a bridle on one of his horses and the doctor leaped on bareback.

What Tom Cover said was true. The moment Tolliver saw the approaching Indians he knew it was a hunting village on the move. They were dressed in buckskins and woolens, spaced out in a long file, many travois toward the end of the line. Only a few women and children were in the group that he calculated to number about fifty.

What John Bozeman said was untrue. He did not

know Indians, but he nevertheless greeted them as though he did. Bozeman was a sturdy, well-proportioned man with a mustache and goatee. He always held himself erect and wore his hat straight on, not tilted or cocked. He smiled broadly and crooked his arm. He received the same in kind from two leathered and furred Indians. From there on it was a mess.

"Must be Flatheads, maybe Kutes from over by the Hell Gate country," he said. "They don't seem to savvy, and I can't get much out of their sign."

Everyone nodded. Everyone smiled, even the Indians who Tolliver thought should have been laughing. After several more frustrating moments, he finally moved his horse to the front and began a series of rapid flourishes. A few "ahs" came from the Indians. Several more riders moved forward and the exchange intensified. Bozeman and Cover, mouths agape, sat and stared.

Tolliver finally said aside, "These fellows are Nez Percé. They come from what they say is the Land of the Winding Waters. From what I can make of it, this place is on the other side of the Bitterroot Mountains, Snake River country. They've been on the trail almost three weeks, came through some heavy snow on one of the passes. Some of these people make the trip every year."

Bozeman exclaimed, "By God, Toby, that's as good as I've ever seen. Where in the hell did you learn to sign so well?"

"Old friends down at Fort Laramie," was the reply. "Came around in the evenings. I sort of got the knack of it."

"You surely did!"

Tom Cover said, "Ask them if they plan on stopping in town; might not be a good idea, you know. Might scare some of the folks."

"They don't intend to stop until dusk," Tolliver replied. "They don't like towns. They'll ride around the other side. This one fellow says there's a white man's village not too far from where they live. A place ten times bigger than our town. He says the place stinks. He says our village must not be so bad. He couldn't smell anything peculiar."

John Bozeman said, "That town he's talking about must be Lewiston, the Orofino Bar country. That's Idaho Territory now."

"Anything else?" Tolliver asked with a smile.

"Wish them well," Bozeman said. "Good hunting." Bozeman made a clumsy gesture or two, a bow, shooting, the sign of a curly cow. One of the Nez Percé politely nodded. Another one grinned and shook his head. Bozeman and Cover turned and galloped off. James Tobias Tolliver, alias Dr. Tobias, alias Big Black Bear, rode side by side with the Nez Percé. The men traded sign for another mile before Tolliver waved good-bye.

The Nez Percé passed. The next morning, three Murphy freighters loaded with buffalo hides came into Bozeman City from the east, a surprise to some of the townspeople who gathered 'round to chat with the three drivers. The drivers were somewhat of a surprise themselves, two breeds dressed in canvas coats and floppy hats, and an Indian woman wearing a poncho and a U.S. Army cavalry hat.

Painted on the sideboards of the wagons in black bold letters were the words "Cobb Freight Line."

A few questions were bandied back and forth from the spectators. How had the drivers avoided the hostiles? Had they passed the forts? How were the soldiers faring? What were the hides worth?

The older of the two men identified himself as Iron Head Comstock. He had been a trader down at Fort Bordeaux for many years and he spoke fluent English. One of the men in the small crowd knew him. Comstock's wife was Cheyenne. She didn't say much of anything except she wanted a cup of coffee. The man who knew Comstock went into the Antler Saloon and returned with three cups, one for each of the drivers.

The third man in the party appeared to be in his early twenties. When he received his coffee he nodded politely and said, "Thank you. Good black joe always best." The men were mildly surprised again when the young man, pointing to the wagons, added, "These my wagons. My name's Charley Cobb. Pleased to meet you." A few of the men smiled.

Tom Cover had come out from Story's Mercantile. Always attuned to business prospects, he asked, "Where you taking these hides, Charley?"

"The place of the fireboats," Charley replied. "Fort Benton, eh?"

"That's the landing, all right," someone said. "Fort Benton, She's a far piece up the trail."

Cover inquired again. "How many hides do you have?"

"Nigh on two hundred."

309

"You didn't shoot 'em all, did you?" Cover asked with a smile.

Charley Cobb replied, "No shoot. I trader, not hunter."

A few chuckles.

After a moment of deliberation, Tom Cover said, "I'll tell you what, Charley. I'll give you four dollars a robe, eight hundred dollars for the load. This way, you won't have to ride up to Fort Benton and sell 'em."

Charley stared at Cover thoughtfully. "What I do with three empty wagons? I go Fort Benton, bring supplies back from fireboats. Many boats coming now up from Omaha. What you think? I go empty?"

"Well, well," Tom Cover said, "we have all kinds of freight going up to Helena. You can pick up a load or two here, get yourself more freight at Helena. Those steamers return freight you know. They take back anything they can carry, hides, furs, lumber . . ."

"I sell five dollars a robe at Fort Benton," Charley put in. "You pay me four. I lose money."

Some laughter. Cover said, "Not if you load up with freight, you don't. I take the hides off your hands here and you can do what you damn well please. Take some of our flour to Virginia City, Helena, and on up to Benton."

Young Cobb, astute and as mentally tough as his late father, calculated for a moment. He finally nodded and said to Tom Cover, "You take hides. I take money."

Good hides were always in demand. Everyone applauded, everyone except a stunned Dr. Tobias who had just emerged from Story's front door. He blinked several times and squinted against the morning sun. No apparition, it was his brother Crazy Coyote! And those other two with him, why it was that trader Comstock from Bordeaux, his Indian wife, too, the one with the ridiculous name, Minnie. Then Tolliver saw the lettering on the wagons. "Cobb Freight Line." Gadfrey! Crazy Coyote, an Oglala warrior, and Iron Head Comstock, a shifty reprobate if there ever was one, here gracing the muddy street of Bozeman City. Charley? Charley Cobb? Well, why not? Dr. Tobias? Good grief, could no man claim his true name!

"Hey there, Mr Cobb!" Dr. Tobias called. And the moment he shouted he knew he had made a mistake.

Crazy Coyote, alias Charley Cobb, almost dropped his cup. He yelled joyously, "Toll-e-veer!" A string of Lakota words, several gigantic leaps, and a warm embrace followed. Iron Head stared at the doctor, not too sure, Minnie either, for they had never seen him in the guise of a white man. He was Lakota, but the name, there was no mistake about that.

"Toby," Tolliver said quickly. "Everyone calls me Toby. That's my name, friends, good old Toby." A few muffled words were exchanged, brief explanations. Some of the people milled about craning their necks, snatching at the conversation. The doctor said loudly, "Old friends . . . old friends from Laramie."

A curious Tom Cover moved in. "By God, Toby, you mean you know these folks? They're friends?"

"That's right, Tom. I knew Charley's father, a trader along the Platte ... came to the fort regularly."

Crazy Coyote smiled proudly. "I go fort plenty times. *Eyah*, I meet doctor at fort. He stay inside."

"Yes," Dr. Tobias quickly interrupted. "That's a long story, Charley. We can talk about it later."

Tom Cover glowed. Little pieces of gold danced before his eyes. He slapped his hands together. "Look here, Doc, you realize what this means? These fellows came up the trail! Charley here traded for these hides, came right up without a hitch. The Sioux didn't touch the boys, by God!"

"Yes, a bit of good fortune, I'd say."

"No, no, no!" Cover said, shaking his head. "Don't you understand? John and I could ride with them when they go back. We could ride right into the forts."

The doctor frowned. "They were damn lucky to make it."

"Luck hell!" Cover retorted. "They traded with the Sioux. The Sioux trust 'em, that's my notion." Tom Cover looked at Charley Cobb. "Are you part Sioux, son? You talk their lingo? That it?"

Young Cobb drew himself up indignantly. With a grimace, he said, "No, man, no!" He jerked off his hat. He had cut his hair, but he grabbed what was left of it. "Sioux get hair. Shoshoni. I Shoshoni!"

"Good grief!" moaned Dr. Tobias. Deception had no end in this land.

Charley, Iron Head, and Minnie unloaded the buffalo hides at a shed behind John Bozeman's office. Cover peeled off eight hundred dollars' worth of greenbacks and left. Watching Charley Cobb stuff the bills into a leather packet, Tolliver said, "Do you know he's going to sell those hides for five dollars apiece? You lost two hundred on this deal, my brother."

Crazy Coyote grinned. "Maybe, Toll-e-veer. Maybe he get only four dollars. Four dollars is what the men pay now at Laramie, eh? Four dollars, he make nothing." The young brave tapped the side of his head. "You know what I pay for hides? I pay two hundred dollars. I make six hundred. He lucky man if he makes one hundred. *Eyah*, I no dumb shit. He dumb shit." He took Tolliver by the arm and led him around to one of the wagons. Flipping back a piece of tarpaulin, he pointed to a big layer of white sacks and a layer of tins. "Look!"

The doctor stared. Coffee. Sugar. Gadfrey, a small fortune! With narrowed eyes, the doctor asked, "Where did you get this?"

"Big trade," Crazy Coyote replied with a grin. "From our brothers, eh? They get from bluecoat and pilgrim wagons. I trade plenty powder, shot, and new shells."

"I see," nodded Tolliver. "And where may I ask did you get the contraband ammunition? Steal it, too?"

"Fort Pierre trades," answered Crazy Coyote proudly. "Iron Head and me partners. We find plenty friends in Pierre. Trade some gold, eh? Buy wagons. Buy hides. We sell this sugar and coffee to gold diggers. Make plenty money, my brother, plenty."

The doctor smiled. A chip off the old block, this young man.

The four hotel rooms above the Antler Saloon were occupied. Iron Head and Minnie elected to sleep in the hay barn next to Donald Blodgett's blacksmith shop. The three wagons were pulled into an adjacent corral. They could keep an eye on them. Charley Cobb threw his robes on the floor of the doctor's office. It was a splendid arrangement. The lamp was dim, the room cozy, and Tolliver listened to the good news and the bad news. There was plenty of both.

The Sioux called the Fetterman debacle "The Battle of the Hundred Slain." Thirteen warriors died, many were wounded. Red Bone and White Wolf saved a few lives but Crazy Coyote said he knew at least six warriors died, among them his good friend Hawk Leg and a young brave called Crow Foot. Tolliver was sorrowed to hear about Hawk Leg, but said he didn't remember Crow Foot.

The two men were speaking Siouan. Crazy Coyote said, "Crow Foot was a Hunkpapa, the son of a chief called Sorrel Horse. He came to our village with some of his people in the Moon of the Drying Grass. He went with Crazy Horse, Hawk Leg, and Yellow Eagle on raids at Big Piney Creek. Sometimes I went."

"The running soldier on the hill?" asked Tolliver. "Was he still there?"

"There were soldiers on three hills," replied Crazy Coyote. "They always made signals with flags. We made our signals with mirrors."

"I read in the newspaper about the big fight," Tolliver said. "I thought it was good strategy."

"*Eyah,* we practiced that two or three times. One time we were ready and the bluecoats gave up the chase." Crazy Coyote sighed. "It was cold. Everyone went back to the village with ice in their blood. We were disappointed."

"You counted coup?"

"I shot many times," Crazy Coyote replied. "When Hawk Leg fell, I carried him away. When Crow Foot fell, I carried him away. It was bad in the village. Red Moccasin came to see Crow Foot. He was in poor condition, shot in the breast. No one could get the bullet free. She said send for Big Black Bear. You, she said, were the only one who could save her man."

Tolliver and his young brother sat on the floor cross-legged opposite each other, a lamp hanging from the ceiling above them. The light was a hazy yellow. Tolliver leaned close to Crazy Coyote. "Her man? Did you say her man?"

"Yes, my brother. Red Moccasin took Crow Foot for her husband three moons after you left. She looked for the sign of the Black Eagle in the south for many days. It was always in the north. She said it was the will of Wakan Tanka."

A big lump swelled in Tolliver's throat. Red Moccasin, a widow at seventeen.

Chapter 20

When John Bozeman learned that three freighters traveled the length of his trail unmolested he believed the army had regained control of the route. Elated, he looked forward to the return of the wagon trains, a new wave of emigrants to populate and bring wealth to the Gallatin Valley. A promising summer lay ahead. John Bozeman was ready. Stacks of sweet-smelling pine lumber were piled high at the sawmill; mortar, tar paper, and windowpane were on the bills of lading at the waterfront platforms in Fort Benton. Mule trains already were on the move. Anticipation always abounded in the spring. Spirits soared, the land rejuvenated, pussy willows bloomed, and grass grew high in the bottoms.

Bozeman's belief in the safety of the trail was not shared by the man known as Dr. Toby Tobias. The doctor hadn't disclosed that a dozen Lakota brothers accompanied the Cobb Freight Line wagons on the lower leg of the journey, that the Oglala Chief Red Cloud was planning a summer of terror. Nor had the doctor mentioned the fact that some of the soldiers were in such poor physical shape they were unable to fight with efficiency. The winter sieges had taken their toll. Scurvy was prevalent. Sioux scouts had observed the men at Fort Smith out on their hands and knees foraging for wild onions. And how could the army "regain" control of a trail it had never owned in the first place? The trail was not safe. He so stated. No argument though, not with John Bozeman, the doctor's friend and benefactor. Bozeman was determined to go.

John Bozeman entertained other ideas, too. He mounted the back stairs to the doctor's office. He scraped a bit of mud from his boots. He had men digging a well on the lot where he intended to build Dr. Tobias's small infirmary and new office. The doctor said good, clean water was imperative; he couldn't do without it.

Tolliver was packing his small bag for a ride out to Bernard Crum's farm. Bozeman came in and reported that the well was beginning to percolate water. Things were looking good; he had ordered piping and a pump for the cistern. Perhaps by late summer, the building itself would be ready. But this wasn't his immediate concern. He wanted Tobias to go along on the solicitation trip to the forts.

"Tom thinks you should go, too," Bozeman said. "You seem to have excellent rapport with the redskins, your ability to communicate so readily, that sort of thing. If we by chance encountered a few of the boys, your presence would be invaluable."

The doctor gave Bozeman a sour look. He said, "My presence, John, would be a hindrance. That's what it would be. The army still regards me as a horse thief. If I go it's likely I might not come back.

I'd end up in the stockade, and getting out a second time would be damned unlikely."

"I'll get you pardoned," Bozeman said.

"What!"

"I have friends in the territory."

"It's not the territory," the doctor replied.

"General Crook back at Atkinson is a personal friend."

"Hmm," mused Tolliver. Fastening his medical bag, the doctor gave Bozeman an apprehensive stare. "Well, no doubt Mr. Crook could help, but when I hold the piece of paper in my hand, John, then I'll believe it. Those fellows back there are still sniffing my trail. I know it."

"Oh, come on, Toby," implored Bozeman, "this ridiculous farce is almost two years old. Who knows you at these outposts? Who do you expect to meet, General Connor? He sure as hell isn't looking for that damned horse. No one gives a hang about that episode. If those boys were so keen on catching you they'd have been on your tail long ago."

The doctor said to Bozeman, "I appreciate the invitation, but I do have other matters that need attention here. I'm a doctor, not a man of commerce. Keeping those soldiers' bellies full is more in your line. You and Cover can handle that end of it. I have a few patients, and I want to see the foundations of that building put in. And I have Martha Crum to think about. She's due anyday now."

Bozeman grinned. "You mean you have Bernie to worry about. Scares the hell out of a man first time he sees a woman giving birth. There's no way on

God's green earth a child can get out of a hole that small."

With a frown, the doctor said, "Sometimes they don't, John. That's another reason I'm staying behind. Life out here can be miserable at times, but it's precious. I just do what I can to make it a little more tolerable."

Bozeman nodded. "I understand. You're absolutely right. We need you. Need that little hospital, too."

"It will be a start." They went to the door. Tolliver said, "You may be right, John. One of these days, this place just might be the crossroads of progress."

"No, that's not what I'm thinking," Bozeman replied. "I'm thinking more along the lines of the *center* of progress. Yes, and I think we better plan on a two-story building. Aim high, that's my motto."

John Bozeman and Tom Cover rode out the next morning for the Yellowstone. Along with high hopes for financial gain, they had a pack mule loaded with enough provisions for a round-trip of twenty days. Dr. Tobias and a few friends waved them off. If all went well, the two men planned on being back in the Gallatin by early May.

All did not go well. On the third night while cooking their meal, five Indians approached from the cottonwoods bordering the river. They were leading one horse. Bozeman and Cover picked up their rifles. Cover, however, didn't like the looks of the Indians so he went over to the horses and began saddling one.

Cover said, "Never know what they're up to, John. Don't let 'em get too close, eh?"

"Saw our smoke," returned Bozeman. "Probably looking for some coffee, a free meal."

Three of the Indians hung behind. The other two began walking toward the camp. Cover asked, "Who are they? Can you tell?"

John Bozeman squinted under his big hat. "Crow. Must be Crow from down the river."

"Crow? Hell, John, those boys are walking. I never saw a Crow that didn't own a horse. For a fact, a dozen. Damn thieves."

"Well, I think I know that fellow in the lead," Bozeman said. "Crows, all right. Nothing to worry about, Tom."

The "familiar" man stopped about thirty yards away, shouted once, abruptly raised his rifle, and fired. Hit in the shoulder, Bozeman lurched once. He cried out, "Damnation, I'm shot! Good God, they must be Blackfeet! Get down, get down? Head for cover."

Tom Cover touched off his rifle. Simultaneously, the Indians returned fire. Cover felt a sharp sting in his left shoulder. In front of him, John Bozeman, struck again, toppled over into the deep grass. One of the Blackfeet had been hit, too, and as Cover backed off fumbling to find a shell for his Springfield breechloader, the three trailing men ran up and assisted the wounded Blackfeet.

Shoulder aching, Cover could do nothing more than run for a hiding place. He ducked under some downfall just in time. A bullet whined through the brush directly over his head. Fearing for his life, he

neaked away through the willows and choke-
herry bushes.

When Tom Cover finally dared to take a look, he
aw the Blackfeet retreating toward the river bot-
om. Trotting ahead of them were Bozeman's and
Cover's horses and the pack mule. When the hos-
iles disappeared, Cover threaded his way through
he brush back to the camp site. His good friend
ohn Bozeman, the man who knew Indians, was
lead.

Tolliver was shocked and dismayed to hear the
news. This was two days after the incident. Cover
had walked thirty miles of trail back to Benson's
Landing on the Yellowstone near one of Nelson Sto-
y's cattle camps, and Story just happened to be
present. He and one of his hired hands went back
and buried Bozeman on the spot. Cover, weary,
grieving about Bozeman's death, came riding into
own on a borrowed horse. He had a very painful
wound. Within five minutes the news spread; within
n hour, Dr. Tobias had been located. He treated
Cover's shoulder. The doctor told him he was lucky.
The bullet had passed through the flesh above the
collarbone. Tolliver said, "Had this been lower or a
ittle to the left, you'd be out of commission for a
month or so. Collarbones are bad enough, but if
hat ball had lodged in your socket, we'd have a real
mess on our hands."

"This is already a mess," groaned Cover. "John
lead, Indians out to prowl?"

"Blackfeet? I didn't realize they wandered this far
south anymore."

321

"They seldom do," Cover replied. "Renegades. Must have been renegades."

"There's a lot of talk on the street, already."

"Angry talk or fearful talk?"

"A little of both. Panic. Hostility. The roof is caving in, that sort of thing. I don't sense any great feeling of sorrow, the fact that a damn good man is dead, a leader. That's deplorable."

"People forget," Cover said. "It doesn't take long out here. A bit of shock at first, some despair, and then it gets to the hand-wringing. They're scared to death of Blackfeet. Killing a man like Bozeman only compounds it, Toby. This might stir up the command, get some of those people at Fort Atkinson moving."

The doctor finished with the bandage and helped Cover into his shirt. "Moving? In what way?"

"Forts," Cover answered. "They've been promising us some protection for over a year now, one somewhere between here and Fort Benton to make the Mullan Road safer, maybe another one on the river trail. Another one of John's ideas."

"Yes, I'd heard mention of it, but I thought it was more of a rumor, some wishful thinking," said Tolliver. "A fort around here never struck me as a great necessity. Protection? Safer?" The doctor opened the door for Cover. "I haven't heard of any concerted effort on the part of the Blackfeet to hamper traffic on the Fort Benton road. And the Yellowstone? One incident? This isn't any Powder River trail, Tom. Protection from what?"

Cover shrugged. "Fear. Pacify the people. John said a fort gives a sense of security to the settlers

322

Like giving a baby a sugar tit. Stops all the fussing right quick." Cover grinned. "Of course, John had other ideas. Promotes growth. Good business for the Gallatin. More mouths to feed. Forts bring towns."

The doctor nodded. Or trouble.

That night, Dr. Tobias was called out to the Bernard Crum farm. He delivered Martha's baby, a boy, and she and Bernie named it John Bozeman Crum.

Dr. Tobias's hopes for a hospital were buried along with John Bozeman's body. Bozeman had dreams; he also had creditors. No one else came forward with an offer of sponsorship so the doctor decided to make do with his rooms above the store. But the hand-wringing of the area residents grew into shouting. They had no time to consider building an infirmary; they wanted protection from the savages. Rumors of congregating Blackfeet, Bloods, and Piegans above the Musselshell River added fuel to the fire created by Bozeman's killing. Shortly, the angry shouts of the people were heard.

Since there were no forts in the area, the acting governor, Thomas Meagher, telegraphed General William Sherman for permission to muster eight hundred men as a territorial battalion. The request was approved and within weeks several companies of volunteers from Helena, Virginia City, and Bozeman City were ready for action.

What action? Tolliver watched in awe. Action against the shadowy Blackfeet wasn't forthcoming. Instead, a few peaceful Flatheads showed up one bright day in May. One of the men was caught stealing a horse. He was hanged. In another "action," two breeds, Mitch Bouyer and John Poiner, came

up the Yellowstone from Fort C. F. Smith with dis
heartening news. There were only two hundred men
at the fort. All of their horses had been killed or
driven off by Red Cloud's warriors. Except for some
hard corn that they boiled to make palatable, the
soldiers were without provisions. If they didn't re
ceive some help soon they were going to perish.

Civil War veteran General Thomas Meagher,
famed leader of the Union Army's 69th Regiment,
the "Bloody Irish," sent forty-two heavily armed men
and ten wagons of food to Fort Smith. Without so
much as firing a shot, the contingent arrived at the
fort on June 10 delivering supplies free of charge,
supplies that John Bozeman had once envisioned
freighting under a lucrative army contract. One of
the guides, Mitch Bouyer, later told Dr. Tobias only
a few Sioux and Cheyenne had been seen near the
fort. Most of the hostiles were on the Powder River
celebrating the Sun Dance and Arrow Renewal
ceremonies.

June faded into July, and the action turned hot
with the weather. One of the doctor's old friends
showed up one morning to pay his respects—Sheriff
Neil Howie from Virginia City. Only he wasn't a
sheriff; he was a colonel in the militia, and his re
spects were very brief. He and a company of men
were on the trail of some horse-raiding Crow, about
a hundred of them.

"Crow!" exclaimed the doctor.

"That's right, Crow," Howie replied. "They raided
several places in the valley. They made off with
more than thirty head."

324

"Smart Indians," opined Tolliver with a grin. "While all the militiamen are chasing nonexistent Blackfeet, the Crow come in and filch a few horses."

Neil Howie frowned. "Your sense of humor hasn't changed, Doc. I want you to ride along with us. They have us badly outnumbered, dammit, and in case there's some shooting, I might need a doctor. You'll be paid for your services just like the rest of us."

The doctor continued to smile. "Your sense of humor hasn't changed either, Neil. I'll admit I don't have too much to do around here, but chasing Indian horse thieves, well, that's a little out of my line."

Colonel Howie returned a thin grin of his own. "I thought that was one of your best sidelines, stealing horses. Now, come on, you're a part of this like everyone else around here. Besides, I'd enjoy your company. So would some of the boys. Probably some of your old friends in this company."

Tolliver eyed him closely. "You mean the ones with the axle grease? *Those* friends?"

"How in the hell do I know?"

"You let that little investigation drop?"

"I beat it to a doll of rags," replied Howie. "Never came up with a thing."

"How about those two stiffs, the cold ones? Who were they?"

Neil Howie shrugged. "There's thirty or forty soldiers missing out of the forts below here, deserters, killed, just plain missing. We buried 'em, didn't we? I don't know who in the hell they were and neither does the army."

"Dead men tell no tales."

"Something like that." Colonel Howie stepped off the porch back to the dirt street. "We'll be riding in another half hour. Will you join me?"

"How much of a lead do those Indians have?"

"Two or three hours, I reckon."

Tolliver thoughtfully rubbed his chin. A little scene from his past flashed through his mind, that long-ago morning when he awoke to find his horses gone, stolen in the night by a Crow coup counter. And trying to mount those flop-eared mules. Gadfrey! He turned away and said over his shoulder, "I'll get my horse and a few things. I have an old score to settle."

Including Tolliver, there were thirty in Colonel Howie's party. Several of the Virginia City men remembered the doctor from his six-month stay in the gold camp but none had been acquainted with him personally. Tolliver rode at the front of the column beside Howie and a militia captain by the name of Bill Nelson. The two men valued the doctor's presence, not only because of his medical knowledge but because he was the only one who had traveled the Yellowstone leg of the Bozeman Trail. This amused the doctor. Tracks of the Crow ponies were everywhere. A child could have followed them.

Several miles west of where the Yellowstone River made a big bend into the canyon toward its headwaters, there were a series of rolling hills. The hills gradually melted into meadowland bordered by trees and river-bottom bushes. Visibility from the top ridge to the river was unobstructed. When Colonel

Howie topped the big hill he suddenly held up his hand. Far below, winding their way to the left of the ferry crossing, were the Crow. At this distance, at least a mile away, the band of horses looked like a tiny water snake inching its way to the sanctuary of the river. The river was no more than a winding piece of silver thread.

Addressing both the doctor and Captain Nelson, Howie said, "If we can catch them crossing they'll be like ducks on a pond."

Tolliver frowned and protested. "No, Neil, I don't think that's a good idea. They'll be moving our horses ahead of them. That's likely to be one big mess. Everyone will be in the water, including us. We just might end up shooting each other."

"What, then?"

Captain Nelson spoke up. "Get down there on the double and charge the bastards before they can find a good ford. Break off our stock, and then it's every man for himself. Let the Injuns take to the water. If we come in shooting, they'll make a run for the other side."

Howie stared at Nelson. "I wouldn't count on it."

Tolliver said, "Nelson's right. Those boys didn't come over here to fight white men. They're not on the warpath. They came to steal a few horses. It's a game with them, one they enjoy. It's honorable, and it's profitable."

Colonel Howie grinned. "Well, I reckon you should know." He wheeled about, gave the men their orders, and cautioned them not to get careless. Moments later everyone kicked away, hell-bent for the flats below, most of them eager to kill redskins.

Tolliver had no such ambition. In defense and retribution, he had killed several men, but shooting had never been his game. Despite his warrior status among the Lakota, he prided himself as being a man of medicine, a man of peace. Yet fate always seemed to intervene. Here he was again, dashing headlong into a confrontation brought about because of horse thievery.

In the brief melee that followed, the good doctor discovered that in perilous situations the parameters of any man's beliefs are as precariously fragile as cobwebs. It was true—the direct, unexpected charge of the militiamen into the Crow middle split off the stolen horses. The accompanying rifle shots panicked the Indians. Flailing their mounts and hunched low, they fled to the river providing the militiamen with poor shots. These volunteer soldiers weren't marksmen in the first place. It was no duck shoot. The Indians scattered like quail in every direction. And there weren't one hundred of them as previously reported by the Gallatin Valley residents. There were twenty.

But there was one Indian pounding down through the river rocks that drew Tolliver's attention, an Indian riding a piebald mare, a strikingly familiar piebald, the doctor's piebald. Tolliver blinked in disbelief. Then his mind exploded. *Wagh!* He became Big Black Bear. Brandishing his rifle and emitting a shrieking war cry, he booted away in hot pursuit. The galloping horses churned the water white, but Big Black Bear caught his enemy about a third of the way across the river where the water was swift and belly deep. He made a sweeping arc at the Crow's head with his rifle barrel and missed. The Crow brave deftly ducked to the other side of his pony. But his leg and thigh were exposed. Black Bear brought the rifle butt down with a resounding whack on the Crow's knee. The leg flew from the stirrup and the Indian disappeared. Reining up, Black Bear shouldered his rifle and stared at the swirling eddy, waiting for a target to show. Nothing. Then about thirty yards across the water he heard a defiant scream. He whirled about. All he saw was a tremendous thrashing of spray, flailing arms, and kicking legs. The man disappeared in the current, only to reappear once again far below in the middle of the river. Another faint scream, and Black Bear saw a dim figure stroking for the opposite shore.

The Bear yelled, "You sonofabitch, I hope you have to walk home!" Turning to the side, he seized the rawhide of the piebald and sloshed back to the rocky shore.

He was met by a concerned but angry Colonel Howie. "Damnation, Doc, are you all right?"

"Perfectly all right," replied Tolliver.

Howie glowered. "You didn't hear a word I said on the hill back there. You took a fool chance. I saw the whole thing. That buck could just as well have turned on you, put some lead in your dumb hide. Damn, Doc!"

"He didn't have a rifle." The doctor pointed to a bow and a bundle of arrows lashed to the side of the Indian saddle. "He didn't have time to string it."

Howie fumed. "They carry knives, you know. Jesus, you're a caution. What the hell got into you? I thought you'd lost your mind, screaming like a banshee and carrying on that way. For chrissakes, you're a doctor, not a one-man army!"

Tolliver shrugged. "Nelson said every man for himself."

"*I* didn't say it."

Tolliver replied sheepishly, "I forgot myself. When I saw this horse, I just plain forgot."

"This horse!" Neil Howie shook his head. He eyed the piebald. "Well, will you please tell me what is so special about this critter? I'd sure as hell would like to know. Does she shit gold or something?"

"She's my horse."

"Your horse, is it?"

"She's no Indian pony, is she?"

Howie took a second look. True, other than the dirty white and black splotches, she was a sturdy, well-proportioned beast, much larger than the typical Indian pony. Howie said, "So she's a big critter . . . stolen somewhere down the line, probably from one of the wagon trains."

"No wagon train," Tolliver said. He moved up the bank and pulled on the reins of the piebald. "Stolen from me almost a year ago. Look on the right rump, Neil."

Howie turned his horse to the side. He saw the dim brand of a circle with a "U.S." imprint inside it. "Good God!" he exclaimed.

"I told you she was my horse."

"An army horse. Wait a minute. The same one . . . ?"

"Well, she's the one I borrowed."

"From General Connor?"

"Yes, now thrice borrowed."

"Judas priest!" Neil Howie guffawed.

*   *   *

By the time the horses were rounded up and the men rested, it was too late to make the long ride back to Bozeman City. Colonel Howie took his men up the river to the ferry crossing where they made an impromptu camp for the night. There wasn't much elation, no boisterous celebration. Though the main objective had been accomplished, that of retrieving the stolen horses, the men knew their military performance had been a poor one, only two redskins killed and several wounded. They had no prisoners to hang from the cottonwoods.

Dr. James Tobias Tolliver assumed his usual calm demeanor and relaxed by one of the night fires. Inside, his nerves jangled like the bell on a lead mule. He had counted coup three times. He had touched the enemy with his weapon; he had unseated him; he had captured his pony. He felt like singing, performing a victory dance around the fire. *Hiyah, ozuye, ozuye, ozuye!*

Chapter 21

Confusion continued to reign. Upon arrival in Bozeman City, Neil Howie was greeted by disheartening news down from Fort Benton. General Meagher was dead. Preparing to depart on a steamer to arrange for new weapons for his militia, the general was reported to have fallen overboard during the night. Or had he been shoved? His body hadn't been found. Since the fiery Irishman had any number of enemies in the territory, especially Southern sympathizers (the communities were rife with these), ugly rumors immediately began to circulate. The territorial government posted a $10,000 reward to anyone who had evidence as to how the "accident" occurred. With the general gone, Colonel Howie and Colonel Charles Curtis now shared leadership of the militia. Howie immediately tried to muster Dr. James Tobias as surgeon of the civilian fighting corps. Tolliver promptly declined. He had no desire to cavort about the countryside chasing any more Indians, especially down the Yellowstone.

By late summer, Tolliver was regularly reading the war dispatches in the Montana *Post*. The Western Union telegraph had been completed between Virginia City and Salt Lake City. Now the news was more timely but it was still nasty. The warriors of Red Cloud and Dull Knife once again were on the attack along the Bozeman Trail. Two separate battles had occurred in early August within days of each other, one at Fort C. F. Smith and another at Fort Phil Kearny. The accounts stated that in both fights, the beleaguered soldiers had repelled the hostiles. (These two engagements were later called the Hayfield and Wagon Box fights. The Sioux called the Wagon Box battle the "Big Medicine Fight" because of the amazing firepower of the soldiers and teamsters. They were equipped with fifty-caliber Springfield breechloaders and Henry repeaters.)

However fragmentary the reports, there was no doubt in Tolliver's mind that Sioux and Cheyenne strategy had achieved its purpose—traffic on the lower part of the trail was at a standstill. Civilian wagon masters refused to make the hazardous trip, electing to stay on the Overland Trail to Fort Hall. Military trains from Fort Laramie attempting to supply the valley forts constantly came under attack. Though outmatched in weaponry, Red Cloud's numerical superiority was winning the war for him. And he owned the trails.

Reports of additional fort construction persisted, and the doctor discovered it was more than wishful thinking. Crazy Coyote, alias Charley Cobb, came trundling into Bozeman City after a very profitable freighting trip from several communities on the Mullan Road. He, Iron Head, and Minnie Comstock took freight to Helena and Hell Gate. They carted mining equipment to Philipsburg and returned to Fort Benton carrying a half-million dollars in gold. Four armed miners made the journey with them. In the hundreds of miles traveled, the only Indians Charley Cobb saw were a few at the docks helping unload steamers, many steamers. Forty were lined up discharging cargo, and young Cobb said a lot of it was marked "U.S. Army."

Tolliver and his Oglala brother sat in the shade of the trees in back of Blodgett's blacksmith shop where Charley and Iron Head had elected to rest a night or two. They had a load of machinery destined for Virginia City.

Speaking in Siouan, Crazy Coyote said, "There were two bluecoats up there by the fireboats. They asked us to come back and haul some of that freight, eh? Many boxes, Toll-e-veer, some packed with glass, some with doors. Glass is plenty bad to carry on that trail."

"Windows," said the doctor. "Doors and windows. Did they say where this material was going?"

"Here," Crazy Coyote replied. "It will come to Bozeman City."

In English: "Gadfrey!"

"This is a secret; a surprise?"

Tolliver grunted. "There's been some talk on the street, that's all, old women's talk."

"That is called gossip," Charley Cobb said in English. "No more gossip, eh?"

"I'll bet that damn Howie knows about this," Tolliver said, "but he's up in Helena at that stupid war camp playing soldier."

"Maybe your friend Story, the man with cows and big store, eh?"

"Maybe."

"Not so good for Toll-e-veer, bluecoats come around."

"Wagh!"

Three days after Charley Cobb left, rumor mushroomed into fact, chilling reality for Tolliver. Amid the shouts and hurrahs of a few gawking citizens, two companies of U.S. infantry wheeled up the dusty street of Bozeman City. A few soldiers marched alongside the heavily laden mule-drawn wagons. Others were perched atop the canvas-covered cargo. Tolliver glumly peered out from his second-story window. He had seen a military train similar to this once before along the Platte River—Colonel Henry Carrington's builders. This contingent was smaller but it was a fort-building outfit, no doubt about it, not cavalry but engineers, infantry, and a half-dozen civilians, probably construction personnel. Several curious locals mounted up and followed. Heading northwest, the long column finally disappeared.

By nightfall, the news was out. The army had pitched camp. Orders had gone out to recruit sawyers and carpenters. The Gallatin Valley was going to have its fort. Tolliver thought of John Bozeman. John would have been happy. It would have been an honor to have the fort named after him, but it wasn't. The army called it Ellis in honor of August Ellis, a Union colonel who was killed at Gettysburg.

Tolliver had never heard of the man. Neither had anyone else in Bozeman City.

By early September a few soldiers began to appear on the street, occasionally patronizing the stores of Nelson Story and Lucas Hamm. But the bluecoats invested most of their fifteen-dollar monthly salary in entertainment—red-eye, gambling, and a few young women who had suddenly sprouted like pine beetles from the saloon's woodwork. And much to the doctor's disillusionment and dismay, the lot for his once promised infirmary now had a two-story clapboard structure sitting on it—not a hospital but a saloon and bawdy house. For Tolliver's profession, progress was not forthcoming.

The doctor existed, warily. In the evenings he occasionally visited the Antler Saloon for a drink or two with friends. Always on the lookout for a familiar face, he fortunately never saw one. What he saw were the faces of new recruits, young enlisted men lacking education or training, hoping to find something better than what they had left back home. For most, this had been nothing. Officers, Tolliver's former peers, were seldom on the street, much less in the Antler. Though unhappy with the present, as well as prospects for the future, the man known as Dr. Toby Tobias began to breathe easier. The gaunt man in the long white robe carrying the scythe hadn't made an appearance either. No bodies around. At least, not to his knowledge.

In the valley, farmers were cutting a good head of wheat and barley; the potato harvest was under way, and the sawmill had a new planer turning out finished lumber. Crates containing six hospital beds and an operating table arrived from the Gibson Furniture Company, prepaid by the late John Bozeman. The operating table went to Dr. Tobias's office, the six beds to Story's big shed. The ever-enterprising Tom Cover volunteered to take the beds off the doctor's hands at a bargain price. He thought he could double his money selling them to one of the houses of entertainment where they could be put to good use. Dr. Tobias was mortified. The transaction was never consummated.

On another sunny day Crazy Coyote, Iron Head, and Minnie Comstock came down from Fort Benton with three loads of hardware and farm implements for Lucas Hamm. Fall was near and Crazy Coyote who had played white man for nine months could no longer tolerate civilization. It had curdled his belly; he was going back home to the Black Hills for the winter. Iron Head decided to make tracks for Pierre with a stopover in the Powder River valley, this to satisfy Minnie's wish to see her Cheyenne relatives. Nostalgia suddenly swept Tolliver. Going home, everyone was going home.

The next morning the doctor made a call at Ben and Alma Thompson's farm to tend one of their ailing children, a four-year-old girl. A bit of a fever and a few spots. Chicken pox. He left some balsam salve to help control the itching and a tea mixture of herbs, including wintergreen, to alleviate the fever.

When he dismounted in front of his office a disconsolate Crazy Coyote was sitting on a barrel under the porch overhang. At each side of the door stood a soldier, one a young lieutenant, the other a veteran master sergeant. They politely nodded. Crazy Coyote shrugged helplessly. Tolliver blinked several times and traced his tongue on the sudden dryness of his lips. Good grief, his time had come!

"Are you Dr. Tobias?" the lieutenant asked.

"Yes, I'm Dr. Tobias." He momentarily stared at the face of the master sergeant, a familiar one, he thought, but he wasn't certain, the droopy mustache, the long sideburns.

"The colonel wants to see you," the lieutenant said. "A matter of identification, sir. Will you please mount up and ride along with us?"

"Identification?" asked the doctor innocently. "Does your commander wish me to identify someone? Or am I to be identified?"

"I think you are to be identified, sir," the lieutenant said.

"Am I under arrest?"

"No, sir, this is only a matter of procedure. There is some doubt about the gentleman's integrity."

"And who is this gentleman?"

"A Mr. McComber," answered the lieutenant. "A freighter."

Tolliver felt his hackles curl. "McComber!"

"Do you know him?"

"Never heard of the man," Tolliver replied.

"Shall we go?"

"At your pleasure."

Crazy Coyote spoke up in Siouan. "They have no big wall at this fort, my brother. If they keep you, I will have you out of there in the morning before the sun shows its face."

The lieutenant looked at Crazy Coyote, then at Tolliver. "What's he saying?"

"It's a nice morning for a ride. He's going to get his horse and follow along, if you don't mind."

"Not at all."

The commandant's office had a long porch, and sitting in the shade on a long plank bench was Jubal McComber. His floppy hat rested beside him, and a big smile spread across his fat face. "Mornin' there, Doctor. Damn, am I glad to see you again! Thought mebee you'd spotted me last night, got yerself all fidgety and went stompin' off like a mule in a canebrake."

Tolliver made no reply. The young lieutenant motioned him ahead and ordered McComber to follow. Crazy Coyote took the seat vacated by McComber. The master sergeant plucked out his pipe, casually examined its charred bowl once, and struck a match. He puffed once and grinned at Crazy Coyote. "They call you Charley, eh?"

"Sometimes they call me Charley," replied Crazy Coyote. "Sometimes they call me other names, not so good, eh? Fuckin' Injun."

The sergeant chuckled. "You're ol' man Cobb's boy, aren't you?"

Crazy Coyote looked up in surprise. "You knew my father?"

"I knew him, all right." Taking a long drag, the sergeant inhaled deeply and blew smoke into the balmy air. "Saved my hide once, he did."

"*Eyah!* Saved your life, my papa did that!"

"Eeyup," was the easy reply. "Bunch of goddamned Sioux was about to carve me up for wolf bait. Killed all my Pawnee scouts and had me next in line. Ol' Barnaby stepped in. Let one of those bucks read me the orders of the day. Angry bastard by the name of Crazy Horse." The sergeant stared down at Crazy Coyote. "You know him?"

Nodding, Crazy Coyote said, "I know him. What name do you go by?"

"Abbott. Sergeant Fred Abbott."

Inside, the lieutenant approached the desk. He saluted once and said, "Sir, this is Dr. Tobias," and to Tolliver, "Doctor, this is Colonel Stubbs."

Colonel Stubbs looked up and stared directly at Tolliver. A small smile crossed his face, and he said, "Dr. Tobias, I'm pleased to meet you." He stuck out his hand. With a deep shudder, Tolliver grasped it. The shake was a hardy one. Good grief, Major Thomas Stubbs! Why, Tom was his old bunk mate back at Fort Reno, his confidant, and at one time the only true friend he had. How ironic. Tolliver's mind raced. Thomas didn't even complain when I stole his damn boots! And now a colonel, commandant of Fort Ellis. Gadfrey!

But before Tolliver could utter a word, Colonel Stubbs stared at Jubal McComber. "Is this the man you believe to be Dr. James Tolliver, an escapee from the stockade at Fort Laramie?"

"It's him all right, and I'm claiming reward jest like I did over at Virginia City last year. No mistake, Colonel. This is the man."

Colonel Stubbs looked at Tolliver as though he had never seen him before. "Your name, sir?"

"Dr. James Tobias."

"Yes, I see," mused the colonel. "And can you prove it, prove you are Dr. Tobias?"

Tolliver glanced at a gloating Jubal McComber. "Can he prove that I'm not?"

"Aw, horseshit!" exclaimed McComber. "Get your hide down to Laramie and I can prove it. Luther's word was the gospel, it was. He knew you to a fare thee well, he did."

"Luther?" asked Stubbs. "Just who is this Luther?"

"Luther Willet, my partner. He knows who this rascal is. Hell, ol' Luther knew him from way back."

After a moment of consideration, Stubbs said, "Well, you better get Mr. Willet up here on the double. If he's the only one who can make a positive identification, he should be here. I know something about this case, Mr. McComber. Everyone connected with it is either dead, a deserter, or out of the army. Where is this fellow Luther?"

"Luther?" McComber stared helplessly at Stubbs, then Tolliver. "Dead, I reckon. Got himself killed."

Colonel Stubbs gave McComber a hapless stare. He said, "Mr. McComber, do you expect me to detain Dr. Tobias, to take him back to Fort Laramie to face a court-martial when no one can testify? A man you only know by the word of someone who is dead? Are you sure you haven't made a grievous mistake?"

"But . . . but this *is* Dr. Tolliver! Shoot fire, someone down there can put a tag on him, I knows it."

Colonel Stubbs tapped his finger on the desk, then half turned and stared thoughtfully out the back window. "Lieutenant Dowd, please call Sergeant Abbott in here." He turned back and looked at Jubal McComber. "I have a soldier outside who knew Dr. Tolliver. Sergeant Abbott is his name. Dr. Tolliver attended him once for a gunshot wound in the shoulder . . ."

"Wal now," McComber said, "that's more like it. Hell, get him in here and let's be done with it."

And directly, Lieutenant Dowd returned, followed by Master Sergeant Frederick Abbott, former aide to Lieutenant Timothy O'Leary.

"Yes, sir," Sergeant Abbott said, saluting the colonel.

"Mr. Abbott, please pull back your clothing and show Mr. McComber here where you were shot."

"In the shoulder, sir." Abbott unbuttoned his tunic and pulled back his underwear exposing the scar of a bullet wound. Everyone took a look including Tolliver who had never seen the result of his work on the Powder River prairie that cold winter day.

Colonel Stubbs addressed the sergeant. "You knew Dr. Tolliver, didn't you?"

"Yes, sir, I did."

"Is this the man who fixed your shoulder? Is this Dr. Tolliver?"

Sergeant Abbott looked closely at Tolliver. Abbott finally shook his head. "No, sir. This fellow doesn't look anything like the doctor who patched me up."

They watched Jubal McComber clatter down the road in his wagon. McComber was a confused and bitter man, a vile man thwarted. But James Tolliver had little to gloat about either. Strange, how his thoughts were so confused. Despite Thomas Stubbs's manipulative intervention, Tolliver found himself lacking in emotion, no elation, certainly no vindication here. A touch of relief, perhaps, little more. Was this his freedom? His repatriation to society? If so, where was the great surge of happiness?

After a moment, Tolliver expressed his thanks to Stubbs. And he asked, "Why?"

Stubbs smiled. He gave Tolliver a friendly pat on the back. "Because it's over, James. Because you've had enough. Because it should never have happened in the first place, the most ridiculous, spiteful charade I've ever encountered."

Tolliver was silent again. Then: "The others? You said they were gone, dead, over the hill. Is it true?"

Thomas Stubbs nodded, and one by one ticked off the dead and missing. Private Ulis Claypool, deserted, his mutilated body found on the prairie; Sergeant Edward Burns and Corporal Delbert Carnes, medical aides at Fort Reno, Burns killed at Fort Phil Kearny, Carnes, a deserter; Major Calvin Mudd, killed on the Platte River trail; Lieutenant Timothy O'Leary, missing somewhere on the frontier; General Patrick E. Connor, retired.

Stubbs added, "The case is closed. It would be most foolish to press it, a waste of the army's time, yours as well."

Tolliver said, "I always assumed the army had more important things to do. My assumption was wrong. Those boys chased the hell out of me."

"No," replied Stubbs. "No, your assumption is correct. The army does have more important things to do, and presently getting out of the Powder River country is at the top of the list. We're moving out of there. We've lost the war, James. Pursuing this folly is about as futile as trying to court-martial you. By winter, it will be all over, something a few of us suspected all the time."

Tolliver stared at his friend curiously. "Over? How do you come by this conclusion?"

"We're going to abandon Kearny and Smith," replied Stubbs. "Plans are already under way. In another year the Bozeman Trail will be history, anyhow. The steel will be all the way to the Utah Territory. The Overland will be history, too. Trains, my friend, trains."

James Tolliver stared across the small compound toward the distant cottonwoods and aspen. They were touched with the yellow and golden hues of early autumn. "Beautiful, isn't it?"

"Yes, a beautiful land," agreed Stubbs.

"A land of lost causes."

"For some," replied the colonel. "And what's your cause now, James? What will you do? The town? Back home?"

Home? Philadelphia? Why, he hadn't thought about it, not lately. Tolliver answered, "I don't know. I've been lost. I'll write my parents, try to explain."

"A holiday," suggested Stubbs. "You should take a long one, rearrange your life. Good tonic."

"Yes, I may go see my people."

"Ye gods!" Colonel Stubbs suddenly exclaimed. He pointed. Crazy Coyote was at the hitching post taking up the reins of the horses. There was General

Connor's piebald mare. "That horse! My God, James, don't tell me! That's the mare that caused this whole mess! And you still have her?"

"Yes, that's the same horse."

"But she's stolen! Branded, a walking invitation to disaster! Why in heaven's name? Why?"

Tolliver shrugged. He smiled faintly. "I don't really know. She's certainly caused a lot of trouble, all right. Nothing better has come my way though. So, I thought it best to keep her." He held up a finger of protest. "Borrowed, Tom, not stolen. Borrowed."

The morning was sunny but the air crisp, and in the shadows along the road a touch of frost covered the first matting of fallen leaves. The smell was fresh, musty, the odor of fall. James Tolliver, the man called Big Black Bear, sat beside his young brother, Crazy Coyote, on the huge freighter. Iron Head and Minnie Comstock were at the reins of the two teams following.

Crazy Coyote had his eyes on the trail but he was attuned to his brother's thoughts. He said, "Do you think the Black Eagle will be in the South? Do you think White Wolf is watching the sky? What about the woman, Red Moccasin?"

Big Black Bear was smiling. He said, "I feel like making a song."

Flipping the reins, Crazy Coyote said, "I thought you only sang songs when you rode alone. This is what you once told me."

"Yes," replied Big Black Bear. "And once you told me your song is a silent one."

345

"This is true."

"I think we have something to sing about," Big Black Bear said. "I think we should make song together." They did. They sang the song of the fox.

"*To-ka la-ka mi-ye ca—ya ya, na ke—nu-la waon we-lo, ya, ya . . .*"